THEA DEVINE

ANGEL EYES

ZEBRA BOOKS
KENSINGTON PUBLISHING CORP.

*To my mother, Claire, and my mother-in-law, Angela
With love to John, Michael and Thomas*

To Carin—in celebration of new life

ZEBRA BOOKS

are published by

Kensington Publishing Corp.
475 Park Avenue South
New York, NY 10016

First printing: August, 1991

Printed in the United States of America

SEDUCED

Rake shut the door meaningfully behind him. "What you must come to know, Angelene, is that your body will not run from what your mind already knows," he whispered. "We are bound, and I claim you."

The air was so thick with his need that she could hardly breathe. The space between them was a heartbeat, and she felt it throbbing like a living thing, calling to her, possessing her, arousing her to forbidden thoughts and longings.

A moment in time only. She would slake the desire and finally have done with it. Why not? She wanted him to act on his pretty speech. She wanted him to claim her one more time, this one time . . .

READERS ARE IN LOVE WITH ZEBRA LOVEGRAMS

TEMPTING TEXAS TREASURE (3312, $4.50)
by Wanda Owen

With her dazzling beauty, Karita Montera aroused passion in every redblooded man who glanced her way. But the independent senorita had eyes only for Vincent Navarro, the wealthy cattle rancher she'd adored since childhood—who was also her family's sworn enemy. The Navarro and Montera clans had clashed for generations, but no past passions could compare with the fierce desire that swept through Vincent as he came across the near-naked Karita cooling herself beside the crystal waterfall on the riverbank. With just one scorching glance, he knew this raven-haired vixen must be his for eternity. After the first forbidden embrace, she had captured his heart—and enslaved his very soul!

MISSOURI FLAME (3314, $4.50)
by Gwen Cleary

Missouri-bound Bevin O'Dea never even met the farmer she was journeying to wed, but she believed a marriage based on practicality rather than passion would suit her just fine . . . until she encountered the smoldering charisma of the brash Will Shoemaker, who just happened to be her fiance's step-brother.

Will Shoemaker couldn't believe a woman like Bevin, so full of hidden passion, could agree to marry his step-brother—a cold fish of a man who wanted a housekeeper more than he wanted a wife. He knew he should stay away from Bevin, but the passions were building in both of them, and once those passions were released, they would explode into a red-hot *Missouri Flame*.

BAYOU BRIDE (3311, $4.50)
by Bobbi Smith

Wealthy Louisiana planter Dominic Kane was in a bind: according to his father's will, he must marry within six months or forfeit his inheritance. When he saw the beautiful bonded servant on the docks, he figured she'd do just fine. He would buy her papers and she would be his wife for six months—on paper, that is.

Spirited Jordan St. James hired on as an indenture servant in America because it was the best way to flee England. Her heart raced when she saw her handsome new master, and she swore she would do anything to become Dominic's bride. When his strong arms circled around her in a passionate embrace, she knew she would surrender to his thrilling kisses and lie in his arms for one long night of loving . . . no matter what the future might bring!

Available wherever paperbacks are sold, or order direct from the Publisher. Send cover price plus 50¢ per copy for mailing and handling to Zebra Books, Dept. 3467, 475 Park Avenue South, New York, N.Y. 10016. Residents of New York, New Jersey and Pennsylvania must include sales tax. DO NOT SEND CASH.

Prologue

Somewhere near Crossville Junction,
Kentucky—Summer, 1880

Rake Cordigan was a man who knew trouble when he saw it. And he damned well knew when to avoid trouble, having spent five fruitless years of his life deliberately, recklessly and relentlessly pursuing it.

A woman was always trouble.

Especially a woman alone, barreling hell for leather down a remote backwoods road in a buckboard.

He reined in on a rise above the road and watched her. Wasn't a man alive couldn't guess where *she* was headed. She'd probably heard of a more profitable and profligate clientele over at Crossville Junction and she was racing to get there before the next girl. Hell, they all wound up there eventually; they came on down from St. Lou where the girls were a dime a dozen and men were more particular—to the place where ladies were scarce and men paid silver and got it done fast.

A woman could clean up in Crossville Junction and be on to the next camp before she wore out her welcome.

None of his damned business.

He was a man who prided himself in never getting involved, either.

But there was such a desperation in her precipitate headlong race down that lonely road that he in-

5

voluntarily spurred on his horse just to keep her in sight.

Damnfool woman. Always trouble. *Always.*

She was shrouded in black and he couldn't tell from the stance of her body whether she was driving her team that frenetically or whether they were on the verge of running away.

The fool was going to dive into the Springs if she didn't get a handle on her horses . . .

She reined up suddenly, violently, jerking the team so hard she almost fell over the side of the wagon; the horses heeled up unwillingly and then broke again, and again she hauled the reins back hard and violently.

Damnfool woman was going to kill herself, he thought sourly, as he nudged his mount down the rise and onto the track. At least she knew when to pull up and in.

Wait . . .

He drove for the trees as he heard a sound and climbed the ridge again on the opposite side of the road.

Someone was following her.

What the hell—

A woman alone could take care of herself.

He wasn't about to play hero.

Probably somebody who hadn't got his money's worth chasing her.

And he wasn't even a little curious to see what kind of man that was.

Hell.

He slowed his mount and picked his way cautiously across the ridge. Trust fate and circumstance to stick him on the wrong side of the road. It was even a fifty-fifty chance whoever was following her might be looking for him. A man didn't get careless for curiosity. He'd avoided main roads for five long years for that very reason, and if he could get behind the seeker, he would head for the hills and the hell with it.

A woman was always trouble.

He reined in and listened for a moment, his head lifted to the wind. She had reached Rogers Springs, and she wouldn't cross over tonight.

6

Whoever was shadowing her could trap her very nicely over by the Springs.

A woman alone.

Damn.

He couldn't leave a woman alone to that kind of fate— even if she were a filly from Cairo or Gant.

There was a place over by the Springs where he could hunker down for the night and get a bead on what was going on.

He reached the Springs about twenty minutes later, still moving with that native stillness and silence he had inherited from his mother's people.

The sun was beginning to drop and he felt the mood of the Springs. There was a turbulence in the air, and the woman had brought it with her.

She stood at the edge of the Springs, staring over the vastness of the body of water as if she did not know how to conquer it. Then she shrugged and turned back to her team and her wagon.

From the distance, he could not see her clearly, and in the shadow of the trees, she became almost indistinct. After a while, he saw the flicker of a flame and smelled the scent of food, and on some level it pleased him that she was so self-sufficient.

But she would not have the wherewithal to deal with the watcher in the shadows who stalked her.

He was aware of the presence from the moment he hid his mount and took his surveillance point.

But the presence wasn't strong, and that puzzled him, and for that reason he crept closer and closer to the firelight under the veil of the encroaching darkness.

She heard something.

"Who's there?" her voice snapped. "Show yourself . . . or I'll shoot."

No response—not immediately, but she knew the watcher was there. The indefinite presence who had made himself felt in indefinable ways.

"Josie?" Her voice was strong and loud, and echoed back over the water. "*Raso?* Come out, damn you—I'm

7

not scared of you or Josie."

She lifted her arm and fired—a rifle, he saw by the firelight—straight into the trees.

"*Damn!*"

"Who's there?" Her bravado slipped into quavering fear at the sound of the disembodied voice.

"*Me.* Damn it, Angelene . . ."

"Bobby? *Bobby!*" She threw down the rifle. "Where *are* you?"

"You're not gonna shoot?"

"Bobby!" She stamped her foot and then turned around slowly.

He could be anywhere in the shadows, in the night.

"You winged me, Angelene."

"I did *not*," she denied stoutly, still speaking to the night air. A twig snapped and he appeared hesitantly from around the back of the wagon holding his arm.

"*Bobby!*" She rushed at him, a flurry of black and kisses.

"I told you I would help you . . ."

"Did I hurt you?"

"You didn't hurt me." He enfolded her in his arms. "You're ridiculous, Angelene. You just didn't have to do it this way."

"Did anyone follow you?"

"No," he said, "no one."

"I'm glad you came anyway," she said softly. "We have to cross the Springs in the morning."

"I'm coming with you from here on in," Bobby told her, as she led him to her campfire and sat him firmly down beside it.

"Have you eaten?"

"Not for days."

She pressed a tin plate in his hands.

Deep in the shadows, Rake Cordigan made a disgusted noise as he settled himself in for the night.

Babies! Goddamned babies. A boy-child probably not even seventeen and a nun, for god's sake, not much older than the boy, either.

A fresh-faced little girl swathed in black with that constricting wimple around her face running like she was chased by thieves through the wilderness. Didn't make sense, but he'd been around long enough to know nothing had to make sense if it *was*.

The two of them together probably had the sense of a buckboard wheel.

Did anyone follow you?

Who the hell could that innocent be running away from?

Josie . . . Raso . . . names that fell strangely on his ear. Names that Bobby obviously knew.

Bobby ate ravenously as he watched, and threw aside his plate.

"I'm tired. We've got a big morning."

"Good night, Bobby," she answered. But she made no move to ready herself for bed.

What was she thinking?

Rake watched her fretful figure long into the night.

Chapter 1

Josie was watching her, she was sure of it.

She hadn't been back a week, and there was Josie, at least once a day, demanding to know whether she was happy to be back with the family again.

"It's good to be with kin, isn't it, Angelene? You missed your brothers all them years you set with the nuns."

And who sent me to the nuns? Angelene wanted to retort, but she kept silent. She wasn't sure how good it was to be with her family again.

She for sure was not home, because home had changed at least a half dozen times in the ten years she had been away. She hadn't wanted to be separated from her family either, but Josie's response to that was always the same: "We're living in rough times in rough places now your Pa's left us, and I want you to grow up to be a lady. You can learn to be rough later. You can't never learn to be a lady later."

None of that speech had struck her as being strange when she was very young. But as she grew older, she found it suspiciously odd that her mother was adamant about educating her to be at home in the very world she herself had so vociferously rejected.

Up until she was ten or eleven years old, she had heard unending tales of the strictures of the world from which Harry Scates had stolen her mother with his own aura of

11

reckless and glamorous freedom. She had gone from a world of wealth and privilege to a world of limitless horizons and dirty mining camps, gold in the imagination and dross in the hand.

She hadn't expected it to be like that. The rigorous life had hardened Josie Scates, and Harry's excesses had cemented her determination. She would survive Harry and the great western promise, and she would raise her children to understand exactly what she had gotten herself into and how they were meant to make it up to her.

She hadn't expected to be abandoned by Harry Scates. When he died, shot in a poker game, she knew what she had to do: she sent Angelene away immediately and used her beauty and wit to help her scrape up the onerous amount of money she needed to support Angelene in the school. But that was a worthwhile investment. She meant the nuns to turn her daughter into an obedient, ladylike creature who would be beholden to her mother for all she had done for her.

Angelene would return with a healthy sense of what her duty was to her family.

Angelene would look up to her mother for all the sacrifices Josie had made for her family.

Josie had begun that story when Angelene and her brothers were very young.

"Your gramma's name is Bellancourt and she lives in a fine big house in the biggest city in the world. Your grampa worked in money, you know, but he eventually died and left her alone. I reckon when Harry Scates came to get me, it made your grampa madder than hell because I was the only child and never had any brothers and sisters like you all do.

"Yes, grampa died a handful of years after your momma came west with Harry, and your gramma was quick to let us know about it. She did want us to come back to that big city and stay with her, but if we'd have done that, you wouldn't be living in these wide open spaces where you can do any old thing your heart desires,

12

isn't that right, Raso?"

"That's right, ma'am," Raso would say obediently. "I can ride to the horizon and back, and you did tell us there wasn't no riding in that New York city except in a park, and what good would that be?"

"Exactly," Josie would say. "And you'd have to go to school and wear stiff collars and proper suits and learn to be in an office or something and I never did like that. Out in the west, I found adventure and *living* right on the edge of catastrophe, and it just made my blood race with health to be part of it.

"In the city, worst thing that can happen is a carriage could bowl you down when you cross the street. The houses are built close up to each other and faced with drab brownstone and you can't spread out, only *up*. And you can only do what you momma and poppa want you to do. You can't go out by yourself, or go riding without a chaperone, and the houses are so big sometimes you could get lost in them. And eventually, you've got to marry who your momma and poppa want you to . . ."

All of which sounded fine to ten-year-old Angelene, who was somewhat disdainful of the various hovels to which Harry's ongoing quest to strike it rich took them.

"If my Harry had found gold, we'd be both rich and free, and that's my aim, my children: to be rich and free—and now your Pa's gone, you have to help me. We're going to send Angelene to the nuns so she can learn to be a great lady, and my sons will stay with me, and we'll find the way to wealth and prosperity."

Angelene was never sure just how Josie found prosperity; the only certainty was that Josie had found enough every year to pay her tuition and keep her relatively comfortable at several convent schools, the first in St. Louis, when the family still lived in Missouri, and the last in Kentucky, after Josie moved them all across the Mississippi River to a little town fifty miles from Portageville called Oak Bluff.

Oak Bluff overlooked nothing, but it was midway between several river-docking points, and a convenient stopover for the itinerant traveller.

Here Josie Scates ran her road ranch, offering hospitality to the bone-weary voyager. This was how her mother had kept body and soul together for ten years, always moving where she could take advantage of the best, most travelled routes, offering a way-station in the least likely place so she could command a premium price for a night's rest.

It wasn't anything elegant, either. Josie's road ranch was a ramshackle log building with numerous bedrooms and one large gathering room. In an ell outside, Josie cooked a plain, filling breakfast while Raso attended to the horses. Tice did the serving and Bobby cleaned the rooms after their overnight guests had gone.

Angelene hadn't seen this latest version of Josie's moneymaking dream until she had actually gotten there. This was a place Josie had bought and refitted about two years ago, moving her operation ten miles beyond her last road ranch and apprising Angelene by letter that she had moved to a bigger and better place, now it was time for Angelene to come home and do her fair share.

She didn't know what she had expected to face when the inevitable call to come home arrived.

She supposed she thought Josie could have done better. Maybe she could have bought herself a respectable boarding house in Oak Bluff, or perhaps Raso or Tice would be out ranching for themselves now and just Bobby would have remained at home.

But this wasn't a home. This was a circus of strangers, entering the door any time of night, sure of a welcome from Josie or the ever-vigilant Raso who never seemed to sleep.

This was leering men bunked up two and three to a room when things were at the most crowded, and incidents where tempers got frayed and guns went off by accident or by design, and it was never any of Josie's business: she didn't see it, and if Raso or Tice hauled a body out back for burial after taking up identifying papers to notify a family, well, that was just how it was.

14

This was nowhere as civilized as the big cities and they just weren't going to try to introduce manners to the rough tough clientele of the road ranch.

"Oh, it ain't as bad as it looks," Bobby would tell her, nonplussed by the uncertain expression on her face. "Momma goes to town about once every two weeks to drum up business. I expect she'll want you to go along too, now you're home. The men generally don't whoop it up so much as you saw last night."

"I hate it," Angelene swore feelingly.

"This is your home now," Josie said flatly. "You have to do your share. That's what we sent you to that fancy school for—so you'd come back knowing your duty and what's got to be done."

"I don't see what I can do here," Angelene said stubbornly.

"All you got to do is look pretty," Josie told her, "and help Bobby keep things neat. That's all the men want: a pretty lady and a clean bed and they'll pay high for it, you hear? That money kept you in Cairo all those years, and now you got to pay me back for it."

Why? Angelene wondered fiercely. Josie had sent her to a fine cloistered school to educate her to come back to *this?*

"Oh, it ain't as bad as you're thinking," Bobby told her again and again. "Momma makes a right fine bunch of money putting up travellers this way. They don't demand much—a bed, coffee in the morning, horses watered and that. Woman comes once a week to boil up the sheets, so you don't even have to do that much. You could sweep up the rooms and help serving, Angelene, and I'm sure Momma wouldn't say another word."

But Momma was watching her, she was sure of it.

And she knew why: she was too quick, too intelligent and clear-eyed, too sane. She didn't belong with Josie and her brothers, and Josie had thought she would return anxious for the reunion and the knowledge that the course of her coming days was set.

"Look at all these bucks," Josie said passionately,

15

shaking a fistful of bills in Angelene's face. "Listen to these dollars, my fine lady. Not even your gramma could get her hands on so much money so quickly. You better show some appreciation for what we've done for you, daughter. No one's leaving the business on account of you."

"Let me leave," Angelene proposed, and she was almost brought to her knees by the scathing blue bolt of her mother's gaze.

"You aren't going anywhere, Angelene Scates. You're staying right here to help out, with me and your brothers. Didn't those fine lady nuns tell you about that? Or maybe they didn't put it quite that way?"

How *had* they put it—when Josie's letter had come? It was time for her to do her duty to her mother. Yes, time to go home and prepare for her future. To listen to Josie and wiser heads. The only future she had was with her mother and brothers, and she would be a very smart girl just to return home without questions or opinions. They wanted Josie to think they had trained her well, and that she would be an obedient daughter and relieve her mother of some of her more onerous burdens.

At first she didn't see that Josie had any onerous burdens whatsoever. She ran a rowdy road ranch on a turnpike to nowhere—or somewhere—obviously those men were going somewhere, and the most difficult thing Josie had to do was keep her boisterous, overgrown twin sons in line.

The horror became clear to her when she finally realized that neither Raso nor Tice would ever be anything more than overdeveloped boys. They had to be told things precisely and then watched to make sure that their chores met Josie's standards and that all of her instructions were carried out.

"Well sure," Bobby told her, shrugging, "you wouldn't have really been aware of it, what with your being away so much. Momma's had her hands full. Wasn't much she could do with two galumphing giants like those two. We didn't see it at first when they were

16

young, but Momma saw it later—they just were never quite right, even when they were born; it just never struck her until later. She handled it right well too, finding a way to take care of us all, and making sure you got the best of things. And she never worried none of us about it, neither."

She felt a twinge of horror, but was she supposed to feel guilty? *Never quite right?* With their odd eyes and their eerie commonality, they scared her to death, her twin brothers; she felt trapped and not a little wary of those two hulking boy-men who turned up in the oddest corners and strangest places and called her "pretty sister," almost as if her name were too complicated for them to pronounce.

They were fascinated with her.

"Pretty sister," Raso would say, stretching out his large thick hand to touch the molten gold of her hair. "Momma-hair."

"Helping Momma," Tice would agree. "Momma's so happy you come home."

She recoiled when their curious hands reached out to touch her, and turned away from the feral gleam in their otherwise bland blue eyes that were similar—too similar—to her own and to Josie's.

She felt as if there was an echo following her. Everywhere she looked, she saw them, one-two, replicas of each other, shadowing each other, stalking her.

It unnerved her in those first weeks when she returned. There was something so primitive about them, so other-worldly, as if they existed in some other place than the one where they were seen.

They were brutish and unkempt and sometimes as silent as snow, and it took her forever to get used to them skulking around when they weren't doing chores for Josie and to finally come to the point where she could just ignore them altogether.

She couldn't, she wouldn't ackowledge them as kin. She felt nothing for them, *nothing*.

But Josie expected her to feel something. "They're

17

your brothers, daughter, no different than Bobby—a mite slower is all, but they have the same good heart to help out their Momma and keep things going. Just like you're going to do, like those nuns trained you."

Oh yes, the nuns: she had now heard more than a week of commentary about how she was to have been trained at school, and how did she tell Josie it all sounded like a lot of meaningless pap to her . . . all that stuff about honoring her Momma and respecting her Momma's dearest wishes to return home—undertaking her duty when Josie called for her.

But she had spent too many years in the clean, spare atmosphere of the school; hemmed in on all sides by structure and strictures, she had learned to be fatalistic, meek *and* rebellious. She had walked out the thick oak doors determined that no one would ever tell her what to do ever again.

"Go help Bobby strip the beds, Angelene," Josie would order her briskly. "Gather up the laundry. Measure up the grits for breakfast. Punch down the bread, will you? Don't dawdle, girl. Tice is waiting for his coffee . . ."

She felt like the princess in the fairy tale who had been given to an evil stepmother when she was a baby.

She did not belong on the Kentucky frontier in servitude to her family. She didn't know where she belonged.

"You just look at it one day at a time," Bobby consoled her one day as she stared at her reddening hands. "Momma's taking in nice money and we're helping her, and then maybe someday we'll just buy a nice house somewhere and she won't have to work any more."

"What about you?" she asked, her voice soft with affection for this practical and very sensible younger brother who acted as though he were years older than she.

"Oh, I got time," he said airily. "I got time to do anything I want, pretty sister. And so," he added meaningfully, "do you."

But time didn't exist on the ranch—at least not in her

18

mind. She measured things by the intervals between visitors, none of whom ever stayed more than two nights. She measured things by Josie's sojourns into Oak Bluff where she never took Angelene—presumably, Angelene thought, because Josie did not trust her.

In fact Josie read her mistrust and her distress clearly, and she didn't pander to it: she just gave Angelene more work.

"Look at my hands," Angelene mourned at one point.

"Happens to all ladies that work," Josie said practically.

"This place is deadly. Those men are no company at all."

"Learn to like being alone, my girl. That's what it's all about, being a woman by yourself with a family you've got to take care of."

"I don't have a family I have to take care of," Angelene retorted grittily.

"Neither did I at one time," Josie said. "And now look."

Angelene looked. In one flashing moment, she saw the Josie of twenty years before, slender, blonde, beautiful with her hungry blue eyes and softly braided hair. The finishing school posture was still there, and the same haughty determination that Angelene herself possessed, but it was tempered with something else: a slashing mouth that had spoken to hard times, a granite chin that always jutted with belligerence, and an overlay of excess weight that now could not support whalebone and satin.

And had never wanted to. Angelene could never remember a time she had not seen her mother in calico and boots which now had given way to practical cotton shirts and divided skirts. The beauty was buried under layers of discontent that was submerged still further under the triumph of Josie's ingenuity at finally obtaining the means with which to live comfortably.

That did not mean she had ever loved the life that she had chosen. But more than that, it did not mean she would ever admit it, even to Angelene. Josie was a stranger to her, and Angelene could not even find the heart to call her "Momma."

But that did not matter to Josie; what she wanted from Angelene was something far different, and it took many months before Angelene understood.

"In the winter," Angelene would say, "what happens in the winter? You don't get so many travellers in the winter."

"No we don't," Josie would agree. "But we've always had enough to get through the winter. We do chores and such, building on, restocking things. I'll whip up a quilt or two, and we'll stuff some mattresses—what's the matter, girl?"

"It sounds deadly."

"It's what a body's got to do to take care of her family, and I've done it a lot of years, Angelene."

"I understand that."

"It's what you've got to do."

"It's not what I've got to do. Why do *I* have to do it?" Angelene demanded stubbornly.

"Because it has to be done. You've got the strength and the energy—and I don't anymore," Josie said, her bolt-blue eyes resting meaningfully on Angelene's face.

"Well fine. We'll just pack it up and go to Oak Bluff and—"

"We stay right here—for now," Josie said.

"I hate this."

"So did I, my girl. Now you know how I felt."

"But you had a choice," Angelene protested. "You chose to go with Poppa."

Josie stared her down. "We *all* stay here—for now."

This time Bobby didn't say it wasn't as bad as she thought, because that winter was the worst thing she could ever have imagined, and it wasn't the bone-chilling cold or the boredom, either. It was the total isolation that was unbroken except for the occasional itinerant traveller.

The winter made Josie morose.

"Can't carry on the way a body needs to," she lamented. "Business is off, and I don't want to move this year—"

"We was moving every couple of years back a few years ago," Bobby amplified as the family sat down to dinner one particularly cold night. Tice and Raso had put a table before the fire in the big gathering room and Josie had put up a pot of stew right over the grate so she wouldn't have to go back and forth to the cold kitchen.

"Because the location is as good as we ever had and meat is plentiful, and—" Josie cast a speaking look over at Angelene, whose face was particularly fretful this evening—"and now we've got Angelene to help, and that makes things easier."

It didn't make things easier for her. Granted, the school had not been a place of luxury, but at least there she had had the company of girls her own age as well as activities to keep her occupied.

Here, at home, there was a never-ending round of chores and now, in the winter, she must put to use all the handiwork she had been taught at the school.

"We'll knit some socks," Josie said one morning, producing a basketful of black wool.

"I hate knitting," Angelene said, not moving from where she stood in the doorway. "I'm not very good at it."

Josie knelt down to stoke the fire. "Neither was I when I started, girl. But when you got to do it, you learn. That's what I did, and now you know how I felt."

She rose up and pulled two chairs nearby the fireplace. "Sit, daughter. Your brothers need new socks and we're going to make them. That's what we do in the winter. I can't tell you how many socks I've made in a lifetime out here," Josie added, catching up a wooden needle and some yarn and tossing them to Angelene.

"I know the nuns showed you how to do it." Her baleful blue eyes never left Angelene's face until Angelene bent her head and began awkwardly tying the

21

end of the skein and casting on the first stitches.

"That's right, girl. A useful skill those nuns taught you," Josie said, her tone muting down to that of a confidante as she sat opposite Angelene and began working her ball of yarn onto a needle.

"You didn't have to do things this way," Angelene said, her head bent over her lap, her voice muffled with just the faintest wariness at making this suggestion to Josie, whom she already knew would never ever admit she had made a mistake.

"Oh no, girl. You don't understand," Josie said, catching the note in her daughter's voice. "It was the only way. See, you haven't been here long enough to understand. Your Poppa and I had Raso and Tice right after we were married, and him fast-footing it all over Kansas and Missouri looking for gold or money or any damn business he could make a stake in. My family just washed their hands of us when I left, and I swore I would never ask them for anything, my girl, you hear? Never. And in return, they weren't ever going to see their grandchildren. And seeing as I was their only child, I considered that was a fair trade for the way they treated Harry and me.

"So that's what you have to understand: when the decision was made, there was no going back. Never. Ever. And when your Poppa died, I found a good way to take care of my family, and I've been doing it, and no one has wanted for anything—least of all *you*. Isn't that right girl?"

Angelene choked. "Yes."

"You see, because if I ever saw them again, I was going to see them with money jingling in my pocket. To say I made the right choice, the good decision. And maybe I will someday—go back and present them with everything I have and how I did it, and the children I'm so proud of because of their loyalty and duty to me. Isn't that right, Angelene?"

Angelene swallowed hard. "Yes," she whispered, her

22

fingers icy and numb on the wooden needle.

"Maybe someday we'll go back to my mother and I'll tell her all the things I did so well. I didn't need them at all, not one bit, just like I told them," Josie said. "Just to show them. Because I raised my children better, didn't I, Angelene?"

She couldn't look at her mother. "Yes."

"They don't think of running away from me when I give them everything right here. You haven't seen that yet, daughter, but it's true. We have everything we could want right here, in our family, and that's how it's going to be, and I'm sure that's just what the nuns told you."

Oh, but they hadn't . . . Angelene drew in a deep shaky breath instead of answering, but Josie wanted every last affirmation she could drag out of her. "Didn't they tell you, daughter? Didn't they?"

"Yes," Angelene whispered because she didn't know what else to say.

"That's just what I paid them for," Josie said with satisfaction as she plied her needle without even looking at what she was doing. "Just what I wanted them to do."

She learned to hide her rebelliousness under a cloak of meekness; being with her family was not much different than being at the school. There were rules and regulations and work and things you could say and not say, and you learned to hold your tongue and bide your time.

She learned not to be upset by her two hulking brothers who continually followed her around, poked at her and called her "pretty sister." She learned to hide her frustration at Josie's determination to continue running her road ranch rather than seeking a more respectable source of income in a bigger, busier town.

"I couldn't make more money if I was working the mines, girl. That's what makes it all worth it—the money."

23

"I thought you had run away from the money," Angelene retorted before she thought about what she was saying.

Josie gave her a long, dissecting look. "I was running away from *their* money, girl. I like my own money very much."

It almost seemed as if she could never have enough to make her feel secure. As the season changed, there was a quickening in Josie that had nothing to do with nature and everything to do with the first influx of travellers down from Portageville.

"This is good," Josie said one evening, her voice reflecting her change of spirit. "Those men will take word right down to Tennessee and up to Lexington about the Scates' ranch and the pretty lady that helps to run it."

"And what *lady* is that?" Angelene asked tartly, not liking at all her mother's tone of voice or the assumption she was making.

"Why, I'm talking about you, daughter, and how you were so nice to that Mr. Benbrook tonight."

"I wasn't so nice to him," Angelene contradicted. "I was being civil."

"You were being nice, just like the nuns taught you, just as I used to be back when we started," Josie said flatly. "You're doing just what I want you to do, daughter. It just comes naturally. You know what it's like and what to expect, and you're doing just fine, just fine, just like I expected."

Angelene felt another wave of horror. This just wasn't what she had expected, not at all. She didn't want to do anything to please Josie; she just wanted to get out of there, away from her lumbering, leering twin brothers, and her mother's veiled allusions that were ringing around her like a tightening noose.

Yes, she had been nice to Mr. Benbrook. He had been kind, a cut above the usual traveller who frequented the ranch. She had almost had half a mind to ask if he would help her, but she didn't know what kind of help she needed. Her one strong need was to get away, and yet, on the surface, no one would believe she had any need at all.

She could not define her uneasiness.

Bobby said, "See? Things aren't so bad."

Weren't they? But what was so bad? A comfortable home with her family, paying guests, freedom from want, security, safety . . . sweet Bobby with his youth and surety, born years after she, just after the death of their father, a baby cloaked in wisdom: *See? Things aren't so bad.*

She still felt wary.

"Where's Mr. Benbrook this morning?" she asked after she had served coffee to the one or two guests who had straggled out to the dining table.

"Oh . . . he had to leave early," Josie said.

"Real early," Tice said, on his way out the back door of the kitchen with a bucket of water.

"That's too bad. I would have liked to say good-bye." *Or good-bye and help me.* But that was crazy; a well brought up young lady did not go asking help of a stranger. Not when she was surrounded by family.

"That's all right, daughter. I'm sure he's taken a nice memory of you on to the next camp. He'll talk about you and we'll get still more business, don't you fret."

That wasn't the point, Angelene wanted to shout, but Josie looked so smug, she just bent her head over the biscuit tin and clamped down on her temper.

She was to be Josie's star attraction. The thought ballooned up slowly like the rising dough under her fingers. She was meant to be a lure for the itinerant emigrant who had no permanence in his life anyway. What did it mean? What could it mean? Why else would Josie keep referring to the notion that the men would talk about her when they talked about Josie's place?

She really was going crazy. It had to be the isolation and the long winter, and maybe her disappointment that Mr. Benbrook had left without saying good-bye.

"You tell 'em down Tennessee way about Josie's place," Josie told her departing travellers. "You tell 'em about Josie's hospitality and her handsome family. Now, don't forget about Angelene, hear?"

"How could they?" Angelene muttered as she hauled dirty dishes from the dining table through the ell to the kitchen. "You've only mentioned it a dozen times or more."

"So what's wrong with drumming up business?" Josie demanded. "Lord, you've got a mouth on you, girl. You don't question what your Momma sees fit to say or do, miss. I spent a lot of years looking forward to having my daughter back with me and you weren't supposed to come home with a chip on your shoulder and all this backtalk in your suitcase."

"I don't like being hawked like some patent medicine," Angelene said stiffly.

"You're a sweet pill for a weary traveller to swallow, daughter, and that's just how I intended it. You'll do exactly what I want and exactly how I want it, is that clear?"

The faint tone of menace in Josie's otherwise conversational tone was abundantly clear. "Yes," Angelene said tonelessly.

"Excellent, daughter. I'm glad we understand each other."

Angelene turned her back purposefully. She didn't understand anything at all, but the time had come to finally start asserting herself. She wasn't going to be her mother's shill for this seedy backwoods road ranch and that was all there was to it, and Josie would just have to cope with that. She, Angelene, wanted bigger and better things than a hard-won life of drudgery on the frontier.

She wanted all the things that Josie had not: the pretty dresses, the social life, the security of one family living in one place at one time. And she wanted a husband, a wealthy husband, so that she would never have to come back to Kentucky or Missouri or wherever else Josie took it in her mind to settle. She wanted one house, a clutch of children and a man who worked at an honorable wealth-making career which could support a home and children—and her, and all her dreams and desires that

26

the nuns never could effectively erase from her mind and heart.

"But don't you understand?" Bobby said as they washed dishes together later on that day. "There's plenty of money. Momma has made a real success of this place. We could do whatever we wanted: she's promised us. A couple of years from now, when I'm just a little older, I'll have whatever I need—because you're back now."

"But you don't understand," Angelene interpolated. "I don't want what Momma wants. This is pure squalor to me after all those years in the convent. We had almost nothing there. A bed, a bureau, a washstand, a desk. Some books. But everything was scrupulously clean and simple, and this is all so . . . how can I stay here?"

"Of course you can stay here. That's what Momma planned. What would happen to Tice and Raso if you went off now? What if Momma got ill or had some kind of accident?"

"What if I wanted to get married?" Angelene threw out just to test reaction.

Bobby shrugged but she noticed his eyes narrowed just the faintest bit. "You don't want to get married, not yet. You don't know anybody, anyway."

This was true, and it had occurred to her even at the convent school that her world was going to diminish even further once she returned to her family. There would be no opportunity to meet anyone once she was back with Josie again.

But there had been Mr. Benbrook, the epitome of the kind of man she would have liked to meet and gotten to know better, and he had seemed to like her too. He had seemed articulate and well-dressed, perhaps wealthy. He had just gone precipitately and she didn't understand it.

"I don't know anybody," she agreed, "and if I stay here the rest of my life I'm never going to know anybody."

27

"Well, you see," Bobby pointed out reasonably, "you're getting to meet people now. All our guests—sometimes we get the real gentlemanly types—"

"Like Mr. Benbrook," Angelene said.

Bobby paused a moment to think. "Oh yeah," he said finally. "Like Mr. Benbrook . . . just like Mr. Benbrook."

And like Mr. Ellingwood who turned up a week or two later. Here was a true gentleman. He wore a suit, he travelled in a carriage and knew just where he was going and what he was doing and he distinctly admired Angelene's blonde beauty.

He spoke kindly to her and she appreciated that mightily. It was a heady feeling, knowing that a man wanted to get close to her, to talk to her, perhaps touch her—even kiss her.

On the other hand, there was also something in the situation that bothered her, that this man of the world, Mr. Ellingwood, would even think he could pursue her to that extent over the period of the several hours he would be at the ranch.

In the end, it was all meaningless, because in the morning, Mr. Ellingwood was gone, as quietly and mysteriously as had Mr. Benbrook.

"Well, a man's business is a man's business," Josie said, sloughing off Angelene's concern and covert disappointment. "No telling what a man takes it in his head to do or when he's gonna do it, daughter. Let that be a lesson. You never know what a man's up to—even when he tells you."

And indeed, what had Mr. Ellingwood told her? He thought she was beautiful; he was overjoyed he had decided to stop at Josie's place. He wanted to talk to her, he hoped to see her in the morning.

No promises there. Nothing but the transient impression of the power of her beauty and the intense feelings such admiration aroused in her.

And all of it was meaningless to the man—if Josie were to be believed.

"Oh, men will tell you anything," Josie said. "You got to fend for yourself no matter what, girl, so you might as well learn to do it now. That fancy education won't serve you well if you have to take care of your family."

"And what will?" Angelene demanded angrily. "Washing pots? Making beds? Living in this stupid hovel miles and miles from nowhere?"

Josie wheeled on her so suddenly and menacingly she almost fell backward. "And what do you think I did all those years when you were away, girl? What do you think I did? Do you think I loved it? Do you think that's what I wanted to devote my life to—beds and grits and two overgrown sons who can't take care of themselves? Now you know, daughter. Now you see. Now you know how I feel. And I'll tell you something worse than that: nothing's going to change. This is how it is, and this is what is going to be. We run the ranch, we make our money and we take care of our own. I did it, and you're going to do it, and that's how it's going to be. That's what I've been waiting for—for you to come home to share the burden with me."

And take it up when you can't do it anymore, Angelene thought, her body rooted in pure horror at her mother's words.

"We'll make it better," Josie went on, her tone softening just the faintest bit. "Together—we can make it better."

No, you mean I can make it better for you, Angelene thought, backing away from Josie slowly, slowly until she was right up against a kitchen cupboard.

"We have money," Josie went on. "The thing is, it's a good business. We have money."

We have nothing else, Angelene thought, her body constricting with a feeling of irreparable loss. *If I don't get away, I will never have anything ever in my life . . .*

"Say *something,*" Josie demanded, planting herself in front of Angelene's slender body defiantly. "You think you're so good, don't you, daughter? Ten years of convent schooling, and you think you know everything about everything. You know *nothing*. Your Poppa never did a thing for this family. I did everything, *me*—everything for your brothers, and you, and Bobby who came so much later. Everything. That Harry Scates was a scoundrel. He abandoned us, and when he came back he had a carpetbag full of foolish schemes that never went anywhere.

"*I'm* the one that saved the family and made the money and kept it together, do you hear, Angelene? And I didn't expect any thanks for it, no ma'am. But I expected that my daughter was going to walk back into my house and at least be on my side when I asked something of her—that was all, Miss Hoity-Toity who can't bear to wash a dish without wrinkling her nose. I expected some kindness to your brothers—they can't help the way they were born, and we have to do for them—*all* of us. I expected a little respect for everything I've done, and what I feel, and all I'm getting is backchat and Miss High and Mighty who would just as soon turn her back on her mother and run off with one of those high-flying bullnoses that spend the night here.

"That's what I get, and I didn't deserve any of it, young lady. You just better buckle down and take things seriously, and then maybe we'll talk—about other things."

Josie turned away, and then looked back. "Maybe," she added ominously, and strode out of the room, leaving Angelene cringing against the cupboard, shaking at her mother's venom and anger and the burden she had placed on her daughter's fragile shoulders.

Chapter 2

Yes, Josie was watching her, waiting for that one tenuous misstep on Angelene's part on which she could pounce. Angelene was now wise enough to temper her rebellious nature and pretend to acquiesce to her mother's wishes.

How hard it was. The work of running the road ranch was pure drudgery unalleviated by any mitigating reward except her odd conversations with the always-busy Bobby, or the appearance now and again of a presentable visitor who would purposefully make known his attraction to her and then subsequently remove himself very early in the morning before anyone was awake.

It puzzled her. It was almost as if Josie were sneaking these eligible gentrified men out the back door before anything could come of a mild flirtation.

Josie surely didn't want anyone becoming interested in her—she could see that. A man of ambition wouldn't want to spend his life on a road ranch in the backwoods of Kentucky waiting for the well-heeled traveller to happen down the road.

The several men who had expressed interest in her had certainly seemed to be very well-heeled.

The thing that upset her finally was that one Mr. Dawkins, who had made a distinct appointment with her for the following morning, disappeared sometime in the early hours of the day, once again mysteriously needing to tend to some kind of business that required an early start.

She couldn't believe it—this time. "Mr. Dawkins was quite specific, Momma. He was coming to breakfast and we were to talk."

"Oh yeah? Talk about *what*, Miss?"

"About things you obviously don't want me to talk about, or why else would all these men run away so fast and hard before daylight?"

"You don't want to hear anything those men have to say, daughter. Trust me, I know. I listened once, and look where it got me. I'm just trying to save you the trouble."

"No, you're just trying to keep me chained to this hellish life you've created here," Angelene retorted.

Josie slapped her. "You ain't listening, daughter. *This* is where a man's pretty words get you. You'll only trade one for the other. You're lucky your momma knows the difference. You're just an educated innocent out of convent school. Those nuns don't teach you anything about the realities of men and their words. You don't know how good you have it: your family that cares, and a momma who takes care of you, and all the money we need. You stop and think, Angelene, and don't open that backchatting mouth of yours before you think about what's coming out of it."

Angelene held her stinging cheek and held back her brimming eyes by sheer force of will. "What if I want more?" she whispered.

"That's what you have to learn, daughter, same as I did. There is no more. Do you hear? There is no more. You just take your portion and you be thankful—just like me."

She felt the chafe of her mother's fingers on her cheek for days, and it only intensified her resolve to find a way to save herself.

"Oh, Momma didn't mean nothing by it," Bobby told her reassuringly. "Like as not you riled up some old memories in her just a little too much. I mean, she didn't have no easy life with Poppa, much as she loved him. He was forever going off here and there and leaving her to make do, and, I mean, how would you like it if that was you? That's what she was trying to get at: any of those men could have abandoned you just the same, you know. You don't want to take up with any of them."

"I guess I don't," Angelene said, more to pacify him so he wouldn't report their conversation to Josie than from any conviction she had on the matter. In reality, she was beginning to believe that enticing one of their gentlemanly travellers might be her only salvation from a life on the ranch with Josie and her skulking brothers and their eerie eyes.

Mr. Greely, on the other hand, looked more like a rough rider than a gentleman, but he spoke so literately, and his eyes never moved an inch from Angelene's face as she went around the table some two weeks later serving dinner.

Angelene really liked him, right on sight, and she thought it was because he had deep, dark blue eyes so nearly like her own. They spoke volumes every time they looked at her.

Trouble was, Josie noticed it too. "Those westerners are the worst, daughter. Don't believe a thing that man tells you. But don't be uppity with him, either. Just go along the middle of the road with him. He likes you. You like him—and you're going to let him take away a nice memory of Josie's ranch—and that's *all*. Clear, daughter?"

"I understand," Angelene said, her gaze swerving toward the disquieting light in Mr. Greely's eyes. But Josie made the same speech every time a man took stock of Angelene and acted interested. She was to be polite and interested in him, and make him feel at home, but not too at home, and smile a lot, and . . . and . . . and—please the fates, maybe one day one of those men might offer to help *her*.

"What's a beautiful woman like you doing in a place

33

like this?" Mr. Greely asked genially. "You belong in some fine house in Oak Bluff with a husband and children."

"Well, what's a fine man like you doing in the back woods of Oak Bluff heading out to who-knows-where, Mr. Greely?" Angelene asked pertly, aware of Josie's hard eyes on her as she cleared the table of the supper dishes.

Mr. Greely smiled at her benignly. "I guess we all got secrets, Miss Angelene. I'd like to have a good guess at yours."

"Nothing much to guess, Mr. Greely. I hate washing dishes," she said carefully, easing her tray full of plates and cups off the table next to him.

But what if she said—*you're right, Mr. Greely, I want to be in a big beautiful house in Oak Bluff with a husband and children, and will you take me there?* She looked into his warm blue eyes and thought maybe she could say that. And maybe she couldn't; she would never be able to tell if a man meant to aid her or abuse her, and that was the trap that held her both ways: she could never leave and she would never know.

Mr. Greely was gone by morning when he had distinctly said he meant to stay for a couple of days to rest his lamed horse, and she didn't know what to think at all.

"He told me that horse of his couldn't travel another foot let alone another mile," she accused Josie. "So how could he have gone?"

"He lied," Josie said. "Go see for yourself."

She did. She ran out to the barn, and she called out to Bobby in a frenzy and Bobby came running like the barn was on fire.

"What on earth, Angelene?"

"Mr. Greely . . ."

"What's the rush? Mr. Greely's gone, you missed him by hours."

"He is not. He couldn't be."

"Angelene—hold onto your skirts now. Mr. Greely left."

"Josie sent him away."

"No. Truly, he just left."

"He was staying for more than one day. He *told* me. He said the horse came up lame, and he didn't even know if he could go on riding him . . ."

Bobby shook his head. "No, no—Raso and Tice looked him over and Mr. Greely was right grateful he could just keep on going as soon as possible."

I don't believe you—she almost said the words, and then she caught them back. What was she to believe? That Bobby was lying? Or that Josie was running every man off the place who evinced the slightest interest in Angelene, who was now to be considered her family's bonded servant?

She didn't know. She didn't know what to think. Mr. Greely had been so certain about his horse, and she had been so sure he would be at the ranch for a day or two, and she was even looking forward to it . . .

It had to be Josie . . . Josie couldn't stand the thought that Angelene might become desperate or brave enough to just leave the ranch with one of those men . . . the ones that seemed to have money and manners . . . the ones that reminded her too much of Harry Scates—

But that wasn't *her* lookout. Her life was her own, no matter what Josie thought, and she knew what Mr. Greely had said and it had to be that Bobby was lying or Josie sent him away.

She couldn't prove either, and in the end, she didn't have to. Two weeks later, someone came looking for Mr. Greely.

"Oh, he passed through a couple weeks back," Josie said airily. "We ain't seen him since, isn't that right, Bobby?"

Bobby nodded.

"Angelene?"

"Yes," she agreed, her voice low. "He was here a couple of weeks ago."

Mr. Greely's friend, one Abner McNab, didn't look at all convinced. He was as rough-hewn as Mr. Greely had been, and more plain-spoken than most, and he was plainly upset over the mystery of Mr. Greely's where-abouts.

"You tell me, ma'am," he put it to Josie. "Ain't no one seed him from Oak Bluff down to Memphis way, and you have to own, that's quite a way for a man to go missing."

"I wouldn't know," Josie said. "Maybe he went in some other direction."

"Maybe he went over Portageville way and crossed the river," Bobby suggested.

"Went to Memphis by way of Missouri, young man?" Mr. McNab repeated disbelievingly.

"Whyn't you stay the night, stranger?" Josie offered. "Maybe you can figure something out from here."

"Maybe I can," McNab agreed warily. "And maybe it'd happen you'd remember something."

"We've told you all we know," Josie said, her voice slightly edgy with impatience. "But you're welcome to stay—no charge, stranger—and see if you can clear this up."

But the only thing that was clear to Angelene was that Josie was impatient for the stranger to be gone.

"I don't want to move again," she heard Josie declare vehemently to Bobby at one point in the evening. "I want that man gone."

"We'll get him gone, Momma," Bobby said, his voice fervent with some kind of promise. "Don't fret none. He'll be gone before you know it. We'll take care of it, truly. We won't have to move. We'll just—make sure Mr. McNab is gone, all right, Momma?"

"I hate doing it this way," Josie went on, her voice muffled. "He don't look like he's got anything worth picking. He's just out to make trouble. I *hate* to do it for nothing."

"Maybe not, Momma. Maybe, since he's Mr. Greely's friend, maybe there's something. We'll find out, I promise. And then he'll be gone and he won't bother us no more."

"All right. We'll do it that way. We have no choice."

"I don't guess that we do, Momma."

36

In the morning, Mr. McNab was gone, just as her mother had said, and Angelene felt chilled all over, both by his sudden disappearance and the memory of the conversation she had overheard the night before between Josie and Bobby.

"The man just *left?*" she wanted to know, her disbelief coloring every word.

"Who knows what a man takes it into his head to do?" Josie said. "Maybe he got some fool idea about what happened to Mr. Greely. There's just no telling. After all, he didn't have a bill to pay."

No, he hadn't, and Angelene wondered about Josie's generosity in the cold light of day; it was almost as if she had wanted to make it as easy as possible for Mr. McNab to leave.

And Mr. McNab had been so adamant about finding out what happened to Mr. Greely, and staying around until he did. Something about that just didn't square, and she couldn't put her finger on it.

Josie refused to talk about it. "The man realized there was nothing more to be done here, and he probably thought—and rightly so—that if he stayed on, I *would* charge him rent."

She hadn't given him one of the more decent rooms either. She had relegated him to a little box of a room at the back of the house, one that was meant for storage, but was used as a spare room when there was an overflow of travellers. Mr. McNab hadn't complained. It was a bed, and there was a hot supper, and Josie had been reasonable and that was that.

And then he'd gone.

Angelene still couldn't believe it, and when Josie wasn't looking, she edged her way out the far door down the hallway to the little back bedroom and knocked.

She supposed she didn't expect an answer. It was still fairly early in the morning, and most of the overnight patrons were still asleep—except for Mr. McNab who had left the premises so arbitrarily early that morning.

She didn't know what she expected when she turned the knob of the door as quietly as possible and pushed in.

What she found was Raso, on his knees, his back to her, scrubbing the floor. On the bed, a heap of sheets was pulled from the mattress, and on them, on the walls, on the floor, on the bed, she saw thick rusting stains of spattered blood.

Chapter 3

Angelene knelt by the edge of Rogers Springs and dipped her cupped hands into the water. It was cold—refreshingly, stingingly cold and she brought her hands up to her face and sipped the water, and then splashed it onto her face.

She shivered as the icy water trickled down her arms and under the sleeves of her habit, and she wasn't sure it was because of the cold or the fact that Bobby had found her so easily.

He lay asleep in the flatbed of the buckboard, his hat pillowing his young, vulnerable head, and she had sat awake all night staring at the fire so that she was now ready to lay down her head and sleep.

The fire had no answers for her, nor had Bobby, and she had been too tired to make decisions or answer his questions or even ask any of her own.

The morning light revived her somewhat. And the water, icy in her mouth made a tingling path of awareness down her numbed arms. She was still alive; she had gotten away from Josie and she had made it this far, and surely that was something to be grateful for.

Bobby was a complication she had not counted on.

But then, she hadn't made plans. She had merely devised a way to get from one place to another as expediency allowed.

But she could see already that she was going to need

39

more than expediency to get her across Rogers Springs. To her eye, it seemed vast and uncrossable and she was only somewhat reassured, as she got to her feet, to see that she could glimpse the opposite shore on the horizon.

Maybe Bobby would know. Maybe it was a good thing that he had found her. She could hear him stirring as she made her way back to the wagon and the cold ashes of the previous night's fire.

"Good morning, sleepyhead," she called out as his fair head popped up over the driver's seat of the wagon.

"You look strange in that habit," he said in a sleep-fogged voice. "If I didn't know it was you, I wouldn't have known it was you," he added as he climbed over the side of the wagon. "What's for breakfast?"

"Oh, I don't know. I've got a little coffee here and some stale bread and some cheese," Angelene said, rummaging around in a bag that she had left by the side of the fire pit.

"I guess the nuns don't have much to spare in the way of food," Bobby said, hunkering down next to her.

She looked up sharply. "What do you know about that?"

"Oh, you know—Josie found out about the whole thing, Angelene. She went right there when you didn't come back, first place she thought of—hey," he temporized as her body reacted to his words by pulling backwards away from him, "I'm on your side."

Angelene bent her head and filled the coffee pot, grateful for the first time for the concealing quality of the veil; she didn't have to look at Bobby, and he couldn't see her face as she made busywork of fixing the coffeepot. She waited for him to go on, and he waited for her to comment.

When she said nothing, he continued, hesitantly now, "I'm not saying Momma wasn't mad, Angelene, but she really was concerned, and she just thought that Our Lady might be the first place you'd go to, that's all."

Dear Lord . . . Angelene held her breath and groped for some twigs with which to start the fire and didn't dare look at Bobby's face.

"Sister Philomena said she had helped you," Bobby said, and Angelene swallowed convulsively. Poor dear little Sister Philomena, her cohort, her champion all those years, to have to be caught in a conspiracy with her, and by Josie of all people . . . she bit her lip and fished for the sulphur matches she had stored in her pocket.

"So I decided to try to find you," Bobby finished, reaching for the coffee pot and setting it on the tentative little blaze she had made with the matches.

Angelene licked her lips. "We need a couple of branches here, Bobby."

"I'll get them."

She hardly heard him. Her eyes were fixed on the flickering flame, and the image of the stone gates of the Convent of Our Lady and its forbidding iron gate as she had approached it the day she had run away from Josie and Bobby in Cairo.

. . . And Reverend Mother Margaret: "My dear, you tell me you need to get to your grandmother in New York, and you are begging for help in outwitting your mother in order to accomplish this end—I just don't understand— what could you possibly expect us to do for you?"

Her tone had been so kindly, so open, but Angelene knew she should have been aware that Mother Margaret of all people would never brook any disobedience, in child or charge. Mother Margaret offered the sane solution: she would send for Josie and Angelene would return home and nothing more would be said.

Angelene had said, "I can't go back home," and she refused to tell Mother Margaret why. As far as Mother Margaret was concerned, that ended the matter.

Angelene was to wait while she contacted Josie.

Angelene couldn't wait. She flew out the door the moment she was sure Mother Margaret was out of sight, and ran to find Sister Philomena.

"I'm in trouble," she whispered urgently through the nun's closed door, and Sister Philomena immediately opened it and let her in.

"Tell me everything," she said calmly in response to Angelene's urgency and desperation.

"My mother is a murderess, and I have to get away from her."

The wonder was Sister Philomena did not think she was deranged. She had no proof, no clues—only what she had seen and what Josie had said and all those awful disappearances, and Josie's obsessiveness about how much money she had—

She sounded utterly senseless as she recounted what had happened since she had returned home; she sounded mad, as if she were inventing things in her disordered mind to account for events that had every appearance of normalcy in Josie's world and none in her own.

Josie's a murderess! The blood . . . the blood—she could still see the blood-soaked room that Mr. McNab had occupied. She would never forget it, and she didn't know how she managed to go back to Josie and pretend as if she had seen nothing.

Josie never knew. *She* thought Angelene was finally picking up the spirit of the thing when Angelene ever so craftily suggested that they might go to Cairo and she, Angelene, would be willing to visit the docking points and stations with Josie to drum up business.

Since she had been so docile and so unfailingly agreeable, Josie had agreed, because she thought Angelene was finally coming around, was finally, as she told her, on Josie's side about things.

It had taken a couple of months for Angelene to bring up going to Cairo, and that after weeks and weeks of pretending to be amenable and resigned to her future, weeks of choking back words she wanted to say, accusations she wanted to make, a month of watching Josie covertly and discovering just who and when Josie struck.

She knew she wasn't wrong, and she knew that Josie, after all these murderous years, fully knew how to accomplish her ends and cover her tracks.

Her only hope was to get to Cairo; there was no one she

42

could trust, no one who could help. She felt even more cornered than before, trapped by a burning tissue of lies and the hope in Josie's eyes that her daughter had finally come back to her.

When Angelene perceived that, she knew that going to Cairo could become a reality.

She had had to school herself painstakingly to accept whatever went on, and to never let Josie become aware of what she knew. When the guests disappeared and Josie said they had gone away at dawn, she accepted Josie's explanation and stopped questioning her. When Josie talked about taking care of her family, Angelene agreed with her. When Josie noticed that she had stopped yearning for a different life, she told her flat out that she was coming to appreciate all the sacrifices Josie had made for her family and after all that, things didn't seem so bad.

Small wonder, after all her bald-faced lies, Josie was willing to go to Cairo. Josie wasn't impervious to admiration and sympathy. She needed that and more from her only daughter, and once Angelene understood that, she knew that Josie would eventually take her to Cairo.

Eventually she would get away.

The hardest part had been the waiting, and it was even harder watching Sister Philomena's serene face by the light of a flickering candle as she listened to Angelene's improbable story without comment, harder still waiting for her judgment. She would either call Mother Margaret or she would help, and for one terrible moment, Angelene could not guess what her decision would be.

And then she said in that same sweet calm way of hers, "I will help you, Angelene. What do you need?"

Now Josie had caught her out, and Angelene could not imagine what the little nun's punishment would be.

My mother killed them all, I'm sure of it, she had told Philomena, and now, as she looked up at Bobby, her

43

emotions under control, she didn't think she was sure of anything.

"I'm coming with you," Bobby said, shoving two thick branches into the little pile of flaming twigs. "You know that, don't you? You can't go alone."

"I can go alone," Angelene said, bending her head again. "No one will attack a nun."

"But still," Bobby said, "you need a man to help you. Besides, I wouldn't mind going east, Angelene. I wouldn't mind going over a mountain and finding something new."

He sounded so wistful, she had to look up at him. He had such a sweet face, such guileless eyes. She couldn't determine at all whether he had known about what Josie was doing, or if he was as innocent as she. He had to be innocent. Who could knowingly live with that?

"Well," he said defensively, "she raised us all up on those stories about her and Gramma. Didn't you ever think she was a little too ornery about Gramma, about not asking for help or anything?"

"Always," Angelene said shortly.

"Me too," Bobby said simply. "So let's go there, Angelene, you and me, let's go to Gramma."

His proposal was so exactly on target, she felt her insides swoop heartstoppingly downward. *How had he known?* Or had it always been his dream as well?

"At the moment," she said evasively, "what we have to do is go across that body of water, and I haven't the faintest idea how we do that."

Bobby looked up and out across the Springs. "Well, we'll just drive the team in and they'll pull the wagon across. Nothing hard about that."

"No," she said, scanning the shoreline once again, "nothing hard about that." But the far shore looked dishearteningly distant and there was really no telling whether the team and wagon could even wade across that formidable looking body of water.

But Bobby seemed so sure . . .

They drank their coffee in silence, dipping the stale

44

crusts of bread in their cups to soften them, and then Angelene doused the little cookfire with the remaining coffee, rinsed the pot and cups and packed them into the wagon.

"I'm ready," she said, but her voice lacked certainty and she wondered what she would have done had Bobby not caught up with her. Surely she would have had second thoughts about negotiating the Springs after getting a good look at the breadth of it.

Bobby began to hitch up the team. "We'll be on the other side before you can think twice about it, Angelene."

Not the sense of a wagon wheel between the two of them, he thought again as he saddled up and prepared to leave the copse of bushes where he had spent the night.

None of his business now. She knew the boy, he wasn't a threat, so that was all right. They would muddle around together and, he supposed, eventually they would get wherever they were going.

He was going back home, to a place where the only thing he had to take care of was himself, his dog and his stock. It was a place with no intrusions, nothing extraneous; a place high and away from the intrusive vagaries of neighbors or itinerant visitors. It was his heaven after a successive five years and more of hell, and he had made sure no one could ever find him, and no one would ever know where to seek him out.

He felt a distinct itch deep in his craw to get there—fast. He couldn't allow himself to be distracted, not for a moment, not even by a woman who seemed to be in trouble.

He had wasted a night and part of a morning on her and he wasn't sticking around one minute more. He had a half day's travel ahead of him still, and a pocket full of dollars, and he knew the fastest way across the springs and it wasn't across the middle.

He wondered why, as his horse picked its way out of

45

the bushes, the damnfool young idiot with the woman was hitching up the horses and not turning the wagon westward up toward Rogers Neck where the Springs narrowed and there was a bridge across.

Then he watched in disbelief as the boy swung his whip high up over the team and began driving them into the water.

They weren't three feet deep in the water when they heard a roar behind them—a voice—someone following them. Angelene turned, her face a study in pure panic.

A stranger! Not her brothers, not . . .

And Bobby kept going, oblivious to the shouts, to her cries, until the horseman was flat out in front of him, blocking the horses so that he had to rein in or just barrel his way over the stranger and his mount.

"Who the hell are you?" he demanded roughly.

"What the hell do you think you're doing?" Rake demanded, splashing over to the side of the wagon. "You fools—you'll drown if you cross the Springs here."

That made no impression on the young whelp, whose face set stubbornly and whose eyes would not meet his. But the woman . . . those mesmerizing blue eyes, that sweet mouth—that face that did not belong encased in a frame that removed it from the realm of sensuality . . .

"Are you sure?" that mouth asked, and her voice was low and husky and like a sweet balm on a wound.

Bobby looked at her sharply, and she turned her head so that the drape of the veil prevented him from seeing her face. Why would she believe a stranger above him after all? Angelene didn't know, except that he was so irritated, and his exasperated expression told her more plainly than words that he had gone well out of his way to warn them.

"There's a bridge up over yonder," the stranger went on, pointing westward. "There's a road back away that meets it, you just follow it down."

46

"What if we don't?" Bobby demanded belligerently.

"Better remove those wheels then, and float the thing across. But mind the current and the horses, because someone's going to go off course."

"Bobby . . ." Angelene put her hand on his sleeve. "Let's . . ."

"Who the hell is he?" Bobby demanded pugnaciously.

"Let's anyway," Angelene said. "Maybe he's right. Maybe we don't know."

Rake leaned across the pommel of his saddle to look her directly in the eyes. "That's right, lady. You don't know."

"How does *he* know?" Bobby shot back.

"He *looks* like he knows," Angelene said pacifyingly, running her curious gaze up and down the tall frame of the man on horseback beside them. He was all brown, from his buckskin boots and clothes right on up to his hands, his hat, his face. But his hair was black, long, unruly over the edge of his collar, and his eyes, under the brim of his hat, were a startling cool gray. He looked like a scout or a woodsman. He didn't look like any of the men she had ever met at Josie's.

He didn't look like a man who talked too much either. He just sat there, waiting, with all the patience of a priest, until Bobby decided to turn the rig and head back up onto the shoreline and the road.

"You'd drown in six seconds when this rig hit six feet in," the stranger said flatly, his steely gray gaze on Angelene's face and veil.

"*I* would?" she echoed faintly, not understanding the implication at first, and then comprehending it all too well. Her dress and veil would pull her down instantly, she would never be able to fight them and get ashore safely, and she felt sufficiently scared by the slightest possibility of it that she tugged on Bobby's arm almost without thinking. "We'll take the bridge. Bobby . . ."

Even he looked a little sick. "All right, all right. I guess we're obliged, stranger," he added reluctantly.

"I guess maybe you are," Rake said, not moving an inch. "Get 'em up, boy. You got a long ride this morning."

Bobby stared at him, and Rake noted his eyes were the same captivating shade of blue as the woman next to him. The boy's expression was one of sheer determination to get the better of the stranger who had appeared out of nowhere and made him look like a fool.

He took up the whip and snapped it over the horses, and reined in so that the team veered to the left and slowly pulled the wagon out of the mud in which the wheels had mired.

Rake watched this slow progression to the shore without making a move to head in himself. He was toying with the notion of letting his mount swim across. He wanted to get as far away from these innocents as possible; he just couldn't take the time to be responsible for all the stupid mistakes they were bound to make.

He didn't want to think of the woman's eyes, that direct speaking gaze, and the quick businesslike way she made up her mind. She would be all right. It was the youngster who would impede her, argue with her, slow her down . . .

Damn.

. . . damn troublesome women—even when they were untouchable. He just couldn't let that puppy get her into another situation that would put her life in danger.

Hell, he was no guardian angel.

Damn those eyes.

When the wagon was out of sight, he urged his horse up and out of the water and took off westward toward the bridge.

She didn't even look down at the water when they crossed the bridge over Rogers Springs, and it was only when they were several miles beyond that Bobby spoke again.

"Do you have any idea where you're going to next?"

he asked in a kind of pettish voice so unlike him that she gave him a sharp look.

"No, I don't," she said shortly. "I was just going to follow a road and see where it led me."

"That's crazy," he shot back. "If you want to go to Gramma's—"

"Who said I was going there?" Angelene demanded defensively. "Who ever said I thought I was going to Gramma's? *You* said—"

"I thought we agreed—" Bobby broke in.

"Well, I didn't," Angelene said flatly. She felt jittery now, and a little leery of having Bobby along on the ride with her. While she had been sure where she was headed when she had started out alone, she wasn't all that certain she wanted Bobby with her if she finally managed to get to New York, though she had been determined to do that. Her plan had simply been to present herself as a member of the sisterhood on her way to a post in New York. Sister Philomena had told her it was done all the time: the mother house periodically reassigned the sisters to places of varying need, and assured her no one would look askance at her travelling alone.

Now she was with Bobby and something inside her made her wary of detailing her exact destination to him in spite of his ready guess.

"And you didn't plan where to stay or how to feed yourself or anything?" Bobby went on.

"I guess I didn't," Angelene admitted reluctantly, clenching her hands under the scapula of her habit. God, it was so hard to lie to Bobby, but she couldn't tell him everything, not yet. She couldn't tell him she had money—some that she had taken from Josie, and another pouchful from Sister Philomena—all of it concealed under the all-encompassing habit. She worried too that if Bobby wanted to know why she had not removed at least the wimple and the veil, she would have no answer for him, nor any reason not to reveal what was hidden so skillfully beneath the trappings of a dutiful nun.

"I figured I would just travel on till dusk and then try

49

to find someplace that would take me in," she added, and she thought that sounded lame, and really too reckless for a woman on the run alone.

"I haven't got any money either," Bobby said. "Maybe it's lucky you've got a rifle. At least I can bag us something to eat."

"We can camp out again," Angelene suggested. "There's still some coffee and some cheese. We could get on that way for a couple of days. Maybe we could even get as far as Lexington."

"I doubt it," Bobby said. "We wouldn't be travelling that fast. We'll just have to take it a day at a time."

She looked at him again, a tinge of uncertainty in her eyes. A day at a time sounded like forever, and it hadn't seemed like that when she had started out. A day at a time . . .

"I guess we will," she said resignedly. "I guess we will."

Damnfool puppy, Rake swore as he pulled up in the underbrush above embankment where Bobby had drawn in the wagon, unhitched the horses and made camp. By his reckoning, they were two miles outside of Marysville, and he would have been happier to see them settled in some boarding house for the night than out on the side of the road with no damn protection and no damn food.

A man just didn't protect a religious woman like that, and she probably didn't know the difference.

Well, he damn well did and the only saving grace of this whole damnfool plan of his following them was that they happened to be heading in the same direction as he.

He had a saddlebag full of jerky and water and a flask of whiskey to keep him company during the night, and at that he was a damn sight more comfortable withal than he had been a lot of times in his life.

It was just a matter of watching them, and making sure the puppy didn't do anything rash or stupid until they had reached their destination.

He didn't even want to know where it was. He just wanted to keep out of sight, follow them to their termination point, and then go home. Wouldn't make any sense to have someone after him too, and even after all this time, it was still a distinct possibility.

He rubbed his face wearily as he chewed on a piece of jerky. A man just wasn't his brother's keeper—but a woman like that . . . with those eyes, damn it—and that innocence . . .

What the hell was the puppy doing now? He jackknifed himself upright as he saw the boy walking away from the wagon, up toward where he was camped.

Swiftly, silently, he threw his gear back on his horse and moved him, with just the faintest rustling of leaves underfoot, behind a stand of trees fifteen feet away.

Within one moment, the puppy was standing at the very spot he had just vacated, looking thoughtfully down on his own camp, and—son of a bitch—the boy was carrying a rifle.

Hell . . . Rake reached for his own gun, and eased his way through the trees to the boy's left where he could get a good bead on both the boy and the camp.

Like as not, he was after game, but still, a man sometimes couldn't be sure . . .

The puppy was just standing there, staring down at the wagon and the flickering fire *she* had managed to coax out of a few twigs enclosed in a circle of rocks.

The boy was listening . . . a right cautious young puppy to lend an ear to his surroundings before he lifted his gun. Commendable to look around a little bit, see if anything was stirring in the underbrush . . .

And—what the hell—the boy was aiming the damn rifle right down at his camp and his travelling companion . . .

Rake moved forward slowly, slowly. The puppy's eye was right on the girl, and he respected the itch of a trigger finger like no man. The intensity of concentrating on his prey took up all the room in a man's mind and heart. The puppy would never see him, maybe he wouldn't even

51

hear him . . . he cocked his gun.

"Ain't no rabbit holes down that way, son."

Bobby's head jerked up and then his flat blue gaze settled on the shadowy figure of the man from Rogers Springs. "I was aiming at a buck across the road," he said, without flickering an eye.

"You'd never get it stripped, cooked and packed in one night," Rake said. "You'd best let me catch you a rabbit."

"None of your business, mister. I'll fend for myself and . . . and the sister."

"No trouble, son. I reckon I'm a far sight more experienced at hunting than you are."

"Still and all," Bobby protested.

"Give me the gun, son."

"I'm gonna need it."

"So am I, if we're going to eat tonight."

"*We?*"

"We, son. Give me the gun."

At least, Rake thought, the puppy was smart enough to know when to give over. He took the rifle from Bobby's tight, resistant fingers, and motioned for him to rejoin his companion.

"Tell her not to worry," Rake said. "Tell her you met up with a force of nature and you couldn't fight it."

But Bobby didn't reappear for at least a half hour and by then he had worked himself up into a fine rage. "That son of a bitch just took the goddamned rifle right out of my hands," he stormed. "Probably went off to sell it in the next town or something. Goddamn it, I guess I'm not much good to you."

"It doesn't matter, Bobby," Angelene said soothingly, but even she was a little distraught. The stranger from the Springs? Following them? She wagered Bobby had not even thought about that aspect at all.

"It matters to me. The bastard took away our protection and our only means of getting food, and damn it—I'd kill him if I had a second chance."

His words rang belligerently in the lowering darkness.

"Here's your chance, son," Rake said, moving out of the shadows and into the camplight. He tossed the rifle back to Bobby and Bobby caught it on the edge of his threat and Angelene's horrified expression.

"I'm obliged," he said stiffly. "I guess I didn't mean that."

"Didn't you?" Rake asked drily. He held up his catch. "Ma'am?"

"We're both obliged," Angelene said, finding her voice. The stranger looked formidable in the firelight: the shadows lengthened his already lean and light-footed frame, and hollowed out the planes of his face so that he seemed mystical and other-worldly. She didn't know what to say to him in the face of Bobby's imprudence, and beyond that, she didn't know what to do with a skinned rabbit and a campfire.

Rake sensed her hesitation. "I'd be happy to transform him, ma'am."

"I'm sure you know just how," Angelene said appreciatively.

"I could've done that," Bobby whispered to her as they watched Rake skillfully cut apart the rabbit, and fish a small pan out from his saddlebags and set it on the fire.

"I'm glad I don't have to do it," Angelene whispered back, and she was even happier that within the hour she was biting into a juicy piece of meat flavored with a little of the whiskey that Rake hoarded in his saddlebags. Bobby was boiling up a pot of coffee for them all, his resentment simmering up in tandem with the bubbling liquid.

"We can't pay you," he said defiantly.

"I'm happy to do it for the sister," Rake said, leaning back against his saddlebag as he finished his portion of rabbit, feeling a moment of contentment at the sight of the woman's face across the campfire.

There was always something about a woman's face: there was such *life* in this one's expression, and something else, and he couldn't quite determine what it was. Regret, maybe. Sadness. Helplessness. Never could tell what pulled a woman to a religious life.

It was just that she was so damned beautiful, and he wanted to ask a dozen questions, and he didn't want to know anything about her at all.

"Tell me your name?" she asked after a long long while, after they had consumed the meat and the coffee and had a bit of the nearly rancid cheese, and after the moon had risen and Bobby had cleaned up and stomped off to bed down in the wagon.

"Best I don't, ma'am," he said consideringly, rather astonished by the feeling he wanted her to know—and he didn't.

"Why is that?" she asked curiously. She had thought, after Bobby left them, that the tension had eased and that the intimacy of the night and the fire would invite confidences, but she didn't know why she wanted that either. She knew nothing about this man. He could be a killer. He could be someone who had just disappeared into the wilderness, out of those who never gave their rightful names again for that very reason.

He was right. It was best not to be curious. It could only lead to questions and more questions.

"I'm glad to lend a hand," he said after a moment, evading her question. "People don't want to know too much around here. You take a man's gratitude and you move on."

But he wasn't so sure about the moving on part. This woman with the speaking eyes was as cloistered from the tribulations of overland travel as she was from the world. He wasn't so sure about the boy, but he didn't want to tell her about the boy. What was the point? There could have been a buck, unrealistic as it seemed that the boy could have killed it at that distance. On the other hand, they were neither of them too well able to fend for themselves and he felt some concern about that. They were like naive, trusting animals—like his own damn dog, for God's sake—naive as puppies, just like he had

54

characterized the boy.

She felt chastised for her forwardness, and yet she felt no fear from him, only a distinct sense of comfort with his long lean body stretched out across the fire from her, his face as still as a wood-carved idol, listening, listening.

She wondered what he was thinking, what he thought about her and Bobby travelling together in such a haphazard way, but she knew—she sensed, he wasn't even thinking about her at all.

A moment later, he rose and began saddling his horse. "Best to leave you now, ma'am," he said quietly, turning to her.

She looked so serene sitting there in the firelight, with her hands folded quietly on her lap, and the shadows molding her face into a Madonna-like mask. Only her eyes moved, following him as he mounted his horse, and shifted away from the camp.

"Thank you," she whispered as he disappeared into the shadows, but she didn't think he heard her. She didn't even think he cared, and she wondered about a man who travelled alone in the wilderness who had such a latent streak of kindness in him when everything about him suggested a man who needed no one nor helped no one.

Maybe he had aided them only because of what he thought *she* was, but what difference did it make anyway? They would never see him again; she was absolutely sure of that.

Chapter 4

He followed them another day, just out of sheer stubborn curiosity and in defiance of his better nature. There was nothing in it for him. When they nooned over near Center Mills, he was a silent watcher in the trees, satisfied that nothing untoward was going to happen.

When the puppy took a half hour to wander around the outskirts of town, he thought nothing of it, except that it was odd the boy would leave the sister alone; on the other hand, she seemed well able to entertain herself. She got some sleep, she cleaned the cookware she had stored in the boot of the wagon, under the perch. And she sat very still for a long, long time, as if she were praying.

They moved on, mid-afternoon, toward Crossville Junction and got halfway there before they made camp for the night. Bobby had picked up some cornmeal as they passed through town, and a flask of water. Rake watched from the shadows as the sister mixed up the cornmeal and fried it over the fire to have with the evening's coffee.

They didn't talk much, these two, but he didn't wonder at that. He was a man of few words himself, and he would not allow himself to speculate where they were going and why and how. He was just concerned about the rifle and how the puppy was going to use it next time.

He reveled in the sounds of the night, the peaceful

stillness underscored by the vibration of insect life and the rustle of trees in the wind.

And a rattle, a faint poisonous rattle somewhere off in the distance—but close, too close, and he was very close to the camp where the boy lay sleeping and the sister sat stringently awake, staring into the fire.

He crept forward once again until he was just inside the circle of shadow cast by the glow of the fire—and he heard it again.

Closer and closer, slithering in the dark . . . "Lady!" he called out to her, his voice soft—and still startling.

Her whole body jerked backward. "Who is that?" Her hand groped immediately for the rifle before she belatedly remembered it was in the wagon with Bobby. "Who's there?" Her voice tapered into pure fear.

"Shhh . . ." He edged his way into the firelight. "Listen . . ."

She froze, both at the sound of his voice and the stillness surrounding them. She heard nothing but the urgency in his voice, and then—the very faint sound of a rattle very near her. Very near. Too near.

"Don't move," he whispered and she could not have moved if something were about to explode beside her.

"I'm going to make a torch," he said quietly, moving cautiously into the circle of light, a thick branch in his hand.

She nodded, still unable to speak, shocked at his reappearance and the imminent danger that could be lurking at her very feet.

He jabbed the branch into the fire and after a long moment it caught, flaring up, shooting sparks and shadowy fingers every which way.

He lifted it and she recoiled, and then Bobby's head appeared over the side of the wagon. "What the—"

"Quiet!" Rake held the torch over his head and slowly thrust it outward and around in a circle, and then downward, still slowly, still turning in a circle, searching carefully the outer area of the camp, and then inward and

57

still inward, until finally he held the torch at hip length and illuminated the ground immediately surrounding the fire.

Angelene saw it first, not three feet away from her, and she reacted involuntarily, her whole body jumping backward as the thing slithered toward her.

The shot was an anti-climax: Rake drew and killed the thing in one economical motion and Angelene screamed as its head separated from its body and went flying into the shadows. She backed up against the wagon, shaking like a leaf.

Rake threw the makeshift torch into the campfire and dredged up another branch with which he lifted the body of the snake and removed it from the camp site and Angelene's horrified eyes.

Bobby leapt down from the wagon bed as Rake reappeared in the circle of firelight. "You!" he said accusingly. "What the hell are you doing here?"

"I was passing through, son," Rake said, brushing him off just as if he were a bothersome puppy and turning to Angelene. "You all right, ma'am?"

She listened to her thrumming heart for a long moment. "Yes," she said finally.

"Good. Then let me suggest you sleep in the wagon tonight and your—companion—keep guard for a change."

"I couldn't sleep," she whispered, her body still shaking. What if he hadn't come? What if she hadn't noticed? And Bobby hadn't awakened?

"I know what you mean," he said. "Good night, ma'am."

"Good night," she breathed, watching him again disappear into the shadows. Every question she had was tamped down by fear, and Bobby himself seemed totally speechless. Or maybe he was just angry because he had not been the one to come to her aid.

She breathed a deep heaving sigh. One day at a time, and who knew what dangers she had yet to confront.

58

What if Bobby were continually no help? She would be better off alone, she thought, thrusting her trembling hands into the pockets of her habit. She really would be better off alone.

"A stupid snake, for God's sake," Bobby grumbled. "I was sound asleep, and where the hell did he come from? You're acting like he's your goddamned savior, and all he is is an interfering son of a bitch."

"Well thank you. It's nice to know how much you value my life. You'd rather he hadn't intervened, either at the Springs or here."

"Oh hell, you would have heard the thing and woken me up, Angelene. Don't make more of your buckskin benefactor than the facts tell you in plain light of day. You don't need his protection, and he sure can't want anything from us. I just hope he's somewhere ten miles ahead of us and on his way."

That was all he had to say in the matter, he thought. He hated the idea that the man thought he could look out for his own sister better than he could, and he said so. "I'm on your side, Angelene; I thought you always knew that. We don't need a third party bumping his nose into our business."

"I guess we don't," she said reluctantly, but even Bobby couldn't know how fully and intensely she still felt the shock of seeing that snake nearly at her feet, and the stranger right there to take the threat away. She still couldn't comprehend it. It was almost as if he were following them—but that made no sense.

The worst thing was, nothing was making sense, and she was beginning to see that her headlong flight toward some shapeless future with her unknown grandmother was nothing more than an unconsidered rebellion on her part.

It might even be better just to go back to Josie. This risky path was full of perils she had never dreamed of

59

when she had begun her journey. A woman alone: how naive could she have been?

And there was Bobby, who was alternately moody and supportive . . . in the end, she had responsibility for him and not the other way around. She was the eldest and she was supposed to have some common sense. Still, she was beginning to think her life was motivated by nothing but fear.

He was behind them by a couple of hundred feet, no more, and he had a bad feeling, a very bad feeling. They were going too slow, and they would not make Crossville Junction by night, and he couldn't figure it out.

The woman didn't know it, either. She sat stiffly beside the boy and she hardly moved; she looked like she was tussling with something deep in her mind and wasn't even paying attention to where he was going or how hard they travelled.

The boy was up to something . . .

The thought tickled the edges of his consciousness. He couldn't allow it in, not yet.

But the boy pulled up too soon to make camp for the night, and the sister never questioned it.

Rake hunkered behind the bushes again, prepared to wait. He was too damned close to home now, and too far away from understanding what was happening with the boy to just go off and leave the sister. He just couldn't do it.

When darkness fell, he felt an ominous thickness in the silence. The boy wasn't talking. And the sister sat, holding her whole body close as if she expected an assault of some kind.

The wagon was parked in the shadows beyond the campfire, and the boy said, "Maybe you should lay down now, Angelene."

Angelene . . .

The lady's name was Angelene. Sister Angelene . . . it

sounded impossibly pure and holy.

She moved out of sight and the boy crouched down next to the fire, listening to her movements as she climbed into the wagon.

Nothing happened the whole of the night, until the light of dawn. Was the boy sleeping? Rake couldn't tell from where he watched, but there was suddenly the most ungodly noise he had ever heard, a howling sound, shrieking high up into the trees and bouncing down again in an unearthly keening cry that startled even his horse, and sent the unhitched team that pulled the wagon into a stampeding frenzy.

"Angelene!"

"Bobby!"

He raced after the horses, hollering at them, stumbling and falling as he raced to grab the leading ropes dragging in the dirt. He fell flat on his face, cursing, shouting, and then he froze as a solitary horseman streaked by his prone body and took after the horses.

"Hell and damn!"

"Bobby . . ."

Angelene knelt beside him, reaching for his arms to pull him to a sitting position.

"Do you know who the damn hell that was?" he demanded furiously.

"Are you all right?"

"That son of a bitch," he muttered, getting to his knees. "I'm all right. Damn it all, Angelene, I feel like a two-year-old child right now, and just look at who's gone and mended my mistake once again."

She looked up and there he was, cantering back toward them, the sun behind him, their two horses beside him with the lead ropes firmly in his large hands.

He didn't say anything as he guided the horses past them and walked them into camp and hitched them up to the wagon.

"They'd have been long gone if I hadn't gotten them," he said without any kind of inflection in his tone when

61

they joined him at the camp.

"I know," Bobby said defensively. "But Crossville Junction isn't too far from here. I could have walked there. I would have done something."

But his guileless blue gaze didn't meet Rake's eyes and he again had the thought, *the boy is up to something*.

He turned to Angelene. "Ma'am?"

She smiled at him uncertainly.

"Maybe you ought to just sign on with us," Bobby said caustically. "Pay isn't too great, though. We don't have a nickel between us."

"I'm going home, boy," Rake said. "I hope you're close to home, too."

But he didn't go but a couple hundred yards beyond them when he finally took his leave, and the bad feeling resonated deep inside him when they started off slowly again.

He hung well back behind them this time, waiting, watching, wary. The sun got hot, hotter than fire this day, and they kept stopping, and Sister Angelene never once protested or asked a question.

The boy didn't want to reach Crossville Junction . . .

The inescapable conclusion hit him in the gut, and he felt a bracing wallop of fear for the woman.

Every muscle in his body tightened as he eased himself slowly behind them, listening, watching, waiting.

It didn't take long. The boy stopped, complaining of the heat, and veered off the road to find shade. He was gratified to see the woman checking to be sure the horses were secured once they had been unhitched from the wagon, and he was even a little reassured to see them arguing and that she was not accepting everything the boy wanted.

Damn, he wished he had asked questions, and he wished he knew a lot of things he was never going to know.

He settled in for the long watch.

* * *

This time, he fell asleep, and he awakened deep in the night, startled by a sound, . . . No sounds . . . Night sounds—

He crouched in the bushes, alert, wary, listening—

He heard it again, ten minutes later, the soft thump of hooves, the distant hum of voices—just a word, a direction, a silence.

He couldn't backtrack in the night. The moon wasn't full, the earth was soft, the sounds of the night compelling.

He waited; he waited until dawn, and as surely as he expected, the sounds came to him again: the thudding hooves, moving cautiously now, a word spoken low. He could hear them coming closer, closer, no more than two or three of them, and his skin prickled.

They were searching, they weren't sure . . .

They were looking for the boy . . .

And the boy had been pulling back, delaying so that he could be found . . .

His bad feeling escalated, along with his sense of the riders coming closer and closer, thrashing through the underbrush to find the subtle approach; they were a hundred feet away from finding him.

Then the boy lit the campfire, and they smelled the smoke, and they veered off toward the scent, passing barely fifty feet away from him, heading toward the road and the smoke fire, with an obvious plan of direct attack.

They were after the woman . . .

He could hear them talking, her and the boy. The boy was peevish this morning, not willing to get an early start.

She lapsed into silence and a wary uncertainty.

Good, he thought; she was on her guard, and he was there, close as two strides of his horse through the bushes. He couldn't warn her, he could only wait.

And listen.

"Bobby, this is crazy. Crossville Junction is about twenty minutes down the road, according to what we were told . . ."

"I'm tired," Bobby said. "I didn't know things were

going to be this hard. I'm willing to go, you know I am, but it's such a long trip, and I don't see why we have to be in such a hurry."

In a way, neither did she. Surely they were a long enough distance away from Cairo that they didn't have to worry about Josie or her brothers giving chase. Surely she should feel secure enough to dispense with her disguise. But she didn't: she felt frantic, and almost justified in demanding that Bobby return to Josie and let her go on alone.

"I don't know," she said finally. "I just am."

"Well, even if Josie were looking for us," Bobby said placatingly, "we have days and days of a head start on her, so stop worrying."

Angelene wrapped her fingers tightly around her hot coffee cup to keep herself from blurting out exactly how much she was worrying, and a distressing thought formed in her mind: it was time to get rid of Bobby.

Dear Bobby, to whom things never looked quite as bad as they really were. She didn't need someone along with her who disputed her intuition of danger. She knew what she had seen and she knew what Josie had expected of her, and more than that, she knew of only one way to escape: she would run as far and fast as she could and somehow find sanctuary with her grandmother, and she didn't need Bobby's help to do that.

Somewhere in Crossville Junction, she would have to give Bobby the slip. They would need supplies; the last time, Bobby had bartered his young muscles for a sack of cornmeal and a supply of water. He had been gone from camp a couple of hours, and had she understood her need to travel alone then, she could have taken advantage of his absence. It made sense, too: he would not be stranded on the road and he would have an opportunity to bargain and trade for a horse and some supplies to get him back to Josie again.

"We need provisions," she said.

"I know, I know. I'll take care of it when we get to

Crossville Junction," Bobby said impatiently.

Good.

"I'm almost done with breakfast," she said. "When do you think you'll want to get started?"

"In another fifteen minutes," Bobby said. "If that's soon enough for you."

"That will be fine," she said tightly to his back as he disappeared behind the wagon. Fifteen minutes—they could have been in sight of town by then, if only they had started earlier.

She sighed as she dumped the remaining coffee over the campfire, and reached to get the canteen with its dwindling supply of water. She shook it, and then poured a small amount into the coffee pot to wash away the dregs. She tipped this over the campfire as well and then scooped dirt over the smouldering embers.

It was then she heard the hoofbeats—a dull thumping in the distance at first, coming closer and closer, and she rose up curiously, her heart pounding.

They were coming down the road. As she moved out into their path, dropping her canteen and the coffee pot, she could just see them in the distance, and she stood rooted by the side of the road as they came closer and closer . . .

And then she saw—the bend of their bodies, the relentlessness of the pace, the hard-driving determination . . .

"Bobby!" she screamed, whirling and running toward the wagon.

He loomed up menacingly from inside the wagon bed. "Don't try to run, Angelene," he shouted at her. "Stop! *Angelene—STOP!"*

"Bobby!" she shrieked, veering away from him, certain he wouldn't hesitate to leap over the side and pin her to the ground. "Bobby . . ." she sobbed as she raced blindly toward the trees, the skirt of her nun's habit crunched in her icy hands, her veil catching in every branch and bush, the dull thud of hoofbeats following her unhesitatingly into the thicket.

Raso and Tice . . . she knew it—her throat clogged with betrayal and mind-altering fear. Bobby had done this to her—Bobby—he had made her into an animal and they were following the scent of her fear, closing in for the kill.

She should have known she couldn't escape Josie . . . she should have known a woman couldn't break the bonds of family without consequences.

Dear Lord . . . they were gaining—she could hear the panting of the horses and the men, the thrash of bushes, the curses of voices now familiar to her—

She saw a break in the trees ahead of her, and she used every last ounce of her strength to heave her aching body toward it, toward the road, toward hell—

She never saw the horseman angling toward her at breakneck speed, she never felt his strong arm literally lift her off the road or heard his authoritative voice growling at her: "Climb up, damnit—hold on, *hold on* . . ."

She was slipping—she grabbed for his arm, his shoulder, she held onto him for dear life, but they were gaining, gaining—her brothers would overtake them and kill them both.

"Let me *down!*" she cried. "Oh, let me down . . ." Let them kill her, only *her*; they only wanted her. She was ready . . .

He didn't hear her, or he didn't want to hear her, she didn't know which. He swerved his horse off of the road suddenly, heartstoppingly, and into the trees again, coming to a jerking halt just beyond view of the road, and dropping her unceremoniously to her feet.

"Climb up now—*fast.*" He held out his hand and she grasped it. He pulled and she involuntarily levered herself upward and awkwardly swung one leg over to straddle the saddle behind him, and before she could right herself, he took off, so that all she could do was grab his waist and pull herself upright as best she could.

A moment later, they were pounding through the trees

again and back out onto the road, leaving their pursuers flailing around in the woods, and gaining a good five minutes head start on them.

But still, she thought dazedly, they would never give up, and she could never be saved. She might just have the grace of a minute, an hour, a day before they finally found her, and whatever the stranger thought to do, he couldn't hide her away forever.

But when she dared to turn around to look, she couldn't see them—and when she did, they were only pindots on the horizon in dogged pursuit, so far behind them her escape was inevitable. Her future was her own.

Her cry of triumph was swallowed by the wind.

Chapter 5

Crossville Junction was his town, his heaven, the place to which he had come and healed his wounds. He had been running then; he supposed there had never been a time when he hadn't been running from one reality or another: his mother's death, the alienation of her people, his father's rejection, and the final grueling comprehension that in his rage, he had become obsessed, habitually drunk, an outlaw, a wanted man, and ultimately on the run from the gang that had spawned him.

He had run from Kansas to Missouri and across the River he had run from the nightmare vision his life had become. He had run from the memories of bodies and blood, from terrorizing the innocent and murdering the strong; he had run. He had run from the family of the gang and the betrayals within, and he had run from the stench of the smoking gun in his hand and the bloodlust in his eye. He never knew if he had killed ten men or one because he lived in liquor-sodden fog in which he was answerable to no one for his actions, not even himself.

He had run: there had been women and a town, whether one town or a hundred, he never knew. It was all a blur in his mind as he expended his rage and his youth up and down the border between Missouri and Illinois as if he could obliterate it, his father and himself.

In the end, his gang pursued him deep into the wilds of

Kentucky until one day he had run up a ridge where he came upon a fallen-down shack with just enough roof to shelter him, and he had fallen into a stupor inside its dark ramshackle comfort. He never awakened until three days later to the smell of dog and a cold muzzle in his face.

There was something about a dog that made a man whole again: a man getting by on instinct and not much else found acceptance and companionship, and a man was never the same again. The animal had saved the life of an animal, and had shown him the way back to salvation and purgatory both.

He didn't leave the ridge for another six months. He hunted with the dog and he built up the cabin and made it livable, and he talked to the fire and the spirits of the hills, and he made a kind of peace with himself about who he was and what he had done, and he reckoned he might stay on the ridge forever.

He hadn't figured on the woman—any woman—and he was amused at the thought of the two of them astride his horse: the recluse and the nun—both cloistered, both on the run.

She wrapped her arms tightly around his torso, too shaken to notice anything but the long strong sense of him in the surround of her arms. He was so warm, so solid, and he had come out of nowhere to save her, as if he had been watching, as if he had known they were stalking her and that Bobby would betray her.

She couldn't bear to think about it: Bobby had followed her purposefully, deviously, manufacturing dreams and determination, giving her exactly what she wanted to hear so that she would slow the pace and in the end escape nothing but the knowledge that her family was inescapable.

He had saved her from that, and she felt, beneath the overlay of shock, a kindling feeling of gratitude that this taciturn stranger had not abandoned her.

Her family had abandoned her ages ago when Josie had

made the one unrelenting decision that had broken any faith a daughter could have with her mother. Josie, who had not batted an eyelash when she sent her three vicious sons to kill her only daughter, one ... two ... three. Josie, intense and obsessed, would never give up the search.

She felt a chill course down the center of her spine. Josie was a murderer; what was one more body added onto the count?

She could not plan a minute beyond this time, this place, as the stranger drove his horse unrelentingly up a sharply graded ridge that looked like Crossville Junction to her, and her feeling of horror was replaced by a tiny shock of foreboding.

It looked as if they were going back into a wilderness from which she might never return.

The horse slowed and began picking its way through a thicket of bushes that covered an overgrown track.

She would be alone with him—he could do what he wanted with her. He could ... he *could* attack her and kill her and *no one would ever know* ...

He could—he *could* be Josie's hired gun, someone she had sent to doubly insure that Bobby carried out his business—

Dear Lord ...

That would presuppose that he knew somehow that she wasn't what she seemed ...

But he didn't act as if he knew that at all—

She began shaking. What did she know of this stranger who had saved her life more than once? Why hadn't he just let Bobby reel them out into the river so that she could drown? Why hadn't he let the rattlesnake bite her? Why hadn't he just let Tice and Raso catch up with her?

Why had he saved her—if he were Josie's hired henchman?

Maybe Josie wanted to finish her off herself ... maybe he was taking her to some secret hideout of Josie's, and she would be there watching, waiting, boasting, deadly ...

Or maybe she was letting her imagination run away with her good sense; maybe he was exactly what he seemed, and maybe he really thought she was who she pretended to be, and maybe he considered such a woman untouchable, and she really was safe.

He wouldn't hurt her, he wouldn't force her. He would ask questions and she would tell him as much as he needed to know and eventually he would help her get where she wanted to go.

Any man would—if he believed her to be a religious.

Josie had nothing to do with it—with him. She was reacting—overreacting—to the shock of Bobby's betrayal, and to a resonating panic at her feeling of helplessness. She couldn't even let go of the man lest she fall off of the horse, and she didn't know where they were going so that even if she tried to escape him, she would surely become lost.

Nor did she feel reassured when they finally came to a clearing that led to a deep dark swath of pasture fronting a rambling cabin built back against a hill.

When he stopped, she dropped her arms quickly, guiltily. He crossed his left leg over the pommel and slid lightly to the ground and stood looking up at her.

"Ma'am?"

"Where are we?" she demanded, her voice evincing just the faintest tremor of uncertainty.

"My home," he said, holding out his hands to her. "Might as well come on down, ma'am. That saddle makes a hard bed."

She bit her lips and looked down at her right leg and she was dismayed to see that the skirt of her habit had hitched up and a good portion of her black-stockinged leg was showing.

That got her moving: she followed his example, folding her leg across the saddle and sliding her body downward, trusting him to grasp her body and bear her weight.

His hands were tight and strong, and his face impassive—and maybe a little kind. She couldn't tell. More than anything he looked tired and worn; his face was deeply tanned and lined with a lifetime of a man's experience. The tenderness of his mouth was hidden by a brush of mustache, and there was no glint of interest in his gray eyes.

He set her down and turned to tend to his horse, and that was more reassuring than anything.

She was sure she looked like a small black crow standing in the middle of the pasture, her knees weak from uncertainty and fear. She didn't know quite what to do. She didn't want to do anything until she was sure that Josie was not lurking behind the solid wood door of that unprepossessing cabin.

It was safer here, in the open, with the blue sky and blazing sun enfolding her in a moment of normalcy and warmth that seemed to negate everything that had happened, everything she had felt.

And he—the stranger—all he cared about at the moment was unsaddling his horse and getting him brushed and fed. He disappeared with the horse into a barn that sat off to one side in a fenced field.

So she was alone, for one moment, and she almost took off and ran into the woods from which they had come. Then he reappeared, his saddlebags slung over his shoulder, and he motioned to her.

She hesitated, turning her head this way and that— there was nowhere to run that he could not overtake her within minutes—and then she moved toward him, her head bent, restraint in her usual eager stride, determined to portray the kind of woman whose disguise she had adopted, and to convince this stranger that his only course was to aid her in her most desperate need.

Wings of an angel . . .

He thought it as she came toward him, when the soft breeze lifted the edges of her veil around her downcast face. He couldn't see her glorious blue eyes, and he sensed her fear.

The boy had called her Angelene . . .

But the boy had betrayed her and he felt a keen edgy desire to know why.

Angelene . . .

Why would a woman with a face so beautiful hide herself away so thoroughly? Why did she slow her walk and fold herself inward and pretend there was nothing suggestive about her when even the flowing robes of her calling could not disguise the womanliness of her?

And yet she hid her fear. Only when she stood directly before him did she lift her eyes to meet his, and her eyes were her soul. She didn't know how to hide behind them.

Her fear and uncertainty were palpable, as was her courage. "What happens next?" she asked, her voice colored with the hope that he had some idea.

He had no ideas. He had never had a woman here; he had never played the role of savior. "Damned if I know," he answered her, "except that you can't go anywhere for a day—maybe a while."

She turned away from him, the wings of her veil hiding the frantic expression in her eyes. "That is impossible," she said finally, certain that he would understand the reasons why by inference.

He felt a curious impatience with her that she didn't quite comprehend the fact that her pursuers probably had not given up searching for her. "You can't leave the ridge," he said inflexibly and she knew argument with him would be futile.

For one moment, she wished she hadn't tricked herself up in this disguise so that she could use some feminine wiles on him. She felt a gnawing desperation just to run, from him, from her past. He was a stranger who would ask questions, and he might even be ruthless enough to concoct plots of his own whereby Josie might reward him for her return.

Assuming he knew nothing about Josie already.

She couldn't take the chance. "I must go."

"They'll still be looking for you."

"I'll go the other way," she said stubbornly. "If you'd just take me to . . ."

He shook his head. "They'll kill you. You know it. Better to wait them out, lady."

She turned her head away again. She didn't doubt they could find her. But maybe she could try to find her own way off the ridge. She could just run until she dropped in her tracks and yes, maybe they would find her. So maybe staying with him would be a preferable solution—if he were not her enemy as well.

She would have to be careful, so very careful. He must not perceive even a hint of the fact she was anything but what she seemed. Oh, but how could she carry off such an impersonation when she was anything but meek or obedient?

No, she could be meek—look at how she had fooled Josie. He would never know. He probably knew nothing about nuns or their religious life.

It might be all right.

If *he* were what he seemed—

If her brothers weren't pounding up the ridge the very moment she was deciding to trust him . . . oh God, her brothers . . . Bobby—

No—*No!* She could not afford the luxury of giving way to her fury over Bobby's treachery. She couldn't allow herself to *think* of it. She wouldn't even tell *him* about it.

She swallowed hard and took a long deep breath to get her anger under control, and then she turned back to him, her face composed once more, her eyes glancing off his and sliding downward again. "Perhaps you're right," she said quietly—*meekly* "I'm most grateful to you."

There was a change of heart in a hurry, and it was a little too abrupt to suit him. "No trouble, ma'am," he said in kind, still wary of that sense of desperation that surrounded her. She accepted nothing, obviously, but she surely had seen the sense of hiding out a day or two in a place where no one would be likely to look for her.

No one ever came up the ridge. She would be as safe here as in a church—maybe safer.

It was an odd thought—the ridge as a holy place, but maybe it was. Maybe he had cast out all his sins, and

74

maybe her presence there would finally sanctify the place and the time and, ultimately, him.

It was strange with the woman in the house. It felt as though something were off-balance, as if somehow the space he had made for himself had lost its symmetry and become irregular, pulsating with unfamiliar emotion all revolving around her.

Yet she was silent, contemplative, unobtrusive, existing in some realm of prayer and quietude.

Still, there was a particular restiveness in her, and a lurking fear and distrust that were mirrored most eloquently in her beautiful eyes, so that when he had finally thrust open the door of the cabin, she had braced herself for what might emerge.

He wondered what she had expected: her whole body froze as she sensed movement beyond the door, and then sagged perceptibly as the dog leapt up and out and raced across the dooryard to hurl himself against her black garbed body and snuffle the ground around the hem of her habit.

She hadn't expected the dog.

The dog surely hadn't expected her either.

He didn't know what he expected, but this sense of disruption within the calm center he had created for himself sat hard with him.

The dog liked the woman. He hovered around her and her raging silence until she touched his head or stroked his nose, and he never took account of the fact that her head was always bent low as if she were praying—or hiding something.

She could be hiding those speaking eyes.

He hadn't much to offer her, after all. The cabin was crude and efficient, but better than anything he had had since he was a boy living with his mother—an outcast even then.

He didn't know how a man made a home for himself. A man on the run didn't have time for niceties—that kind of man didn't even know the rudiments of creating a safe haven: he left it to others to create it.

But when he had found this place, he had found a haven and he had begun, slowly, to inhabit it from the outside in. He had constructed the crude furniture—a table, a chair, a trundle bed, a cabinet to hang his clothes. He had paid a woman in Crossville Junction to weave the rag rug he had placed in front of the fireplace. He had carted in the cookstove and built the shelves beside it, and when he got interested in feeding himself, he had scrounged up some pots, a coffeepot, some dishes, food, some canned goods. After a while, he had built a bed and put a small heating stove up in the loft above the long room, and he had used that as his bedroom. Finally he had bought some rough-woven cotton material and hung it over peg-supported dowels to create a curtain over the windows.

This was his home, and every time he entered it, he felt it enfold him. He felt a sense of place and a center that contained all that had pulled him outward and all that was destructive within him. Here, he felt at one with himself, and cleansed.

But now the woman would impose her needs and fears on the flat calm of his days, and he could not guess for how long she would stay, or whether she would just bolt out the door and disappear into the anonymity of the night and into the hands of those who pursued her.

He had given to her the space that was obviously his: the length and width of the bed swallowed her slender body as she huddled in its center, his rough woolen blanket wrapped around her tightly, her body straining to keep awake and listening hard to the sounds of the night and seeking the one unfamiliar sound that would alert her to danger.

But all was quiet. And *he* was quiet. She hadn't expected that he would be a quiet man. It was almost as if he had nothing to say beyond the most basic communication with her.

Or maybe he just didn't *want* to say anything.

And he hadn't asked questions—not yet, at any rate—nor did he require her presence. He had left her alone, and she found it odd to be alone until it occurred to her that he was respecting her outward guise, and she found that to be good—very, very good. She wouldn't talk much either. She would keep to herself, and in the end he would believe whatever story she concocted and he would offer to help her.

Still, it was harder than she thought it would be to sit across from him as he dutifully fed her dinner. She found her impulses warring between looking at him unabashedly, and keeping her eyes downcast and behaving as self-effacingly as a woman of the cloth.

But she found the silence stifling, and she knew it was because she was used to the noise of the road ranch and her continual bickering with Josie. She felt as if she needed to fill the silence, but she knew how dangerous it was to begin to talk and open herself up to questions and explanations she did not wish to make.

What a wild scheme she had devised, thinking she could just disguise herself, escape Josie and somehow make it to her grandmother's home in New York.

She hadn't the faintest idea where New York was, and now it looked as if she was to get no further than the attic of some reclusive mountain man's cabin.

And she still didn't know whether the man had anything to do with Josie. She didn't know anything, she thought later, as she listened to the night noises and quelled all the uncertainties and fears that clamored just beneath the surface of her wavering confidence.

She didn't even know if she would be alive in the morning.

She knew for sure she would never sleep.

But the dog woke her, nudging its muzzle against her face and licking her dry lips fervently so that she had to raise herself upright to escape its enthusiasm.

The dog . . .

77

The man. The sun outside the window at the far end of the attic space. The chill of the morning mountain air, hardly mitigated by the diminishing aura of warmth she felt from the little stove nearby.

He had lit the stove . . .

She shuddered as she jumped to her feet. He had been up there sometime during the night, and the thought that he could have prowled the room, lurking at her bedside, positively scared the wits out of her.

He could have found out somehow that she wasn't what she seemed. But how? How? Her sleep-fuddled mind couldn't think of one thing that would give her away, save perhaps that she had slept in her habit and she had not removed the veil. But that was a precaution, and after all, what could he know of the habits of a religious? *He knew nothing at all.*

He had just wanted her to be comfortable.

The simple explanation. The probable one.

She touched the grizzled head of the dog. "Do you have a name, I wonder?" she murmured to steady her frazzling nerves. Does *he* have a name?

She didn't want to know it.

She didn't want him to know hers.

The only thing she wanted to know was that it was safe to attempt to continue on her journey, and she knew it would not be as easy as that.

She smoothed her clothing, made sure that her habit and veil were presentable, and then, with the dog leading the way, she walked cautiously down the rickety attic steps.

Angelene . . .

Angelene of the speaking eyes and the beautiful face that did not belong within the confines of a nun's wimple. Angelene, *Sister* Angelene, who had been followed by the boy, delayed by him, and chased by two murderous men. What could those innocent angel eyes have done to warrant the demand of her life?

The whole of the first day, she was so still and quiet he barely knew she was there.

Except for the air: the air moved in agitated waves around the stillness of her; her pent-up emotion was like a bird flapping its wings in futility. Her words needed to fly, and he refused to ask the questions to release them.

He wanted to think.

He knew what it was to be desperate, to be hunted, to be dangerously on the edge of capitulating to something beyond oneself, something that had the allure of the flame and seared like the devil. He had been to that place and further than that, and when he finally understood that succumbing to his dark side meant death, he had never wanted to tell a soul.

It was so strange with the woman in the house.

She sat on the trundle bed by the fireplace, her head lowered, and did not move the entire day—except when the dog nuzzled her, except when he asked if she wanted food, except in the one or two odd moments when he caught her looking, those angel eyes calculating where she was, what she was doing, what he was doing—and something else, perhaps? Then her head would bow again and an onlooker would believe she was deep in the midst of pious prayer.

Maybe she was. Maybe there was no other solution for her. Maybe she was atoning for other sins.

Maybe her destiny was to be one with the earth.

Or—the unbidden, forbidden thought—one with him.

Chapter 6

He was an extraordinarily busy man for someone who lived alone on a high ridge. She was consumed with curiosity to know what it was that kept him so busy, and she couldn't move two inches from the trundle bed where she had ensconced herself on the preceding morning.

She didn't know how she was going to keep still for an entire day. The dog nudged her, demanding that she play with him.

The man went in and out at periodic intervals, and she couldn't be sure that he wouldn't walk in on her in some unguarded moment when she chose to look out the window, or tried to find some clue as to who he was or what he intended to do with her.

But he was a man who lived in such rustic simplicity, she could almost believe he was what he seemed.

She was not, however, and so for that first day she kept her head bowed and her mouth shut. It was the hardest thing she had ever had to do.

It gave her too much time to think, and she didn't need to think. She was desperate to *act*, and her rescuer didn't seem to find it imperative to do anything at all.

He hadn't even asked her name, or why Raso and Tice were pursuing her with such a vengeance. But she had figured it out. Josie had thought she would tell. Josie thought she might have told Mother Margaret, and that she would tell anyone else she could, that she would find

80

a Sheriff and they would come looking for her and expose her and all those killings, all those men—those missing, long-gone men. No one knew what had happened to them, and that poor Abner McNab . . .

My mother is a murderess . . .

She couldn't see herself confessing any of that to her taciturn savior; he would think she was crazy. He thought she was pure, innocent, pious.

So why didn't he have any questions?

Did he know everything already?

Her hands turned cold thinking about it. He had been so conveniently *there* everytime there was a problem. Bobby resented him. Bobby . . . damn Bobby—maybe it *had* been an act. How could she know after the way she had trusted Bobby and he had led her into a trap?

She was going to go mad. Maybe she was already mad.

Why else would she watch him covertly when he came into the cabin to attend to feeding the dog or replenish the cask of water or to boil up yet another cup of coffee in an endless consumption of cups of coffee throughout the morning?

Why else would she almost open her mouth to speak, and then think the better of it and lower her eyes once again so that when he passed all she could see of him were his long denim-clad legs moving purposefully toward the door with the dog following in his steps?

Why else did she feel she couldn't say one word without exposing herself to those opaque gray eyes into which she could not even bear to look directly, lest he discover just what a liar she was?

The first day passed into one long fraught nightmare of trying to maintain the character of the woman she was supposed to be.

She couldn't do it for more than a day—she was sure of it; she had to convince her silent savior that the best course was to get her away from his isolated mountain cabin as fast as he could. Instantly.

She was going to scream if the silence stretched out much further. She jumped up suddenly and began pacing the long room to expend that fury of energy and frustration.

And he caught her.

Her back was turned to him for that one moment when he entered the cabin; she whirled as she heard the tick of the dog's paws and her beautiful eyes widened—with guilt or fear, he couldn't tell, nor did she have time to control or hide the determined expression on her face.

Damn those eyes.

"Sister?" he said, swinging a well-worn saddle off of his shoulder into the corner of the room by the door.

Dear Lord, now what had she given away? She frantically grasped at maintaining some composure, but those cool gray eyes seemed to take in everything, just *everything*, and it was almost as if she had nowhere to hide, nowhere to go—except by his decree.

Now she was out of character and she had to distract him somehow. "I must leave," she said, her voice firm, her resolve just on the edge of collapsing altogether.

How did one convince a rock to move? It would take an avalanche to initiate any expression in that impassive sun-browned face. The eyes unnerved her; they seemed to see right through her, as if they knew all her secrets.

"Those men are still seeking you. They will kill you if they find you now, and they *will* find you if you leave the ridge."

He was so sure! No one could be that certain without knowing—*something*. "You can't know that," she said defiantly.

"Nor can you," he said heavily. "Do you really want to take the chance?"

Well, did she? To anyone she might have said that action was preferable to doing nothing. But doing something meant merely carrying on as she had begun: a woman alone travelling across the frontier, hoping to find her way to a place she had never been, praying that her disguise would save her from assault.

Naive of her to think anything could be that simple.

"One sometimes relies on luck," she countered cautiously.

"Not prayer, Sister?"

"And one prays—and *hopes*," she retorted tartly. "But prayers and hopes don't always solve problems." Oh no, she was talking too much—she could see his eyes light up with interest at the nun who believed in luck and hope as much as the dogma of her church, and she had to turn away from him lest he infer much more from the expression on her face.

She knew what it was: it was worldly, not innocent, too revealing. There was something about the face being framed and thrust forward from that confining crown of the wimple and veil that made it so susceptible to responding. If she were what she was supposed to be, she would bow to the wiser master and retreat into her prayers and that would have been the end of it.

Of course she had aroused his interest by questioning his decision.

"Becoming a target won't solve yours," he said tightly. "If they kill you, you'll never be able to hope or pray again—Sister."

Her back stiffened. "Of course," she said slowly, turning to face him again, mustering every ounce of her nerve to quell her frantic need to *move*. "You're right. I *am* anxious, but I'm not foolhardy."

"I didn't think you were," he agreed warily. She was talking too much now, this nun with the beautiful face and speaking eyes, and her words were too temporal and there was no mysticism in her practicality. Her desire to stay alive was very much of this world, and he understood that most human of emotions only too well. "You're safe here, Sister."

She wanted to turn away from his mesmerizing gray eyes and impassive face. She couldn't have dreamed up a better savior than he: he seemed to have no interest in her whatsoever and that, however welcome it was to her, was also disquieting.

There was an aura about him. He seemed calm and quiet and yet he radiated something hot and potent; she sensed danger emanating from him, contained and deliberate. He wasn't just some illiterate mountain man with a good heart. He spoke from experience: he had lived another life.

But then so had she; they were hiding things, both of them. This was an unholy alliance, and he was not sheltering her out of the goodness of his heart: she felt it as he waited for her to acknowledge his assurance that she had nothing to fear from him.

All she could do was nod her head.

"For as long as need be," he added stringently, just to see how she would react. He was beginning to become very curious about the woman behind the religious facade, in spite of himself, in spite of her. She was struggling even as he spoke to maintain her pose of serenity and composure and she was not succeeding very well. She was a woman with a purpose, he thought, on her way to somewhere that had nothing to do with convents or church dispositions.

"Surely no more than a day or two," she said finally.

"You must tell me, Sister. Only you know why those men were looking to kill you." So he said it finally, and every instinct within him pricked up as her face set and she turned away from him again.

"I can't tell you," she said stiffly, and she really thought that was better than claiming she didn't know anything even though he might infer that.

He didn't. She felt his restiveness even with her back turned: he couldn't believe at all that she had no idea why she had been hunted down. "You *won't* tell me," he contradicted, keeping his tone of voice even and non-censurious.

He was too intuitive, she thought despairingly. "Is it a condition of your sheltering me?" she continued, bowing her head so that she would appear humble rather than frightened by his perception. She couldn't make herself turn to face him, and she felt that put her in a bad position: her very lack of nerve would compromise her. Nevertheless, she could not look him in the eye—not yet, not about this.

She felt him measuring her question as if there were qualifying points at which he would accept or not accept what she chose to tell him, and she swallowed hard. He might hoist her right up on his horse this minute and take her to town, and then where would she be, with her brothers possibly still on the loose and not knowing a thing about where to go next?

He answered her finally: "Not yet, Sister. Not yet." Still, there was a promise in that reluctant tone. He meant to find out, and she could either continue lying to him or he would allow her to leave, and her only choice would be the lesser of the two dangers.

It was evident to him, because he had learned to be a patient man, that her confession would come when it would come.

Every clue was building up into an indisputable conclusion: the nun was frightened, she had a secret, she might not be what she seemed.

And she felt secure in her veil, certain that it was a wall between her and the secular world, a particular necessity if indeed she were not what she seemed.

She seemed intent on maintaining her aloofness, her mystery. She had not as yet asked his name, nor anything about him, and he found this fascinating. She felt the same as he: the less either of them knew, the less they were inclined to ask questions.

But the questions were piling up nonetheless, and while he was used to silence and introspection, he perceived that she was not and that all her effort this day of avoiding questions was directed toward avoiding his eyes, avoiding *him*, while she watched him as covertly as he watched her.

She was praying that he did not ask another question, that he would allow her merely to stay by and that eventually he would offer to take her to Crossville Junction and see her to whichever direction she wished to go.

But now that the thought had come that the woman could be other than she seemed, he found himself observing little signs that proved the case, that made the point that he would have to address sometime soon.

Her hands were restless, her angel eyes ever moving, never still. When he caught her unaware, he saw the crease in her brows, the perplexity shaping her mouth as she bit her lip when deep in thought; he saw her beautiful eyes staring straight ahead, somewhere to the future, he saw her hands clench into fists time and again, helpless, frustrated. He saw her pacing with an elegant posture that spoke of some kind of schooling beyond that of a convent novice; he saw the impatience in her step, and the sway of her body that was unconsciously feminine and alluring. He saw, because he was looking for it, the curving shape of her body beneath the shapelessness of her habit, and the length of her leg encircled by the swirling black folds of material as she strode agitatedly around the room.

Yet the moment she became aware of his presence, she lowered her head, her eyes, clasped her hands and folded herself inward, her body still as a statue of the Madonna.

"You will need some time and privacy to take care of your personal needs," he said to her that night as she awaited her share of the plain-cooked dinner he was preparing.

Her hand snapped up, her eyes immediately on guard. *Personal needs? What did he mean?* Not the obvious; surely not the obvious—she hadn't given a moment's thought to it, and here he was thinking of everything, as if he meant what he had said: she was truly going to stay there, with him—for a while.

"I have no tub," he went on blandly, watching her face. "I myself—forgive me, Sister—bathe in a stream down the ridge. Perhaps you wish to take advantage of that . . . ?"

"I—" Well, what *would* a nun do? She hadn't the faintest idea. The dog came up to her and nudged her hand, and she was grateful for the momentary distraction as she furiously tried to think of an answer. She would want to wash—she *did* need to wash, she had just forgotten about it in the crush of events. And now . . . maybe he was trying to trip her up somehow.

"A pot of warm water," she said faintly, hoping that sounded reasonable, "a cloth . . . that would be fine." She patted the dog's head and rubbed his ears. *Personal needs*—who would have thought? A woman was a woman, even in a veil.

She looked up as he set two bowls down on the table and her gaze glanced off those inscrutable gray eyes. He sat down opposite her without a word and began to eat, and she felt a pang of conscience.

This self-sufficient recluse was now waiting on her, serving her, and solicitous of her *personal needs* as well. She didn't know what to make of him, with his dog and his lonely life and his patient silences.

And his eyes, those skewering, *knowing* eyes—she knew he was just waiting for her to tell him the things he would not yet question.

She dipped a spoon into the stew he had cooked up: beans mixed with meat and stewed tomatoes and poured over cornbread. Plain food, too heavy for her unnerved stomach, but she forced it down anyway.

She could do this, she thought, as she pushed the spoon around the bowl; maybe if she had something to do she wouldn't feel so edgy and restless. She would have an outlet for the explosive turmoil within her, and she could, in some measure, pay him back for his rescuing her.

"You must let me do the cooking," she said suddenly, impulsively.

His cool gray gaze never flickered. "You, Sister?"

"Why not me? I can cook at least as well as you, and I was accustomed to preparing meals at—" she stopped abruptly; she had almost given it away, had almost said, *at my mother's road ranch.*

But he wouldn't let it go. "At *where*, Sister? Surely I should have the benefit of some recommendation before I turn my stove over to you."

"I should think it would be enough that I volunteered to do it," she countered tartly. "At the *mother* house, of course. I was accustomed to take my turn in the kitchen and I will be happy to take my turn here."

Oh, be still my thundering heart, she chided herself. He had to be able to hear it, to see it. She thought it just might pound out from her chest, it was racing so fast and so hard.

He leaned back in his chair and regarded her with an interested light in his flinty gaze. "You are leaving the mother house?" he asked plainly, curious to hear how she would elaborate on this first piece of personal information she had volunteered.

Yes, she growled inside herself, *I am leaving the mother house*—that was a wonderful way to put it, perfectly apt. "No, the mother house to which I am returning." A better answer, an excuse for her journey, a smokescreen to hide the reason for the vicious pursuit by her own brothers.

"Which is where?" he asked coolly.

Oh damn where—where? The only place that made sense—the place to which she wanted to get: "New York," she said unflinchingly, but her heart had not stopped its wild erratic pounding, and she felt he could see right through her habit, and right through her.

"That's a far piece for one *young* nun to travel, Sister," he said, his tone mirroring his obvious disbelief.

"One goes where one is sent," she retorted with just a trace of that spirited tartness in her voice again. Oh, and she was so tempted to add more, to pile another story on top of the one she had told just to wipe that skeptical look off of his tanned face.

"And you have been called to . . . New York," he stated before she could say another word.

"Exactly." She couldn't renege now.

88

"Where presumably, you will take over the cooking chores once again."

"I should think so." Damn him.

"Well then, you must practice, must you not, Sister?"

"I would be grateful," she agreed, but every sense within her screamed to attention as he gave in to her story and her request so easily. Too easily.

He smiled, a mirthless smile, a ruthless smile, and it occurred to her that a man who had secluded himself so thoroughly might indeed be a man who had a reason to hide, a man without mercy, a man without honor as well.

A man to whom her puny disguise would be meaningless.

For one long fraught moment, she pictured him as the outlaw he might well be: implacable, unfeeling, inexorable. His face as a map of experience, stony, lined, pitiless in its impassivity, his features strongly marked and set off by those stone-hard gray eyes relieved only by the sensual curve of his lower lip.

He was not at all unnerved by her deepening blue stare.

Not what she seems. A curious nun, a contradiction among many inconsistencies, including the questions she would not ask. She did not yet even know his name, but she would cook for him. A restless nun, wrestling with secrets.

It was time, he thought, to pry some out of her.

"Sister?"

He had startled her. "Yes?"

What had *she* been thinking about?

"Do you have a name?"

She froze, and threw out the first words that formed in her mouth: "Do you?"

She dearly wanted to keep her secrets, he thought. And she really hadn't meant to ask: she looked horrified that she had even asked. She hadn't intended ever to know who he was if she could help it. Already things had gotten too personal for her. But he sensed her question had been a defense, to buy her a moment while she considered whether to reveal her real name or to invent one.

Her thoughts flew every which way, her first instinct to give him the name of Sister Philomena. But he had followed her and Bobby for some length of time, he might even have heard Bobby address her by her right name. And she couldn't bear to add that lie on top of all the others.

"I believe I have a name, Sister," Rake said in answer to her query, declining to give it just yet, watching her composure slip away inch by inch, and her struggle to retain it.

Oh, damn him. So clever to turn things so that she must ask again. And she must. "Well, what is it?" she demanded testily.

He smiled again, a small flash of triumph in his lean tanned face. "I'm called Rake Cordigan, ma'am."

Rake Cordigan. She rolled it around in her mind, on her tongue. A hard sounding name for a hard-bitten man. "Mr. Cordigan," she acknowledged him formally. "I am called—" instant decision— "Angelene. *Sister* Angelene."

"Ma'am." He nodded his head in a mannerly way.

She bent her head over her cooled bowl of beans and meat, refusing to ask another question or to hear one more personal thing about him. She knew he was waiting for it, and she lifted the spoon to her mouth and filled it with cold beans and sauce.

The silence stretched on between them. The dog nuzzled around Rake's legs and her skirt in turn, seeking a morsel of food, and she wanted to ask if he ever fed the animal, but even that was too much for her to know.

She ate the sopping cornbread and the scraps of meat, refusing to meet his cool, cynical, *steady* gray gaze. She could feel it pouring all over her, heated, skeptical, certain of her lies and perfidy.

She raised her head finally, unable to stand it, seeking to attack, the best defense she could think of. "So, Mr. Cordigan—how many days did you say we would have to remain here?"

Again that smile, faintly amused, always aware. "I didn't, ma'am. But I should think a week—maybe two . . ."

She shot bolt upright from her chair. *"Never!"*

He shrugged. "I don't know, Sister . . . Angelene." Ah, the name, the first time he had said it aloud, and he liked the sound of it in his voice and he disliked the note of fear in her adamant dismissal of his estimation. "Those men could be anywhere around; they could be staking out a place in town just to watch, hoping you'll come by in a week or two when you think the coast is clear. Men who are killers are moved by mighty powerful reasons, ma'am, and they don't easily give up."

No, they wouldn't, she thought mordantly, especially men like her brothers who were moved solely by their loyalty to Josie, and Josie's desire to remove the threat of the daughter who could send her to jail and beyond.

"Perhaps . . . not," she admitted reluctantly.

"You need to give it a little time, Sister," he went on, slanting a curious look at her thoughtful expression. "Surely the . . . mother house hasn't fixed a timetable for your arrival."

She looked distracted. "No, no—of course not. Sometime by the end of the month . . ." But that was *her* timetable, now to be scrambled up and tossed away by the enigmatic Rake Cordigan.

"Then you will stay as long as is necessary," he said with finality, caught by the unguarded expression of dismay in her eyes.

Trouble. He was spiralling down into it deeper and deeper with her, and he knew it, but he couldn't stop it now; he had saved her life and now he owned her. It was a feeling as elemental as the earth, and it stunned even him who had sought no grounding, no possessions, no frame around which to rebuild his life.

It was those eyes, those innocent, worldly, guileless, knowledgable eyes. Sinless eyes. Lying eyes that bent away from his in concert with her facile agreement with him: "You're right. I'm know you're right, and I do appreciate everything you've done for me so far."

Easy words: he recognized them when he heard them. Not a lie. Not the truth. Not what she seemed. Now he had committed himself to finding out the truth. Her truth.

And maybe his own.

She was really scared now. Now she had a name by which he could call her. Now, in spite of herself, she had fully entrusted herself to his protection, which went right down to his providing a bowl of hot water for her bathing convenience the following morning.

Dear Lord, how *did* a nun attend to her personal bathing? So much unwrapping and unhooking, and what if he ventured up the steps while she was in the midst of it?

Then there was the question of the money she had secreted under her veil. She would have to hide that somewhere. She could not wear that headband of silver and paper around her head for unending days and weeks.

How had things become so complicated?

The worst part was, she had no mirror, so that when she was finally finished scrubbing herself and had donned the habit once more, she could not tell, as she wound herself into wimple and veil, whether she had tucked away every strand of her abundant golden hair.

She rushed, because she had promised to prepare breakfast for him this morning, and it was evident he was awake and doing whatever it was he did already.

The money, the money . . . she had sewn it into a strip of white muslin, and in her frantic hands, it now felt heavy and obvious. It seemed that there was not a place in the whole attic loft where she could conceal it. No loose floorboards, no containment space behind the little stove, no niche in the rafters, not even under the scrap of rag rug at her feet by the makeshift bed. Not even under the mattress, which was supported by a grid of ropes beneath it.

No—maybe under the mattress—just for this morning until she had time to think about it . . . She heard the "tlick" of the dog's nails as it slowly and patiently climbed the bare wood steps to the attic loft, and that decided her.

Carefully she lifted the mattress end by the wall and she meticulously laid the strip of muslin across four of the cross-ties and then set the mattress back over it, and sat on it.

Then she thought, what if he came with the dog, and what if, from the upper steps, he could see just beneath the bed, and what if there were just an end of that muslin band dangling down—and *what if—?*

She held her breath, her heart pounding furiously with fear. What if—?

The dog was alone, and he slowly made his way across the floor to where she sat, her hands tightly clasped, and he nudged her cold fingers and licked them, and she swallowed and reached out one hand tentatively to touch him, expelling her fear.

Just the dog, after all. She rose up, collected the bowl of now-cold water, and carefully made her way down the steps, turning once at just the spot she had envisioned to see whether any damning ends of muslin hung from the ropes, and then, reassured, she called to the dog and tremblingly made her way downstairs to the cold parlor and the cold cookstove.

Time didn't exist in this place, she thought as she stoked the fire she had built in the firebox of the stove. There wasn't even a clock in the place. There was only the sun, risen higher than she would have liked to see, the cold cookstove chiding her, and the absence of Mr. Rake Cordigan who had obviously warmed the wash water someplace else and then sent his dog after her.

Where was Mr. Cordigan? What did a man do who lived secluded on a mountain ridge with an old wise dog and the barest of necessities?

She prepared the coffee and set it to boil. She found cornmeal, oats, grits, a couple of fresh eggs sitting pointedly in a bowl, a tin of tomato sauce, a bucket of freshly pumped water.

But where was the man?

She couldn't begin to cook anything lest it cool before he returned, so she mixed the grits and found a pot to heat the tomato sauce and set that next to the coffee to heat slowly. Then she went out to find him, the dog obligingly by her side.

"Where?" she whispered to him as she stood in the dooryard. Beyond the swath of green near the house and the fields adjacent to the barn she was surrounded by forestation as far as her eye could see.

"Where is your master?" she asked him, her voice firmer now, because without the dog she would never find him. The most logical thing to do, she decided, was to head for the barn, otherwise she might get lost on the ridge altogether.

There were open fields beyond the barn, fenced-in pasture that had been meticulously cleared and tended, and a track—thank heaven, a track, easy to find, easy to follow.

The dog knew the track. He bounded on ahead of her, sure of his way, sure she would come behind him; still, he raced back occasionally to ascertain that she was trailing after him, and then he ran ahead of her, showing her the way.

The track curved and then eased slowly downward, a descending path through a sun-dappled bower of leaves and thick tree trunks, ending suddenly at a stone wall centered by a three step stairway.

She stopped at the plateau of the stairway where the dog joyously awaited her, her heart pounding once again.

What was she going to say to Mr. Cordigan when she finally saw him?

She should *not* be pursuing him in the depths of the woods. She should have stayed back at the cabin and awaited him. She was not supposed to be curious or impatient or aching to escape him.

She took a tentative step downward, envisioning herself from a bird's eye view as the one dark spot on the landscape, black and mysterious, as obvious as a gunshot in the Eden of her savior's garden.

She stepped downward again—one more step, just to see, and then she would return and she would wait for him, patiently, obediently . . .

Another step. He had left her alone. She could have bolted out the door, she thought, but that idea had just never occurred to her.

How sure had he been that she would never leave without him—or did he just not care?

She moved slowly through the bushes below the staircase, the dog now snuffling around her hem. She was beginning to think she was sure of nothing other than the reality of the dog and the heaviness of her habit and the glare of the sun directly ahead of her through a copse of bushes that led to a clearing beyond.

She was too curious, and it had to be her fatal sin, the thing that would trip her up in the end. She crept closer to the sun, entranced by the unearthly light—one more step and she promised herself she would turn around and go back.

Through the bushes now she could see the glint of sun on water and she felt a jangling in her memory . . . *forgive me, Sister* . . . and she remembered—his bathing place.

Then she saw him, limned against a golden glow, breaking water with his long sinewy arms, rising from the depths like a god from below, long, strong, sun-browned and naked.

Chapter 7

Black on green, black on green, a combination made to be seen, her mind chanted and her heart pounded. How could he not perceive her haunting him in the bushes?

She sank to her knees, aware of the dog beside her, the one thing that might give her away. She dared not touch him, or shush him. She dared not watch the man beyond the bushes, and she couldn't take her eyes away from the sight of him.

He was so completely different from her, and so utterly himself, that she felt a keen awareness of his masculinity pierce her very vitals.

She had never seen a naked man before, and the darkness and the mystery of him captivated her. Where she was full and round, he was lean and hard. Where she curved, he was long, strong and muscular. Where her most secret self folded inward, his thrust outward from a thatch of crisp hair, which extended in a long line from his heavily furred chest.

She was mesmerized by the tautness of him, the darkness of him, the unknowable secret of his maleness, the thing in him that was the savage despoiler of an innocent woman like her.

She had been warned about men, and yet the naked power and potency of this one did not send her fleeing in fear; instead it held her in fascination even as she understood that he personified the danger of all men, about whom she had been warned.

The sisters whom Josie had paid so well had *taught* her nothing at all of men. She had learned everything from books, deliciously forbidden novels of mayhem and romance, and from whispered conversations in the deep of the night when the ranch-raised girls would detail their expert knowledge of what really went on between a man and a woman: of course, they really knew about horses, but they claimed the principle was the same, and their endless discussion of it was both fascinating and repugnant to Angelene. All that wrangling conjecture on the physical nature of a man and how it connected *them*, and now the reality of it had nothing to do with imagination whatsoever.

It had only to do with her response to this sudden covert view of his nakedness, and it was the most alluring thing she had ever seen. She was greedy for every movement of him as he bathed himself and swam here and there in the wash of water he had called a stream.

What was it about that body that could penetrate the soul of hers? How was it done, and what did it feel like? Her insides curled, yearning for the answer. He was as flesh and blood as she, there was no stain on him.

There was only the forceful virility of his nakedness and her invasive presence coveting the sight of it.

She held her breath as he finally rose from the water and began walking slowly to the shore, the perfect form of his body blotting the sun for one breathtaking moment, lord of all he surveyed.

Lord of her . . .

No!

She meant to turn her eyes away just then and to get back to the cabin as quickly as possible, with or without the dog who had remained still and silent by her side.

But she was riveted by the contrast of the small clean cloth in his large hand moving swiftly all over his burnished body, blotting away the wetness in a brisk no-nonsense motion.

A man's rituals, as inviolate as a woman's, as graceful

97

and unfathomable, elusive and yet known in the very depths of her being.

She had to get out of there. She was enchanted by the vision of his nakedness at one with the sun and the earth.

He threw down the cloth and bent to retrieve an article of clothing, and she was caught by the fluid motion of his body and the supple curve of his back and buttocks as he slowly straightened upright, his shirt dangling in one hand.

The dog growled, and he paused. Angelene almost jumped out of her skin. She threw herself flat on the ground as he turned, sure he would see the flat black of her habit against the rich green of nature.

"Eh, dog?"

The dog growled again, and Angelene thought her heart would stop because he would just come get the dog and find her laying prostrate behind the bushes as if she were worshipping at an altar.

"Come, dog!" he called, and the dog looked hesitantly at the prone figure of his companion and then turned in the direction of his master.

"Come, boy!" he called again, and the dog leapt to attention and raced through the bushes, leaving Angelene with her nose in the grass, fighting the abject terror that he would discover her spying on him and that the dog was, even now, leading him right to the spot where she lay.

If she turned her head, would he see her?

She had to chance it, she had to know what he was doing and whether the animal would betray her.

Slowly and painstakingly, she eased her head around just enough so that she could get a view of the bank of the stream.

He was not there.

Dear lord . . . she expected to hear his voice at any moment . . . Sister? *Sister?*

She bit her lip and turned her head still further around.

Oh yes—thank goodness—he had dressed, he was

98

tucking the shirttails of a clean white shirt into his trousers as the dog nipped up at him, and then he hunkered down to rub the animal's head and grab his boots.

Time . . . she had a moment's time, and ever so slowly she began to crawl away from the bushes toward the stone steps.

"Come, dog!"

She heard his voice from farther away as she reached the wall that housed the steps, and she got to her feet and raced behind a nearby tree, certain he and the dog would appear at any moment.

But there was silence—then a whistle, and a forceful bark way in the distance.

She had to take the chance: she had to jump up those steps and race for the cabin before he turned back.

She didn't know how she was going to look him in the eye after spying on him like that, after seeing him in all his pure raw maleness.

The wonder was that she was standing serenely by the stove, a bowl and spoon in hand mixing the grits, her eyes dutifully lowered, the firebox blazing and the coffee boiling merrily away when he finally walked in the door.

She understood then, the moment she confronted him again, that her need to outwit him overset everything else, even her growing guilt at having this covert knowledge of him.

All she had to do was *not* think about it.

But her heart was still pounding painfully. She really could not look him in the eye.

"Good morning, Sister." His voice was as neutral as ever.

"Good morning, Mr. Cordigan. I thank you for the water."

"No trouble, Sister. I put it up over a little campfire down by the barn while I was watering the horses."

Horses . . .

She dumped the mixture into a pot and set it on the stove. "Coffee is ready, Mr. Cordigan." This was absurd;

99

he was right behind her with his cup and she barely had room to move out of his way. No—out of the way of that lean clean body—oh, no, to be thinking like that . . . she turned abruptly and her nose jammed right into the vee of his shirt, against a tuft of coarse hair and heated skin.

She took a deep breath to speak, and inhaled the indelible scent of him; she heard his voice—"Sister?"— and then he moved out of her way to the opposite end of the room.

The cooking . . . oh yes, the eggs, the tomato sauce which had cooked down appreciably in the time she had gone. The coffee. Was she supposed to like coffee? She felt desperate to drink a cup, to have something in her hands so that she could concentrate on it and on not betraying her edginess to his all-seeing steely gaze.

"Sister?"

"Mr. Cordigan?"

"You seem right at home around a cookstove."

Think fast—stay in character—"Mine is a *working* order, Mr. Cordigan."

"And no vows of silence, Sister?"

Damn him. "Not in mitigating circumstances, Mr. Cordigan. Or would you prefer that?" she added tartly as she broke the eggs into a bowl the way she would have liked to break them into his face.

"I'd prefer to know why those hombres were looking to gun you down, Sister."

"I can't tell you today, either," she said smartly, punctuating her retort with the sound of the eggs steaming onto the griddle.

"What *can* you tell me today, Sister?" he asked skeptically.

"Nothing you don't know already, Mr. Cordigan."

"That's not a damned lot, Sister."

"Because there is nothing for you to know," she said in irritation.

"Well, we do disagree on that one, Sister. I know three men were after you, and one of them was pretending to be your friend all the while he was trying to kill you—"

She wheeled around in shock. *"What?!"* Her heart denied it, instantly, vehemently. Not kill her. Bobby had wanted to slow her down maybe, but not kill her; he had wanted to leave that to the others . . .

"Kill you, Sister," Rake said implacably, again watching her face, her eyes, the mirror of her thoughts and soul. She knew it too; she turned away again as the words sunk in, words that gave life to the thing that had happened that she hadn't wanted to name.

"He wouldn't have killed me," she said, her voice muffled, her head bent over the frying pan with the burning yellow of the eggs. She groped for a spatula and wielded it forcefully, digging it into the smoking remains of the eggs viciously, angrily.

"Sister, you were there, and you saw what you saw, you know what you know."

"The eggs are ruined," she said distractedly.

"Dog will eat them," Rake said. "Just pool that sauce over the grits and serve them up, Sister."

"I'm not hungry," she countered, mashing a spoonful of the stuff into a bowl and pouring the sauce over. "Here."

She pushed the bowl across the table, unaware he had come up right behind her, and so she turned again, and her body swiped by his and she almost fell over.

"Of course you'll eat," he said firmly, taking another bowl and preparing it exactly the same way as she had his. "Sit down."

"I can't."

"You won't. I have told the truth of what has been going on and you refuse to see it or to look at me, for if you look, Sister, *you* must tell the truth. But you have no choice about that: you will tell the truth sometime because you will find it will become necessary. I am a patient man, Sister. I have learned that one hard lesson in all my years. So I invite you to sit and join me in this hard-won morning meal."

She sat, still unable to meet his cool gray gaze, feeling as though she need not say another word, that he knew everything already. —*"he was trying to kill you"*—Bobby, Bobby—not kill her, surely *not* . . .

He fed her, patiently as he would spoon-feed a baby because she would not lift her spoon or her face for the anguish she felt inside. Her divided selves fought, the one begging for the confessional, the other restraining her impulses, opting for keeping the secret from a man who may be part of her life for no more than a week or two at the most. He had no reason to know any more than he had conjectured already, and she had no reason other than her gratitude to give him the gift of her confidence.

She swallowed the thick cereal convulsively as he gently tipped the spoon against her dry lips, thankful for the coating of sauce that made digesting it possible. She barely tasted it. She tasted the bile of the defeat of her plans and all the possibilities achieving it would have meant. It was likely now that she would never get past the town of Crossville Junction, or perhaps never get past *him*.

She was still not safe with him; if he ever discovered her lie, if he ever found out that there was no holy innocence protecting her, what might he do?

What would any man do? There were no laws up on the mountains, no judge to pronounce the right or wrong of what a man living in solitude might do. He was his own law, and she was his subject now, even dressed in religious cloth.

"How will you know when it might be safe for me to leave the ridge?" she asked suddenly as the question occurred to her. After all, if he were his own judge, he alone had the right to say, unless she wanted to chance finding her own way down the mountain to the safety of the town. And she didn't want to do that, not yet; she did think it was likely her brothers had not given up their search. But she also thought it was possible that Mr. Rake Cordigan could decree that she would never leave the mountain.

He didn't answer, and all of her fears rushed right into her heart, her mind, her speaking eyes.

"Two weeks, three? A month?"

"Sister . . . you know the men, you know how dangerous they are. You tell me."

How clever of him to reverse the tables. She bit her lip. "I can't tell you anything." This was getting to be a refrain. Her stiff lips could barely utter the words, but they were words that committed her to nothing, even if he did not read them the way she intended.

"Won't, Sister. I think we agree on that. Won't." Stubborn angel eyes, holiest of all beings to sequester yourself away from life like this. How could those men want to murder her? *Trouble.* Her eyes flashed with anger at his probing. There was too much involved in this, and the woman was not what she seemed.

But he was a patient man, hadn't he said so? He had learned patience in the camps of his childhood when he had always stood apart from the others, always different, always alone. He had learned it in the waning days of his separation from the disaster of his outlaw life when dark and light merged into one long painful awareness of existence and nothing more beyond that. He had learned well. He had had time.

The woman had time as well. The men would not find her, and eventually he would find the truth of the killers and of the woman.

She could not compete with that surety. She felt wildly uncertain of what to say next when denials were so futile, and she could convince him of nothing.

"We don't agree," she said sharply, trying once again to distract him from delving into the question of her brothers and their pursuit. "Nor do we agree on how long I must immure myself here, Mr. Cordigan. I find that intensely distressing."

"Then pray, Sister. Pray those men don't find their way onto the ridge and that they give up and go away," Rake said caustically. "Although my own experience has been that killers never give up and they never can be ignored until one or the other is dead."

"*No!*" she cried out involuntarily, shaken by the

instant vision that the end of the story might come to the choice between her life or theirs. *"No!"*

"Could you kill, Sister Angelene?"

"Stop it!"

"Could you? Could you pick up a gun and aim it at the boy puppy—what was his name? Bobby. Could you shoot to save your life, Sister?"

She saw it even as he said it and her whole body shook with the force of the possibility of it. She hated him. She felt like attacking him.

"Could you?" she demanded, her hand instinctively reaching for an empty pot as if she might hurl it at him.

She felt the hot grasp of his hand on hers before she could lift the thing, and she raised her eyes finally to meet the molten emotion in his.

"Yes I could, Sister. And I have. And," he added dispassionately, disengaging her hand from the handle of the iron pot, "I think you could too."

So, she thought, huddling on the trundle bed in the makeshift parlor, she had accomplished nothing and he had scared her half to death in the bargain. Now she was alone with the hulking dog and her wayward thoughts and she felt like she could be broken into a thousand pieces and scattered to the wind.

There was no reality anywhere. If she were not what she seemed, neither was he. What kind of man secluded himself on a mountain ridge with a dog and couple of horses and talked about the nature of killers as if he knew what he were talking about?

Someone who had been one?

No, no—she couldn't allow herself to think that because it would mean she was in even more danger than she thought she was.

If only she *could* pray . . .

She had never felt so hampered by anything as she did by this cumbersome habit and the behavior necessitated by it. Even so, it was her key to safety, now more than ever, and she couldn't let his words, his assumptions, his unnerving eyes deter her from her original purpose.

She had just never intended to be sitting in one place at one time for the space of more than one day.

"Sister Angelene?"

She started as his rough-edged voice broke into her thoughts from somewhere just beyond the door, and she twisted around to get a look at him. "Mr. Cordigan?"

He had changed his shirt to something dark and plaid with the sleeves rolled up, and he carried his hat in his hand, and it was as if he had paused in the process of heading someplace else because a thought had occurred to him. "Can you ride, Sister?"

That was not the question she was expecting. "I beg your pardon?"

"I asked if you can ride, Sister. Surely you had a life somewhere before you chose to cloister it in a convent."

How clever of him. It took her one moment to see beyond the surface of the question. Any answer would provide him with clues to her past and to the purpose of her flight and her pursuers. What a devious man; and yet, how calculating was she in comparison? She was rightfully matched with this man, she thought, and he was taking her on, nose to nose, head to head.

"I do not ride, Mr. Cordigan."

"You only cook."

"And pray, of course," she shot back.

"Not a nurse, Sister?"

"No."

He wasn't going to let up. She felt that little frisson of enveloping fear. When the questions honed in too close to things she did not want to reveal, she knew her silences would say more than words.

"Nor a teacher?"

She bit her lip. "A teacher . . . of sorts, Mr. Cordigan."

"Of children?"

"No."

"Of culinary skills?"

105

"Mr. Cordigan!"

"And they sent you so young—where did you say, Sister?" Oh, damn it—he could scent fear a mile away: the room was suffused with it now.

"I *didn't,*" she said in a strangled voice.

"And you would mind very much saying, wouldn't you, Sister?"

"It has no bearing on anything, Mr. Cordigan."

"Except your presence here, of course. But that has nothing to do with reality anyway, does it, Sister?"

Nothing to do with reality? How close was he to divining her secrets? She licked her lips nervously. She could deflect his questions so easily if she chose to pull poor Mother Margaret and Sister Philomena into her deceptions. And yet, she still had some conscience abut that. At night sometimes she thought about Sister Philomena and what the cost might have been to her for giving aid to nothing more than a rebellious former student. She thought about a lot of things at night, but in the day, nothing looked clearer and everything got more and more tangled because of her need to maintain the fiction of her identity.

So it seemed reasonable to talk about the convent school in Cairo: he would never go there to check her story, it was real and her familiarity with it would permeate her little fiction and convince him and forestall any more questions.

Simple as that.

So why was her voice so scratchy as she answered his question?

"I was sent—so young, as you say, Mr. Cordigan—to a convent school in Cairo, just on the border between Ohio and Kentucky, to assist Mother Margaret who runs the school in her effort to educate all of the children in the area. It was an open school, sir, and all were welcome. There were well-to-do boarders and there were children from the streets of the city, and it was those I helped care for. Now, do you have any other questions?"

"And you came from New York?"

"No, I am returning to New York. I entered the convent in Missouri; the mother house is in New York." No, that didn't make sense—maybe it would to him.

"I see."

Oh no, that implacable voice again. "Yes, Mr. Cordigan, I hope you do." Best to take that self-righteous tone with him. If she caved in under his questioning, she would be at his mercy.

"Those men—former children of the convent orphanage?"

Now he was baiting her. "There was no orphanage, Mr. Cordigan."

"So this little band of strangers came out of nowhere to persecute an innocent woman of the cloth on her way from one cloister to another? And she just happened to know one of them well enough to *travel* with him? Sister . . ."

Dear lord, worse and worse—he had compressed every one of the inconsistencies of her story into one telling accusation . . . and now what?

Silence, golden silence. Because she was counting on the fact he wouldn't coerce her? Because she was sure he still believed that she was what she seemed to be? And how long could she maintain that fiction under such astute and perceptive questioning?

"*Sister?*"

She bent her head again. She couldn't even claim his assumptions had no bearing on anything. He was too clever, and she was too naive. It was beginning to look as if she would not leave that cabin without revealing everything to his satisfaction and laying herself open to other suppositions . . .

Laying herself open . . . yes, to that compelling masculinity that she had totally refused to think about, that she had resolutely pushed deep into the recesses of her mind so it would not distract her from the deadly game of wits she had to play with him.

But he was real, and the contradictions in her situation were real, and he was a strong, silent, quick-witted man of

107

experience who had chosen to seclude himself on a mountain—what could that mean? That he *was* dangerous and he was *not* kind-hearted or charitable, and her danger was real from all sides. She was going crazy. One well-placed question by this enigmatic stranger and she fell totally to pieces.

Why? Because she *was* guilty?

No, she was a survivor, pure and simple.

"I have no answers for you," she said finally.

"Wrong choice, Sister."

Implicit threat? It did not matter. Whatever happened, she could not let go of her guise of an untouchable woman; she had to protect that at all costs, with all the lies and all the deceit she could muster.

"*My* choice, Mr. Cordigan," she retorted sassily, before she realized that what she had said was as good as an admission.

"I knew that, Sister."

He knew too much. She had to get away from those piercing, knowing eyes and the suppressed knowledge of that powerful sun-browned body.

"Mr. Cordigan . . ."

"Yes, you pray, Sister, and you find the gumption to give me the answers to my questions, and then maybe we can proceed from there."

"The only place I want to proceed *to*, Mr. Cordigan, is the nearest town so that I can get on with my journey."

"A journey to nowhere if those men kill you, Sister."

"I bow to your assessment of the situation, Mr. Cordigan."

"You are not a prisoner, Sister."

She raised her head at that, and the electric blue of her eyes almost bowled him over. "Am I not, Mr. Cordigan?"

Bold angel eyes; he wondered how she could look him so squarely in the eye and lie so convincingly. He had never met a woman like this before: she was both bold and innocent, devious and desirable. He wanted to contain all those qualities in her and he wanted to crush out all her secrets and deceit.

Oh yes, she was a prisoner—a captive every bit much as he, to emotions he didn't know he had, to feelings that had never had a name. He just couldn't take the chance that she wasn't what she seemed even though every instinct told him differently.

He couldn't dissemble when it came to that. "Perhaps that is the truth of it," he said warily. "But then, I would be the only one admitting it, wouldn't I, Sister Angelene?"

Clever, clever man, turning it around on her again, waiting for the answer that would give away something, anything to his deductions. How did she combat that with equally clever words and distract him once again?

"But I am not here of my own volition," she countered provocatively.

"The truth of that is had you acted on your own volition, you would be dead," he shot back. "And so we come to the beginning of things again, Sister. Who were those men and why do they want you dead? Perhaps during your *enforced* stay here, you might bring yourself to give me some good reason for my putting my life on the line for both rescuing you and holding you *captive*. I hope it has occurred to you that I did not have to volunteer to do either."

He left her then—he was a man who knew exactly how to deal out his cards, blow by blow, and how to add dimension upon dimension she had not even considered, except that she didn't—she *couldn't*—believe in his altruism. He didn't look unselfish or beneficent. He looked ruthless and hard-hearted and there was no reason whatsoever for him to have prevented her brothers from assaulting her.

But neither had she asked him for either food, shelter or help; he had just run all over her like a steam engine, and she supposed in gratitude he felt she ought to confide in him; but the simplest answer was to relieve him of his responsibility for her.

In fact, that was the only answer. To that end, she decided, this very afternoon she would begin to explore

109

exactly how she could leave the ridge, *of her own volition*, and alleviate his onerous burden.

She bore watching because he had cut too close to the bone with his questions and conclusions.

His first chore that afternoon was to scout down the mountain, and to that end, he took the dog and the one mount that needed thorough exercising, and he thoroughly scoured the forest and the trails leading down to the one viable track that led around and down to town, and he found nothing: no broken branches, no tracks, no footprints, no sign that anyone had ventured up the mountain anywhere near the ridge.

So far.

But it had only been three days.

It felt like months.

He walked the track, sending the dog on ahead to scratch out the scent of man, and the dog came back, whining a little, begging for approval.

They climbed back up the mountain to the ridge, seeking clues to the vengeance of the murderers, and he found none. The ridge was secure. The woman was safe.

But not from him.

As he approached, still on foot, the clearing which led to the cabin, he saw her through the trees, and she wasn't just wandering aimlessly.

She was trying to find the approach by which he had brought her up to the ridge, and that she had remembered this much proved to him what a guileful and calculating woman she was.

And not what she seemed. A woman who had been cloistered most of her life would have none of these resources, none of the cunning to deflect his questions and seek her own answers. This was a self-reliant woman, a woman who created her own means to accomplish her purposes.

He admired that, he really did, but it was obvious he

110

couldn't let her find the hidden track down the mountain.

He motioned to the dog and sent him galloping through the trees to emerge from an outlet fifty yards beyond the actual track, and he noted with some satisfaction that the appearance of the dog startled her. For one moment her beautiful face expressed a gratifying combination of anger and dismay.

Then she saw him and she immediately became composed and dispassionate, right on down to the sang-froid note in her voice as she acknowledged him. "Mr. Cordigan."

"Sister. This is quite a way from the cabin."

"One needs exercise, Mr. Cordigan. In the convent we called it recreation, and I was accustomed to walking during those times." Well, she *had* been. Not for her the hours spent knitting or sewing or doing genteel watercoloring in the wood-beamed parlor. Reading had been disallowed as well, except for spiritual or biblical books, and she and her classmates had smuggled in any amount of gothic novels of romance that they had read secretly by the light of candles.

She knew there wasn't the faintest hint of insincerity in her voice as she offered him this excuse, but she could see plainly that he did not believe her either, and it was just pure luck that he had come up and found her exploring at the very moment she least wanted to see him.

Well, no matter. She knew that somewhere through this unbroken line of trees there was a way out, and she would find it.

However, to him, "accustomed to walking" had an ominous ring to it, and it wasn't too long a step to envision her plowing her way down from the ridge on foot one day in the future when he had left her too long to her own devices.

She was a dangerous woman, this Sister Angelene, and there was nothing meek or obedient about her: she was

111

fearless and just a little too curious, a deadly combination that had nothing to do with religious principles and everything to do with proving she was not what she seemed.

"Of course, Sister. Recreation is important for the soul," he said blandly, disregarding her sharp intake of breath.

"I tend to think you have no soul, Mr. Cordigan," she said tartly, allowing him to guide her back toward the cabin reluctantly. She had no excuse whatsoever to justify her wish to keep walking when the cabin itself was still a good distance away. Besides, the pressure of time meant nothing here; tomorrow would do equally as well as today to continue her explorations.

But her verbal explorations were something else again. He didn't even take offense at her acid words, and she found that disconcerting.

"I think once I might have agreed with you, Sister," he said after a while. "I think I found a soul up here on the mountain." He looked down at her, a faint smile edging around the corners of his mouth. "Maybe you'll find a soul too."

"There is only one kind of 'soul' up on this mountain ridge, Mr. Cordigan, and that is 'sole', as in alone, and that is strange to me after years of being part of a community." There, more convent clues for him to nurture so he would be deterred from questioning her walk. Anyway, there was a kernel of truth even in that lightly glossed-over statement: she was used to being around many more people, either at the school or at the road ranch. She didn't like this solitude or the sheer physical solidity of her self-appointed guardian.

This was a man worlds removed from the men she had met at Josie's ranch, nothing like the gentlemanly Mr. Benbrook or that nice Mr. Ellingwood—and oh, how she wished she had not recalled them to mind. Death equalized everything: possibilities, desires, dreams, a daughter's loyalties . . . a brother's choices . . .

Of course she had to keep on the path she had chosen.

112

Bobby wouldn't give up, neither would Josie. She *had* done the right thing, and perhaps she still had a chance to make it through, if only she didn't break down under this stranger's keen scrutiny and kept firmly in mind what she was escaping from and what she was heading toward.

"But Sister, you are never alone," Rake said gently, obliquely, watching her lovely face dissolve into an expression of perplexity for one of those long combative moments until she understood the reference.

She hated him for alluding to that higher power which was always supposed to reside within her. Her unruly tongue *would* trip her up on that point, she thought frantically, when she was hardly the picture of a pious nun to begin with.

"You are right," she acknowledged, almost choking on the words, and she knew that wasn't lost on him either. He had the most extraordinarily penetrating gaze; she couldn't avoid it either lest she reveal her outright fear of his perception. She could give him this point, much as it cost her, and she knew he must be asking why someone such as she would ever complain of being alone.

"And of course the One who watches over you assured the fact that you would come to no harm. Don't you believe that, Sister?"

This man was endless; he would just *never* stop. "Of course, Mr. Cordigan." She had no choice but to agree; he had brought all her protestations to a standstill. The next course would be his pursuing the question of her attackers yet again.

If she were so smart, she should forestall him . . .

"I suppose I might assume then that you are a gift from heaven, Mr. Cordigan."

He smiled at that, the same slow edges-of-the-mouth smile she had seen moments before. *A gift from heaven.* The part of him that craved balance and symmetry and oneness with his surroundings felt the benediction of that thought, and a mystical union with the woman who had created it.

"A gift of your presence, Sister," he contradicted

113

gently, because he was also not one to accept what he had not earned. He had chased after her grudgingly, and now he was determined that she would not leave the mountain shrouded in the lie. There could be no grace for a man like that.

"As you say, Mr. Cordigan; you know I'm grateful."

"I know you're frantic."

"We have nothing to talk about, Mr. Cordigan," she said tensely. *Why* did he have to spoil one moment of accord between them? "I refuse to consider myself imprisoned here. I took a walk. I am returning to the cabin. I will spend the afternoon at my bedside . . ." *I will be bored to tears* . . . "and I will prepare dinner. Presumably tomorrow you might see fit to take me into Crossville Junction. I *must* continue on to New York as quickly as possible."

"Thank you, Sister. I know all these things. It is not yet time to leave, and believe me, I am more anxious than you to see you safely on your way."

He tasted that falsehood in his mouth. She looked utterly deflated by his words: she had nothing more to argue about with him now. But that didn't mean she wouldn't find something.

Audacious angel eyes . . . gift from heaven—

Invocation from hell, most likely.

He wasn't nearly done with her yet.

Chapter 8

The problem with living in proximity with such a man was that it was too easy to become curious about him—there was hardly anything else to think about except when he would allow her to leave—and she found herself wanting to know why he lived so isolated on this mountain ridge, and what he spent his time doing, besides his usual and uncommon practice of bathing in the stream every morning. She was starting to ask questions just to fill the intermittent long silences, and in doing so, she knew she was forgetting what she was supposed to be except when something called her attention to the physical representation of it—like cooking the edge of her veil in a simmering pot of soup.

Even so, she knew she should not begin to satisfy her curiosity about Rake Cordigan. It was dangerous to do it; it made him into a person with feelings, emotions—and a past that he wished to discuss as little as she.

"But why does a man choose to live away up high on a ridge like you do?" she finally allowed herself to ask him at dinner that night.

As she watched, those cool, penetrating gray eyes turned inward for a long, hard, considering moment, almost as if he were deciding whether he should answer this question or not.

That irked her for some reason: she resented that he could pound and pull away at her about her secrets and

115

her contradictions, and she could not require one answer to one question from him.

But he answered, and she found that answer equally unsatisfying.

"A man wants to get away from civilization, Sister, particularly when he finds it isn't any too civilized. Surely you've felt that yourself?"

Well, she must have, if she were what she was pretending to be; so she didn't have any answer for that. "What about the dog? Did you bring him with you?"

"No ma'am. He found me and took care of me, and he taught me a whole lot about being civilized."

"Does he have a name?"

"He's used to being called 'Dog' or 'Boy'. Sometimes it's good to leave a thing natural, Sister."

Cryptic, maddening answers.

"And so you go to town, maybe . . . once a month, Mr. Cordigan? Or maybe more often so that you might hear of whether there's anyone strange in town?" Well, that was bald and blatant and . . . who knew what he thought about this spate of questions she was handing him with the evening's soup.

"About once a month, Sister, but of course the first thing we want to be sure of is that no one finds the way up the ridge."

"Of course," she murmured caustically, because she had the firm sense that Rake Cordigan was enjoying himself hugely at her expense. He wasn't going to go anywhere or check up on anything yet, and so it was left to her to check up on him and find the way to thwart him and the approach to the ridge. Fine. She could do that, although she wished to heaven she were not hampered by something as visible as her cumbersome habit.

"And how do you determine whether someone has found the path up the ridge, Mr. Cordigan?"

"You just look around you, Sister. Everything in nature tells a story, and everything is obvious when it has been disturbed. The break of a branch, the scattering of leaves, rocks, pebbles, the imprint of a hand, a boot, the remnants of an animal's excretion—you have only to see what is before your eyes."

The man was crazy: was he really talking about clues to unwanted visitors lurking in animal waste?

"Well, that makes it easy, doesn't it?"

"It really does, Sister."

And he really was serious!

Or he meant to discourage her further questions.

"And so we'll just fool everybody by staying here and *never* going to town," she added trenchantly. Damn him, damn him. She had a thousand questions suddenly, all of which she had to forcibly tamp down. She didn't want to know anything else other than when her days on the mountain would be numbered to no more than two or three.

"Sister, you're getting carried away."

"I'm *being* carried away, Mr. Cordigan."

"You'll be carried to your grave if you insist on being reckless."

She slumped back in her chair. "It always comes to that, doesn't it, Mr. Cordigan? Whether those men meant to attack me are combing the woods to find me."

"Since you are the only one who knows *why* they want to find you, perhaps you can tell *me*," he retorted, and when she started to speak, he held up his large hand. "I know, Sister. You can't tell me anything. You don't have to. The facts speak for themselves."

He left her with that, and she fumed the whole night about how cleverly he had circled around her and come straight back to the issue of the discrepancies in her story.

She was beginning to believe that her disguise hadn't fooled him one bit; it had only lulled her into thinking she had. While she wore it, she felt holier than him; she did not have to deal with her very secular response to his baiting and his powerful maleness. But still, she felt like an animal caught in some kind of trap he was just waiting to spring.

There was something about his attitude toward her: it

117

was both respectful and mocking at the same time.

He was playing with her.

She was playing with fire.

In the morning, every morning since the healing of the pain, he was accustomed to go to the stream at sunrise to perform a ritual of greeting the day. He understood that the very act of doing it harkened back to something in his childhood, some time-honored observance that ultimately he did not wish to discard, and that it was part of the final acknowledgement of himself that he wished to embrace rather than to destroy.

He watched the sun rise over the horizon, having fully divested himself of his clothes, his boots, his anger, his frustration, his pain, the last vestiges of the day before. Everything fell by the wayside each and every morning when he went to the stream.

He offered no devotions to the sun at daybreak: that was a duty of his youth that he did not carry into manhood. Rather, he gloried in the wonder of the physical nature of the earth, the sky, of man: that the sun arose each day in its place, and that he, a man with his own volition and desires, could choose to come to the same place each day to pay homage to the unvarying elements of nature.

Part of this daily renewal was the cleansing, and every day, every season, he bathed himself in the stream and emerged resurrected once again, revitalized in his body and purified in his soul.

He could not remember when, after he had stumbled up onto the ridge, he began coming to the stream. Perhaps, in the beginning, he had gone merely to cleanse away the weeks of dirt, vomit and grease from his battered shell of a body. Perhaps he had continued going because it cooled his rage as well, and then perhaps the sun had found and warmed his spirit and infused it with life.

Every morning, he knelt and cupped that water of life

118

into his hands and poured it onto his face and into his mouth as a sign that he lived, that he felt, that he had survived.

He relished the silence.

It had taken him a long time to come to that; at first, he had hated the emptiness and the chittering sounds of nature all around him. But he had learned, side by side with the dog, that it was himself he hated, and the emptiness was deep within him that must be filled.

The dog had shown him. The dog demanded nothing of him, and gave everything to him. When his soul was engorged with rage, the dog came to him with understanding eyes. When he was worn out with his hate and fury, the dog lay down beside him and kept him warm. When he collapsed under the burden of the futility of everything, the dog nurtured him and gave him a reason to keep on going. And when he was ready to reach out to something beyond himself, the dog was there for him to touch.

The dog became his companion, a creature of supreme intuition and upstanding morality. The dog saw him in his deepest anguish, his darkest hours, in the lightening of his most unbearable pain when the sun healed his heart and made him whole, and the dog loved him throughout, and the dog only saw the good in the man, the thing that responded to the need and the giving of the animal, which in turn responded to the need to give of the man.

It became so clear to him after a long time, and yet the dog waited patiently until he came to the knowledge, and he loved the dog for that as well.

After a long time he was able to bear the accusatory silence, the one in which he stood as both judge and jury of the actions of the man; he could hold on to the dog and he could view his past, and somehow, he could make peace with it. Somehow. But the path there had been laced with violence and fury, even against himself, sometimes so much he could hardly bear it, sometimes so much that the sole punishment *was* to endure it with the weight and pain of the full knowledge of all he had done.

The water cleansed him, the sun became a benediction; his torment dwindled into a gnawing ache of remembrance.

Every morning he bathed at the stream. In the winter, he shucked his clothing and wrapped himself in the warm cloak of his childhood, the buffalo robe, and it brought back a clamor of memories of a time that was to him both good and bad, the time in which he had stood both inside and outside the two different worlds that sought to claim him.

The scent of it surrounding his hardened, healed body was the sign to him that he had finally claimed himself.

He wore it on the coldest of days, finding in the ritual of the stream, in winter and in summer, his purest connection to the nature of man and the thing that humans believed was greater than man. Perhaps he did too, for there was no greater joy in his healing than to stand naked in the elements and reveal himself fully in just this way.

He had not altered any of his customs since the woman had come, but he had the wary, disquieting feeling that she could—and might—intrude upon him at any time, and it lent credence to his gut sense that she was not what she seemed.

She was a curious woman, not a prayerful one. She was a woman who was used to working, whose hands were accustomed to stroking, kneading, mending, mixing, holding. A woman whose very walk spoke of her innate impatience to get somewhere. She was not a woman of calm inner peace. Nor a woman who would sit still in contemplation, accepting her lot, her fate, at the hands of a stranger.

She was a sharp-tongued woman with angel eyes, and the spirit behind them had nothing to do with spirituality.

He found himself thinking about her too much during his precious mornings by the stream, and he was annoyed that the balance of things had been so upset by the coming of the woman.

He wasn't even sure what he was going to do about her. Trouble, women were always trouble.

Naked, he waded out into the stream on this third morning, oblivious to everything but the pleasurable lap of the sun-warmed water against his bare legs. He bent and cupped the water into his hands, and he drank from it and then smoothed it over his face and neck.

From behind the copse of bushes that edged the stream, Angelene watched in fascination equal to the time before, her eyes riveted on the ripple of the pure hard muscle of his arms and the beauty of the curve of his back and buttocks as he arched his body toward the water to take the living wetness of it into his hands.

On the rocks beside the stream, she could just see his clothing, and in her heart, she knew—she just knew— that if she could only find the approach to the ridge, she could steal those clothes, and his horse, and she could be on her way to New York, rid of him and her family forever.

The other thing was, he was gone a good part of the day, and she knew that he was somewhere on the ridge, but still, he was nowhere around.

So she should feel perfectly safe in trying to find that path that led off of the mountain. She should have no qualms about searching every inch of the stand of trees that surrounded the long swath of pasture that led to the cabin. She shouldn't feel as though his eyes were everywhere and that he could see everything she was doing.

That would make him omnipotent.

. . . you are never alone . . .

She felt that way about *him*, damn him. He could pop up anywhere, anytime. He could find his way right through her disguise to her vulnerability and then where would she be?

She had no choice: she had to find her own way out, just as before, and she had to bide her time for as long as it took, just as she had with Josie.

Oh, but *waiting* on this hellish mountain ridge where there was nothing else to do but pretend to be endlessly in prayer, or pet the dog, or just sit outside and watch the trees grow . . . she didn't know how she was going to contain her bursting desire to get going.

She was sure he could feel it. She was certain the whole cabin was explosive with it.

She felt a searing resentment that he was so sure she could not find her way off the mountain alone.

Damn it, damn it, damn it—why had she been so oblivious to the idea that there would be repercussions to her ill-conceived plan to escape Josie?

She wandered out toward the stand of trees hundreds of yards away, her head bent, her pace slow, so that if he were watching, he would perceive the religious in prayerful contemplation.

Or was it too late to don that disguise now, with her potent questions and her fulminating anger?

She didn't know, and it was made worse by the fact the dog came bounding after her, as if she had invited him to walk with her. The dog knew; she was sure those soulful eyes saw even more than his master's.

"Where is the track, dog?" she asked him idly. All she needed was the clue.

The dog barked.

Damn it again. He was signalling his master, no doubt. The man had obviously trained the creature well.

She felt a deep futility engulf her. She hated the dog, she hated the lie, she hated Josie and she hated her brothers. She hated the father who had died too soon, and the grandmother who had never known her and who could not save her.

She hated the man who would not yet let her go. She hated him for his strength, his surety, his naked beauty, for the threat he was to her, for the time he was taking out of her life, for his smug maleness—she hated him.

It was good to hate him; she would never be sorry to escape him either. There was a horse somewhere on the

122

ridge, she was sure of it, and his morning ritual left him assailable—*if* she could keep her eyes off of him and on her ultimate goal.

But she had to find that break in the trees that enshrouded the track away from the ridge, and that looked impossible. There wasn't a thing that seemed different to her.

A tree was a tree . . .

. . . everything in nature tells a story . . .

Every tree for hundreds of yards around the pasture looked the same to her.

. . . see what is before your eyes . . .

She could hear him saying it, she was sure he had been mocking her. What was before her eyes but an endless vista of greenery?

Or had it been a challenge?

How *much* had she given herself away?

"Sister?" His voice was *behind* her, and she swung around, startled, and in that moment, she saw him on blessed horseback, she saw the break in the trees, and she saw freedom.

"Recreation, Sister?"

She was sure he was mocking her. He had come because of the dog, she was certain of that too, and it pranced around his legs as he slowly dismounted.

"Of course, Mr. Cordigan. The routine of the day is what holds one's life together, don't you agree?" Better to attack than to let him get a toehold into her reasons for walking out exactly where he had found her the day before, and at a disadvantage too.

"No, I don't," he said flatly. "It is still dangerous for you to wander around here alone, you know."

"But you are so sure that no one can find his way to the ridge, Mr. Cordigan."

He shrugged. "Maybe not. Anything is possible if someone is desperate enough, or asks enough questions, don't you agree, Sister?"

He saw the flash of anger in her speaking eyes before she got a hold of her unholy temper.

"Anything is possible," she said—meekly, she hoped. He had craftily turned her away from the direction she faced when he had come up on her, and now he subtly forced her to begin walking with him, all the while facing the cabin, so that she could not take note of exactly where she had been.

No matter, she would find it again, she *would.*

"I think it is time to ask more questions, Sister."

She barely heard that for her concentration on the landscape as they walked. And then his words sank in, and she bent her head in frustration. She did like the all-concealing veil that allowed her a long moment to let her thoughts catch up with his words, but she hated the fact he was gnawing away at her story like a dog with a bone.

She had to get away from him.

She slanted a look at the horse he was leading. She didn't know a lot about riding a horse, but surely she could manage to stay on this one if she immobilized Mr. Cordigan by stealing his clothes.

She had to do it soon—tomorrow . . .

She missed his next words.

". . . are those men?"

"Excuse me, Mr. Cordigan?"

"How desperate are those men, Sister?"

"They seemed desperate to me," she said airily.

"Sister . . ." he said sternly.

She turned her face away from his. "I don't know."

"You knew the boy."

So, he had come to that.

"The boy knew me," she said desperately—not a lie, not really. A half-truth, and how could she tell him it was her own brother?

"From the convent?"

They were almost at the cabin.

"From *where,* Sister?"

She remained mute, her head bowed.

"You can't tell me," he paraphrased cuttingly.

"We have been over this ground, Mr. Cordigan, and I am in great pain as you scythe through it all over again. You have only to show me the way off the mountain, and you need not concern yourself about me ever again."

"A pretty and proud speech, Sister, even while you're trembling in fear. You value your life or you would have run right back into the fray and let them kill you. Now, *who were those men?*"

His gray eyes held no sympathy for her, who she was or what she might become with her confession. His face went stony with impassivity; he would not judge her either, but she could feel that he was coming closer to the truth—her truth, and she was no match for him whatsoever.

There was only one thing he would do once he found that out: he would make her pay in the only way a man knew how, and she weighed that against the burden of the lies that came so easily from her mind and heart.

The lies won; the half-truths were formed even before she finished her consideration of the consequences.

"They are my enemies," she said, and that was truth, she felt it as she said it, and her sincerity was borne on him as well. Whoever they were, they wanted her life, and it didn't matter to them who she was or what she was. Why should it? Why should it matter to him?

He didn't understand how someone like her could have made such enemies so young.

"Why?" he asked uncompromisingly.

Her heart sank. There wasn't one way to explain that with even a grain of truth in it. She didn't even have time to invent something: what could she conjure up that would be even remotely believable? His questions were like little traps, underfoot, quicksand, sucking her under before she knew it.

"I can't answer that," she said finally.

"That doesn't wash any more, Sister."

"You have no right to ask questions, Mr. Cordigan."

"Somehow I feel I have some rights somewhere in this, Sister."

"And next I suppose you will tell me there is some ancient mountain belief that if a man saves a life, the life owes him."

"No, I believe it goes that if a man saves a life, he owns that life, Sister."

"It's a pretty poor possession, Mr. Cordigan."

"But rich in mystery."

"*You* are the enigma, Mr. Cordigan, a man alone on a mountain with no company but a dog, and travelling some very out of the way roads to come to a place where you were able to lend some assistance to a helpless woman."

"Not so helpless," he said, "and surely less immured than you yourself, Sister, with no knowledge of the ways of men—or killers. Or so you say."

Back to that, neatly turned round again by his words and inescapable logic.

Well, enough was enough. She wasn't scared. She didn't think she was scared. She could even look him in the eye as she issued her meager little threat.

"It comes to this, then, Mr. Cordigan. You take me to Crossville Junction tomorrow, or I will find my way there by myself."

He laughed. It wasn't much of a laugh—more like a derisive bark, but it was fuel to her determination.

"I would love to see you do that, Sister, I really would." He issued the challenge fully conscious of the deepening resolution in those darkening blue angel eyes.

"And so you shall, Mr. Cordigan," she said dampingly, stupidly, she thought later, because of course there was something in her not-so-meek tone of voice that rang true to him, and so he didn't let her out of his sight for one moment from the time they returned to the cabin.

She accompanied him to the barn where he unsaddled his mount, brushed it down and watered and fed it. It wasn't the only horse there, either: the stable could house a dozen or more, and there were two in adjoining stalls, caught wild, which he was in the process of breaking.

"You live alone on this mountain to chase and tame wild horses?" she asked in disbelief.

"Easier to tame a horse than get along with people," he said cryptically. "Come, Sister. You will want to choose tonight's meal."

Choose? she wondered aggressively, but then, for the last two days, he had presented her with the evening's fare on the worktable for her to fry or bake or whatever she chose to do with it.

This time, he led her to the cistern where he stored his fresh meat—two days' worth, no more, in the summer— his eggs, a block of oleo wrapped in wax paper. Behind this was a storage shed filled with dry goods and canned goods: beans, flour, vegetables, coffee, baking soda, root vegetables, tins of sauces and fruits—he lived well, this recluse of the mountain who caught and trained horses and had but one dog and now a reluctant woman as his companions.

"There is a little beef here to be used up, some potatoes, carrots, parsnips . . ." he piled the items into her unwilling arms. "You have another night on the mountain, Sister, if you fully intend to leave. I hope you aren't ungracious enough to refuse to continue preparing the meal."

She felt like stamping her foot. He was treating her like a recalcitrant child, and moreover, he chose to pull up a chair beside the work table as she set about flouring the meat that he cut up for her, and he chose to keep an implacable eye on everything she did.

She made choices as well. She chose not to speak and not to be baited by his twisty little darts of information seeking. When she had mixed up some biscuits and put them in the oven beside the stew, she chose to sit in the chair opposite him and bow her head in a gesture of piety and silence.

It lasted for all of ten minutes.

"Sister, you haven't sat so long and so still in prayer since you got here. I suppose you're asking for special favors?"

Impossible man! She took a long deep breath to try to contain the throb of fear that shot through her. Her disguise was crumbling all around her minute by minute and she wanted nothing more than to leap up and pace around the room and shout him down.

She clasped her hands tightly and bit back a smart retort.

"The only thing I pray, Mr. Cordigan, is that *you* favor me with silence," she said finally, lifting her head and meeting his cool gray gaze.

"Indeed, Sister," he agreed, his voice laced with irony, "in silence there can be no questions."

He had caught her off guard: her beautiful eyes reflected the look of a hunted animal—he was stalking her and she knew it, but still, she gathered her wits in the blink of an eye, never at a loss for words.

"Or perhaps we both have much to answer for, Mr. Cordigan."

Her malice flicked him ever so slightly. This was a woman who had dealt with the world, however much she wanted to pretend she had not. And she *was* pretending. He just didn't know how he could prove it.

"And so you hide behind your profession of faith, Sister."

"As you hide behind your profession of being a good samaritan, Mr. Cordigan. And—" And—? She cast around wildly for some cohesive thought to attach to that negation, one that would distract him away from the notion *she* was concealing anything—"and it is becoming quite obvious *you* are not what you seem."

Oh there, he reacted physically to her words. She had cut close to the bone then and she was glad of it.

He let her savor that little triumph because he could not refute her words, not as they applied to himself or to her.

128

Then again, he liked watching that calm serene mask of the obedient nun settle over her beautiful face. It was a most interesting expression, compounded as it was of a purposefulness edged with a small smile of satisfaction that just flirted around the corners of her mouth. The darkening blue of her eyes lightened and focused, and every inch of her body directed itself to whatever task was at hand.

He didn't need to watch her to envision just the way her body moved, or the grace with which she bent over the stove to check the woodbox or the oven. He knew exactly the stretch of her arm by which she reached for something, and the drape of the material that outlined its young fresh shape.

She had too many faces, this young nun, and not a one of them rang true. But still, he could not take the chance, he couldn't . . . she played the part well—*when* she played it, when she chose to play it. And the look on her face was right, when she didn't forget to keep the mask firmly in place.

Was it obvious *he* was not what he seemed?

He appreciated that, and he meant to keep the long drawn-out silence she had imposed because it was plain to him that she would break under it sooner than he. She knew nothing about silences, or the deep inviting well of oblivion and revelation. She could never sit still long enough to begin to delve into the silence to find the self.

They ate in silence, and she fidgeted, unable to find even a flicker of expression in his face that might tell her what he was thinking.

She hated that inward-turning nothingness more than anything else about her enforced captivity, which was about to end.

She couldn't wait to get away from those eyes which seemed to see everything. They followed her every movements as she cleared the table and placed the dishes in a cask of water to soak. They never left her as she moved across the room and peered out the door into the mesmerizing darkness into which she could read nothing, see nothing.

Above all, they climbed the steps with her as she ascended to the attic room, the dog at her heels, and she was as sure as anything they watched her as she prepared for bed, and prepared for the events of the coming day. She wasn't sure that he didn't forsee the ending of it all more clearly than she.

Chapter 9

She awoke with a start, and for a moment she wasn't sure whether it was the dog nuzzling at her dangling fingers or the sound of a footstep on the stair that had jolted her into consciousness.

It was still dark, and earlier than usual, she thought as she petted the dog abstractedly and groped for the edge of the cover. She swung herself slowly into a sitting position and felt for the veil which she had laid at the foot of the bed.

Well, that was almost over. Four days of sleeping with the tight constraints of the wimple around her head were quite enough; she hadn't dared remove it, even in darkness, even after she was relatively certain he wouldn't violate her privacy: she just couldn't take the chance.

She felt for the little stub of a candle that sat in a bowl on a shelf by the bed, and for a match with which to light it.

There in the flickering light, by the steps, she saw the usual steaming bowl of hot water, just where he left it every morning. This routine had been unvaried for these three days since he had offered her the bathing water. He always set it just at the top of the stairs, and always some little time before she woke up.

But today he had come just a little early: she was not mistaken. The first light of dawn had not yet broken, and

131

she wondered why today was different as she stooped to look out the small attic window into a blank gray day.

Today would be different only for her, and as she washed herself carefully, she went over in her mind the exact plan she had half-formulated the day before. In essence it was simple: she would appropriate a horse and secure it somewhere near the pasture, and then she would track the bold Mr. Cordigan down to the stream and appropriate his clothing so that he would be inconvenienced and delayed while she made her escape.

It probably would make sense to bury whatever extra pairs of pants he owned—if any—that she could find.

That wasn't a bad idea at all, she thought, as she retrieved her money belt from beneath the mattress and undressed herself enough so she could fasten it around her waist.

The only thing that could spoil everything was the dog. He pattered after her down the steps, and snuffled at her hem as she dumped the cooled water outside the door.

He followed her to the cookstove and sat by approvingly as she made the coffee as usual by the light of the flickering kerosene lamp, and regarded her curiously as she tried to decide what to do about him.

Best to lock him in the house, she thought, at least while she was taking the horse to the pasture.

She had thought that would be easy to accomplish, but the one horse did not want to go anywhere and stubbornly resisted her inexperienced coaxing.

The other, docile and rather sleepy, watched her ministrations disinterestedly, and then pulled back when she tried to put a rope around its head.

Damn, damn—how did a person steal a horse? In the dim light of the stable area, she couldn't tell a bridle from a lead rope or which end of the horse was the right one, for that matter.

Her novice hands reached for a length of leather and metal and somehow forced it over the second horse's head, and somehow, in her desperation, got it out the door without anything catastrophic deterring her from her purpose.

By this time the sun had risen, and she was sure the enigmatic Mr. Cordigan would be down by the stream taking his morning bath. She had spent too much time with the horses, and cursing her own ignorance. She would have to post her mount closer to the house than she intended, and she would not be able to search Mr. Cordigan's closet for other trousers to squirrel away someplace he would not easily find them.

Damn and damn again, everything was going awry when she had thought everything would be so easy.

At least the sun was up and the day was bright, blue and warm.

She paused for one moment by the track that led down to the stream: she had locked the dog in the cabin and she had not heard a sound from him, not yet, but it seemed possible to her that he would resent being confined and he could ruin everything by his protests.

But she couldn't hear anything, not a whine, a snuffle, or an offended bark. She hoped he was sleeping—she prayed he slept as she started her tentative way down the path to the stream.

Now, her sole job was to keep herself low to the ground where he could not see her, and then cleverly steal away his clothes.

Easier plotted than done. As she neared the copse of bushes where she had hid out before, she could see him in his habitual stance, naked and open to the water and the sun, close by the bank of the stream, too close to where he had carefully laid his clothes and his boots.

She would have to wait; she loathed waiting, and today his ritual bathing held no fascination for her. He was her jailer, nothing less, and she would do anything to escape him.

She waited. Sooner or later he would plunge his body into the stream and sooner or later she would snatch his clothes and the thing would be done.

133

If only she weren't wearing the accursed habit which she was sure would slow her down immeasurably. She would have to make certain he was very far out in the stream before she even dared creep toward the embankment for his clothes.

She watched as he stood, as he bent and scooped up the water in his hands, as he drank it, feasted on it, smoothed its wetness over his face and chest, as he cupped it to his body, and finally waded into the wet warmth of it until it enfolded him completely.

His back was to her, his mind and heart utterly engrossed by the pleasure of the water, and she knew the exact moment to move forward and forward again, around the bushes and then up onto her feet, in a crouch, and then forward again in a crab-like scuttling walk, closer and closer to the pile of clothing, and the exact moment when to reach out her arm and grab the lot with a snap of her wrist and fold the bundle against her body.

The woods surrounding the stream were so still: she was the intruder, scurrying like a big black insect to the safety of the tall bushes a hundred feet away.

She thought she would die, her heart was pounding so hard and fast; she didn't know if it were from fear or exertion.

She crawled to the nearest tree, and wound herself into an upright position behind it. From this vantage point, slightly above the line of the concealing bushes, she could just see him; he was deep enough in so that he would have some trouble getting out if he should catch sight of her, and he was far enough away so she could get a good start on him.

She waited another moment, another. It was almost a shame to disturb the peace of the morning with her subterfuge, but she had learned already to take her chances when she could.

In the next instant, she moved slowly and very carefully toward the stone steps, angling herself so that—she hoped—the tree was between her and his view from the stream.

Up the steps now, bending slightly, feeling like the thief she was, she kept her eyes resolutely fixed on the pathway ahead of her, resisting the horrible urge to turn around to see if she were still safe. Better not to know if he had detected her movement beyond the bushes, or if he had caught sight of her tip-toeing blackly through the bushes.

Better *not* to know.

Better to take it one step at a time . . .

She froze.

An unholy howl split the silence, once, twice—a whimper—a hooting . . . the dog, the damned dog—the one thing on which she could not count.

He howled again, a long mournful "o" that echoed all the way down the path to the stream, again and again, dolefully, plaintively, insistently.

She didn't waste another moment bemoaning her luck: she ran.

In the sun-warmed water of the stream, he felt the ineffable harmony between himself and his surroundings. Here, nothing about the woman seemed disruptive; here, he reveled in the power of his body moving within nature and taming it the way he fully expected to tame the woman and make her own up to her lies.

It was all one now as he basked in the wet warmth of the stream. The woman would never attempt to leave the mountain ridge, despite her threats; he was certain she was well aware of the risks and that the men who sought her had most assuredly not given up the search.

Surely she knew he was less a danger to her than anything that awaited her in Crossville Junction.

Or maybe he wasn't. Maybe he was dwelling too much on her beautiful face and her changeable temperament. Maybe he was reading too much into the fact she didn't seem to bend her knees in prayer as often as he thought was proper. Maybe he had wondered once too often just how she slept at night, and whether she removed those constricting headpieces, and what she looked like beneath the forbidden wall of veil and habit.

Maybe he had just been totally enslaved by the sea-change of colors reflected in those angel eyes that were so direct and innocent and worldly all at the same time.

He knew nothing of women, not women like her. He knew the shy, beckoning girls of his childhood who sought other boys with fervid desire, but never the outcast who would take no part in the ceremonies that would mark him a man among his peers. He knew the wanton women of the frontier who followed the armies, and the prospectors, and anyone who would pay for the pleasure of their company.

They lived in sumptuous hotels in burgeoning towns, they lived in boxcars along the railroads, and they plied their trade in wagons along the trails, and when they stopped somewhere, they made sure the competition was light and neat, and sometimes, in a frenzy of jealousy, they chased a newcomer right out of town.

He knew all about women like that. They were good for an evening's comfort, a sigh in his ear, their hand in his pocket. He had eased himself among those women in every small town from Kansas right on through St. Lou, cushioned in the arms of ripe willing women who issued no rejections and told him no lies.

He had never loved a woman in all his long life, and if there had been one among the maidens of his youth who had made his heart pound faster, he had known instinctively she would never be his for safekeeping. The outsider who had never had a dream, never fulfilled his destiny as the son of his mother and the orphan child of his uncle had no place among the chosen of the men, no choice among the maidens as a husband or provider.

He had shown early on that he would provide nothing. He had shown only the fury and resentment of the displaced and nothing his poor anguished mother could ever do, or the patient uncle who had become his second father, banked the rage of the child abandoned by his father and disconnected from the world into which he

136

had been born. He had reviled everything in that ninth year of the return of his mother, lonely and destitute, to her people on the plains.

But why did he think of that, this day, this morning as he was thinking about the woman. What was it about her that was not what it seemed. It was the thought of the woman that had sent all these bitter memories flaring back into life, and the acknowledgement of the woman that made him remember he was a man.

Nevertheless, he was a man of honor now: he lived by his own stringent code and he would not break it. The woman was safe, no matter who she was or what she was—but he was rather startled to see that the merest thought of her could provoke an actual physical reaction in him.

He felt immediately suspicious of it and instantly waded into deeper water where the shock of the wetness would dampen his vigor.

The dog howled, a long protracted yowl of discontent. He stopped and turned toward the sound of it.

Again and again, followed by an agonized whimper, an angry hoot and another hair-raising howl that sounded as if the dog were mortally injured.

He clambered out of the water toward the embankment where he had tossed his clothes.

No clothes . . .

Only his boots lay there, like fallen soldiers.

He squinted up toward the sun, toward the barn and he saw her then: a black dot against the green landscape, laboriously racing up the path, her arms encumbered, and he could guess exactly with what.

Damn the woman and her recklessness. Damn his stupidity in not believing she would take up the challenge. She was a clever one, she who was not what she seemed, and he vowed to find out just what she was behind the cloak of an innocent's piety.

He moved like a streak through the woods, ignoring the scratch of the underbrush, reminded forcibly of the games of his childhood where he competed and emerged triumphant, but still never whole. He felt like a child pursuing the woman through the woods, and he felt that vindictive male exasperation that she, so chaste and virtuous, had gotten the best of him.

But not for long. He was gaining on her, and she was hampered mightily by her long skirts and the fact that she could not use her arms.

He was fleet and encumbered with nothing more than his desire to defeat her. His nakedness was no impediment; it harkened back to the games and rituals of his youth, and the tension in him was a welcome friend— the will to win at all costs.

She was about a dozen yards ahead of him when he saw that she realized he was behind her. In that moment, she tossed away her burden, lifted her skirts and ran for her life.

He leapt after her with a growl, gaining on her, pressing with the advantage of his speed, his unobstructed movement, his pure male power.

So close—he could almost reach out and grasp the end of the long black veil that flew out behind her.

If he grabbed it . . .

Not quite close enough . . .

He pushed himself and thrust himself forward at her, his hands closing around the edge of the veil and pulling, pulling hard as he met resistance from both her forward-hurtling body and the material itself, anchored to the headdress beneath it.

Again, one more hard, horrific yank, and he vaulted his body onto hers at the very moment he ripped the veil and wimple away from her head. She tumbled forward, with his heavy body hard on hers, her thick blonde hair streaming out behind her like spun gold.

She lay face down in the dirt of the path, savoring the moment of pure incandescent calamity: she could be in no more submissive posture than this, with her secret

138

revealed and the man who could be her enemy straddled naked across her back.

She wondered if it would do any good to demand he let her up. No, no good at all. She felt his large hands touch her hair, and then his fingers comb through its lustrous length.

She closed her eyes. This was the worst. She could not explain away the hair, and she could feel his wonder in it as his hands stroked it and felt its texture.

His preoccupation with it didn't distract her for one minute from her awareness of his nakedness. His heat radiated out all over her, surrounding her, scaring her. She had never ever been at the mercy of anyone to whom she had so blatantly lied. He could call her on every word she had said to him from the moment he had appeared at the Springs. She couldn't conceive of what words she could use now that he would even remotely believe.

It was safer to take refuge in silence.

The dog was making enough noise for both of them and three more people besides.

She felt him shift, and then her body being rolled over so that she was lying on her back with her eyes focused squarely on the thrust of his manhood so devastatingly close to her face.

If she moved, she would come nose to nose with it, and she hated him for forcing her to face up to it.

"You have the advantage of me, Mr. Cordigan," she said tartly.

"I prefer to think you've taken advantage of *me*," he answered in kind. "Sister . . . or is it that you are someone's sister and that is the whole basis for this pretense?"

He was too astute and too formidable, rising up like a pagan god over her prone body. He would sacrifice her, too, sooner than save her. His nakedness was potent and scary, and the power of the flesh of his manhood was something utterly unknown to her, and something not to be assimilated easily in subjugation.

It was not the same, being confronted with it before her very eyes, as it was seeing it from afar. Above her, his bronzed nakedness radiated a primitive savagery, untamable by woman. He held himself with an elemental power that seemed totally unconquerable. He was mighty and at one with the sky above and earth below.

He had vanquished *her* and there was nothing she could do to escape this force of nature. He was wholly there, aroused by his conquest and she felt one melting moment of terror that his anger and mounting desire could overcome his civility, and all that she had feared would come to pass.

It was such a powerful thing, this thrust of muscle and flesh, so immutably *him*, and yet strangely apart from him, as if it had a life of its own. She couldn't imagine it in conjunction with her. She couldn't imagine wanting it a part of her or how to make it a part of her.

She wondered what it felt like to touch, and then she recoiled, horrified she had even thought the forbidden thought.

He waited patiently, watching those expressive angel eyes assessing the situation, assessing him, *all* of him, in relation to her.

Angel eyes. Angel hair. Her beautiful face and mouth that close to the essence of him . . .

His question unanswered—he had forgotten it, watching the mobile blue of her eyes seeking still another way out.

Wondering if he would demand the ultimate price.

He was wondering too, given the assault on his senses by the very revelation of her lie.

Her body felt so soft, so giving beneath his.

Who would know, in the woods?

The dog howled again, and he rose up abruptly in one graceful movement. "Get up," he commanded, his voice raspy with impatience.

He held out his hand and she grasped it reluctantly and let him pull her to her feet.

"To the cabin," he directed, pushing her ahead of him,

140

disgusted with himself for his near loss of control. "Where is the dog?"

"I shut him away," she said defiantly, still disoriented by his change of heart—she knew she had read his intent in his eyes. She knew what she feared: All possibilities were alive now, as he prodded her impatiently toward the cabin. He was not ashamed of his nakedness. It almost seemed as if he ignored it.

She couldn't ignore her fear: it must be palpable to him. But she could read nothing in his stony expression now. His cool gray gaze was shuttered and his lips, beneath that thick brush of a mustache, had firmed into a thin hard line.

He thrust open the door of the cabin and the dog burst out with a yelp of gratitude, hurtling his body hard against his master's. He knelt then, and let the dog nuzzle him while he rubbed its bony head affectionately, and then he looked up at Angelene.

"Get inside."

"I—"

"Just get inside, Sister of Angels."

There was no arguing with that tone of voice. It was deadly, and she had the grim feeling that she was not the first who had ever heard it.

She went inside to be greeted by the smell of overboiled coffee.

Damn, she had forgotten she had put on the pot. Maybe she needed it too, something strong and hot to fortify her against his anger.

The dog bounded in, and he followed just as she was pouring herself a cup.

"That isn't hardly strong enough to give you the backbone you need to face me, Sister."

She didn't turn around at his words; she nudged away the dog who had padded over to her hopefully to try to make amends. "Perhaps it will heat up my words," she said, but she still couldn't make herself turn to look him in the eye.

"Your words have been inflammatory enough," he

said drily. "Just who the hell are you?"

She turned to face him then, leaning her shaking body hard against the worktable while she took a reviving sip of coffee to give herself a moment to assess his temper.

Well, the latent anger was there and he hadn't made a move to cover himself, so she was at a disadvantage having to *look* at him. Oh, she could look at his face, yes, but who could look at a man's face when he flaunted his body so casually without shame?

"My name *is* Angelene," she began, as her eyes slid involuntarily all over his bronzed muscular frame. Damn it.

"I don't doubt it, with that hair," he interjected. "Go on, Sister of Angels."

"Don't call me that."

"But that's how I see you—Angelene. Earthly and holy, all at the same time."

She bit her lip. "I *am* on my way to New York."

"I marvel at the coincidences, Angelene."

"And I *do* need to get there as soon as possible," she added with just a touch of desperation. None of it sounded true now, and she wondered fitfully how little she could tell him so that he would believe without her having to tell him the whole.

But why not tell him all of it? What could he do, besides ravish her and then turn her back over to Josie and perhaps demand some kind of reward.

She made herself look into his implacable set face, and she knew the man was an outlaw and he might stoop to anything.

"Of course it becomes clear now why those men were chasing you," he said mockingly, noting her clear-sighted appraisal of him.

A little dart of fear pricked her stomach. "Indeed?" she murmured, trying very hard not to give anything more away. What could he have deduced from that meager bit of information she had just fed him? "Just why is it clear, Mr. Cordigan."

He smiled, but it was a cold-blooded smile, on a par with that tone of voice she never wanted to hear again. "Because you're not a nun, Angelene."

Of course. Murderers chased women all over the place all the time. It was perfectly clear. If she weren't a nun, it stood to reason she *was* something else, something that incited men to murder.

She knew she was something else: she was a gambler—and she was scared. It was unbelievable that she was standing in an isolated mountain cabin trading barbs with a naked man who might or might not attack her.

His nudity was so distracting: she couldn't keep her eyes off of him. "You don't know that," she parried willfully. She knew it *would* have worked, if she hadn't been so strong-willed and tart-tongued.

"I know that," he said softly. "Your eyes are too curious and too bold, Sister of Angels—among other things."

Her eyes swerved away from him immediately. "Why don't you get dressed?" she said abrasively, reacting to the fact he had caught her looking at him once again.

"I can't do that, Angelene. Some wood nymph stole my clothes."

"She would be happy to retrieve them for you."

"That would not make me happy at all, Sister of Angels. I am perfectly content to have nothing between us but the naked truth."

"Yes, you've made a point of baring your soul to me," Angelene muttered derisively.

"So it is now time for you to divest yourself of the lies and half-truths, Angelene."

She stiffened. "I don't know what you mean."

"Plainly, I mean for you to become mortal again, Sister of Angels. Please remove the rest of your habit."

Oh no, oh no: her heartbeat accelerated painfully. No, she couldn't—he couldn't *make* her . . .

"Angelene . . ." That tone of voice again, the one that must make men tremble, let alone women. There was a thread of steel underlying it, and a threat of violence, the

143

same danger in him she had sensed days before.

She could not back down, she could not show fear, and she didn't know if she could pull off the right tone of impertinence either.

"I'm not in the habit of undressing in front of strangers, Mr. Cordigan."

"No, you're merely in the habit of dressing them down, continually. But now it is time for you to dress down, Angelene, and if you don't, *I* will take care of it."

That was clear enough. But so must she be clear. "I won't do it."

What could he do, after all, an unarmed man with no clothes on? She found out in a minute: he strode purposefully across the floor, grabbed the edge of her shoulder and gave one mighty pull. The whole dress came apart in his hands to leave her standing with her last defense in shreds.

She felt a frisson of pure horror. She had totally forgotten about the muslin money belt tied around her waist, and it was the first thing his darkening gray gaze lit on, and she held her breath in fear of what he might do next.

"Well, well, Angelene. Here we have the ultimate truth," he murmured, tossing her habit into a corner of the room where the dog began sniffing it. "A dozen stories could be fashioned from the fact of your possession of a money belt and a nun's habit."

"I could tell you a thousand and one stories, Mr. Cordigan."

"You are beautiful enough to play Sheherazade to my lord, Angelene. After all, you are prisoner in my kingdom."

"And like some fat naked pasha, you have no right to keep me here," she rejoined daringly.

"It's my mountain, Angelene."

No arguing that, or the look in his eye as he surveyed her skimpy chemise and black cotton stockings. She might just as well be stripped naked: there were no secrets left to hide. He had destroyed her disguise and

144

found her identity all in one brutish pull of his determined hands, and now he and his rambunctious manhood were enjoying every moment of it.

There was something horribly unnerving about defending her honor before a man who seemed to have no honor whatsoever.

The only weapon she had left was words.

"It's my story, Mr. Cordigan."

"The first of many, I'm sure."

"Mr. Cordigan . . ." she began in a fury of frustration.

"Sit down," he said, interrupting her, motioning to the cot opposite the fireplace.

"I don't want to sit down. I want you to get dressed."

"I'm perfectly comfortable."

"I am *not*."

"It must be the weight that you carry, Sister of Angels. I will take it, and you need not worry about it." He held out his large hand.

"I—" Oh Lord, her money, he wanted her money, and he could tear that flimsy muslin belt off her as easily as he had ripped away her black dress, as easily as he could pull off what was left to shield her ever-diminishing modesty.

She untied the strings and handed the belt over to him.

"Now sit, Angelene."

That thread of steel permeated the politeness of his tone. He knew it—he had used it deliberately and it was well that she obediently lowered herself onto the cot and looked up at him defiantly.

He needed some distance from her now; his body felt pummeled by his ongoing reaction to her blonde beauty that he could not gratify. But his nudity kept her off-balance and suffused with fear of the threat of it, so demonstrably visible.

She did not know he was a patient man. Of all the things he had learned in his self-imposed exile on the mountain, he felt this was the most life sustaining: that time and justice were on the side of the man with patience.

He needed every ounce of self-possession now that he

145

knew this woman of the angel eyes was no pristine postulant. He wanted her, instantly, torturously, the way he had never wanted a woman before, and without knowing who she was or what she was.

Now that her beautiful face and glowing, glowering blue eyes were surrounded by that mane of spun gold hair and the supple body hidden by those voluminous nun's skirts turned out to be the body of a wanting and perhaps wanton woman, he could allow himself to feel the steeply banked desire that had haunted the three nights and days she had been with him on the mountain ridge.

His nakedness, with which he meant to subdue *her*, became both a powerful weapon against himself and a threat and a promise to *her*, neither of which he was sure he could fulfill.

He paced around her warily. It was another woman who inhabited the body that had once belonged to the nun. She was Sister of Angels no more, and he cursed the isolation that had not taught him how to deal with a woman's wiles, wits and guile.

Her intelligent gaze followed him every which way, resolutely fixed on his face, ignoring the cat-like stalking of his naked body, and he didn't suppose he had thought she would fall on her knees and worship the latent power in him. It seemed more likely she would resist it.

In fact, he felt the more powerful urge to keep her with him, no matter what were her wishes, no matter what the cost.

He picked up the thin muslin belt and hefted it in one of his large hands. It was heavy with coins, which did not necessarily suggest a lot of money, but did suggest gold, and the notion perhaps she had stolen her booty from the very men who pursued her.

He ripped open the thin muslin cover and a quantity of silver fell to the floor, along with a small golden heart suspended from a chain.

He heard her catch her breath as he hunkered down beside her and picked up the slender gold chain in his large rough hands. Of everything, this was the most meaningful to this woman of the angel eyes, a small gold locket on a chain.

He flicked the catch and the heart divided to reveal a photograph: a heavy-set, stolid looking woman with a thin mouth and gray hair, dressed in plain black.

He looked up to see Angelene's hand extended toward him.

"Who is this woman?"

She hesitated a moment, but she saw no harm in answering him in order to retrieve the locket. "My mother," she said, unaware that her reply sounded to him rigid and unemotional, and that he heard in her response a connection to himself and his past and the things from which he had tried to run.

He canted his hand and poured the chain and locket into her palm, still crouched beside her, watching her intently as she closed the trinket into her hand tightly and refused to meet his cool gray gaze.

"Now, what is the truth, Angelene?"

She refused to look up, she couldn't look down without fixing her eyes directly on his powerful body. She wet her lips speculatively. There really was no point not to tell this savage whatever he wished to know. In every way, she was at his mercy and she still couldn't tell if he were friend or foe.

She could feel his intense interest in her words.

"It is just what I have told you, Mr. Cordigan. I am on my way to New York, and I adopted the disguise so that I would not be attacked because I am a woman travelling alone." There, that was good, and true as far as it went.

"And the men?"

Oh yes, the men. But really, the problem was explaining away Bobby and how she came to be travelling with him. She just couldn't bring herself to admit her relationship to those men.

Her silence strained his tolerance. He felt a creeping rage in tandem with his growing desire. His naked body sought only to betray him. He wanted to prove what this woman was and then to take her. No innocent could have

147

devised such a scheme. She was—she had to be—a cunning town tart, fleeing from the consequences of her actions, not above stealing, not above lying to get what she wanted. A Circe, pulling an innocent puppy into her toils.

And he, fool that he was, knowing what women were, had been dragged in right along with the boy. He had been too lenient, giving her too much time to make up a thousand and one stories that would prevent him from seeing the truth.

He rose suddenly, his body stiff with an angry lust, and he circled around her, once, twice, three times.

"The men, Angelene?"

She refused to answer. The men, her brothers, sent to kill her—it was a worse story than any she could devise, without any redeeming ring of truth.

She felt him behind her suddenly and she stiffened.

He felt like shaking her. He clenched his hands as the palpitating waves of his simmering anger spilled into sheer fury. He had to make her tell him the truth.

"The truth of the matter is," he said coldly "you stole the money from them, and you sought to hide from *them* with your disguise, and you roped that puppy into helping you escape from whatever town you were running from. That is the truth that fits the facts, Angelene, isn't it? Isn't it?"

He felt like shaking her. He clenched his hands as the palpitating waves of his simmering anger spilled into sheer fury. He had to make her tell him the truth.

She felt his hands grasping her hair. She felt him pull her head back so that she was braced against the hard heated thrust of him. Her breasts thrust forward and her mouth came into alignment with his implacable angry mouth, speaking words that hardly registered as he lowered it to meet hers, to take what he envisioned others having had before him.

She squirmed against him frantically, her fingers tearing at his rough hands and his forceful invasion of her mouth.

She knew nothing of men and kisses and the heat of arousal that came from a man's possession of the most tender recesses of her mouth. Her body rejected and welcomed it at the same time, a concession to her passionate nature and her best instincts of survival.

His harsh wild wetness caressed her with no thought to her need or her innocence. He knew this only as a prelude to what came after: in moments, she would grant him everything and he would lose himself in oblivion once again.

But in another moment, he felt the frenzy of her anguish at his heedless violation of her mouth and he wrenched himself away. This was the kiss of an innocent—he had known it, and wanted to refute it because he wanted her. But there was time for that. There was *time*.

He was breathing so hard and heavily he could hardly speak. "What is the truth now, Angelene? What is the *truth?*"

She was positively shaking with fright, and something else that she didn't want to define. She tasted of him, she could still feel him in her mouth, reaching for her, playing with her, assuming in her an experience that was all too seductive and all too easy to feign.

Her body felt explosive, and yet deep within her, she knew as well that his overpowering her was the last thing she should give into, in spite of that little kernel of response flowering within her. All she could do now was tell him the whole truth, and withhold nothing—except herself.

She just couldn't get around how it sounded.

"Those men are my brothers, sent by my mother to kill me."

It sounded crazy.

"And the young one as well?"

"He laid the trap. The other two are not capable."

"Except of shooting a gun? This makes no sense, Angelene."

"No."

"Why?"

Why? A thousand reasons why—or maybe just two: Josie had wanted her to stay, and she hadn't wanted to. That was the crux of it: she was to be Josie's aide-de-camp, murderess in training to take over when Josie fell by the wayside, and presumably she would have had to swear to care for her brothers as long as they survived as well.

Now she knew—she could pull the whole thing right out from under Josie, or maybe Josie was doing a good job of that all by herself, since people were becoming suspicious of the mysterious disappearances of friends. Maybe it couldn't have lasted more than another month or two.

Maybe her own defection was just an excuse for Josie. Getting rid of her would put them in a fresh location with a new and ready clientele full of money and the ambition to strive westward.

She laid it all out for him, just like that, and he plainly didn't believe her.

"You've been up on a mountain too long, Mr. Cordigan," she said tightly, still veering her gaze away from his insistent nudity.

"Or you're an excellent storyteller, Sister of Angels," he muttered, "and I swear I don't know which."

"What does it matter?" she asked desperately. "All I want is to be on my way."

"But that is not what I want, Angelene."

She felt color positively wash her cheeks. "That is obvious, Mr. Cordigan."

"I suppose it doesn't matter what the story is," he went on, ignoring her tart comment. "It only matters whether those men are still hunting for you."

"I'll take the chance."

Of course she would—she didn't even have to think about it twice. Just as she hadn't thought about the consequences of disguising herself and running blindly from a pair of murderers and an erstwhile beloved younger brother. Or trying to outwit *him* with the meager weapons she had at hand.

Her innocence dismayed him, because within it she wielded the most powerful weapon of all, that he had to respect it.

That didn't mean that he couldn't try to change it. All it meant, simply, was that he would not let her go.

"No," he said finally. "For now you will stay here with me, Angelene—and never a moment out of my sight."

Chapter 10

He meant it. She slept on the cot beside him while he slept on the floor, covered in a silky tanned buffalo robe, and in the morning when she awoke, he was beside her, clothed now in some kind of cloth pulled between his legs and draped over a piece of rawhide tied around his hips.

The coffee was ready, and a thick chewy biscuit to go with it, and he sat across from her, consuming it, watching her carefully as if he were seeing her for the first time.

But of course, he was. She was no longer inviolate. All curtains got pulled back eventually, and now hers had opened to reveal a woman beneath the draperies of make-believe. She was too well aware of his visual fascination with her hair and her face, and the limp cotton undergarments that hung from her limbs and outlined them as clearly as if she were naked.

"You will let me dress," she said at one point.

"I will make you a dress," he told her. "In a day or two."

Now he was a stranger again, remote and almost mystical in his removal from the plane of his being a man and she a woman. He had clothed himself to reflect the fact, and she found herself thinking about what lay quiescent and powerful beneath the drape of the cloth covering, and she didn't want to think of that at all.

She thought of the kiss, the heartless, forceful,

demanding feel of his mouth possessing hers as if he expected she would welcome the wet heat of his seeking tongue.

She felt less repelled by the memory of it than curious. Was this what women did, the accepted custom of a caress, the foretaste of that which she had been instructed to resist with all her might, even her life?

No, she couldn't think this way: that man had meant to use her in just the way she imagined if she had been the slightest bit willing. She knew her virginal kiss had saved her, but she couldn't be safe for long if she were to remain on the mountain with him indefinitely.

"What kind of dress?" She dearly wanted to know since he would not let her mend the voluminous black habit he had virtually destroyed.

"An appropriate dress," he said, sidestepping any discussion of that neatly. He didn't have to offer her a dress at all, but he forebore to point that out to her. "You will come with me in the morning to the stream to bathe."

"I? Bathe?" she repeated falteringly.

"Now," he added firmly, taking her cup and setting it aside.

He was not unkind or harsh with her. He merely insisted she accompany him to the stream, and together, she in her chemise and drawers and drab black stockings, and he in his draped covering and barefoot, made their way down the path beside the barn to the stream.

She knew, with a sinking heart, what was to come.

"You will undress, Angelene."

It was that tone of voice again, the steely one, the one reflected in the stone-hard gray of his eyes and the set of his lips beneath that brush of mustache.

She felt assaulted on all sides: the sultry heat of nature surrounding her, the seduction of the thought of bathing, the elemental power of the man who demanded this of her—it all came down to one thing: he could force her, and she would have no control whatsoever.

She stood by the side of the stream and slowly pulled

the ribbon from the neck of the chemise as he watched, again with that remote and cold gray gaze, as if he only wished for her to cleanse herself.

She slid the sleeves down her arms and off, pausing for a moment before she let the soft material drop from the taut thrust of her breasts.

She had to close her eyes: she couldn't bear to look at him as she untied the tape of her drawers and removed them, and pulled the horrible stockings from her legs with two quick swipes.

This was worse than anything she had ever been warned about. The physical possibility was no match for her imagination.

"Angelene." His voice was rock hard with determination not to give in to the seductive sight of her, naked and tearingly afraid.

She opened her eyes. He had not removed the cloth that covered him, and he held out his hand to her.

She bit her lip and extended her own trembling one. He grasped it firmly and propelled her forward toward the water. When it lapped against her feet, she almost jumped into his arms.

A moment later, she was in its warm depths up to her waist, a naiad, naked and alluring, luxuriating in the wet warmth of the water.

He watched her; he gave her the soap to wash her body, her hair, and he said not a word, and his silence was so impressive, she nearly forgot he was there.

But then she looked up, and found him watching her, and the expression on his face was both one of impassivity and repressed desire, and it frightened her all over again.

Still, he made no move toward her, only to hand her her underthings so she might dress again, and after—and she took this to become the tenor of their days—he took her to the barnyard, and let free the horses. Setting the dog to guard her, he went about putting them through their paces.

His anger, when he had found the one she meant to use

for her escape, had been volcanic and contained. She hadn't made it and it took him very little time to reach that point of understanding within himself. She would remain with him, just as he desired, and that was all that mattered in the end.

She sat on the fence and watched him, lean and bronzed, with only a piece of material wrapped around a rawhide belt to protect him from the wild horse he sought to tame.

The sun washed him in a mystical glow, his dark skin contrasting with his still darker hair and mustache, and the flinty lightness of his eyes. Every muscle in his body rippled as he moved, following the horses, feeding them signals, tamping at them with some kind of long birch wand when they headed off in a wrong direction.

He handled them so skillfully, she wondered if he couldn't handle a woman as well. His corded legs were so long, he could kneel in obeisance to someone he adored, but he looked like a man who had loved nothing and no one in all of his life.

Yet his hand was kind—to the dog, to the horse, to herself when he perceived the virtuousness within her, and he had saved her life.

She didn't know what it meant, but on this first day when the curtain had been lifted, she was reassured by the sight of the man touching his horses, and playing with his dog.

"You must have come here a very long time ago," she said to him.

"Long enough ago, Sister of Angels, and perhaps too long," he said thoughtfully.

"From where?"

"Why must you know, Angelene?"

She shrugged. She had thought, now he had made clear she was as good as prisoner here, that it would help to know something about him, so that he would seem less a mystery and more open to scrutiny. But of course he would rather be surrounded by the mystery. It kept her off-balance, and she was certain, with his brusque dismissal of her question, that this was exactly what he intended.

She found herself watching him nevertheless. There was something so primitive about him, the way he moved, the carriage of his body. His posture was impeccable, every inch of him aware of his surroundings, his eyes seeing everything with a calm clarity that missed nothing.

But his face was not a map of calm contentment. It was long and thin and deeply etched with lines, its saving grace his firmly marked brows, cool gray eyes and the firmness of his mouth.

There was no humor in this face: there was a lifetime of pain and acceptance, and perhaps a little hope. She found herself becoming more and more curious about him by the hour, covertly watching him, admiring his body, trying to read whatever she could catch in his expression.

"You will take me to Crossville Junction eventually, won't you?" she asked idly that evening as he sat across from her, cross-legged, on the floor.

He really never wanted her to leave. "I don't know."

She felt a horrible flash of anger. "I don't owe you my *whole* life, Mr. Cordigan."

"No." But he hadn't thought past this one day. "Yes, you are most anxious to travel on to New York. Do you have any idea where New York is, Sister of Angels?"

She drew in her breath in a hiss. "East. It's east of here, and you get to it by train, and surely you haven't immured yourself up here so long that you don't know that."

"Oh, I don't know a lot of things, Angelene, but I do know that you won't leave here until it is safe."

Her heart crashed with a sick little thud. "You mean that."

"I don't want you to die."

She supposed that was as generous as the man could get, *if* he meant it. "Perhaps you should come with me, just to see."

156

His eyes lit up. "Perhaps I should, Angelene." He shifted his body, and lifted one leg so that it was angled in front of him where he could lean his weight on it.

Her eyes moved involuntarily, following his movement, settling for one brief unsettling moment on the bulge between his legs just revealed by the upended flap of material, and she wondered crossly why she was thinking about that so much.

It almost seemed, after his blatant display of the previous day, that he was deliberately hiding himself from her, but that seemed fanciful and a little shocking.

Nevertheless, he had remained covered when he had bathed, and he had neither undressed or changed the whole of the day.

"You are going where in New York, did you say?" he asked after a moment, just to keep words between them because he needed something to douse the heat of his desire for her. The way she sat across from him, with her long blonde hair falling in a cascade down one shoulder to cover her breast, intrigued and aroused him. His mind was full of the feast of her nakedness, and his whole engorged yearning to savor the feeling of her beneath him, crying for him, wanting him.

But he did not know how to love a woman like this, a woman of innocence and acidity, and he could only play with words and not with feelings.

"My grandmother," she said, swallowing hard, aware of the way he was looking at her, shamed by her own curiosity about his body. "My grandmother lives there, and she will help me."

A bold statement that was. She didn't know that at all for a fact.

"How can she help you, Angelene?"

"She will find me a wealthy husband, Mr. Cordigan, and that will remove my mother from my life forever." Oh, her voice was so firm, so sure that this grandmother existed in reality, and that the trip to New York was a mere trifle to be accomplished in minutes, let alone days or weeks.

157

Her words hit him like a punch to the gut. She was on a quest to find a man who could save her from her family.

And he was the man who had saved her life.

But a wealthy man. Yes, a woman like her, reared in innocence, would want the trappings that were in and of themselves meaningless. She would want dresses and a fine home, servants perhaps, life in a place that meant no hardship whatsoever, with someone who could provide the things for her that she had never had.

Yes, he could see that.

He could see her, limned in the dimming light of the evening, precious, angelic, speaking hard words into a still harder consciousness.

He could help her achieve that.

When he was ready.

And he was not yet ready to let her go.

She knew it. Somehow she knew it, and she wondered how she could lure him into taking her where she wanted to go.

The next day passed in the same manner: he woke her with coffee, they walked to the bathing place, she stripped, he watched, and together they waded into the water. He did not remove the concealing material, and when she was through washing, he gave her back her underthings, and they went on to the horses.

He did not talk much; he was still grappling with her desire to meet and marry a wealthy man.

She did not talk much: she felt wary and unsettled because she could read nothing in his face, nothing in his words. She hated herself for being aware of his naked chest and his long legs, for thinking of that long dark kiss which was meant to test her, to scare her, and the thought of which now aroused her.

She felt his hot gaze resting on the peaks of her breasts pressing against the thin material of her chemise, and she caught herself seeking the tell-tale evidence of his feelings in his eyes, in the hidden place between his legs.

He gave her a comb, and then settled down to the pleasure of watching her work it through her hair.

158

"Why do you sit like that?" she asked him through a tangle of blonde curls.

"This is my way, Angelene."

She liked his way. The bend of his crossed legs spread them wide to give her an unobstructed view of him, and she took advantage of the veil of hair to look him over closely, pleasurably, imagining his powerful male essence quiescent behind the cloak of material.

"Why do you hide in this place?" she asked him, lifting her head, lifting the curtain of shining golden hair, lifting her arms so that her breasts thrust forward in all innocence—or maybe not. Maybe she wanted to invite his gaze, his desire to see behind the secret of her clothing the way she wanted to see behind his.

She didn't know what it was about two people together like this, a man like him with all that subdued power and taut maleness, and a woman like her, who knew nothing except the things on which she had spied in secret, and the hot hard forceful kiss that had been meant to make her capitulate and instead had enslaved her.

"I do not hide, Angelene. I live."

"Strange to live alone," she murmured, bending her head again, and slanting her gaze toward the impatient movement of his lower torso.

"I am not alone now, Angelene."

His voice was husky with the rising heat between them. She threw back her head and let her hair cascade down her back in a molten stream.

She could almost feel his yearning to bury his hands in it. She set aside the comb.

"But when you are alone again?"

"I do not think that far ahead, Angelene. I take each day as it comes."

Each day savored, she thought, putting her head down to rest. She understood that; she was savoring each moment, every point at which she could watch him unguarded, could recreate the kiss, could feel her mounting sense of yearning, define it, enjoy it, and lay down to sleep with him nearby her side.

What had happened in the space of a day?

At the stream the next morning, she was conscious of not hurrying through her disrobing; she wanted him watching now, but with her full knowledge, and her full engagement in the act of undressing for him.

Today the thought did not shock her at all. Today she wished to savor the moment and her building curiosity in him and those tenuous strange hours they had spent together.

Her breasts swelled with excitement as she slowly pulled out the bow that tied the neckline. She felt his hot gaze settle right on the taut tips of her nipples as she pulled the material away from her upper torso, and she turned toward him as if he were the sun.

"Why don't you get undressed too?" Or did that sound coy, blatant?

"I am comfortable as I am." But his voice rasped with emotion.

"What do you call that thing?" She untied the tapes of her drawers and let them fall from her hips.

"This is a breechclout," he said evenly, but he swallowed hard as the thin material clung to her body and she sat down on a nearby rock, crossed one leg and proceeded to delicately roll down one stocking and remove one leg of her drawers in full view of his avid gaze.

"I have never seen anything like it," she murmured, slanting a look of pure feminine guile at his bulging loins.

"It is the symbol of my childhood, Angelene, of a man who wanted that freedom but still did not know his place."

She stood up, dropping her clothing on the ground beside her. "Does he know it now?" she asked breathlessly.

He shook his head as he met her glowing gaze. "No. He must still find it." To say that cost him much pride. This was angel eyes, with a knowing look deep down within that was older than Eve; and it came from the same place as his knowledge of his place, his part. It came from a

160

place where things like this did not matter at all.

Nevertheless, he knew ultimately they were of importance, especially in the world beyond the mountain ridge.

She turned away from the naked emotion in his voice and bent to retrieve the soap before making her way slowly into the lapping water.

He followed the movement of her body, his face impassive once again, his eyes burning with the knowledge of the difference between himself and his angel of innocence who was slowly discovering the heart of her desires.

He knew it from the very way she moved, so different from a day or two before. He saw it in the way she had willingly removed her clothes, her eyes clinging to his, and the uninhibited way in which she washed down her naked body, aware of his controlled emotion, and the living light in his gray eyes that took every detail straight to his heart and manhood.

She turned her back to him first and soaped down her arms, her legs, her buttocks, under the fall of gold hair, around to her chest—she turned slightly to give him a better view as she slid that wet soap down her breasts, first one and then the other, and then the lean flat table of her hips and stomach, her thighs, and finally soaking the luxuriant thatch of feminine hair between her legs.

When this was done, she tossed her head so that her hair fell over her face, and she bent and immersed her head in the water for a long moment to drench her hair before applying the soap to it.

Then she rubbed it in thoroughly, as she raised herself upright, and the sun adored her lavishly soaped nakedness, warming the thrusting peaks of her breasts and her sleek long legs and gold-spun hair until the moment when he, still as a statue on the shore, could almost not stand it, and made a move to follow her into the water, to take her there in primitive triumph.

At that very moment, she immersed herself totally in the water and it was as if the very spirits of the sun and

161

the stream ordained that he would not fulfill his desire. He stood in awe of the ways of nature.

When she emerged from the stream, she was trembling with cold, a temptress turned shivering innocent.

He retrieved her underthings for her, and made her sit on the very rock where she had tried to entice him, and there, he dressed her in her well-worn chemise and tied the ribbons together over the alluring mounds of her breasts that pressed so seductively against the thin material.

He crouched down in front of her and lifted her long silky legs into the thin cotton drawers, unbending to the provocation of the sweet heat of her femininity inches away from him. He drew on the long black stockings to cover her naked feet and legs.

She watched, her tormenting gaze never leaving his expressionless face except to rest intermittantly on the thick hard protrusion between his legs.

She savored every touch of his large rough hands and the way his cool eyes tried to avoid looking at the tempting tautness of her nipples as he drew the ribbon ties of her chemise tightly together. She knew he tried hard not to caress the silken shape of her legs as he lifted them to slip on the horrible thin cotton drawers, but she felt the slide of his fingers against her skin nonetheless.

"The sun warms you," he said, raising himself to his feet so that she had to look up at him.

"Yes," she said tautly, unable to keep her heated gaze from skimming away from his shadowed face to his broad chest and, covertly, still downward.

His body fascinated her; it was all taut and angular, his hips just at her eye level, and the low-slung belt with its tormenting flap of material just below that.

She felt power emanating from every inch of him; all of him radiated an unconscious male strength, latent, potent, formidable. She couldn't match it, could never equal it, and she felt the pull of it and the need for it, and an unthinkable yearning to submerge herself in the mystery of it.

He moved away from her, tantalized beyond endurance by the sheer scent of her femininity, and by his sense of her sultry curiosity.

Her hair was a tangle of flat wet curls tumbling all around her blazing angel eyes, her posture preternaturally tense, almost exaggerated so that he would notice it, so that he could claim it, and he knew she was very well aware of what she was doing.

But—a wealthy husband, the thing she wanted, planned for, ran to with open arms. She had a future, and she had nothing here on the mountain except a man with a past who had consorted only with whores.

She shimmied with the voluptuous heat coursing through her body. She could see him so clearly and cleanly silhouetted against the sun, fighting with his desire, his conscience and whatever else moved and motivated him, leaving her the freedom to visually explore every inch of him and feel the hot mystery of his most potent and secret manhood.

She didn't understand either, but the moment he concealed it from her, it became a thing of ineffable fascination, the memory of the size and feel of it against her provocative and arousing.

From where she sat now, with him etched against the light in the distance, she could see the distinct thrust of that aggravating flap of material that so teasingly covered the lusty power of him.

She hated him for doing that to her, and she reveled in the fact that his covering himself had made her so much more greedy for the sight and touch of him.

Then, almost as if he had sensed what she was thinking, he abruptly turned and strode toward her, the whole of his repressed desire firmly outlined to her hungry eyes.

He saw that look, and he thought that if he were anyone else but who he was, he would have taken her right there on the rock and spoiled her forever for the wealthy husband she wanted so badly.

And spoiled her for himself as well, he thought

belatedly, and that thought almost stopped him cold. He wanted her for himself, and he didn't know how to take her; he only knew how to suppress his desire and his anger.

He came so close to her she could almost reach out and touch the throbbing evidence of his desire. "You're still cold," he said, since he didn't know what to say. "We'll go back to the cabin."

She tossed her head edgily. The cabin. Yes. It would be close and warm in the cabin, hot with promise, and deep with mysteries still to be uncovered.

The dog did it. As they approached the cabin, he came racing out of nowhere and leapt first into Rake's arms and then threw himself against Angelene, his claws raking the front of her chemis, pulling it and tearing it irreparably.

Rake's mouth thinned to a hard uncompromising line as he motioned Angelene into the cabin, his eyes consciously avoiding the saucy bob of her naked breasts. The damned dog was a mind reader.

Inside, it was hot, hotter than she would have supposed, and the air caressed her bare breasts and they swelled in sensual anticipation.

An amazing thing, her body. It knew the things she did not know she wanted to know. It knew she wanted to discard the torn chemise, and it knew she felt so hot that she just wanted to remove everything she was wearing because it would upset and torment him.

And it knew especially that she wanted to reach beyond the realm of temptation into the reality of her ballooning hunger to discover the secrets of her burgeoning carnal cravings.

She pulled off the offending chemise and tossed it onto the cot, and then she sat down and matter-of-factly took off the damp drawers. Her stockings, too, she supposed, although she liked the look of them against the nakedness of the rest of the body.

So did he. She felt the scorching heat of his flinty gray gaze as she slowly slanted a look up at him. He was transfixed by the sight of her long legs encased in the thin opaque black stockings, and as his eyes painstakingly examined every inch of her naked body, she felt a gush of pure enveloping desire.

She wanted to rise up and go to him and press herself tightly against his hot bronzed chest and that thick jutting essence of him, but she had the almost errantly funny thought that she would trip over the stockings. Well, she would just have to secure them somehow.

She groped for the shreds of the chemise and pulled the ribbon from the neck. She looked up at him, and yanked its frayed length into two pieces, and then slowly and deliberately she pulled each stocking up toward her thighs and tied each one delicately with a piece of the ribbon.

Then she leaned back, and lifted one leg and then the other, and ran her hands over the black shrouded length of them to make sure they were smooth-fitting and tight against her skin.

She felt his explosive movement toward her, and then he checked it.

He was a man with an iron will, she thought tightly. She twisted herself more firmly upright and played with crossing her legs just as he habitually did when he sat on the floor, and she knew he was watching every wriggle and writhing movement of her body until she finally got it correctly.

And now what? Nothing she had done had tempted him one foot past the threshold where he still stood, enraptured and enraged.

She jabbed an exasperated hand through her tumbled hair. It was just a little damp, ready for combing. She leaned over the side of the cot, rooting for the comb he had given her, giving him an unfettered view of all of her volatile nakedness.

"Comb my hair, won't you?" she asked him prettily, extending the comb toward him. Begging him, maybe, to

165

come close, to see all she was offering.

She felt his indecision and she felt like stamping her foot. Here she was, utterly luxuriating in the sense of her nakedness and the tight feel of the ribbon garters against her skin, and the shimmering heat of his unguarded lust, and he was going to refuse to even touch her.

But then he moved, and like a cat he came up behind her cautiously, warily, and he took the crude comb from her hand.

She immediately braced her arms so that she could lean backward, knowing full well it was a movement that would arch her back and thrust forward her taut-nippled breasts.

She learned fast, this angel of innocence, what would tempt and torment a man past all control. He was nearly there now, with his full voluptuous view of her luscious nipples and the wanton spread of her stockinged legs that revealed the lush mystery of her.

This close, he was enveloped by the sultry carnality of her need; and he could have taken her there as he had taken many others, with a grasp of her hair, and a seeking lunge down her firm naked body, a dark hot kiss, and then volcanic oblivion. What did he know about an innocent angel who presented herself with the aplomb of the most hardened street woman?

He touched her hair, the golden hair damp with desire and dreams, hair for a wealthy man to possess, and not a man whose gold turned to dross.

She wriggled with pleasure as his hand tentatively lifted her hair.

It was silk, smooth silk, slick with spots of dampness, redolent of the scent of soap and the perfume of her body, and he just wanted to bury his hands in it and feel it against his skin.

He felt himself elongating still more at the very thought of it, and he wondered how, in the space of four short days, she had gone from being untouchable to the very essence of caressable femininity. The line had blurred so quickly: innocence to innocent to hopeful

166

seductress who knew too well what to do and how to entice a man. Who would not capitulate to those luscious breasts or those long enthralling legs and the thought of them wrapped around his pumping body?

He pulled the comb slowly through the sleek texture of her hair, once, twice, again, reveling against his will in her throaty groan of enjoyment.

Trouble. If he went on a moment more like this, he knew he would give in to her intoxicating innocence.

He moved closer to her, daring his jutting manhood to send him over the edge. It would be a battle of mind over body, he thought ruthlessly, and he would not be seduced by the angel of innocents who thought she momentarily wanted the man of hardened experience.

She wanted the man of hard cold cash.

But even his awareness of that could not stem the tide of pure visceral desire that washed over him as he played with her hair and his thoughts.

He wondered what she wanted of him.

She seemed to know exactly what she wanted. She canted her head backward so that her hair swung downward and caressed his secret tumescent manhood.

It was as if the tendrils of hair could feel the rock hard length of him and convey the sense of it back to her. Her lips parted and she strained backward, reaching for him in mute demand.

He grasped a handful of the liquid silk of her hair and bent over her, his eyes feasting on the naked perfection of her, his mouth slanting over hers unerringly, hovering, unwilling to make the final commitment to take her and explore her.

He could submerge himself in her femininity and lose her to the lure beyond the mountain.

Perhaps you should come with me, just to see . . .

He growled low in his throat at the resonant echo of her provoking words and his mouth closed hard over hers, his left hand constricting around her luxuriant mane of hair, his right arm pulling her tight against his towering manhood.

His marauding tongue possessed her in a wild swirling release of desire: it was overwhelming, and it gave over nothing to the delicacy of her sensibilities. And yet it was different because she welcomed it, demanded it and met it with the ferociousness of a tigress who had captivated some new prey.

Deep, deep within the flood of passion, she felt the connection between the volcanic fury of this kiss and the yearnings of her naked body. She turned toward him eagerly, seeking the wetness and the tight molding of her body against his.

That was enough. For those long, luscious moments that he held her against his raging need and he explored her mouth with unrestrained intensity, it was enough, violently fulfilling, voluptuous in its arousal—and unsatisfactory in its consummation.

She reached for him then, twisting her body so that she could splay the palm of her hand and fingers against the tight hard muscle of his thigh and the wonder of all that compressed power. Her hand trembled with it, moved with it over the hair-rough skin of it, slowly, insinuatingly feeling the texture of it and the secret place to which it led.

He felt it, the tenuous exploration of his leg, her fingers firming against taut flex of muscle and becoming bolder, and still bolder—and he wrenched himself away from her entwining hand and her mouth with the last vestige of conscience clanging in his craw.

"I will not do this," he rasped, thrusting away the temptation of her clinging hand and clinging scent.

"Don't—" She felt as if he had tossed her adrift and there was nothing for her to hang onto. She felt shamed, instantly, that he couldn't bear to kiss her, didn't want to take her and do with her whatever the culmination of their dark ferocious kiss might lead to. She felt cold under the flay of his lacerating gaze and the mask of impassivity that slipped so easily down over his face.

But she had done nothing wrong: she had done nothing she hadn't wanted to do or that he hadn't wanted to see. She couldn't for one moment suffer under the notion of any kind of dishonor to herself or to him by her actions. She wouldn't let herself: the explosiveness between them was real, in the air, waiting to be ignited.

She raised herself up into a sitting position on the cot, but he had already strode out the door, seeking the cool air like a conflagration sought water.

She didn't know how he could want her with such ferocity and then clamp down so tightly on that volcanic need; he couldn't, not if he felt anything at all what she felt, she knew he couldn't.

She got up slowly and walked to the door just to watch him wrestle with demons of which she had no conception.

When he became aware of her, he saw her braced elegantly against the threshold of the cabin, naked, black stockinged, her hair tumbled and clinging to one bare breast, the angel of innocents, innocent no more.

In the morning, the feeling of something supple and pliant being laid over her bare skin awakened her.

"What—?" She pushed at the thing groggily, and then she became aware of the smell of the coffee, the crackling of a fire in the fireplace, the dog licking her outstretched hand, ever present and immutably there.

And of course *him*.

She shook herself awake. "What is this?" she demanded, turning so that she could see him face to face in the early morning light.

His expression was stony as ever. "Good morning, Angelene."

"What *is* this?" she demanded again, lifting her head now to try to see what the thing was.

"It's a dress, Angel of Innocents."

She couldn't believe her ears—or her eyes. "A— dress?"

"A dress—for you to wear."

"Oh really? And why must I wear this dress?" she

asked, her voice sweetly defiant. "Because you want to cover me? Because I am so ugly? Or because you might become distracted from whatever great purpose you have here in hiding on this mountain? Take it away."

But that imperious command got her nothing. She raised herself into a sitting position and drew the soft piece of deerskin up toward her chest. "It's very *nice*, Mr. Cordigan, but it's not my *style*," and she threw it over her head onto the floor.

"What is your style, I wonder," he murmured, getting to his feet to retrieve the dress, and then she saw that he had donned something that looked like the legs of pants which were attached to the belt of the garment he called the breechclout, and her interest pricked instantly.

He wanted to hide more from her; he was afraid of his feelings, of her.

He threw the deerskin dress at her. "Put it on, Sister of Angels."

"I won't, I'll go naked today too, Mr. Cordigan, and you don't have to look if you don't want to."

He didn't know how to fight with her. He picked up the dress and laid it across the foot of the cot. "As you wish, Angelene."

She abhorred the bored disinterested tone of his voice. This was going to be worse than last night, when he had spent the entire night camped outside the cabin door.

No, it *wouldn't*.

But somehow her ardor did not flare as fast as she thought it would with her pacing around the stove and worktable doing the mundane chores of the morning with the dog nipping at her stockinged feet.

There was even a point at which it didn't seem that important, and she wondered about the fickle nature of her own desire, and the waxing and waning of his.

She brooded on it as she sipped her coffee until it came to her that the thing that excited her most about him was the fact he had clothed himself and hidden himself away from her.

Perhaps she needed to hide her body away from him.

But it was very hard to ruminate on these things in the closeness of the cabin which now worked against her purposes. She could do nothing without his knowledge, and she certainly was not going to don the offending dress he had so painstakingly fashioned for her sometime in the early hours of the morning while she slept.

Upstairs in the attic where she had slept before he had found out her disguise there was a thin cover overlaying the bed. She supposed she could wrap herself in that and just sit still as a statue all day long until he came to his senses.

She doubted it, but she had to try. When he left her in the care of the dog while he went to check his horses, she scrambled up to the attic and pulled down the cover so that when he returned, she was sitting once again on the cot, swathed now in a bilious green cotton blanket.

She looked like a little old grandmother sitting there hunched under the uncompromising folds of the blanket—except for her exasperated expression and unruly tumble of golden hair.

"A wise choice this morning, Angelene. It is cool outside."

"I trust you slept well?"

"I did. Did you?"

She wanted to shout at him, no, I did *not*; I didn't understand why you left me like that. "Comfortably enough, thank you. Tell me, am I not to bathe this morning?"

"Later, perhaps—unless you would like to wash now. I can heat the water . . ."

"Later will be fine," she said tensely. She just didn't understand. He was acting as if nothing had happened between them. *Nothing*.

No. She reached over and fingered the hem of the dress. The dress meant that something had happened, something cataclysmic that he did not want to have happen again. But *why?*

"When did you do this?"

"Early in the morning. I know how to make my clothes

in the custom of my childhood, Angelene. A dress is not so hard with one piece of leather and a knife. It slides over your head, you see, and you belt the sides closed."

"Yes, I see." In the custom of his childhood.

"Not quite the thing to go travelling in, I grant you, but a reasonable piece of clothing to wear on a mountain."

"Along with a green blanket," she added, smiling faintly.

"I could cut that in the same manner," he said seriously.

"I—" She caught herself from saying something rash. She hadn't much choice after all: her black nun's habit lay in shreds in the barn, and her torn underwear had been folded neatly away somewhere in the cabin. She supposed she could insist on trying to make something out of the heavy dark material of the habit, but she did not want him to get any ideas in his head about her sewing or mending things or any kind of caretaking other than cooking.

She had meant what she told him, she thought in surprise: she was determined to get to New York and find her grandmother and after that, marry a wealthy man.

So why was she feeling so bereft because of his rejection?

She didn't know: she just understood that she had violently wanted something from him the previous day, and the intensity of that voluptuous feeling overrode everything else.

It had come straight out of the way he had kissed her, and the way he looked at her, and the unconscious way he flaunted his lean bronzed body. No one could be immune to that, not even someone as innocent as she. And nothing she had ever known before could have prepared her for it, nor could mere words have done justice to those unimaginably powerful feelings that overset her judgment and control and made her *want* the very thing she should be resisting with all her might.

All that hidden molten emotion that made her want to

172

torment him as she became increasingly aware of the power of her femininity against the potent force of *him*. The wonder of it—two such disparate people, the one who could easily take, the other who could just as easily goad.

She understood what he wanted; she comprehended not at all those hot luxuriant feelings within herself that only wanted to provoke him into some kind of explosive action. She only understood *how* to do it, and that she *wanted* to do it.

"So we're just going to spend the days to come sitting here?" she said abruptly, moving impatiently under the threadbare folds of the blanket.

"Well, no. I expect you're in more of a tearing hurry to get to New York now," he retorted caustically.

"What do you mean, *now?* I've always been in a hurry to get to New York, and now you've kindly delayed me by more than a week."

"There was nothing kind about it, Angelene. I saved your life and I've probably saved it again by insisting you stay here until you can be sure those brothers of yours won't come skulking up the mountain after you."

"And when do you suppose we can be sure of *that*, Mr. Cordigan?"

"Maybe *never*," he growled, stalking out of the cabin and into the sunlight. Damn her, damn her, damn her—always in a rush to get away from him and toward some dream of a life of opulence and ease. And another man. Another snake-handed man looking at her. Touching her. Kissing her. Reaching for her naked compliant body in the dark and . . .

Absolutely never.

Well, she showed him: she didn't move from the cot the whole day except to take something to eat. Now they were deadlocked in a fierce heated anger and she couldn't understand for the life of her why *he* was angry.

She had every right.

173

She didn't even know why she was determined to consummate the very thing she had been afraid would happen.

It didn't matter now. The day died, the moon came up, the supper was a thin gruel with biscuits, singularly unappetizing, and the fire warmed the room once again as the cool of night descended.

She had gotten no further in convincing him it was time for her to leave. She didn't believe she could convince him of anything. Look at what had happened to her ill-fated disguise.

She slept.

And sometime deep in the night, she awakened, called by the mystical impulse of her unfurling womanhood. Her whole body was alive with suppressed longing, billowy with expectation.

The whole room was stuffy, cloying, hot, the embers of the fire still glowing, still giving off heat, muted, blazing beneath just like her naked body under the constricting cover.

Moonlight filled the room and the sense of something else—his presence, and his suppressed desire, alive, awake, suffusing the room with his effort to smother it, to keep his body in check, his longings to touch her stifled.

It was like a living thing in the room, the struggle of the man against his emotions and he was losing, he was losing.

A man who had chosen to live a solitary life on a mountain had no right to so forcefully invade the precious life of someone who would never share his own. A man who lived alone on a mountain knew nothing of the innocence of a woman who was Sister of Angels; he only knew of women who invited such attentions and held their hands out for payment afterward.

Still, everything about her had been a blatant invitation this past day or two, and he wondered if she even knew it.

No, the look in those knowing angel eyes had told him

she knew it; she just did not know what it was to set off the powderkeg of her sexuality.

Even as he thought about the possibility of it, he wanted to reach across to her in the dark, and he wanted to touch her, just touch her—in the dark where it was easy to be bold and nothing could be taken unless it were offered freely.

In the dark, in the dark, the mind played tricks on a man and he could imagine that she lay there, breathless, intent, hoping . . .

In the dark, all things were conceivable. Primitive desires could be unleashed and it would be as if nothing had ever happened.

He wanted this woman of the angel eyes as he had never wanted anything before.

He sensed her subtle movements in the dark, and the long luxurious stretch of her body in her awareness of him and his keening need.

He felt every muscle knot up with his effort to restrain his own incendiary desire. She was but a breath away, her body shimmering with heat and awareness. He felt it, he could almost touch it: she was on the edge of the precipice as surely as he. One committment to action would determine death or transfiguration, and not even he was so all-seeing that he could choose his fate.

But he had chosen already. In the dark, in the closeness of the room, of their bodies, he could "see" with that ineffable sense of knowing that came from his childhood. She was temptation—aroused, provoking, inciting, waiting—and she would be his downfall.

Angel eyes, his for now: this was the moment she had always feared and now perhaps the moment of both their truths.

He rose up on his knees, silently, fluidly, rock hard with resolve and contradictions. He reached out his hand and lifted the concealing blanket and touched her hot bare skin.

She writhed against his hand instantly, gorgeously feminine in her response to him, arching herself against him subtly, hardly even aware of her volatile invitation.

He bent over her then, seeking her mouth, anchoring his hand and claiming her body for his own.

His mouth slanted against hers tenuously, his mustache roughly caressing her lips before his own mouth touched them.

This in the silence, the filling sense of him entering her, hungry for her as he had never been hungry for a woman before and then the hot enveloping whole of him conquering her, teaching her this in the dark: feelings, rushing unimaginable feelings aroused by a man's questing tongue and her own tentative response to understanding it, mastering it, beckoning it—tempting it.

The tension of the preceding days exploded in a fury in her mouth, greedy with want and reckoning. Only this could have been the end of her futile attempts to escape her past and him: in the dark, she never wanted to run again, she only wanted to pursue this evanescent descent in to a pure opulent submersion of her senses. She never wanted him to relinquish her, and she willingly gave herself up to the undulating swell of desire which washed over her shimmering naked body and coalesced in lush wet center of her very being.

Oh this, in the dark—her tentative hand reaching out to wind around his broad, rock hard shoulder in a mute acceptance of his dangerous kisses.

His mouth hovered above hers for one explosive moment. "And now, Angel of Innocents?" he murmured, his voice rough with some pulse-pounding emotion. His hand moved on her hip sliding heatedly around to cup her buttocks as he enfolded her body with his own, covering her, owning her with that one act of possession.

He was so long and strong and he fit against her so perfectly, chest to chest, hip to hip, thigh to thigh with the tense probing length of his manhood thick, hard and demanding between them.

Mouth to mouth they lay in the dark, and she

176

wondered at the granite length of him that fused so elegantly with the contour of her quiescent body, and the sudden unbearable shimmer of excitement that coursed through her at the feel of him nudging her, thrusting gently against her in concert with his forceful, demanding kisses.

She was stunned by her ravishing arousal; this she had not expected in the dark, that she would come to know what it meant to want the more, that a man's nearly naked body covering hers could incite a positive quagmire of desire which would pull her toward an ultimate surrender as hazy as the oncoming dawn.

But still his kisses, oh his treacherous, heated kisses. His arms folded so tightly around her nakedness, crushing her so tightly against him formed a complete little world in the dark that had nothing to do with reality and everything to do with the incandescent yearning ballooning within her.

And he knew just how to arouse it too, with long slow hungry kisses, and with the artfulness of not exploring her naked body and letting the torrid teasing thrusts of his ramrod manhood torment and provoke her.

Soon, soon, her tentative hands began to move, to touch the wonder of his naked muscled torso, to cling, to demand, to hold as she lifted her hips in the mute ancient enticement of Eve.

Angel eyes—the temptress of his heart, the vixen of his soul—his driving need to possess her escalated with each tentative thrust of her hips. Her gorgeous, bewitching body understood and overpowered every coherent thought within her as he deliberately began his torrid and thorough exploration of her nakedness.

She had been waiting for the feel of his hands, the slow slide of his probing fingers on her hot naked skin, stroking her from the curve of her hip to the sleek roundness of her thigh, lifting her, cupping her buttocks, letting his fingers sink into their softness to range over every curve and crease of her lower torso.

She moved with him, against him, inviting his carnal

177

caresses, her body shifted mindlessly, suffused with the pleasure of his touch; she moved to ease his way as his questing fingers sought the crown of her welcoming fold, and when he touched her there, she jolted against him in pure panic.

The sense of him there, his fingers poised to possess her, and the naked essence of her open to him and only to him both excited her and terrified her, and she did not know which was the stronger emotion.

Her traitorous body did: the shimmery glow of his caresses had led to this one moment when he would explore her feminine soul; she had known it—she wasn't ready for it.

His mouth eased and his kisses and she pulled him back against her lips. The hot, wet comfort of his kisses enslaved her all over again, arousing her to the feel of his waiting fingers gently canting against her seductive sex, never moving, waiting, tantalizing, tempting because he did not attempt to possess her and she could feel him not moving, not probing, not *taking*.

Her awareness of him *there* unfurled into a ravishing ripple of erotic need, fed by his kisses and her powerful sense of his own thick desire for her.

It seemed suddenly as if he had been waiting for her forever and that she had always wanted this one ineffable moment of knowledge, and she arched herself against his body and against his hand and invited his caress.

His fingers moved, his body moved, rolling her toward him so that they faced side to side; he stroked her then lightly, tormentingly, letting her feel the pleasure as he flirted with the outer edges of her provocative femininity.

She moved restively against him, seeking surcease as her body became acclimated to his caresses and his control.

Ever so slowly he insinuated his fingers into her sultry heat, and her body stiffened against this erotic penetration, and her hands grasped his shoulders tightly in discernible agitation.

He had never taken a woman like this before, with patience and kindness and this deep desire to arouse her past the point of coherent thought. He felt the grip of her hands keenly and he wrapped his free arm around her tightly and seduced her mouth all over again to quell her protests and arouse her enthralling passion.

Her hands fought with him, pushing at him, clutching him, snaking a path of resistance and capitulation all the way down his naked chest across his ribs and down his belly.

And then her fingers brushed the potent forceful thrust of his desire and her body gyrated wildly away from him again. Her movement deepened his carnal caress and she went exquisitely still as she realized it.

They lay together like this for several long voluptuous moments as he played with her mouth and tongue and let her assimilate the feeling of his fingers deep within her.

Once again, he chose not to move, not to take, just to let her experience the intensity of this carnal possession of her, and once again her feelings, her emotions and her body became his ally in his patient pursuit to claim her: he heard her moan, "Oh, don't—" and then her hips bore down on him hard, unwillingly, mindlessly, and he growled into her mouth, "Lift your leg—*now*," and she unerringly wound her leg around his thigh and shifted herself upward in another attempt to escape him.

But she felt herself opening to him and in a different way, where he had more purchase to explore her and to find new and different delights to seduce her all over again. It was almost unbearable—his seeking fingers found the throbbing center of her hot velvet core, caressed it, stroked it, enslaved her with it until the most unendurable spasm of white-hot silver crackled through her entire body like a bolt of lightning, sending an unending stream of sensation from her head to her feet.

It wasn't going to end, never, ever—and then it ebbed down and down and away and she bucked against the feeling of him still within her and tore her mouth away from him in a frenzy, sobbing, "Oh my God, oh my God, what was that . . . what was that?" But she knew, in the dark blackness of acceptance of the pleasure, exactly what it had to be and could not be of itself the thing she had most feared.

That was poised lightly and gently against her hand which still flexed with involuntary contractions of pleasure, and *that* a moment after her convulsive release was thrust naked into her hand and she clutched it without thought as he claimed her mouth once again.

"And now, Angel of Angels," he murmured against her lips, "now you fly with me," and he pushed her gently onto her back and spread her legs gently and she felt the whole hot length of him lean into the thick bush of hair that concealed her ultimate secret. He pushed gently at first, but then, as he gained the barest entrance, he thrust himself forcefully into the momentary resistance of her innocence, and then hard and deep into the textured heat of her velvet sheath.

She moaned as he effected the first long lunge to conquer her, and then her body felt soft and liquid from the lush residual pleasure of her culmination—and then the pain shattered the pleasure, sharply, quickly, incisively . . . and then it abated and he was nestled deep within her, more intimately than the first time. It was like nothing she could ever have conceived.

She wanted to get away from it—fast, and she couldn't because he was so decisively *there,* and she could feel every long hard inch of him, invasive, thick, overpowering, and for long moments she could not understand how this had anything to do with the other.

Then he moved and a whole new set of sensations supplanted her first desperate feelings: the long slick slide of him against the wet lush warmth of her, the opulent movement of his body and the way her own body suddenly wanted to move with his, the weight of him so perfectly aligned with her, and ultimately, the stunning urgency of his race to the final release—the unceasing pumping and driving of this rock hard extension of himself deep within her again and again and again, as if he knew exactly what she felt, what she wanted when she herself did not.

Her body felt fathomless, weightless, everything centered on that gossamer tenuous feeling between her legs. She wanted to reach out and capture it, and she could only capture him, his nakedness, his male essence, his mouth in a savage kiss that matched his own.

She would take the feeling, and pull—pull—unwind it to its very core—it was coming, exquisite and tantalizing, it was there—she would pull, hard, and it would come, spiraling all around her, dazzling, churning, primitive, different, different than the first, better, melting, blending, blinding—she lifted herself again to wrench the last cascading sensation from his movement—and he groaned. In one aching, lunging thrust, he found release in a long drenching eruption of passion.

She awoke the next morning covered and alone, and when she opened her eyes, she saw him rearranging that awful flap of material between his legging-covered thighs.

Dear Lord, between his legs . . . for a moment she could see clearly in her mind's eye the whole of him jutting aggressively forward from that thatch of coarse hair, a warrior of muscle and skin, all thick, hard and seeking, bold in its aspect, stunning in its ability to give pleasure.

What about it fascinated her? It was the strength of it in conjunction with the pure raw power of his body; it was the shape and size of it, the animate movement of it, as if it were a thing apart from his body, and the quiescent state of it that could quicken in urgent arousal.

It was the secret of a man's soul and this morning, in the aftermath of its telling passion, she felt a resonant connection between it and her most intimate womanly self, and she wanted only to look at him and touch and marvel at the part of himself he had given to her.

"Don't do that," she said softly, and he looked up to find her watching him intently, braced on one elbow, inutterably desirable, intensely alive after his carnal possession of her deep in the night.

"Why not?" he murmured.

She bit her lip. How brazen could she be? And yet, why could she not desire him as freely and openly as he wanted her?

The forbidden nature of their desire enticed her. Who would know up on the mountain what she might have done in the deep of the night or in the semi-darkness of the pulsating dawn.

He wanted her again too: she saw him elongating even beneath the concealing flap, and she whispered, "I want to see you," and his intractable male member responded to the husky, unconsciously seductive note in her voice by thrusting achingly forward to demand that he comply with her command.

He had to restrain himself from taking her forcibly now, and this was something new to him: a willing woman who did not know how to comply with the rules of equal exchange. This was the innocent wielding her new found power, enslaving him, binding herself irrevocably to probe the depths of her own passion.

There were repercussions to moments like these, especially for a man who had lived too long on a mountain. "Are you sure, Angelene?" He could barely utter the words through his shuddering urgency to possess her.

"I'm sure," she whispered silkily. How could she not be sure after last night? She felt ripe with surety that she wanted to experience again the mystical hot pleasure of the night before. "Can't you see I'm sure?"

"Tell me, Angelene."

She looked up at him with glowing eyes. "I want you to possess me just the way you did last night," she said huskily, daringly; how could he refuse? She threw back the cover to invite him to her side.

He knelt beside her, clamping down hard on his first primitive impulse to mount her and drive himself into her until she bucked and begged for more.

She was a goddess lying there with her golden hair

streaming over her luscious breasts and her hand tentatively reaching out to the granite hard evidence of his desire.

And if she touched him there? Oh, she wanted to touch him there, why couldn't she touch him there—her hand closed around his towering length beneath the constricting material and she felt the constriction of his muscles and reveled in the faint soughing groan deep in his throat.

Her feeling for it streamed out from her in the touch of her fingers that sought the living heat of him beneath the civilized covering of *the custom of his childhood.*

She wanted to see him, she wanted him to pleasure her again in the same way he had in the deep of the night, and she wanted him naked and open to her the same way she was naked and open to him.

She inserted her fingers through the layer of material to nestle in the coarse wiry hair that surrounded the base of his pulsating member. Oh yes, this delicate probing aroused something vital and explosive in him, a thing that was very good to know.

"Angelene . . ." he growled, and he wrenched her hand away from his body and levered himself onto her, his hands lacing themselves through her gilded hair, his mouth penetrating the soft recesses of hers with the force of a man taking exactly what he wanted with the knowledge that nothing less than this fierce invasion of her mouth would do. Nothing less than the strong and tender exploration of her body, with his growing comprehension of just where she wanted to feel his hands and just how long she needed his urgent caresses, and finally, how absolute was her own need to replicate their explosive union of the night before.

This time, he took her swiftly, his need as primitive and volcanic as the night before, with nothing to impede his perfect connection with her pliant nakedness.

She was so perfect, so all-enfolding, so hot and willing for him, her long arms wrapped around him, her long black-stockinged legs bracing her body to lift with his movement, to shimmy and writhe against him as her own

183

pure perfect pleasure escalated with his.

Her kisses were perfect, hot and wet and every bit as abandoned as his, ferocious with her own need; she had taught him already that she was no delicate angel: she was a woman, and she wanted him and his manhood, and on the mountain nothing mattered but that.

"Show me how to kiss you," he muttered between long hard kisses that left them both breathless and panting with urgency.

"You know how to kiss me," she whispered against his lips and the wiry scrape of his mustache. "You taught me to kiss you and I want only the way you kiss me."

He could lose himself in a woman like this, he thought, as he drove his way to another wracking climax on the heels of the glittering spasms of hers. He could keep her with him forever.

"Don't dress," she whispered to him as he pulled himself away from her. "I want to see you all day long. Don't hide yourself from me."

He didn't think it was possible for him to grow hard with desire again so soon, but her words made his manhood jut to attention once more.

"Is that what you want?"

"Almost more than anything," she murmured.

"Everything removed? Even the leggings?"

She contemplated him for a moment, because his long legs were still encased in the deerskin leggings, and she liked the aspect of him being partially covered and still revealing his potent naked essence to her.

"No, leave the leggings. I like the leggings."

"As you wish, Angelene." *Anything you wish, Angelene*, as his lusty male member agreed fully with her decision and made itself very visible.

"Tell me what I may do for your pleasure," she asked huskily as she enjoyed the sight of him slowly elongating before her eyes.

Everything, he thought tautly, as his desire for her spurted to life once again. "It would please me to see you naked all day long," he said, his voice raw with his new

184

need. "It would please me to have you welcome my kisses and my desire to possess you—but you see, Angelene, that desire may come when a man least expects it."

"I like seeing it," she murmured throatily.

"But would you welcome it?" he asked harshly.

She arched herself toward him, angling out one long black shrouded leg to give him a full view of her wanton willing nakedness. "Come kiss me," she commanded, her voice tinged with the rising urgency of her excitement, "and find out."

He found out. He found she wanted his kisses all the time, that she loved the feel of him in her hands, against her body, deep within her velvet center. She loved watching him, loved the darkness of his skin and the hard muscularity of his body; and she especially loved looking at his thick quiescent manhood, and cupping it into her hand whenever she wanted to.

He found he wanted to kiss her all the time, that he wanted her touching him and he wanted to touch her; the need was ongoing and compelled by her deliberate flaunting of her sensual nakedness.

If he went to the barn, she followed and demanded his kisses in the earth-rich scent of the stable. If he mounted his horse to exercise it, she pretended to pout because he had not spent the time mounting her. If he played with the dog, she would tease him by getting down on all fours and wriggling her tempting body to demand he play with her and caress her too. And when he sat quietly cross-legged in contemplation, she taunted him with her willful nakedness by laying on the cot and caressing him with her heated knowing gaze until his virile manhood stiffened into a jutting ramrod of passion. Then she would come to him, and stand straddling his folded legs, mutely begging for his lush possession of her. And he would make her wait, just a moment or two or longer, until he finally raised his hard-muscled arms so his hands could grasp her buttocks and ease her downward, downward, downward until he filled the sweet need of her body and the sweet heat of her mouth.

He could not get enough of her, and his naked readiness and her wanton nudity incited them both to an urgent excitement several times a day.

Sometimes he would idly kiss her to find that just the taste of her aroused him beyond all control; sometimes it was just the sight of the taut naked nipples thrusting from her breasts; sometimes it was the way she walked, or when she bent over to pull up her stockings, or when she crouched, her legs spread invitingly, in an enticement to exploration and more.

He took her everywhere in the cabin and beyond—in the rough narrow bed in the attic, on the cot, on the floor, on the worktable, in the barn, in the woods and the water. One day he stripped the stockings from her legs and buried his head between them to caress her with the ultimate carnal kiss, and then he dressed her again in the same black stockings tied with the same frayed ribbons just so that he could slide his hands all over her long silky legs and then have the pleasure of undressing them again whenever he chose.

"And how was it," she asked one time as she nestled tightly in his arms, against his chest, and played lovingly with his nakedness in the afterward of his possession of her, "how was it when you went to town and paid a woman after all those months on the mountain."

His whole body pricked up at the sound of something in the tone of her voice. "I don't wish to tell," he said at length. "It was different."

"How different?" she wanted to know, her fingers trailing a tingling path between his legs.

He didn't stop her; her feathery caresses were working their magic. He spread his legs further apart, his excitement growing because of the tenor of her questions and the sweet rubbing motion of her knowing fingers between his legs and against the heat of his lengthening erection.

"Why do you think a man goes to town?" he asked roughly. "Because he wants release, my innocent angel, and he wants it hot, hard and quick. And in town, there

186

are women who will ask no questions and demand no caresses for the privilege of entertaining a man with a certain sum of money."

"And so," she went on with that same taunty tone of voice, her hand becoming bolder and bolder between his legs with each succinct word, "a man gives over his money and then what?"

"He goes to a room," he said thickly, "by which time he is eager and ready to possess whatever woman is waiting for him within. He doesn't look for a face or a kiss or an eager hand. He wants the only thing he has come for: the darkness of the room and the darkness of the act."

"And what is her name, this woman who waits for you?"

"She has no name."

"She has no name *now*," she contradicted in a whisper, "because I want to be your town woman." And she did; the thought of it excited her all over again as she played with him and rubbed him and heightened his desire and his urgency with the caressing slide of her fingers down deep between his legs and all over his massive erection.

"*No!*" Yes—he wanted her all over again and he didn't care which way or how or what stories or games she wanted to play.

"Of course I will. Look—you are a man with an enormous appetite for carnal possession. You feel like you are going to explode with your need for a woman. You are stiff with wanting, your mind is full of the thought of a willing naked woman. You've even unbuttoned yourself to let free the hot hard source of your gratification. And there is a woman waiting who is eager for you to possess her with every last inch of your urgent need. And now—" she moved away from him as her voice slid down into a sensual whisper, "all you need to do is go outside and demand that she admit you, and that she let you take her just the way you always do."

He moved out the door in a carnal haze, shuddering with the excitement of playing the game and the ultimate coupling to come. He closed the door behind him, waited

187

a moment and then rapped on it, hard. *"I'm coming in."*

"Have you paid?" her voice came floating out, seductive and hard-nosed all at once.

"Enough," he rasped.

"I'm waiting," she conceded, and he burst into the room, strode to the cot where she lay, grasped her hair, and straddled her naked body.

"Are you ready?" he demanded, his voice rough with both the familiarity of it and the temptation to lose himself in it as the line blurred between his past and his present.

"I'm always ready for you," she purred, in a wicked imitation of what she imagined his town woman might say. She felt his hand slide under her body and then he hauled her backward against his hips. She could feel the hard probe of his manhood, and then the sweet surprise of his complete possession of her from this reverse way.

"Angelene—I can't do this," he whispered, his voice ragged.

"But it feels wonderful. I want you to do it. I want you, just like this—" she felt him move, she felt the tenseness in his body as if he were about to explode, and it was clear to her that the words heightened his arousal, and the words could push him straight over the edge, "—I want you any time, all the time. Take me now, take me . . ."

It took three short heated lunges before he spent his passion and collapsed on top of her.

"I swear to you, Angelene, it was never like that."

"No," she said with some satisfaction, "it was better."

"It was only a game."

"No, it was a recreation of an experience, and I wanted to know. And now, when you're ready, I would welcome your kisses and caresses, and your complete possession of me—if you're able."

He found, to his astonishment, that he was.

Chapter 11

When would it end?

She never thought about it; it was almost as if they were the only people on earth—the first two people on earth, naked and blessed.

Another week had gone by in the carnal excitement of their desire for each other, and she thought of nothing else but the fury of his passion. It left room for nothing else, and she realized, if she thought about it, that perhaps she didn't want to cope with anything else.

If she thought about it, she would have to determine a time to leave him, and in these halcyon last days of summer, that did not seem even a remote possibility.

But then she began to wonder about the seasons, and how he spent his days, and whether his life had room for another being, especially one as demanding as she.

She had learned a lot about herself up on the mountain with him. She had learned about the mystery of the connection between a man and a woman and the depths of passion a woman could command.

She had learned how to incite a man's passion and she had learned how to quench her own.

She had learned how to give and how to take, but more than that, she had learned something about the nature of man.

Or rather, this particular man, and there came a day when she could for a moment look at him dispassionately and wonder whether it were possible to leave him, or whether he could be part of her world at all.

And then she was shocked that she was thinking that she belonged in a place so different from his. She couldn't allow herself to think that because it would mean that she was getting ready to leave, and that she wanted to go on to New York and play out the dream she had nurtured for so long.

Dreams were not possible on a mountain.

Maybe only *his* dreams were.

One day she took the dress he had fashioned for her and tried it on. It fit over her head like a serape and it hung almost to her feet. Attached to one side was a deerskin tie, and she wrapped this around her waist and adjusted the sides so that there was no gap.

It was a very primitive dress . . . *in the custom of my childhood* . . . and she understood suddenly with a shock exactly what he had been trying to tell her with that one phrase.

Still . . . what could that matter, that a man was born on the plains of a primitive people. He had been well and truly civilized by now and he surely was no nomad moving with the buffalo to find food and sustenance.

So what was he, besides a man who had chosen to live on a mountain?

An idyll could only last so long before the questions she had chosen to ignore presented themselves with stunning reality.

Time stopped on a mountain ridge; there were no clocks here, nothing to beat out the hours or the days except the setting of the sun, and even that had melded into the rising of the moon and waxing and waning of this uncontrollable desire they felt for each other.

How many weeks had she lost to her journey east? How long ago had Tice and Raso given up on finding her and just disappeared? And when had she given up on herself in this morass of passion they had created together? She would never give up. She needed her money, she needed her *life;* she began frantically searching for the money belt of silver, to bind it to herself before he discovered it missing, and that she still meant to leave.

This was no life for her up on a mountain. And soon he would realize it as well.

He knew it the moment he walked in the door, fresh from his morning bathing, and saw her in the deerskin dress with her spun gold hair plaited into one long braid that hung down her back.

She embodied, in that one stunning moment, everything he had ever dreamed of, and the thing he thought he would never find. But her acceptance of the dress meant a complication he hadn't planned on, and questions he had never meant to answer.

His angel eyes, attired in a dress, was another woman, the woman he had coerced up to the mountain, not the woman who had turned into a temptress before his very eyes.

And this woman, this clothed and civilized woman, was the one who was on her way to somewhere, seeking some kind of better life for herself. She was not the woman who teased and tantalized him. She was not a woman who would willingly stay on the mountain with him.

He cursed himself for ever having made the dress.

"And so—" he murmured, feeling the thing come to a sickening deadening end for him. He felt ludicrous, suddenly, dressed in nothing, dressed to invite tumultuous caresses that might never again come.

"The custom of your youth?" she said, touching the deerskin tie around her waist.

The impassive mask slipped readily over his face; his eyes turned inward, remote, unforgiving. "But you know what I will say already. I am of the People of the Plains. My father was a white man, and my mother a woman of the Sioux. We were with him for nine years before he abandoned us completely and forced my mother to return to her people. And this is why I know the customs of my youth, Angelene, and why I rejected them as well."

"I see." But she didn't.

"There were times when the Plains conception of the unity of the body to the earth was the savior of my soul," he went on, his voice flat and emotionless, his nudity a hindrance no more. "A boy-child can't come to this symmetrical balance of living as late as I did and come away fully believing in all of it, or any of it. I had no father, no name, none of the things the other boys had, no mother when it came to that—she withered away and died, and when I went to my father, he denied his son, Angelene, and that, above all else of my youth, was a gut-wrenching blow. I spent nineteen years with my mother's people and I learned the ways. I accepted what I could earn, but never was I part of them, and yet, forever, they are a part of me.

"I wear their clothes, I worship the sun, I revere my animals and—as I know now—my woman, and I curse the missing years of my life when the two sides of myself were not in harmony with each other.

"And that is why I came to the mountain, Angelene. I found the dog and I found my soul, and now I have found you, and you now know about me."

"And you now know that I could not make a quiescent Indian maiden any more than I could make an obedient little nun," Angelene said slowly and painfully. "I cannot stay on the mountain."

"No," he said with a bald honesty, "I never thought you could."

Her heart sank right down to her toes. "You will take me to Crossville Junction then, and give me my money and the locket? I need the locket, you know, so my grandmother will know who I am."

"In a day or two," he agreed and his voice was so weary-sounding, so shattered with suppressed emotion that she reached out her hand to touch him.

He shook his head. "No. You found out something about yourself and about me today, Angelene, and it makes a difference, and the rest is as if it were the dead ashes in the fireplace: not to be resurrected for another

192

brief flaring moment. Do you hear?"

"I hear," she whispered, her throat clogged with tears. What had she done? But she knew—she had taken their fairy tale into the realm of reality where it couldn't stand scrutiny, and for that the prince would never forgive her.

She wore the dress, and he gave her the money, and fastened the gold locket around her neck so that she would not lose it. In the intervening days, he never again appeared before her naked, and he made her a pair of moccasins—in the custom of his youth. He had no hard buffalo hide with which to fashion a sole, so he cut the whole from one piece of soft leather, whole hides of which he seemed to have stored in the barn, and he shaped the leather to an outline of her foot that he marked on the floor with the dead ashes of the fire.

It was simple then to draw the cut piece of leather over her foot and puncture several places along the instep and heel to insert rawhide ties to secure it to her foot.

She didn't know how to thank him.

At that, it was better not to try to talk. The air was thick with things unsaid and memories unspoken. It was just as well to have a clean but painful break than to try to justify it.

The end was still the same: he lived on a mountain in near poverty in a manner filled with silences and work and she needed to have the silences filled and the surety that her mother could never touch her ever again. If she had lost sight of that in the stimulus of the preceding days, she was sure she would have come back to her focus eventually. At that, he never would have married her, and surely he could never have dealt reasonably with Josie on any level.

And at the best, she was a woman in control of her sensuality—and a woman who would cry herself to sleep for months to come.

But she was awakened by a cry, somewhere in the

193

distance, something she thought she dreamed, except for Rake's alert jump to the window, and then furiously shaking her to consciousness. "Hurry."

"*What?*"

"Damn it—" He pulled her out of bed. "Get to the barn—*now!*"

She eased her way out the door and to the side of the house. He stood just within the threshold, watching until she slipped past the window, and then focusing his attention on the fog-shrouded distance.

He had heard the cry—he knew the cry; he had the eerie sense of being stalked, as if the cry were the one and only warning he was going to get.

The waiting was impossible. The dog and his rifle stood staunchly by his side. It was only a matter of time.

From behind the cabin, Angelene could barely see into the foggy dawn light. Thank the heaven she had slept with her clothes on last night—at his insistence. She had been so angry at him, both for being adamant about it and for taking his place across the room from her where he could watch her and guard her and never come near her again.

Trouble. The keening cry that broke the morning meant trouble, she felt it in her bones; her heart pounded fearfully as the stretch of waiting lengthened and lengthened, and the only thing she could think to do was to try to ready a horse in case she should have to escape.

It wasn't possible anyway: they reared up at her touch and she couldn't get near them, and for the first time she was scared for her life.

What was Rake Cordigan doing, hiding away in the cabin when he could have been in the stable saddling a horse and helping her get away?

She drew in a sizzling breath as she hovered just inside the barn door.

Then she heard the howl of the dog, a blood-curdling cry, shots, the hiss of an object thrown through the air, and she damned the man's orders, and raced back around to the front of the house.

She saw them, riding hell-for-leather across the pasture toward the house, the stench of burning grass and wood beating a trail alongside them—Raso and Tice—and guns and murder in their eyes.

The dog raced out, oblivious to Rake's forceful shout: "*Boy, NO!*" His words were seconds too late, and above the sound of a gun firing was the scream of the dog as the bullet entered his heart.

"*NO!*" Rake screamed, an unearthly wail of grief and rage. "*Boy! Boy!*"

And riders were gaining, the one lighting another torch and hurling it with its ominous hiss right toward the cabin.

"*Rake!*" The hysterical scream was her, those feet were hers, carrying her toward him to stop his madman's dash toward the oncoming riders.

She hurled herself at him in a hail of bullets and he shook her off. "Those sons of bitches . . . get away, Angelene—go away; they killed my dog, and I'm going to kill them—"

"*Rake—*" She ran at him and toppled him to the ground. "*Rake—*"

"The dog, the damned . . ." He heaved his body up and rolled her over.

"You can't—"

"*I damned can!*" he roared. "I'll kill that son-of-a-bitch . . ." He raised his rifle and took aim as the riders bore down on them, trampling over the dog and veering away from the cabin to circle back again to where their prey lay obligingly in the dirt. "Those bastards, those . . ."

"*Rake!* They'll kill us, you hear? They'll kill you, they'll—they're murderers—Rake!"

He got off a shot, close enough so it spooked the horse of one—he couldn't tell which and it didn't make a difference they were so alike—and it reared and screamed. But the other kept coming and Rake took aim again and fired, and a gratifying spurt of blood appeared just as the son of a bitch aimed at him.

Then he became aware of the stench of burning wood, and he turned to see the cabin ablaze. "Angelene . . . the horses—"

"I don't know—they wouldn't come . . . you have to . . ."

"You first—I'll cover, and I'll kill the bastard if I can."

She ran, hunched over and in pure fear for her life. She heard the crack of the gun behind her as she circled wide around the burning cabin.

It was only a matter of minutes before the grass caught and the flames beat a path to the barn.

Damn the horses—where was Rake? Another shot, and another and she couldn't tell anything from the sounds, except that this day might be her last on earth.

She crouched inside the barn door, watching, waiting, never expecting to see him crawling in the grass around the side of the blazing cabin.

"Angelene—"

"I'm here."

He got to his feet and raced into the barn. "We've got to get out of here." He threw on the blankets, the cinches, the saddles with a self-preserving fury that scared her.

She caught back a sob. "I know. The horses, they wouldn't come to me . . ."

"Don't talk." He swung himself up onto one of the horses and held his hand out to her so she could mount the other. "I'll leave those bastards here to die, and if they survive this, I'll go hunting for them, I swear it, Angelene, and I won't rest until I kill them. Hurry now."

She heard an ominous crackling, suddenly, from behind them.

"Don't look."

"The barn—?"

"*Don't look.* Just follow me."

But she didn't have to look; she could smell the acrid smoke as it smouldered in the old twisty beams behind

196

her. She hung on for dear life as he led her through a maze of stalls and out a back entrance to the barn.

They came into blessed light and a smoky hell.

Everything behind them was ablaze, and anything in front of them could catch at any moment.

Still he had to work his way around to the track off the pasture. And he couldn't go—the grass was burning.

"Oh my god, *Rake*—!"

"We'll make it, Angelene—I promise you."

"But *where?*"

"Anywhere. I know the mountain and those bastards don't, so you'd better mourn them now, Angelene— they'll never make it out alive."

But then, she wasn't sure they would either. Her mount was skittish under her inexperienced hands and leery of the scent of the fire. In the end, Rake took her up on his horse, and let the other one go to find its own way down the mountain, a decision he wasn't any too happy to make.

"I'll pay you for him somehow," Angelene promised, wary of the fit of her body against the explosive anger of his.

"When you marry the wealthy man you so ardently desire," he countered caustically. "I'll be waiting for your draft, Angelene. I think that would be a fitting end to everything."

He found it disturbing to hold her in his arms this way; his memories of her were too close and painful as it was, and he had already resigned himself to letting her go.

As the horse picked its way cautiously down the mountain, mere steps ahead of the moving conflagration, he felt as if the fabric of his life had been ripped to shreds and there wasn't a single thread he could pick up and use to mend the shocking tear.

It was worse in town. They emerged from the smoky acrid forest of the mountain smeared with soot and coughing violently in the fresh air, with the horse almost ready to keel over from all the smoke she had inhaled.

Of course there were some in town who knew him as the recluse of the mountain, and there were some to whom he even spoke, like the owner of the mercantile store and the man who ran the livery stable who often was either in need of a horse, or knew of someone who was.

But no one knew Angelene, and the sight of the two of them together, mounted in tandem on a sorry soot-clotted horse, looking like two primitive tribespeople who had lost their way caused no end of curiosity and comment as they proceeded cautiously down the main street to one of the two places where Rake was known.

"The man's name is Carter," Rake told her, as he dismounted with some little difficulty off of the rear of the horse. He held out his arms to her and she slid down from her seat unhesitatingly.

As her moccasin shod feet hit the ground, a man burst out of the store. "You! I was scared to death for you when we saw the mountain got on fire."

"I am much obliged, Mr. Carter, but as you see, we made it safely to town. This is Miss Angelene, Angelene, Mr. Carter."

"Ma'am." His eyes swept over her, her homemade dress, her thin leather moccasins, her thick blonde hair, and she didn't know if he just dismissed her or was being gentlemanly as he turned his attention back to Rake.

"Was two men up and looking around for you, son. And they didn't never give up."

"Maybe now they will," Rake said, nodding toward the mountain.

"I'm damned," Carter said.

"They killed my dog."

"Damned sorry about that, son. They were sure desperate to find you."

"They did," Rake said, "or maybe I found them. No matter now. I have a different problem now. I need to put

Miss Angelene on the first train going somewhere east and I know you're the man who can tell me how to do it."

Carter turned back to Angelene, and she felt acutely uncomfortable as she wondered what questions lurked behind his affable expression and keen blue eyes. "Where you headed, ma'am?" Nothing in his tone indicated any disrespect to her. If he thought she looked odd, or that her appearance in town with the reclusive Rake Cordigan was the stuff of speculation, he did not show it. His tone was solely that of pure helpfulness, and she thought gratefully that he had surely seen sights more peculiar than her in his years running a mercantile store.

This was one of a block of stores down a long dusty boardwalked main street, and if there were a train station anywhere nearby, she thought, it was well-hidden. "New York," she said succinctly, and that did cause his eyebrows to raise.

"I don't rightly know, Cordigan. There's a through-train due here in about an hour that'll get her to Lexington. I expect she could connect through some way from there." This time, however, he sounded doubtful, as if he were uncertain about the thought of someone like her travelling so far so fast with no plans whatsoever. In fact, he had thought she would be asking for through passage to Kansas or Missouri, and he didn't know what to make of her at all, or the fact that she had appeared in the company of Rake Cordigan.

"That sounds fine," Rake said. "What does she have to do?"

"Just go on down to the station and wait. Stationmaster'll tell you what to do. I know he'll be there today; we're getting in a shipment ourselves."

"Good. Now—before we leave, we have to get Miss Angelene outfitted properly," Rake said, his cool gray gaze amplifying the thought: back to where she belongs, and she read it distinctly in his eyes and his edgy expression. "We don't have much time, Mr. Carter. You

199

make the choices and she'll change at the station."

More and more curious, Mr. Carter thought, as he heaped two sets of underthings, stockings, two dresses, a hat, a purse, a shawl in quick order on the counter.

"Shoes," Rake said, and Mr. Carter found a pair of high button boots. "A nightgown," Rake said, and a moment later, a simple gown of gauzy lawn with smocked decoration sat on the pile of clothing. "A suitcase," Rake said, and Mr. Carter found a nice used carpetbag that he was willing to give her, and he piled all the articles into the bag, including with them some soap, a brush, powder, a mirror.

"On my account," Rake said, taking the handle of the bag authoritatively.

"It's done," Mr. Carter said, calling out after them as they left, "Good luck, Miss."

Angelene bit her lip. She didn't think there was any luck involved, and as the moment of leaving came closer and closer, she wasn't even sure she wanted to go. A train in an hour! A suitcase full of clothing she hadn't even chosen for herself which would change her from a buckskin princess to a reasonably clothed young woman on her way to somewhere.

"You have your money?" Rake questioned roughly as they paused outside the store.

He was just dying to have her go. "Yes, it's tied around my waist."

"Good. I want you to transfer some of that to your purse when you change so you'll have money for necessities."

"What does that mean?" she asked angrily.

"I mean necessities; I don't know what I mean, damn it, Angelene."

"Good."

"Just mount up, Sister of Angels. Time is getting short."

I don't want to go.

No, I do want to go. I want you to go with me.

200

She was shocked by the thought. But how could she leave him, her savior, her lover?

What would he ever do in New York?

What would she?

She was crazy. She couldn't bear to leave him.

"Come with me," she said suddenly, impulsively, desperately.

He reacted explosively. "You're crazy! Damn, get on the horse, Angelene, or you'll miss the goddamn train to wealth and happiness."

"I mean it, come with me." The idea bloomed and blossomed and positively overwhelmed her.

He didn't think twice. "No, Angelene," and he swung resolutely up onto the saddle and tied her bag to the saddlebags and extended his hand to her. "Now, Angelene."

Her heart pounded furiously. *Why not? Why not?* "Just to Lexington," she went on, trying to keep the coaxing note out of her voice, anything but begging him when she wanted desperately to do just that. "What will you do here? You couldn't go back up on that mountain for a week, maybe more. What will you do?"

He hadn't thought about that. He hadn't thought about anything but getting her to Crossville Junction and getting her out of town. Maybe he thought he would go back up the mountain and scour the whole of it to be sure those murderous brothers of hers were dead, and if they weren't, maybe he thought he'd finish the job.

Or maybe he thought they would finish him.

"I don't know," he said finally, veering the horse off of the main street, and down another long dusty road. "I don't know."

Further along down this road, she saw warehouses, all packed together on both sides of the road, one after another, all bearing painted signs, names of companies or indications of the nature of the storage facility. Then this road widened out and turned right and she could see the glint of dark rail and the open space beyond that was demarcated solely by the horizon.

Two small square buildings sat on either side of twin streaks of railroad track a hundred yards beyond the turn point, and Rake nosed the horse right up to the nearest one.

He squinted up at the sun. "I reckon there's about a half hour until we see a train coming through. Time enough for you to get dressed, Angelene."

"All right." It wasn't all right, nothing was all right. She had never thought for a minute she would feel like this. "Is anybody inside?"

"I wouldn't think." He lifted her down from the saddle and dismounted and preceded her inside.

It was a small square place divided into three rooms, one of which was obviously the stationmaster's domain, one a waiting room, and the other, some kind of all-purpose room which contained a stove, a chamber pot, a bed, a wash basin.

Rake put her bag in there and closed her inside.

With a sinking heart and shaking fingers, she unpacked the bounty of the bag and chose the set of underwear: a pretty cotton chemise, the overskirt that was boned to support the impractical and very small bustle of both of the dresses—the only frontier concession to fashion.

She chose the more serviceable of the two dresses, a plain jersey flannel in blue and black stripes, with a high collar and plain black buttons and a little pleated flounce around the hem. The shoes went nicely with that, and the plain lisle stockings. The little purse was black too and she put into that the soap, the powder, the brush and the mirror when she had done fixing her hair, as well as a handful of money to both pay her fare and have on hand for "necessities."

She hated him.

She made sure the money belt was tied securely around her waist again and overlaid with the tape ties of the boned underskirt so that nothing could dislodge it from its hiding place.

Finally, she took the hat, a plain black crepe with a little pleating on the crown, and she set it on her head, and felt a moment's gratitude to Mr. Carter for his sensitivity.

She felt like a woman who was truly on her way somewhere. She repacked the remainder of her wardrobe very carefully, and she reluctantly put away the little mirror. She was finally ready to face Rake Cordigan again, armored and confident.

When she emerged from the little side room, he could not believe his eyes. The differences between them were palpable: she looked as elegant as any sophisticated and wealthy woman, and he looked like some primitive ruffian who had just hauled in a catch of buffalo on the plains.

He turned instead and looked out the window. "I reckon the stationmaster will be here soon."

"No doubt." She put her bag on one of the benches and sat herself down sedately. It was amazing how differently she moved in conventional dress, and she marveled that it had taken no time at all to get used to unconventional dress, and she wondered what she was going to do when she finally met up with her grandmother and she turned out to be a woman who insisted on the most rigorous propriety.

She fingered the locket beneath the neck of her dress. How fortunate she was to have Josie always with her to remind her of what she did not want. How lucky she came back to it not a moment too soon, before she had made a fool of herself for someone like Rake Cordigan who probably would have turned out to be no better than her own father.

No, this way was better, it *was*.

"They're coming," Rake said, his voice that same remote non-committal tone she hated. "They're coming fast." He sounded puzzled, and she joined him at the window and she saw what he was seeing: a battered old buckboard roaring up from the east, the driver pushing the horses hard to make the station.

"Two men," Angelene said in surprise.

"Carter's man most likely if they're shipping in goods for him."

Yes, the recluse of Crossville Junction had all the answers, she thought. So much the opposite of her own father who moved from town to town looking for the easy buck until Josie put her foot down. She didn't know which was worse.

The buckboard barreled down the station road and then they could hear one of the two men shouting: "Hey, Cordigan! You there, Cordigan?" and as the wagon jolted to a halt, the younger of the two jumped out and raced for the station house. "Cordigan!"

"It's Ray, Carter's man," Rake said, exercising his inbred caution before showing himself at the door. "What is it, man?"

He was a very young man, maybe even Carter's son, and he was breathless with fear. "Those men—Carter said to tell you—they made it down the mountain, man. They're comin', they're askin' questions and they know . . ."

"Hell," Rake swore. "Damn—"

The stationmaster clambered up the steps, an older man, wiser, more cautious. "Carter stopped me going through town, Cordigan. Don't know where or how, but he sent the kid, said for you to tell him what you want to do."

Angelene clenched her fists. *Come with me.* She heard herself as clearly as if she had spoken aloud.

"Son of a bitch—"

"Come with me, Rake." Yes, she said it, and he looked utterly thunderstruck, as if he had forgotten all about her. "Come with me."

Hell, damn! He wheeled on the boy. "I need money. Take the horse down to Carter and tell him the stationmaster is going to finance me a ticket and he's going to buy my fare, and he's going to use whatever he can get for that nag to pay my tab, got it?"

The boy nodded.

"When is that train due?"

"Hell, man—take a breath and listen," the station-master said, and they heard it then, the mournful wail of the train whistle in the distance.

"Will you give me the ticket?" Rake demanded.

"I'll do it," the stationmaster said. "Boy, you take that horse and the wagon back to Carter when we finish loading up. I'll take Carter's word you're good for it, man. Now come on over here so I can make out your tickets."

"Two tickets," Rake shouted at the boy who was already at the door. "Tell Carter he's paying for two tickets, you got that, boy?"

"Two tickets, Mr. Cordigan, I got it. Carter said whatever you want—" and the rest of his words drowned in the hissing clamor of the train arriving in the station and steaming to a halt.

"Boy's gotta unload," the stationmaster said, furiously writing and snipping at two pieces of pasteboard. "On you go now; I'm trusting Carter means what he said."

"He means it," Rake said. "Hurry, Angelene—"

She didn't even have time to think; he was coming with her, he was, and how she had accomplished that miracle she would never know. Or maybe she hadn't; maybe it had nothing to do with her, and everything to do with her tenacious murderous brothers, and he was just going into hiding until they got tired of waiting him out.

He had been right about them all along. They had kept at it until they had found her, and maybe the only way to deter them *was* to get as far away from them as possible. *That* was probably the only reason he had decided to go with her.

They scrambled into one of the four narrow passenger cars of the train, her suitcase bumping the back of his legs as he shifted his way down the long double rows of strange looking people until he found a seat that would accommodate both of them.

"I can't believe this," she whispered, sinking down onto the worn upholstered bench.

"It's too believable," Rake growled, his face turned toward the window, his eyes scanning the distances for any sign of her brothers. The unbelievable thing was that two hours before he had been flirting with the suicidal idea of going after them, and then when it was possible to confront them, he had chosen life—and Angelene.

At that, he didn't know what he had chosen. There was nothing for him anywhere but up on the mountain, and maybe, he thought morbidly, a sojourn on a train with Angelene was even more self-destructive than facing the blazing guns of her killer brothers.

Chapter 12

—

The train chugged out of the station, slowly at first, and then not fast enough. Then it seemed as if the town had suddenly disappeared and there was nothing but land, sky and horizon to the right and left of them.

Someone collected their tickets, and then sometime along toward dusk, they pulled in to another small station where they were offered a fifteen minute respite for personal matters and to purchase food.

The things a novice traveller never even would have thought of, Angelene thought, as she took the time to stretch her legs, and watched interestedly as the other passengers hurriedly scooped up neat packets of dinner that were being sold on the platform by women who looked very local and very poor.

She dug around for some coins. Rake Cordigan had been a singularly uninspired travelling companion for this first part of the trip: he hadn't said a word, almost as if he blamed her for his decision to accompany her, and she was tired of looking at scenery to avoid looking at him. At that, she could eat, and she proffered the fifteen cents being asked for a picnic box of fried chicken and fixings without bargaining and took it away with her back into the car where Rake still reclined, keeping a wary eye on their seats, her bag, and—had she known—her.

"I brought food," she said breathlessly.

"Smells good."

"For you too."

"I'm not hungry, Angelene."

"You're not *anything*," she said crossly.

"Oh, I am—I'm damned worried about this plan of yours to continue on to New York."

She took out a piece of chicken and bit into it. It was hot, deep-fried, salty and inutterably *good.* "It's a perfectly sensible plan. My grandmother lives there, and I know she'll be happy to see me."

"You know damned nothing, Angelene, not even to try to conserve what little money you have. You don't even know that your stash will take you as far as New York. If it didn't, what would you do then?"

She bent her head over the chicken. "It was enough," she said at length.

"And minus what now? Two bits?"

"*Less,* and what could you possibly know about it from living up on a mountain, Mr. Cordigan?"

"You don't even know but that your grandmother might not be alive," he continued inexorably.

"She's alive," Angelene said firmly. "My mother talked all the time about going back and showing her just what was what and who had gotten the best of things in her life. *She's alive.*"

"Damn it—give me a piece of that chicken—"

She looked up at him then, and he never wanted to see that expression in her angel eyes again. "Only if you pay your fair share, Mr. Cordigan."

He stared her down, only because he knew how to do it better; he had had years of practice, years of turning himself inward and presenting a cold and calculating face to whomever got in his way.

And then he dug into his shirt pocket, and he tossed her a silver dollar.

She didn't say a word: she handed the box across to him.

The train started up, they finished eating and she packed the box away. Only then did she take the silver dollar and look at it.

"I hope your Mr. Carter paid the fare, Mr. Cordigan, because I can just see some sheriff boarding up the train with a telegraphed warrant for your arrest. You could have paid the passage yourself."

"I could have," he agreed, "but neither of us knows what kind of money we're going to need on this ride, and I'm a man who errs on the side of caution—always. You only need one hard lesson, Angelene, and you carry it with you for life."

"So you're saying I haven't learned any of those lessons?"

"I don't know, Sister of Angels, have you?"

"I've learned at least *one*," she said pointedly, and tucked the dollar meaningfully into her purse.

"Tell me about your brothers then; maybe I should know what I'm getting into on this journey."

"I hardly think they're going to come roaring up to you in some way station in the middle of the nowhere," Angelene said tartly.

"Well, I don't know about that myself, Angelene; they did spent a good two weeks scouring the town and that mountain for you. You said they were murderers, and I owe them for the dog," he added darkly, his expression turning inward once again. He hadn't forgotten; he had pushed it mightily to the back of his mind, and he wouldn't let himself grieve—not yet, not yet.

When it was time, he would go back to the mountain, and he would bury the dog in the manner of his youth, and he would feel that things were in balance once again.

"Tell me about those men, Angelene."

She couldn't deny him then, and not because of that deadly steely tone of voice. She too would never forget the sight of the dog running toward her brothers and the casual way in which one of them had obliterated its life. She felt his grief, she negated her own.

"They're my brothers, older than me. One is Tice, one is Raso, and the last I knew before Bobby hunted me up just outside the Springs, they were all in Cairo where I left them."

He tried the names in his consciousness, two of them sounding familiar—Raso, Bobby—somewhere, sometime during this nightmare, she had said those names and he had heard them, and so Bobby was the puppy who had tried to delay her so the others could catch up. Or maybe he had even been trying to kill her—but she didn't know that.

He knew it.

"Bobby is the youngest," she added, as he said nothing, "the one who was with me at the Springs."

"I remember Bobby," he said tonelessly. "Go on."

"My mother came from this grand family who lived in a mansion in New York, and when she met my father, she chose to go west with him because it seemed so romantic and exciting, I guess. It turned out to be a bitter disappointment. My father had no skill at anything—he couldn't hold a job, work a mine, own a ranch, run cattle. Nothing. He was a gambler, Mr. Cordigan, straight and simple, and when he died, my mother refused to request help from her parents. She was an only child, you see, and they had tried to prevent her marriage, and her pride would not let her admit to them that they had been right. Rather, if she ever did go back, she would go in high-handed style, with dollars falling out of her pockets, just to show them.

"When I was about nine, just after my father died, my mother sent me away to school—first to a place in Kansas, and then finally to the convent school at Cairo. I hardly went home; she and the boys were always moving from this place to that, so I never knew where she got the money to keep me at school, and frankly, I liked it a great deal better there than I would have at home with her. I didn't even know her, I hadn't spent above a month at any given time over the years in her company.

"But the day came when she did want me to come home, and to a place that she considered pretty well permanent: she had started up a series of road ranches, you know—places for travellers between towns, and apparently she had finally found the perfect location and she was ready to welcome me back to the family.

"I thought perhaps she was ready to begin a more legitimate life in a burgeoning town somewhere, but all she kept telling me was she had found a good way of life right where we were, doing a business that made her plenty of money, and all she expected was that I was going to come home and help her.

"None of my wishes were to be taken into account on that score. Particularly since my twin brothers Raso and Tice had proved to be not quite right—and my mother only realized it years after they were born. I expect she felt trapped and then maybe determined.

"What she wanted was to hand her legacy on to me and to be sure that her sons would be taken care of for as long as they lived.

"And mother thought the only way to do it was *her* way, which was a way that precluded asking anyone for help and a way that provided her with mountains of money, Mr. Cordigan, all of it stashed away for that day she would return to New York in triumph to prove that her way had worked.

"I don't think she was ever going to go. I think she could never get enough money to satisfy her lust for having it and proving her parents wrong. I don't think she ever would have told me where it was, either, if I had chosen to stay.

"Of course, she expected a meek and obedient convent-educated young woman who would not ask questions and do as she was told, whatever was required of her. And she got me instead, and she found me terribly unsympathetic and embarrassingly rebellious.

"But still, Mr. Cordigan, I think she did have hope I would come around.

"I truly didn't see how. A convent, Mr. Cordigan, is a very moral place. The commandments are very strick and stringent, and when you have these parables of morality drummed into you for nine years or more, you can't condone very much, not even for the sake of your mother.

211

"But she would never have understood that part. I was just to bow my head, agree that she had lived a hard and horrible life and that my sole duty was to make it up to her, and then, when she became infirm, take over and continue the business she had started."

"And what business was that, Angelene?"

She smiled tightly. "My mother is a murderess, Mr. Cordigan. She lures travellers to the road ranch and the more obviously well-to-do ones never see the light of the next day. She even meant to use me as an inducement so that the men would talk about the place they had seen me, and more travellers would come. I don't know which of them did the dirty work at any given time, but I think all of them at one time or another killed guests."

That, she thought as she paused in her narrative, had not been nearly as hard to tell him as she had thought. He hadn't moved a muscle throughout the whole story, and she couldn't tell if he were shocked, disgusted or thought she was a liar.

It sounded so improbable: a dust-gray, once-proud woman reduced to murder. It sounded like some dime novel that would end happily somehow.

She bit her lip. "I came upon Raso cleaning up the blood of a man who had come looking for a friend who had disappeared from the ranch."

That sounded good, he thought skeptically, blameless Angelene—angel eyes—innocent of innocents *came* upon a brother mopping up blood. It was impossible to believe; it was a nightmare story made worse by the fact that she hadn't told him any of it from the time he had taken her to the mountain. Now he was the one who had lost the most: his beloved dog, his home, his mountain, and she had gotten the chance to continue on this journey to her mythical grandmother who might or might not exist.

Trouble. Women were always trouble.

"And so you ran," he prompted, keeping his expression remote and noncommittal.

"I fooled mother into taking me to Cairo, and I got help

212

at the convent: the habit, some money, the wagon. I never dreamed that mother would send Bobby after me."

"And you never killed a soul," Rake finished for her.

"You don't believe me."

"It's an impossible story."

"More than your own, o man of the mountain who could not live in the custom of his youth and couldn't find a place with the father who did not want him. What did you do in those intervening years, Mr. Cordigan, that you should wind up on a mountain with only a dog for companionship and talk so painstakingly about finding a soul?"

Clever angel eyes, he thought, they missed nothing, and her woman's ears heard everything in defense of the course she had taken. Wisely too. It made him proud, peripherally, that she had been his woman, however briefly. Now, he could choose to tell the truth or he could choose the lie. All men had secrets, and women too. He didn't need her forgiveness, nor had she asked for his. He had only asked for the truth and she had given it to him. He, he supposed, could do no less.

"I was a murderer, Sister of Angels, as tortured and vicious as your mother, your brothers—or you—"

"No!" Her cry was involuntary, and she raised her hands, almost as if she thought she would ward off the naked truth of what he told her.

"Angelene—"

"No . . ."

And she never even thought about what the people around them were hearing of this conversation. *"I don't believe you."*

"You do," he said heavily. He knew it, he saw it come, from her rank denial to her turning over in her mind the things she had said to him which linked with his confession: she believed it.

"Those days are long gone, Angelene."

"I know," she said quietly, but still—hadn't she witnessed him with the gun, aiming forthrightly to kill the killer? Could the identity of one get crossed with the

213

other? What if she had known that on the mountain? What would she have done then?

She put her head wearily against the high uncomfortable bench back. "Tell me."

He shrugged. "I went to my father and he refused outrightly to acknowledge me. But after all, he was well known, he was the governor of Illinois and he lived in a fine house in Springfield and not in the mud huts of my youth. He looked at me and he saw degradation and the life he had deliberately left behind. He never saw me: he saw my skin and he saw his past, and he denied them both.

"Nor could I return then to my mother's tribe. She was gone; my uncle was disappointed in me for a list of imperfections too numerous to mention which all centered on the expectations of my mother's people. I never could live up to them, not even when my mother was alive. I was in a rage, in a place between those two cultures who did not want me, and I was young—too young and too easily influenced. I wanted action, plain and simple. Hard riding, explosive action.

"So I chose my course, and when that path led to debasement and destruction, I found the mountain, and the dog found me, and eventually, Sister of Angels, many years later, I found that I am the sum and substance of the two people who spawned me, and I could not kill it away, erase it, destroy it, deface it or hide from it. It simply *is*, and this is the soul I found on the mountain."

"Yet you could kill again," she pointed out.

"I am not stupid, Angelene. I also found that I very much wanted to live, and when a man is a killer, he truly wants to die."

"And a reformed killer uses any means at his disposal to stay alive."

"You could say that, Angelene. But then so would a woman whose family seeks to kill her, wouldn't she?"

He had an answer for everything, she thought, but then she wasn't surprised: he had had so many years to think about things, high up on a mountain, where he made friends with his animals and the man in town who could do him the most good.

He was either the cleverest man she had ever met or the most cynical, or maybe both. She was too tired by then to come to grips with the revelations, too tired even to castigate herself for letting herself be possessed by a man about whom she knew nothing and who turned out to be . . .

But then what have I turned out to be? she thought. It was too confusing, and in the end, it probably didn't matter. He would leave her in Lexington, as she supposed he intended, and her future would be secure from there. Her grandmother would welcome her, and men would fall at her feet, and she would have only to choose the one she wanted, and the past would recede like the nightmare it really was.

Well, maybe that was a bit simplistic. In the morning things looked more complicated than that: they had arrived in Lexington and the train station looked impossibly formidable because she had never been in a city that size in her life.

Rake had, but how much did he really remember of that journey to denial, to the mansion where his father ruled a politician's sanctum and wanted nothing to do with a wild-eyed, primitive-looking half-breed man child who was hardly coherent and deadly serious? He remembered nothing of that torturous day except that the way he had gotten to his destination was by asking questions.

All he needed to do was find the golden train that would take Angelene to the city of wealth and power and well-to-do men who wished to be husbands.

No easy task, that. This was a train station full of well-dressed and purposeful people, none of whom were willing to give in to the sincerity of the tall, dark buckskin-clad stranger with the long hair and mustache.

And he saw the way the men particularly were looking

at Angelene, who, although her dress was not the latest fashion, was still beautiful enough to attract attention in spite of it.

He didn't like that one bit. Men were men no matter what city or small frontier town they inhabited; under the skin, they all wanted the same thing—one beautiful, willing woman, and a woman like Angelene, travelling alone, was fair game.

She had been damned right to trick herself up in the one outfit that would guarantee a safe journey.

Damn it all, she had been right about a lot of things.

She wasn't going five feet out of that station without him, he decided, and he surely was not going to let her go on to New York alone.

"I don't damned know what a pullman is, except that it costs a lot of money and it guarantees you some privacy, and it's worth it," Rake said impatiently as they jostled through the crowd seeking a car number to match the one on the ticket he held.

"I do believe I don't care what it cost as long as I don't have to share it with anyone else," Angelene said breathlessly, as she almost ran to keep up with him.

"I didn't say you didn't have to share it—here we are—" he stopped abruptly three quarters of the way down the line of cars. "Here is your ticket to a life of luxury, Sister of Angels."

She took the ticket hesitantly, and looked up at the railroad car. It looked massive, crowded, a whole corral of people already elbowing their way up into this and other cars behind and in front of it.

She was going to be a woman alone now, after spending an educational night with the mountain man prowling the mysteries of the railroad station, instead of finding accommodations like everyone else.

Well, she had found out exactly what she had been afraid of from the first: men were curious and men were not kind, and she wished she had stuck to her original

216

plan of travelling in disguise.

Now she had to share some kind of compartment which was supposed to offer some privacy and some kind of bed in place of the uncomfortable benches they had shared on their journey to Lexington.

"Up you go, Angelene, let's see what this thing looks like." He cupped her elbow and pushed her forward, and picked up her bag along the way. Three steps up and into the vestibule of the car, and then a left turn into its corridor which was lined with compartments with glass doors, each with a number corresponding to the tickets, and each with two benches, richly upholstered, placed opposite each other.

"Number what?" Angelene asked, above the noise of the jostling crowd.

"Number ten."

That compartment was at the far end, and they burst through its door with a clatter. Angelene gratefully closed out the noise of two dozen other searching passengers.

It was a small, square room with two benches and a small water closet tucked behind one of them. There was gaslight on the outer wall, and curtains and a shade on the windows and the door, and under the benches there were drawers to store one's belongings. There was even a little closet tucked behind the opposite bench, along with a full-length mirror on the door.

Angelene looked at herself in the mirror and could not credit what she saw. She did not know herself; she was thinner, more dressed up, more worldly than the girl who had fled for her life four weeks before.

It seemed a lifetime ago, even as easily as she could talk about it; it remained with her always, and yet sometimes it seemed like something from a nightmare.

And then, behind her, Rake, so tall and bronzed, so out of place and yet still a part of it in a way she could not define. He looked different as she viewed him through the mirror, and she didn't know if the reflection was the distortion or the actuality was.

217

Whatever Rake Cordigan was, he was a man who looked weary, and vexed, and not a little resigned, and he had lost more than she could ever imagine when he brought her down from the mountain.

Now he was about to walk out of her life forever.

He looked at her across the small space of the sleeping compartment, and he thought about the myriad of things that had happened since he had followed her and Bobby to Rogers Springs. He thought how unlikely life was, and how one never could hide from a destiny that was uncertain at best; and he thought about how the woman across the room from him had been his adversary, his captive, his angel of innocence, his lover, his princess, his angel eyes.

He knew above everything else, no matter what he felt, that he would never let her face the end of the adventure alone, and he thought perhaps that was his own saving grace: that he had finally found something else outside himself to care about, so much so that he wanted to be beside her when she finally discovered the ultimate truth—that there was no grandmother, there was no wealth, and there was no New York.

Meeting her eyes in the mirror, he pulled out the second ticket from his pocket, the one he had neglected to mention that he purchased for himself.

It was four days' travel to New York, with stops in West Virginia, Washington D.C. and Philadelphia.

She didn't quite know how she was going to spend those four days in such closeness with him when she had been perfectly prepared to be alone, but the whole first day he slept, after they had figured out how to convert the benches into beds, and she sat staring out the window watching every vestige of her former life fly by.

Six weeks before, she had been a naive and scared child, running from the threat of an omnipotent mother. Now she was a woman, in every sense of the word, and the man who had saved her life, ripped away her disguise, taken her innocence and called her Sister of Angels was the very man who was helping her implement her plan to defeat her mother once and for all.

A reformed killer aiding the daughter of a killer . . . it even made a peculiar kind of sense. They were allies in their own particular kind of hell, each of them running from a past, only she hadn't stopped yet, and he—he had found a dog and a deep abiding peace on a mountain.

She had taken that away from him, with her carelessness and deceit, and she wondered what more he had to lose and what, if anything, she had to gain on this uncertain adventure into unknown terrain.

They had little money now between them, and the bulk of it had to be saved for a possible return trip to somewhere, much as she wished to deny that possibility.

For the rest, they had to eat, but they had agreed that neither of them wanted to frequent the dining car, he because he looked like a misplaced member of a wild west show, and she because she did not wish to appear at alternating meals in one or the other of her two dresses.

The only solution to that seemed to be for her to make a daily foray to the dining car rather than pay any of the accommodating porters to deliver whatever viands they selected to their compartment.

She was hungry now, on this first afternoon of travel, and she hadn't slept much either during their enforced overnight stay at the train station.

But still, she felt a certain excitement to be on her way to a place unknown that held such promise for the future.

It was the second day that proved to be much more difficult. She was the one who was tired, and she had to change out of her dress to preserve whatever freshness remained in it. She had to put on that nightgown, which was light as air and almost as revealing, and she had to face that remote gray gaze of his as she climbed into her bed. She didn't know how things could be so very different and still quite the same.

He still wanted her, and she didn't know how she could justify wanting him when what she needed was a powerful husband who could ward off any threat from Josie.

Nothing had changed in that regard, she thought with a weary resignation as her body told her an entirely different story. Had she thought she could just bury the memory of his possession of her and go on with a search to find the right man to marry? Or was that naive of her too, to think, she could just march into her Grandmother's house and demand her hospitality and her help—and, moreover, that she finance a wedding should one be forthcoming?

When she listened to her little inner voice talking like that she thought she must be ragingly out of her mind. Nothing about the whole story sounded in the least plausible, especially the part about Josie.

What had she thought she was going to tell her Grandmother?

She hadn't thought, and she couldn't think because Rake's cool gray gaze continually made her feel uncomfortable.

It wasn't anything he did, either. He hardly spoke; he watched her. Or he just watched life, she wasn't sure which. During the day, when the curtain and shade were pulled up from the door window, he watched the passersby with equal intensity.

"Why do those people fascinate you so?" she asked him.

"I don't think they do. I think I fascinate them," he said, but what he really meant was that *she* fascinated him and that his memories were as deep and thick and strong as hers.

But she didn't want that said, and he did not say it.

Sometimes she saw a deep abiding sadness in his face and she knew he thought about and he mourned the dog, and that he would never forgive or forget the killers who destroyed him and devastated his mountain.

He thought that perhaps the time had come for him to leave the mountain and that she was meant to be the

220

agent of change, wherever it would lead him, but he would grieve for the dog as long as he lived.

On the third day, the air between them thickened with awareness as they shared coffee and biscuits and two unmade beds. He had removed his shirt the previous night to wash and he slept without it and now this morning, she was faced with the taut expanse of his hairy chest and his unsettling eyes, lukewarm coffee and her undeniably volatile body which suddenly became very aware of him once again.

The space between them, which was minuscule at best, suddenly constricted still further until it almost seemed that she was just a heartbeat away from being drawn into his arms and the opulent oblivion of her sensual nature.

"No!" She literally jumped up onto her bed and backed away from him because there was literally nowhere else to go.

And he knew it. He looked up at her, faintly amused, the Indian warrior at rest, sure of his conquest and undeterred by denial. "Sit down, Angelene, or you'll pop right out that window."

"I feel like jumping," she grumbled, sliding down into a small huddle in the window corner of the bed.

"You could jump this way, Angelene, and then at least you could be sure someone would catch you."

"Someone did catch me once," she said goadingly, "and he got more than he bargained for."

"Now who are you to say *what* the bargain was? Maybe he sold his soul and he never did find it on the mountain like he thought."

"Don't say that," she said violently. She *had* to believe he had found his peace there, because otherwise . . . otherwise . . . he could still be what he always had been.

He shrugged. "It's my story, Angelene. I suppose I can tell it—or reshape it—any way I like."

"I'm the storyteller," she protested.

221

"I'm fond of the stories you tell," he agreed. "Particularly the one about the town—"

"*Stop it!*" Dear Lord, the man meant to drive her mad, she who knew how powerful and sensual words could be. "Don't *do* that."

"It's too easy to do, Angelene. You can't possibly believe that your determination to find a wealthy husband will sever the connection between us."

"There *is* no connection," she said fiercely, squeezing herself more tightly against the wall, hoping perhaps that the lazy knowing glint in his eyes would not move one inch from her mutinous expression.

False hope. She couldn't hide a thing from him behind the gossamer drape of her nightgown as she futilely folded her arms across her breasts.

"And yet you run."

"I am not running."

"And you seek material things as evidence of a man's desire."

"This is ridiculous. I have met no man who can offer me the things *I* desire."

"But you have, Angelene," he said quietly, and she drew in her breath with a tight hiss.

"I met a man who could offer me a mountain, if he had chosen to do so, and a solitary life far removed from everything I was used to. That was *all*." And she dared to meet his cold gray gaze after uttering *that* denial. Surely she would have the nerve to do or say anything else after that.

"What you were used to," he repeated mockingly, explosively, levering himself up off of his bed and onto hers with the suddenness of a bomb. "You were used to being no better than a servant, Angelene. You were used to seeing men disappear before your very eyes—isn't that what you told me? You were used to the fact that your mother was preparing to sell you off eventually to the highest bidder."

"*No! No!* She never said that!" she protested violently.

"*I* say that, Sister of Angels."

222

His line-ravaged face was very close to her now, his gray eyes keen with his incisive knowledge of her and what he knew of the world and now of her nature. He knew her. He knew Josie. He knew everything.

"So I sold myself off to save my own life," she finished trenchantly, unwilling to let him see that deeply into her soul. What had she given up on the mountain?

What would she give up now?

She had to repudiate everything that had happened between them—all that time together on the mountain.

Because he couldn't say he would never have touched her—she saw it in his face. He couldn't even say he wouldn't touch her now.

Her words resonated between them like the thick clotted sound of a muffled bell, and then he reached out his hand to touch the satin gold of her hair. "You sold away nothing but your birthright," he murmured, "and you clothe every feeling with a lie."

She slapped his hand away. "I understand that isn't the way you would prefer to see me lie."

The light in his eyes turned to gray stone. "I can accommodate you standing as well, Angelene. If you would care to lay bare all those concealed feelings."

"*I* can barely stand to have you near me," she retorted grittily, as he made an angry movement toward her.

"Can you *stand* to have me?" he asked softly, dangerously lazy as cat stalking its prey.

"I can't stand any more of this nonsensical talk," she snapped, desperate, scared of his power, his cat-quickness.

She thrust out both arms suddenly, pushing them right into his chest. He fell back, startled, and she jumped off of the narrow bed, and darted into the little washroom.

A moment too late. He was so fast, he wedged his body into that small space quicker than a jackrabbit and her heart fell to her stomach.

Here the atmosphere was cloying, compounded of the scent of him and the perfume of her rising excitement.

There was something so primitive, so elementally male in this moment of heated pursuit, and it had nothing to do with words or anything she wanted beyond the walls of this pullman car.

Now he was close and she could inhale the very essence of him, and she could see the stone in his eyes soften to something more knowing, more appreciative— the soul of the conqueror who had cornered his prey.

She could feel herself wavering, the memories of her body more forgiving than the desire of her heart. And she had begged him to come with her. Words didn't matter; she couldn't, in that breathless hot space between them, recall a single thing she had said three minutes before.

She became intensely aware of her naked body beneath the thin veil of her nightgown. She felt her breasts jutting out, almost as if they demanded his caress. She felt the overpowering sense of excitement as his eyes changed, his body heated up, and the physical evidence of his need stood tellingly between his legs.

He moved into the slender little washroom and shut the door meaningfully behind him. "What you must come to know, Angelene, is that your body will not run from what your mind already knows," he whispered. "We are bound, and I claim you."

The air was so thick with his need that she could barely breathe. The space between them was a heartbeat, and she felt it throbbing like a living thing, calling to her, possessing her, arousing her to forbidden thoughts and longings, to wanting the things she could never tear out of her mind or her consciousness.

A moment in time only. She would slake the desire and have finally done with it. Why not? Why not? Words were no armor against him. He was too determined, too patient, too all-seeing. He saw *her*.

It was such a small space for the explosive need of the two of them. One more time. Just . . . one more time.

She wanted him to act on his pretty speech. She wanted him to claim her.

But he didn't move; he leaned back against the narrow

door, his arms folded across his broad chest, watching her, his rampant manhood goading him, his clear-sighted mind pointing out every little detail about her that made her so desirable to him right now, this moment.

Those angel eyes, soft with yearning. The shadow of her feminine hair readily visible beneath the thin drape of the nightgown. The curve of her hips and breasts beckoning his hands to touch, to explore. Her firm lush mouth waiting—begging?—for his kiss.

I want to see you . . . words that had echoed in his dreams—in the one great impossible dream.

This was the only way to end the dream: he must make love to her when and where he could and store up the memories for a lifetime.

Even the most patient of men could not have suffered such an end. It went beyond anything a man should be asked to do. Kindness would mean nothing in the aftermath. There would be *nothing* when she finally left him, and he felt a concurrent swelling anger of resentment that this was all there would be.

Damn it, damn it, damn it . . . the injustice of being the man who could never offer enough—

Enough except . . .

He ripped apart his pants in one motion and reached for her in the next moment, stripping away the thin nightgown as if it were a piece of thin paper.

This was how a man and a woman came to each other, naked and vibrant with need; this was how it was when nothing else remained, not mutuality, not desire, not hope.

This was the finality of it—the dying moment when all there could be was pure raw hunger and the inescapable memory of what had been and what could be no more.

She was breathless with the force of it; she hadn't even conceived she would feel any lingering depth of yearning for their tumultuous coupling. But it was there, shaded over with words, with determination, with the ever-present knowledge that neither of them could escape their pasts, their future or what they were.

She could never go back; there was only the moment and the pitched excitement of her need to be claimed one more time, this one time.

She had never felt more the supreme connection between his maleness and her femininity. The waiting for the one ineffable moment when he would touch her, take her, was perfect; so intense, so opulent that when he finally took her face into his hands to kiss her, she almost swooned.

He gathered her up, he gathered her in, and she opened herself to him wholly, ecstatically, and he took her, canting his body to accommodate hers and possessing her with one ferocious sliding motion that fused her to him forever.

She exploded with it wildly, frenetically, instantly in small convulsive spasms that went on and on and on, her groans of pleasure lost in the filling lust of his mouth, in the feel of the solidity under her grasping fingers and in his potent maleness deep within her shuddering core.

It was too much even for him in his mindless drive to culmination. Her heat, her desire, her inimitable response to him and the naked essence of what he was— he could read it all in her glowing angel eyes, he felt it in her readiness to open herself to him and in the wild heated kisses of her provoking mouth.

She made no promises, nor did he, and in the end, his punitive desire never to reach completion and keep her there with him always came to nothing.

As the last rippling paroxysm of her release swirled into oblivion, he found his, slowly, endlessly, in a drawn out moan of sheer reluctance.

And a moment later, the train screeched and wailed and jolted to a clattering halt deep in the recesses of the New York terminal, the end of the line—the end of his dreams and the beginning of hers.

Chapter 13

And so, finally, New York.

And the moment became as if it had never been, lost in the steaming smoke of their entrance to the city. The door closed behind them as firmly and finally as Rake closed the door to the Pullman cabin when they left, never to be spoken of or referred to ever again.

The incoming platform discharged them into a maelstrom of humanity, everyone rushing or pushing in one direction or another in an endless swirl of motion.

Angelene had never seen anything like it before in her life. She felt helpless before such purposeful chaos and grateful she could lose herself in it in their quest to exit the terminal.

The whole was huge, bustling, confusing. It reminded Rake too much of the city where he had sought out his father, and he wasn't a bit astonished to find out that Angelene had no idea where her Grandmother lived.

Neither had he known where to find his father.

No one took particular notice of them as they followed one and another knot of people who seemed to be heading to an entranceway and instead wound up at the ramp of the next train due to leave.

It was a marvel, this Grand Central Depot, all brick and marble, with numerous pavilions, each of which contained a huge clock exactly at the center. They could go nowhere in the building without at least knowing the time.

And the time was running out, fast.

They had debarked from the train at four o'clock and had spent a good half hour searching for an entrance before they finally found one that let them out onto a vast avenue lined with imposing brick and stone carved buildings that seemed to reach to the sky.

Out here the air was muggy and suffused with smells and noise that assaulted them like a battering ram.

"So how does someone find out where her Grandmother lives?" Angelene wondered mournfully as she surveyed this new rush of people and now horses, carriages, drays and horse-drawn trolleys.

"I hope you at least know her name," Rake said dryly, not a little daunted himself by the sheer density of the population that roamed the street at close to five o'clock on a summer afternoon. "How did you hope to find her— by yourself?"

"I don't know," Angelene said faintly. And in truth, she hadn't even thought that far ahead. She supposed she had thought that New York would turn out to be a little city the size of Cairo where everyone knew each other and she had only to ask any stranger in the street for directions to the home of Mrs. Horace Bellancourt.

But this—this was like a foreign country where they didn't know the language.

And the hour was getting later.

Rake chose the direction and they walked a little until they found an identifying sign. "This is Fourth Avenue and that—" she pointed the other way to the intersecting street—"is Forty-second Street. Neither street name is meaningful to me."

Worse than that, both streets seemed to extend into infinity, with no end or beginning to them.

It irritated her that they looked as raw and gullible as she felt at that moment. And stupid, too. She felt inutterably simple-minded, and green as the pasture on the mountain ridge that existed no longer. She felt like every passerby knew it, and that no one would offer to help.

"Maybe there is some kind of listing of city residents," she said hopefully.

"This is possible," Rake agreed, "but we haven't got time to figure out where to find one. And I'll tell you, Angelene, I do not want to spend the night in that terminal the way we did in Lexington. We have to find out where your Grandmother is, and fast. And if that means asking everyone we meet if they know who she is, then that is what we'll do."

And they did it. For one solid hour they accosted passersby and asked if anyone of them had heard of Mrs. Horace Bellancourt.

The majority had not, and were in a rush and didn't care to pursue the matter. One or two allowed that they had heard the name but they did not know in connection with what. Finally they thought they had found an agreeable couple who might help them and who actually seemed to know her Grandmother's name.

"Yes, of course. Bellancourt," the woman said. "You know, Willy, one of them *rich* Bellancourts, the Fifth Avenue Bellancourts."

"Right," the man said, "I knew that name was familiar. Just right, Mary. Fifth Avenue is the ticket. That's where they all live, lady. You just take a cab on down that way and ask anybody where the old lady lives. They all know."

"A cab?" Angelene repeated faintly. She didn't know what a cab was, and Rake shrugged when she sent him a questioning glance.

It wasn't lost on their hopeful couple, either.

"A cab," the man said, "you know—one of those covered carriages like the one over there. Maybe you'd like me to call one over for you?"

Angelene looked at Rake and he nodded. The man motioned them over to the curb, gave a piercing whistle, and called, "Hey you—cabbie!" at the very instant Angelene felt a wrench at her arm. She whirled to see the woman running down the street, her purse in her hand,

and before she could even understand what had happened, the man had taken off in the opposite direction with Rake in pursuit.

She felt like sinking through the sidewalk. She didn't dare move, lest Rake not be able to find her again.

He was back within moments. "No chance of getting him. It must be a set play with them, and they arrange to meet someplace in between. Angelene! Don't lose hope now."

"But my money—"

"There wasn't much left anyway, and I still have some. We will be all right, but we need to find some officer of the law to report this theft."

"And we'll have to ask someone to find out, won't we? I suppose two thefts in a day is normal in a place like this?"

"Don't make assumptions, Angelene. Read the signs first. All the clues are in nature."

"There is no nature here. There is only un-nature."

"Then we'll go back to the terminal and we will find someone connected to the railroad to give us the information. Maybe we should have done that in the first place."

"Or maybe we should just go back to Crossville Junction," she said morosely.

"But there's no money to do that now," Rake said gently. "We really have to find your Grandmother."

"That's a very nice description," the police officer said, as he obediently took notes and tried not to stare at the man in the outlandish costume. The man was tall, bronzed, calm and purposeful, the woman edgy and unnerved—and damned beautiful. What a pair. Innocents in the snakepit of the city. And the only news he had for them was that there was no way the police could apprehend the thieves.

"You know there's a million people in this city, lady," he said, choosing to speak to Angelene in order to calm her fears. "And maybe fifty women and a dozen men could fit that description. I wouldn't look for an arrest any time soon."

"No." The man spoke now. "We don't expect that. It's enough that you know that visitors are being preyed upon. What you can do for us, however, is locate someone we have come a long way to see."

"Hey, this isn't a Visitor's Bureau, mister."

"I'm aware of that. But we lost all our money and we need this help."

The officer supposed he couldn't deny an out of town visitor that, but he felt strangely reluctant to offer. "What's the person's name, mister?"

Angelene answered him. "Mrs. Horace Bellancourt."

The name made him sit bolt upright. "Really," he said cautiously. "How are you acquainted?"

"I'm her granddaughter."

"For real," the officer breathed. "I'm damned. You know, I think you two are running the larceny ring here, you know that? What a deal! You find the right story to get you into a place you can case for the biggest richest names in town. How many other precinct houses have you visited tonight, honey? A half dozen? Building that list of names you're gonna try on your visit here? Not too wise of you to dress so distinctly, mister. They'd pick you out of a line-up in a minute."

It was another world, another country. Angelene didn't understand a word the man was saying, only that his implicit sympathy had changed to something venal and cold and he wanted nothing more to do with them.

"You two get out of here, and don't let me hear about your making that claim anywhere else around town, lady, because I'll lock you both up so fast you'll think you're riding a fast train to hell." He tore the sheet from his notepad and ripped it to shreds before their eyes. "*Out!*"

Rake whispered, "Don't run," and he guided her slowly, and with dignity out the door to a shaking halt on the steps of the precinct building.

The sun was setting now, and all of her hopes, and the

231

very thing he had feared seemed to be a reality: the woman did not exist and neither did the city in which she lived.

Read the signs. Surely there were no colder, more hard-hearted people than existed in this city, Angelene thought disconsolately as she and Rake made their way back to the terminal in the oncoming dusk of this futile summer day.

She read the signs all right: a fool and her dreams were soon disillusioned.

"Take heart," Rake told her. "Consider that police person's reaction to your Grandmother's name. He knew it. He was protective of it. He did *not* say there was no such person. Angelene—*are you listening to me?*"

Read the signs . . .

"I hear you. He didn't deny her, did he? He didn't seem to want us to get in touch with her at all."

"Yes. He knew where she lives."

"And he cautioned us about trying to get her address from any other precinct station, didn't he?" *The signs were there.*

"Emphatically," Rake said darkly, still in thrall to just how similar these circumstances were to his own in Illinois those many years ago. Then it was merely a matter of asking the question. Everyone knew the socially significant families in town. Homes were known as the Smith house, or the Jones residence. The politically important had been moving targets for anyone who chose to camp on their doorsteps, including one enraged half-breed son. Everyone knew the limestone mansion of Brandon Cordigan, the governor of Illinois.

"And so," he said after a moment's thought, "this is what we're going to do. We're going to take the advice of that nasty couple and find one of those cabs, Angelene, and I just wager that the driver knows exactly where your wealthy, socially prominent Grandmother is."

Maybe he had been hoping this suposition was erroneous. Or maybe he hoped the old lady had died long ago. What he didn't expect was the imposing pile of white limestone similar to what his father called the Governor's Mansion in Illinois to be the town home of the woman who was Angelene's grandmother.

Here was the embodiment of Angelene's dream of a life of luxury as far from her mother as possible.

Providing, of course, that her Grandmother acknowledged her.

She had been so easy to find. Too easy.

"Oh yeah," their cab driver had said, "all them little old rich ladies live down on lower Fifth."

Common knowledge for vulgar wealth. Mr. Horace Bellancourt had made his from untidy things like stock speculation and investing in foreign soil and uptown Manhattan real estate. Everyone knew that.

And so they finally stood in front of the imposing walnut double doors that rose at least six feet over their heads, and Angelene shifted her bag, squared her shoulders, commented that she thought the time was not *too* late, and—and this was the hardest part—lifted her hand and firmly pushed in the doorbell.

To which there was no answer.

"It can't be more than seven o'clock. Surely she wouldn't be asleep now," Angelene fretted, and pushed the doorbell again, this time with a hint of frantic impatience.

Still they waited.

"I am *not* backing down those steps," Angelene swore, her voice gritty with uncertainty. Besides, the steps were so wide and white and marble, and the whole of the front of the house was enclosed with a marble fence as if that could shut the owner away from the sights and smells and noise of this peculiarly busy street.

On top of that, the house sat squarely on a corner and

rose five stories over her head, and she just would not let it or her Grandmother dwarf her. Not after coming all this way.

As usual, she hadn't a clue as to what Rake Cordigan was thinking. She didn't even know how she was going to explain him.

The door swung open quite suddenly and a tall super cilious man in blue livery stood on the threshold. "Miss?"

Angelene drew herself up. "I wish to see Mrs. Bellancourt."

"Mrs. Bellancourt is not available, Miss. Perhaps you would like to leave your card?"

"I don't have a card. Tell Mrs. Bellancourt that Angelene Scates is here to see her."

"I can certainly tell her, Miss, but I assure you that she—"

"I assure you that she will want to see me," Angelene said with more certainty than she felt. The damned butler's haughty gaze was making her feel more and more like a piece of vermin who had crawled out of the street. He meant to close the door on her too, as nicely as he possibly could.

"I'll be certain to tell her, Miss," he said, making the move to close the door.

But Rake was quicker, sliding his body between the butler and the latch. "The lady will wait while you announce to Mrs. Bellancourt."

The butler didn't lose a minute of his composure. "Ruffian's tactics will get you nowhere, sir. There is nothing in this house of value to you, and there is a foot patrol that checks up and down the street hourly."

"I'm sure that's true," Rake said, "however, there is something of value here for Mrs. Bellancourt. Now you kindly tell her that Miss Angelene Scates is waiting out side her door."

The butler turned and tugged at a bellpull just inside the doorway and immediately a young woman dressed in somber black appeared.

234

"Please awaken Mrs. Bellancourt and tell her that a person called Miss Angelene Scates is camping on her doorstep," he directed her with that awful trace of disdain coloring his every word.

She curtsied and scurried away, and the butler turned to them with expression on his face that said plainly, *now you'll see.*

The wait was torturous: her Grandmother could deny knowing the name altogether. The minutes ticked by with agonizing slowness, with the butler becoming excessively restive and hoping, no doubt, an officer on foot patrol would put in an appearance before his mistress.

And then they all heard her voice, far away above them: "Scates? Scates? Dear Lord, dear Lord, where *is* she? Josephine! Josephine!" Closer and closer she came, her richly modulated voice demanding Josephine, and Angelene's heart sank. She had never once thought that her Grandmother might still be yearning for the daughter she had lost all those years ago.

"Where is she, Borden, where is she?"

And then the woman became visible in the anteroom, a robust-looking woman in her sixties with yellow-gray hair and a thick but well-dressed body and slightly jowly face that seemed to reflect the essence of Josie.

She stopped short when she caught sight of Rake's tall frame blocking the doorway. "Who is that person, Borden?"

"I don't know, ma'am."

"And where is Josephine?"

"The person's name is *not* Josephine, ma'am."

"Not Josephine? But—"

Angelene squeezed through the doorway. "It's *Angelene*, Mrs. Bellancourt, Angelene Scates."

"I don't know any Angelene Scates," Mrs. Bellancourt said perplexedly. "Do I, Borden?"

"I tried to tell the person so, ma'am."

"Yes, well thank you. I did think you were someone else," her Grandmother said. "You must have made a mistake."

235

Angelene put out her hand. "No, no ma'am, I didn't make a mistake. My *mother* is Josephine. I'm your granddaughter, ma'am, and I'm hoping you'll be kind enough to let me stay."

Well, she didn't suppose she thought the old woman would jump up and hug her and make her welcome.

"Nonsense," her Grandmother said, "Josephine had boys—didn't she have boys? Well, twin boys, I think—at least that is what I seem to remember and that's the last I heard. How do I *know* you're Josephine's daughter, girl? I never saw you before in my life and now you've disrupted my entire household—*and* my sleep."

Rake said, "Perhaps we should go inside and discuss it, Mrs. Bellancourt, rather than make a spectacle out on your stoop."

"Dear Lord, *what* is this person? He looks like a buffalo. Who is this man, Borden?"

"He neglected to state his name, ma'am."

"Well, then—*who* are you?"

Angelene jumped right in. She was sure she hadn't intended to say one word. She had intended to let Rake walk down those steps the moment her Grandmother accepted her. She just couldn't have him around telling her what she wanted or didn't want. She really had decided she *couldn't.*

"Why, Grandmother, surely you recognize my brother —Rake."

He choked. He thought he would fall right down and die. *The little heathen.* She knew damned well what she wanted: she just wasn't brave enough to take it.

"I don't recognize anything, Miss, except—come to think of it—wasn't one of Josephine's twin boys named something odd that began with an R? Oh, but never mind. That proves nothing. My dear girl, I don't know what you're up to, but you'll have to leave."

Angelene felt a chilling frisson of horror. If the old woman made her leave, Rake would surely strangle her.

236

"Please ma'am, if you could just look at this—" She rooted around for the locket that was tucked away beneath the prim little buttons of her blue and black striped dress. "Please look."

She held out the locket suspended from its chain which she could not unfasten without unbuttoning her bodice as well. She flicked the catch so that the little heart divided to reveal the picture inside.

"I don't know the woman," her Grandmother said decisively, but she edged nearer just to be sure.

Angelene felt the situation slipping away from her. If she failed to identify the photo, she would lose everything. Her Grandmother could claim she would never know Josephine, not after all those years, and so this daughter must be an imposter.

So she had to recognize Josie's photo herself. She *had* to.

"My dear girl, I've given about as much time as I've given any tradesperson trying to sell me a bill of goods . . ." her Grandmother began and then her robust voice petered out for a long moment. Then she said, "Oh dear . . ."

She moved still closer and finally took the little locket into her hand. "Oh dear . . ."

She looked up at Angelene, whose beautiful blue eyes glistened with sympathy.

"All right," her Grandmother said abruptly, dropping the locket, "this is my daughter Josephine," and Angelene let out a surreptitious breath.

"Thank you, ma'am. She gave that locket to me when she sent me to convent school some ten years ago. She must look very like how you remember her."

"Very like," her Grandmother agreed, bending her electric scrutiny to bear now on Angelene. "You have the look of her, you know."

"And she has the look of you," Angelene ventured daringly.

"Yes," her Grandmother said, sounding suddenly tired. "Borden—I am too weary to argue with this person

237

tonight. If you will put both her and her brother in the guest wing, I believe in the morning we can straighten this out. No—" she put up her hand, "I truly do not believe that my Josephine's daughter would walk away with the silver. But, if it makes you feel better, you may keep guard over the connecting door, or assign someone else to do it. Now," she turned to Angelene, "what is your name again, child?"

But she knew very well what it was. Her name was granddaughter, and it was manifest in every gesture, every tilt of the head and the sweet low register of her voice, its timbre so closely matched to her memory of Josephine's.

It was almost too much to take in, at this stage in her life, and all she could think to do was to return to the privacy of her room and say a prayer to her Maker for returning to her the treasure she had lost, so long ago.

Chapter 14

They followed a stiffly disapproving Borden through the reception room and a series of doors that led to a long opulent corridor at the end of which was a steeply winding staircase. He led them up this stairway to the second floor hallway.

Here there were three stately doors surrounded by classical carved woodwork painted white, one directly opposite the staircase, the other two to the left of it as they stood on the landing.

The whole door was carpeted in a rich Chinese carpet and furnished with elegant and dainty side tables that held brass or cut glass bowls full of fresh flowers. On the pristine white walls, interspersed between the doors, there were massive gilt-framed paintings of bucolic landscapes, and on the far wall that backed the hallway, one formidable-looking probable ancestor.

Borden threw open the door opposite the staircase. "Mr.—Rake . . . ?" he said delicately, motioning Rake to enter the room.

Angelene peeked around the door as Rake entered the room as if he had been walking into rooms like this his whole life.

Everything, from the thick carpet underfoot to the massive bedstead, armoire and dresser spoke of luxury and caretaking of the most lavish kind. Everywhere, there were little touches of refinement: a small jewel-toned painting over a matching washstand, an extendable mirror placed discreetly where it commanded the best light, the grooming implements placed handily by the shaving stand, the towel rack closeby which was overlaid with a coverlet matching the bedspread, the bench by the armoire where a man could sit and remove his boots easily with the help of the bootjack placed cleverly on a hook just underneath.

And finally, there was a gleaming carved walnut fireplace along the connecting wall, with a good-sized leather chair beside it. A small table next to it was stacked with a selection of current magazines and the daily paper of preference of the house.

"Now Miss—" Borden didn't wait for a thank you or a gesture of appreciation since he thought the whole idea of putting these scruffy beggars in the guest wing was just a lot of sentimental nonsense on the old lady's part, brought on by an attack of guilt over her long-gone daughter. How cleverly the two had gained entrance!

They were lucky he didn't have to wait on them or have anything to do with them at all, short of making sure they didn't steal away during the night with the valuables of the house in their arms.

He showed Angelene to the last door along the corridor, and she caught her breath as she walked into the room. This one, though less massively furnished, was no less spectacular. It had floor to ceiling windows on either side of a similarly carved walnut fireplace, and its reed-posted canopy bed faced directly opposite. This room was also carpeted plushly and had a full accompaniment of closet and dresser space, a dainty dressing table with mirror, the requisite washstand, bed bench and instead of a leather chair beside the fireplace, a chaise lounge. The room was illuminated by an ornate brass fixture hanging high over her head that diffused flickering gaslight like a warm soft amber cover over the whole.

"There's a bell-pull, Miss, should you wish anything, and of course, in the morning, Mary will see to your needs. Good night, Miss."

240

"Good night, Borden," she said imperiously, trying on her new role, the one she was sure she would assume in the morning when she finally sat down for a long talk with her Grandmother.

She was sure he shuddered, but perhaps that was only the effect of his having to pick up her bag and place it inside the door.

He pulled it closed as quickly as possible, as if there were something contagious in the room, and Angelene felt a distinct sense of wanting to put him in his place.

She walked around the room, touching everything, reveling in its refinement and elegance, astonished that the pitcher on the washstand contained hot, hot water, a luxury that reminded her painfully of the mornings when Rake himself heated her water and delivered it up the attic steps for her convenience.

Rake!

Dear Lord, now how was she going to face him, alone, and explain to him just why she had made him her brother? Perhaps she wouldn't.

It was too easy anyway to just make herself comfortable in the very surroundings her own mother had renounced. She would never for the life of her understand why.

This home, the woman who was her Grandmother were everything she had ever hoped they would be. And her Grandmother would help her, she knew she would. She just didn't know what she would do about Rake . . . or what he was going to do to her.

But she was going to find out soon. She hadn't even had a chance to unpack her meager belongings or wash the grit and grime of travelling and her anxiety from her face, when he rapped sharply at the door and let himself in, shut the door softly—dangerously softly so no one would know he had even entered her room—and leaned back against the pristine white-painted wood, his arms folded against his bare chest.

241

He had shaved, she noticed irrelevantly, avoiding those lancing gray eyes and focusing on the thing about him that wouldn't hit her like a blow to the stomach.

"*Brother*, Angelene?"

"Better than guardian angel," she retorted.

"And surely better than Sister of Angels, always supposing you would have been desperate enough to present yourself to her in your holier-than-thou nun's disguise."

"Oh, *stop* it!"

"In which case, you would have had to forsake all this luxury and the dream of a wealthy husband, and what a sacrifice *that* would have been. Anything humble and sincere pales in comparison, and nothing else can equal it. Your instincts were exactly right, Angelene, find the grandmother, abandon everything else—even hope."

She was shaking with anger at his words. "Well, I'll tell you what, you noble savage, you just go right downstairs and tell that awful butler you are *not* my brother and let him send you packing. Damn you, I didn't do it to hurt you."

"No, you don't know why you did it, Angelene, and that is the most disturbing thing."

"And you do," she demanded stormily. "You're so wise from all those years of contemplation on the mountain. Who are you to talk of renunciation?"

"And who are you to put the one thing between us that puts our footing on totally forbidden ground?"

"If you deny it, there will be *no* ground," she said furiously, desperately. "That horrible butler will pull it right out from beneath you."

"I can read the signs," he said evenly, "and I'm not going to deny it at all, Angelene. And do you know why? Because this is the world I could not enter ten years ago. This is the world of my father, and I am of a mind to learn how to move within it. Perhaps I might even find a suitable woman. Perhaps we might have a double wedding."

"*I hate you.*"

"A man has his dreams too, Angelene."

242

"You didn't have a single dream before you took me up on that mountain."

"Maybe," he said softly, "maybe *you* were my dream, Angelene."

Yes, but now he had dreams enough for two men and a taste of the very same thing that had lured her from the life Josie would have chosen for her. She couldn't picture him as anywhere else but part of a landscape, on a mountain, riding with the wind.

They were the same in this: they wanted the forbidden, they had tasted the forbidden, and when she thought of all the things she had done with him on the mountain, she could not believe that she had yearned for the forbidden with all the passion in her soul.

Her return to this house, this destiny, had been forbidden, and now the stricture she had placed upon him had transformed him into the forbidden.

She wondered if there were ever to be an end to her duplicity.

There was, however, an end to the time allotted for her to toss and turn in her bed. At eight o'clock promptly, she heard a rap on the door, followed by the appearance of Mary, the smart little maid from the night before. She carried a tray in her hands containing coffee, chocolate, croissants, butter, eggs, ham, biscuits.

"Good morning, Miss. Your breakfast is here, and when you have done, I will draw your bath for you."

"My—bath?"

"In the room next door, Miss. The guest bedrooms share the bathroom. Mr. Rake is having his bath right now."

Oh, dear Lord, Rake—bathing.

Mary set the tray down on her knees and fluffed her pillows as she leaned forward. "There now. Now Miss, I know you brought little clothes with you. Would you like me to press something for you?"

243

Her tone was so respectful, with none of that looking down her nose at the alleged poor relative tone in it, that Angelene agreed to have both dresses pressed so that she could make a choice later on.

Mary whisked those away, and Angelene sat back in her bed, a cup of chocolate warming the palms of her hands, and thought about the kind of wealth that could provide the facilities for bathing indoors.

Then she thought about Rake, his tall frame folded into some kind of tub, naked, slick with soap—had she really wanted to pretend she had pushed away everything that had happened on the mountain? What if she got up and walked in there now, then what?

Why was she thinking like that anyway?

She drew a deep shuddering breath. She hadn't forgotten *anything*, including the fact that she willingly gave him up because he could not offer her the very luxury in which he was now steeped.

Who had made *that* possible?

She ate some of the eggs and ham and croissants, and drank the coffee appreciatively.

The die was cast now.

She couldn't turn back, and Rake had obviously decided that neither could he.

An hour later, she seated herself across from her Grandmother in the smaller of the two parlors on the second floor of the building.

They were alone, in the small alcove of a bow window that overlooked Fifth Avenue, seated at a small round table on which was laid a beautiful lace tablecloth, a vase of flowers and place settings for two.

Her grandmother was dressed in beige rose crepe edged with ecru lace, a color that lightened her skin and her sallow look. She had abundant hair, now that she could be seen clearly in the light of day, which was pinned up into an elaborate knot on top of her head, and she had the sharpest blue eyes Angelene had ever seen.

244

"I don't like that dress."

Angelene had chosen the second of the two dresses provided by Mr. Martin when they left Crossville Junction, and she couldn't have said she liked it either. It was plain blue serge, made to withstand the rigors of travelling and the scrutiny of a Grandmother who probably could see too much.

"Neither do I," Angelene said frankly.

"Well then, you won't be averse to my doing something about that, will you?" her Grandmother said briskly.

"Grandmother—ma'am . . . please be sure."

Her grandmother gave her a baleful look. "I'm sure, young lady. Now you must tell *me* everything."

"Yes ma'am." But where to start, and how much had her Grandmother inferred by her untimely and inauspicious arrival?

She told her almost the whole, about how she had grown up and all the stories she had heard about her Grandmother at Josie's knee, and how she never could understand why Josie had followed Harry into the unknown, and how she had vowed she would never do the same, and the aftermath of that, when Josie insisted that her work was with the family, and she had no choice at all about her future.

That wasn't a lie, either, only a very expurgated version of what had happened. "And I decided that my best course was to try to come to you," she finished, "because I grew up wanting the things that mother had run away from, and I never thought it was fair that I could have no choice about it. And then—and then . . ." she looked up and she saw Rake hovering on the threshold of the room, looking refreshed and cleansed, and skeptical as always.

"And then my big brother Rake found out what I was planning to do, and he thought I was a little crazy, and the only way I would ever get here was if he came with me." She smiled up at him brilliantly as he entered on that line. "And so he did."

"Rake, Rake, what kind of name is that?" her Grandmother demanded, motioning for Rake to take a side chair and draw it up to the table. "Rake Scates? That's what Josephine named you?"

Rake sent Angelene one of his cool gray looks that positively flickered with amusement and demanded that she come up with the answer since she had invented everything else.

"Well—well, no. It's just a nickname of course. His name is—" she frantically rolled through a list of names in her mind, none of which *wanted* to begin with R, "*Richard.* And he looks just like Harry, don't you think, Grandmother?"

"I don't remember what Harry looked like," her Grandmother grumbled, taking a long sidewise look at Rake. "No, I don't think he looks like Harry or Josephine in the least. And those odd eyes—"

"No, no, Grandmother," Angelene said hurriedly, "his are the color eyes that change in the light. Like my father's."

"I don't remember Harry at all," her Grandmother protested again, though Angelene was sure she had never forgotten him. "Now, how old are you?"

The question startled her. "I'm twenty."

"Good, very good. A good age, the age at which your mother should have had the world at her feet, and instead she chose to put her feet in boots and kick the world. But that's another story. You, however, came to me because you chose not to follow your mother's way, and I'm glad of that, Angelene. But now you must tell me exactly what you expect me to do for you."

Gutsy old lady, Rake thought, watching Angelene's eyes brighten with anticipation. Oh, angel eyes, he thought, who could have guessed you'd walk right into the place and conquer the old lady as thoroughly as you have conquered every obstacle in your path—including me?

He himself had seen no resemblance between Angelene and the tiny photograph in the locket. But then he hadn't been looking with a mother's eye, the suspicious eye that saw no likeness between him and Angelene or anyone she remembered. He found himself admiring Mrs. Horace Bellancourt; she was no fool, but she would not be concentrating on him when she had Angelene on whom to spend her energy and, he guessed, many years of unrequited love.

It was her face that he watched minutely as Angelene outlined exactly what she had in mind.

"My mother, of course, cannot be happy with this turn of events," she began as a preface. "On the other hand, I had no reason to suppose you would so readily accept me into your home, Grandmother, and I'm so grateful."

"Nonsense," her Grandmother sloughed off her appreciation. "Go on."

Angelene hesitated. How bald-faced could she be about her desire to marry wealthy and well, she wondered. She didn't want pots of money expended on her, not really. What she wanted was the introduction to a better world, a better life, a chance at meeting a more refined kind of man. A man of power who wouldn't need anything her Grandmother had to offer because he had everything himself. And so, first and foremost, he would become her shield against Josie and whatever schemes *she* might cook up. But that was later, much later.

"I expect I want exactly what you wanted, what my mother wanted," she began again, feeling her way through what had to sound like a set of purely money-grubbing desires. "I want marriage, a home, a family. I just don't want it down some dirt road in the middle of Missouri. That's what mother chose eventually, Grandmother, and it was a life where she ultimately had to find a way to salvage and support her family after my father died. She keeps a road ranch, kind of a sleep over ranch for travellers who aren't overlanding on the major trails. She does very well with it, you understand, but that's all there is. My brothers help, and mother had me slated to come to work there too, and—"

She couldn't look at Rake because of how thoroughly

247

she had sterilized this version of the story. "Anyway, I never wanted that. I wanted what my mother willingly gave up. We didn't see eye to eye on that," she added in a masterpiece of understatement that caused Rake to choke into his delicate china cup.

"I see," her Grandmother said, her keen eye taking in every nuance of expression on her face hungrily. It was Josephine's face, so many years ago, and she had so many pictures of the young Josephine with just such a look, just such a gesture. It was almost painful to watch, and yet it was exhilarating: Josephine had come back to her, and she never meant to let her go.

"Well my dear," she said at length, "it will give me great pleasure to assist you in this regard. You have come to me at exactly the right time. It is August now, and we have three and half to four months to prepare, and that's very good. That's excellent, in fact. There is only one barrier to your achieving what you want and that is that you have not travelled in the upper echelons of New York society where you might have had many distinct advantages. Of course, had Josephine sent you to me sooner . . . well, that's neither here nor there. Let me put it bluntly. I suppose I could conceivably launch you into society here in New York were it possible to invent some story about the fact you had been in a nunnery or something all these years, but since that isn't the case . . . the next best thing, my dear, is England."

"*What?*"

"The English love American girls, my dear, especially those backed with money. Look at Constanza Morales and her sister. They had nothing. They went over, they charmed the Prince Regent with their spectacular looks, flamboyant way of dressing and excellent kitchen, and before you knew it, Constanza landed a peer of the realm—well, he had a while to go until his father died, but still—and, in any event, she makes a tidy little business of doing introductions for those not acquainted with the social scene. After that, it is only a matter of interesting the Prince and then everyone else becomes interested, and your success is assured."

"It sounds like a fairy tale," Angelene said drily.

"Well, of course it is. And here is your fairy god-mother complete with wand to make you into a princess before you can blink. And *you*, young man," she barked at Rake.

"Yes, ma'am," he said, startled, immediately straight-ening up in his chair from his posture of utter stupe-faction at the ease with which Mrs. Bellancourt would be able to transform Angelene into exactly what both of them desired: the eligible young woman she had never had the chance to present.

"You look like an inside-out buffalo. You can't go gal-livanting all over the city like that, let alone come with us to England—which, by the way, I expect you to do. There is no better chaperone for a young beautiful woman than her own brother. I will make an appointment for you with Mr. Bellancourt's tailor."

Rake raised his hand to stop this steamroller of energy from just bowling right over him. "Ma'am—"

"Grandmother will do, young man."

He looked at Angelene, and those gorgeous angel eyes were blazing with negative emotion that told him as clearly as words, *don't do it, don't let her do it, don't accept.*

"I'm most grateful, ma'am. I would be delighted to be my—*sister's* chaperone." It was amazing—there was no balance, no symmetry here at all, except that Angelene was in this place with him. He felt as if he were careening off the earth and into a place that might well have been meant to be his destiny. He felt fatalistic about it, calm, once he accepted the fact that he would allow Mrs. Bel-lancourt to adopt him in exactly the same way she meant to adopt Angelene.

"Well, that's settled then, and there is so much to do. You must tell me first, Angelene, if you have any skills."

She raised her eyebrows in perplexity. "Skills? Sewing, I can sew, Grandmother, and play a little piano. I love to read, I can clean house moderately well, and I can cook—"

"No, no, my dear. *Skills*—lawn tennis, riding, dancing, bicycling—no? Do you swim? My dear, we truly have much to do. And that is in addition to providing you with a wardrobe. That first, of the instant. I need Mary." She reached for a bell-pull. Mary immediately appeared.

"My notepaper please, Mary, and a footman to carry a message. We will want to see M. Dumiere at his convenience today in order to choose a new wardrobe for my granddaughter. And then, in addition to that, right away, you will send to Mr. Darlington at Mr. Bellancourt's club, and request he join us for dinner in order to aid us in choosing the most up to the minute instructors for my granddaughter. Let me see—pending his reply, I will need to change the menu, and then of course, Mr. Scates must be sent to Mr. Bellancourt's tailor immediately for something ready to wear, because he cannot appear at my table looking like the innards of a cow. Thank you. And now, Borden."

He appeared after another sharp yank of the tapestry pull.

"Here you are, Borden. I will need a driver this afternoon, after lunch will be fine. And I wish to inform you that Mr. and Miss Scates will be staying with me indefinitely. And—oh yes, I wish to have you unpack the family albums, Borden. I should like Miss Angelene to see the old pictures of her mother and the way things used to be."

They had a respite just before lunch, and Angelene fled to her room. Her grandmother was like a whirlwind, lifting everything in her path. It was almost too much, and too soon, when yesterday morning she had been both confused and confined by a desire she could not comprehend in a pullman car thirty miles outside of New York.

The last person she wanted to see was Rake, so naturally he was waiting for her in the stairwell.

"Well," she said nastily, "here's a man who fell off a

250

mountain who has been elevated to heaven instead."

"The very place where the deserving Sister of Angels has finally been given her wings, and has found paradise on earth. My heaven is here, Angelene," he said quietly, touching his heart. "I have no need of what your grandmother offers."

"But you'll take it: I saw in your eyes that you were going to go right along with it."

"For your sake, Angelene, nothing more."

"Why don't I believe you?" she demanded stormily.

"Perhaps because you know if I touch you or kiss you, you will never go to England."

"You have that entirely wrong, *brother* of the devil. Nothing will stop me from going to England."

He smiled then, a small, pleasurable, *smug* little smile. "This truly sounds like a challenge, Angelene." He took a step closer to her, and reached for her. She didn't back away. He grasped a thick handful of her lustrous golden hair. "Nothing can stop me either," he murmured, centering her unresisting mouth right at the perfect angle beneath his. "Try to stop me, Angelene," he whispered, seeking the truth in her angel eyes, and the denial on her lying lips.

She groaned as his mouth settled uncompromisingly on hers. It took so little to evoke her latent yearning. It wasn't fair. She would never be able to put it behind her and she would never be able to resist it. It was the predatory stalking of the hunter, and it was the probing molten possessive kiss of a lover, the one she didn't want, the one she desperately wanted to forget.

The one he never wanted her to forget.

He eased his mouth away from hers triumphantly. "Go to England, Angelene—fly like an eagle before you come back down to earth and realize that a man's worth is not measured by what is in his pocketbook."

"Nor in his skill in seducing a woman," she retorted tartly, wrenching herself away from him. "You're a rich man there, Rake Cordigan."

251

"And you are poor in spirit not to recognize the wealth at your command. It will come, but I hope the cost is not too high."

"The price is too dear," she said acidly, struggling to maintain a semblance of calm. It was too difficult to deny what she felt with vehemence on the heels of such capitulation. Her legs felt weak, and little darts of fury kept jolting her internally in the aftermath of her intense arousal.

Anger was her only weapon. And propriety: who, after all, had been the one to recast him into the role of her brother?

It was all too ludicrous trying to balance that permutation with learning how to become the kind of woman a wealthy man would want to marry. It was even possible she had created the situation to distance herself from him. She had *not* expected that her grandmother was going to ask him to stay.

The mask of impassivity settled over his face. "As you wish, Angelene. I can afford to wait."

But it was about all he could afford in this atmosphere of extravagance that seemed to have no bounds, and he protested mightily at the amount of money that Mrs. Bellancourt was prepared to spend on the barbarian in buckskin whom she thought was her grandson.

"You have no conception of the amount of clothes a man needs in this social scene," she pointed out to him.

"No, ma'am."

"And at the very least, you need several suitable suits for dinner and day wear—and of course this all seems strange to you," she added with an odd little note of sympathy in her voice.

"Well, ma'am, you have no conception of how countrified it is where we were living." A roomy enough statement, no untruths there, applicable to mountains— or road ranches.

"To be sure. But now you are here, and of course you want to do me credit."

"As best I can, ma'am."

"Good. Then let's go shopping."

But what she meant by shopping was an activity so far removed from his sphere of knowledge that he felt like a wanderer in a strange land with no familiar signpost to guide him.

The first stop was the tailor's, and he saw with dismay that Mrs. Bellancourt meant to *leave* him there, with Borden, for a round of measuring, draping, fabric selection, and alteration of two sample ready-made suits, and the ordering of a half dozen more in various colors and materials.

Before he could protest, she was off with Angelene to someplace called McCreery's, uptown at Eleventh Street, to select a small ready-to-wear wardrobe of several day dresses, underwear and one evening gown before she took her to M. Dumiere for the very serious business of choosing a wardrobe with which to travel to England.

"And even this is just a minimum; I would infinitely prefer to have you dressed by Worth—at least for evening wear, and it would be well worth a stopover in Paris to take the time to have a half dozen gowns made up for you. In fact, I think we will. We will have M. Dumiere forward your measurements and description in advance of our arrival to be sure that we get an appointment and that no time is wasted in the choosing of fabric and a selection of styles."

"Grandmother—" Angelene protested softly. She was like a thunderstorm, gathering momentum as she moved, crackling with energy and a purpose she had not had in years.

"Don't be silly. I would have done all this for your mother, had she let me. I am thankful to be able to do it for you."

"But it's too much—and Rake—he's never been out of leather for as long as I can remember." Well, probably not; she was having a hard time envisioning his long lean body keeping still for one moment of being measured by some clerk. Neither of them had ever been *in* a store larger than the Clark Mercantile store, and the very size

253

of McCreery's positively assaulted the senses.

There was just too much to look at; every counter displayed a selection of wondrous things, from ready-made hats and scarves and gloves and jewelry on the main floor to robes and shirtwaists, coats, slippers, shoes, boots, unmentionables, purses—she couldn't count the number of things—on the second. And there was even a separate department for menswear *and* household furnishings.

"This," her grandmother said, fingering a pretty nightgown made of fine muslin, with a high lace collar and rows of tucked pleats down the front, "is a mere stopgap, to fill in your wardrobe until M. Dumiere finishes the rest. Now, we'll start with the nightgowns, and actually it does make more sense to purchase these ready-made—except of course for the ones that will be in your trousseau. So, tell me, which styles do you like?"

She chose five gowns, two of muslin, the pleated one and one with an embroidered yoke, another of cambric, with a lace collar, sleeve panel, and wristband, two of plain cotton with tucks, scalloped edges, and lace decorating the collars and cuffs.

They went on to look at underwear, and here her grandmother insisted on seven sets of chemises, underdrawers and over skirts, all of fine cambric, muslin and cotton and all trimmed with tucks, pleats, embroidery and lace, finer than anything she had ever owned in her life, and more extravagant. Then she chose two corsets—only at her grandmother's insistence and over her own protest that she had never worn one in her life.

And never would, she vowed, as she ran her fingers over the stiff contours of the thing, and felt the heavy boning buried deep within the material.

Then she must choose a set of steels—one for dresses that had the attached bustle, the other without, to support the narrower morning dresses and informal skirts that were next on the list.

The array was dizzying, the choices staggering, and total of the bill was mounting faster than a river at flood stage and they hadn't even gotten to looking at the more elegant dresses yet.

That was perhaps the most enjoyable—here a ready-made suit with brocaded silk trim, there a beautiful silk dress with three lace-trimmed flounces and a short draped overskirt, a silk dress with velvet collar lapels, matching sleeve cuffs, two panels of brocaded silk and bustle caught up with a matching velvet bow, a dress of seersucker in blue and white stripes with lace trim, another of sateen with a draped overskirt trimmed in lace, a walking suit made of homespun with a pleated skirt and velvet collar and cuffs . . . and then a collection of skirts, made of chambray, satin, poplin, plain, striped, lace-trimmed, braided at the flounce, utterly beguiling just for their lack of pretension and need for the inescapable bustle support.

With these, she chose an assortment of shirtwaists and jersey jackets, shawls, hats, stockings of cotton, lisle and silk in white, black, blue, flesh colored—daring. And shoes—a pair of house sleepers, a pair of sturdy oxfords, button top boots, and a most elegant pair of evening shoes.

And a trunk. A three foot wide barrel-topped tray trunk, leather covered, with separate compartments for hats, shirts and jewelry. Then one parasol of pongee silk with a deep lace edging and one leather purse—and finally they were done.

And they still had to go to M. Dumiere's!

"Well, of course!" her grandmother said. "This is a mere week's worth of clothing, just to wear around the house."

And M. Dumiere was equally exacting. Between him and her grandmother, they figured she would need a minimum of two weeks' worth of dresses for daywear, so as not to be seen in the same costume *too* frequently, a half dozen evening gowns, several morning gowns—these were not quite as important in terms of how often she wore them—a riding habit, most important, and especially that it be form-fitting and complementary to her figure, two costumes for afternoon tea, being sure that at least two of the day dresses would pass muster in case Madame's granddaughter was fortunate enough to be invited more than twice, at least two high-necked, long-sleeved dresses for receptions and theater, and two ball gowns, besides.

And the fabrics: silks, brocades, velvets, chiffons, laces; and the colors: from subdued to gaudy, gold, purple, black, gorgeous combinations: cream against bronze, royal blue against black, fuschia against cream.

And the endless measuring: every inch of her body, the circumference of her neck, her arms, wrists, fingers, ankles; the slant of her buttocks, the size of her feet, everything in proportion and properly neat.

It would take weeks . . .

"Weeks that will be spent learning the skills that will make you good company," her grandmother said; she was still chipper, bright with excitement and exhilaration, as delighted as a child at all they had accomplished and not in the least fazed that they would be returning home six hours later than they had left it.

"You go right upstairs and change," her grandmother instructed her, and Angelene wanted to beg an hour's rest in between. "Dinner will be served promptly at seven, my dear. Please wear the sateen dress tonight. I'm sure everything has arrived and Mary has put it away.

Then Mary came to brush her hair and draw her bath and lay out the clothes that were hung so neatly in her armoire, as if an army of elves had been put to work while she and her grandmother were gone.

"Aren't they lovely, miss? McCreery's has the nicest things."

She had never heard such a tone of longing before, and it struck her that this girl would never be able to afford even one of the dresses that she had so frivolously chosen at her grandmother's encouragement, that Mary would always be on the outside looking in, while she, Angelene, was now on the inside looking out.

She infinitely preferred the comfort there, and she

would never understand how her mother had so willingly given it up.

"Richard! *Richard!*"

Rake wheeled abruptly at the insistent voice behind him, wondering who the devil this Richard was. Angelene's grandmother stood on the threshold of the parlor, decked out in lace-trimmed black silk and expensive perfume. "Good evening, ma'am."

"Good evening," she said, coming briskly into the parlor, amused at the sight of him eyeing himself warily in the pier mirror over the fireplace. He looked so uncomfortable—and so handsome, and he had the broadest shoulders she had ever seen. She wondered what Mr. Bellancourt's tailor had made of him. But she knew. The beautifully cut and fitted suit told her.

"You're brown as an Indian, Richard," she said critically, although she admired the way his tanned skin contrasted with the white of his shirt and the severe black of his suit.

Richard? Richard—she was calling *him* Richard? "Comes from working outdoors all my life," he said easily, maybe a little resentfully if he decided to dig deeper into what she meant. He decided not to. She was just a rich and sad little old lady who had needed and now finally had some family. But who the hell was Richard . . . ?

"Tell me about that," she said, motioning to one of the two brocade covered sofas in front of the fireplace.

He really didn't know if he could sit down. He had never been so buttoned, tied and belted into anything in his whole life. He lowered himself gingerly onto the pillow.

"Tell you what, ma'am?"

"About your mother. A son's perspective is always different, don't you think?"

No, he didn't think, and he didn't have a clue as to what she wanted to know either. *Richard . . .*

"It's hard to say, ma'am. I mean, I'm that much older than Angelene and . . . and we were raised to see the necessity of both staying together and finding a way to earn some money. And that's a thing I would be doing all of my life anyway, so . . . I reckon I didn't see it in quite the same light as Angelene." What a piece of work that little invention was—a patchwork of everything Angelene had told him underlaid by the pure terror of her determining he was *not* Angelene's brother. She would, if he didn't get any more specific.

"Yes, I know that," she said impatiently. "Tell me about Josephine."

"Ma'am," he said, temporizing—he didn't know a clue to anything about Josephine, let alone the details she was hungry to hear, "I can't tell you about *Josephine*. She is Josie, and she's a hard-working woman who's been bitter all her life, and I don't know if it's because she regretted the course she chose or if she was just plain ornery. She talked about . . ." About? About? What would a rich little girl run away from? The very things that Angelene was embracing, he knew. ". . . about choosing freedom, ma'am, and I reckon she's about as free as a woman can be." And that *was* the truth, if she had done all the things of which Angelene had accused her.

"Freedom is not slogging around in the middle of nowhere, raising a family because your drunken gambler husband couldn't take care of you," the old lady retorted heatedly. "She couldn't still be talking about that, she *couldn't*."

And he remembered what Angelene had said. "She was never coming back, ma'am, and she was going to make so much money, she would prove you and Mr. Bellancourt were wrong."

"Did she?"

He rubbed his face, again to give himself time to sort through his meager recollection of Angelene's story. "I believe she thinks she did," he said gently, but even his considerate tone did not ease the blow, and she slumped backward almost as if she had been punched in the

258

stomach, just for an instant, and no one would have noticed had he not been looking directly at her.

Then she squared her shoulders and popped the next question. "What about you, Richard? You're more than old enough to be on your own. Why did you stay with her?"

Richard, Richard, damn Richard . . . why would she keep calling him that? And how the hell did he know why he had stayed with the redoubtable Josie? "She needed my help, ma'am," he said, and he thought it sounded lame and even evasive, but for some reason it was an answer that pleased her on some other level.

"Then you decided to help Angelene?"

"Maybe I wanted to come east myself, ma'am."

"It must have been a hard choice."

"No. I mean, Josie and Bobby and Tice and Angelene would not have had anybody. It was an easy choice, but it was one in which we had to deceive Josie because she never would have let Angelene come."

"I see," the old lady said, and she hated what she saw: these two children had somehow stolen away from Josephine and her wishes and desires and dreams, and somehow they had come halfway across the country so that Angelene could fulfill hers in spite of her mother.

It made her very sad that Josephine had held the grudge all these years when she herself had forgotten about it the moment she and Horace received word of their twin grandchildren. Well, maybe she hadn't forgotten about it, but she certainly had set it aside in hopes that Josephine would reconsider and come back to her family sometime.

And now one of those first-born grandsons was here, delivering the message she had never wanted to hear— that Josephine never wanted to see her again. Thank God Angelene had had the sense, the courage and the spirit to defy her mother.

"Grandmother?"

Angelene's voice, uncertain, from the doorway. They both looked up at once, and she felt a wallop of dismay;

her grandmother looked inutterably sad and Rake looked . . . she couldn't tell—guilty, maybe, and it was obvious they were having a very confidential conversation and she wondered just how much her *brother* had given away.

"You're supposed to stand up when a lady enters the room, Richard," the old lady nudged him, and he got to his feet gracefully and without haste.

"Thank you, ma'am. I'm afraid I'm going to need a lot of help in that quarter."

She was pleased at his candor, and she rose herself to meet Angelene halfway as she walked curiously into the room.

So her grandmother was calling him Richard. How sharp she was. She bent to kiss the old lady's cheek.

"How lovely you look, Angelene. That blue picks up the color of your eyes perfectly."

"I feel very elegant. And you *look* very elegant— Richard," she added, extending her hands to him so he was forced to grasp them briefly.

"And brown as an Indian," he murmured in an undertone. "What a perceptive grandmother we have."

He released her hands and looked inquiringly at the old lady who nodded, and invited Angelene to take a seat with them.

She sat down every bit as cautiously as had her brother, the old lady noticed, and it was a sad commentary on the nature of the things they were used to.

"Mr. Darlington will be joining us soon," she said lightly, "and Richard and I were just discussing your mother, Angelene. I am hungry for details, and it seems there aren't very many."

"No. I'm afraid she was very unforgiving of the fact you did not want her to marry my father, Grandmother. Everything else was only to prove she had made the right choice."

"I can't bear to think," her grandmother began, and then her voice broke. "Oh no, no—I wasn't going to allow myself the luxury of imagining how things could have been, I really wasn't."

"Of course not," Angelene said instantly, sending a bolting blue glance over at Rake, even though she could see he felt every bit as nonplussed as she.

"You do look just like her, Angelene. It's almost like having her back here with me again."

"Thank you, Grandmother. That is a lovely compliment." But she wasn't sure it was: what if the old lady meant to keep her here forever, just like Josie had meant to keep her at the ranch?

The old lady took a deep breath. "And so," she sniffled, "ah—here is Mr. Darlington."

Borden escorted the gentleman into the room, a portly man of medium height with graying hair, ruddy skin, wire glasses and the twinkling look of a Christmas symbol.

He was the eternal guest at the homes of sundry society friends when they needed a witty conversationalist, a man who would not be a threat to the woman guests, and someone who was not a burden to his hostess.

He had been Horace Bellancourt's best friend, and the one-time suitor of Horace's wife. He hadn't been quite rich enough to marry her, but he was wealthy enough to have remained her friend, and he would have married her in a minute if she hadn't still been in mourning for both Horace and her willful daughter.

His shock was palpable when he saw Angelene. "My dear—she's Josephine thirty years ago, Amelia."

His comment shocked *her;* there was too much of Josephine in her, and it felt like her mother inhabited her skin and not her.

"Yes," Amelia said, "and now you see why I invited you here tonight. These two children have been raised like savages, and we need to put our heads together to find the right instructors so we can prepare to take them to England in December."

"Wonderful timing," Mr. Darlington said, his precise

261

eye taking in every detail of Angelene's dress and bearing and the faultless cut of Rake's suit and his ramrod posture. "Wonderful. Any help you require, my dear Amelia, and with only one condition."

"And what might that be?" she asked, not a little archly.

"Why, I must be allowed to come along too."

The disquieting thing, Angelene decided, was both Rake's appearance and his ease of movement within these very unfamiliar surroundings. He looked as if he belonged among the heirloom pieces of furniture, the molded and gilded high ceilinged rooms, and at the dining-room table draped with linen, lace, gold edged china and thick, heavy silverware.

He didn't speak much. He listened, he watched with that peculiar intensity of his and there was just something about the look of him, particularly in *civilized* clothes, that was just devastating.

The man was positively dangerous, a chameleon. It just seemed impossible to her that five days before they had been fleeing from a burning mountain top and her two murderous brothers.

How did a man like Rake Cordigan, stranded between the world of his childhood and the hell he had made for himself, come to a mansion in New York and ease himself into it as if he had lived there all his life?

It was the clothes against the bronzed skin, that threw his muscular face into high relief.

Or had they just trimmed his hair?

No, it was more than that, and she wasn't sure where it came from: it was a certain fatalistic acceptance of the inescapable.

Of course, a man alone on a mountain repenting of his sins had a lot of time to think and to move into a certain harmony with what his life had been and what it would eventually become. He had had a lot of space to accommodate the unexpected as well—like her, or like being coerced by circumstance into a situation hundreds of miles away from his nominal home and sliding into it with such a quiet dignity that it was hard to imagine he had known anything else.

Even so, they were both walking a precarious line. She had lied to suit her own purposes, and he had played into the lie because she had given him no choice, but now she wasn't sure that she didn't want him to make some excuse and take the next train out of New York and back to Kentucky.

The threat was she still wanted him, and never more so than when she looked across the table at him fingering a crystal goblet full of ruby red wine and moving with charismatic confidence in the world she had coveted.

Or did she feel resentment that he could enter with no penalty whatsoever and make such a success of it?

Or was it that she knew that if he really were what *he* seemed, he would be the personification of everything she wanted?

Nor did she think it was ironic that her observations and questions circled back to the idea of wanting. She knew exactly what exuded that power that enfolded all who sat around the table. She knew his kisses could still enslave her, and that secretly, she wanted all his kisses, and more.

She had to convince him not to come to England with them: it was the only course. He would be a distraction and an interference and he would hate it anyway. If he came, she would hate it too.

She would hate him for the rest of her life.

Chapter 15

The program her grandmother wished them to follow was comprehensive in the extreme and it was to begin the following afternoon, when Mr. Darlington could make arrangements to have one or another of the instructors they had settled on come to the house and begin lessons.

"And you, young man," her grandmother said peremptorily, "you must never again appear in public in that cow suit you arrived in."

"Yes, ma'am," he said obediently, amused but just a little cowed himself: he hated the suit they had stuffed him into and moreover, the stiff collar of the shirt made him feel like a stick figure, and he didn't know how he was going to accustom himself to wearing the like of it every single hour of the day.

And Angelene, strutting around in that satiny puff-skirted concoction with lace and ribbons and bows—that was not his Angel Eyes. That was a doll that her grandmother had bought to play with, an object from which she would pull the last ounce of value for her dollar.

He saw it already: the old lady would twist her and turn her this way and that like a puppet, changing her clothes to suit the occasion, or her personality to fit the purpose.

"And Richard—*Richard?*" Her insistent voice came at him again.

"Ma'am?" Damn, it was time to take stand against this Richard thing before it really tripped him up.

"I want you to call me Grandmother."

He slanted a look at Angelene, whose eyes widened slightly. He wondered what she expected, having handed the invention of him to her grandmother full blown with a name and a history that included her.

"My pleasure, ma'am," he said at length, "but I have to insist that you call me Rake."

"Well, I can't *do* that," she said just trifle testily. "It sounds so—unrefined."

"Maybe it is, ma'am, and maybe *I* am, but that's the name I answer to, and I feel very strongly that it's going to embarrass you mightily when I don't answer in public when someone calls me Richard."

He could see she felt a grudging tinge of admiration that he hadn't backed down, and he wasn't ashamed to say what he was. But she wasn't going to back down either.

"I can't possibly speak that unspeakable name."

"You can try, ma'am."

"Well, I *won't* then."

"Your decision, ma'am."

She was a little discomfitted to see an impassive mask slide down over his eyes, his face, a stolid acceptance of her refusal, and she didn't know quite what to do. In her world, people bartered, they offered alternatives if one were not acceptable. But she had never dealt with savages before, and she thought perhaps they had a different code of ethics, one that had nothing to do with saving face or making concessions.

And then she thought it was probably all Josephine's fault, raising her children in the backwoods of whatever place she had chosen to hide out, and of course they didn't know any better.

"We will need a teacher of etiquette as well," she said to Mr. Darlington, and he nodded sagaciously. The boy *was* intractable, but one wasn't born knowing the social graces; they had to be taught, and preferably by a mother who had been raised the right way and married the right man. A teacher of etiquette was absolutely essential.

"We'll talk about this another time," she said haughtily, rising from the table. "And now, you will excuse me, Angelene my dear, and, I trust, your *brother*. Mr. Darlington, please come with me."

She exited the dining room, her head held high as any queen.

Rake pushed himself back from the table explosively. "I have had enough of this."

"I hope you have," Angelene said accusingly. "I hope you decided you should just pack up your cow suit and go back to Crossville Junction."

He really disliked her in that moment. He remembered everything and she remembered nothing, and the only thing he read in her darkening blue eyes was her devilish intent to pursue the course she had chosen. It wasn't enough to have found her grandmother and an ally.

"Oh no, Angelene. That's not my intention in the least. I intend to *pack in* everything I can get from *our* grandmother and use it to my best advantage."

Oh, she hated that tone of voice—the steely one, the one she thought he had left back in the ruins of the mountain when he had chosen to come with her. It was the outlaw voice, inflexible, unshakeable, and it was permeated with the portent of treachery.

She got up slowly from her seat. "Don't ruin this for me, Rake Cordigan."

"My dear *sister*, don't you ruin it for me."

"I don't trust you," she hissed.

"And who can have faith in you, Angelene? You wear two faces so well now that you have discovered the values your mother rejected. Maybe she was right, Angelene."

"*No!*" She wheeled away from him, unable to even consider his conclusion. "*No!* She was never right and she was always rebellious and you have no right to say that, when you are duplicity itself, Rake Cordigan. *Who* is the impostor in this house?"

"Who made me into one? Who jumped headlong into this over-stuffed house and the empty life of this woman, tell me, and who did it as deliberately and calculatedly as she begged me to come with her and then found the most rational excuse for me to stay."

"You are *crazy*. You could have bowed right out. You could have said—"

"I could have said *mother* needed me, couldn't I? I could have said I was in a tearing rush to get back to Missouri to take care of the daughter that woman abandoned because I'm such a dutiful *son*; and that's what you would have loved me to do, wouldn't you, Angel of Innocence, so you could just gallivant all over the social scene and find some moneyed milksop to marry you."

"That's exactly what I wanted, you savage, and instead I got you and your presence obligating my Grandmother to spend *her* money unnecessarily on *you*."

"Oh, Sister of Angels, how precipitate of you to count on *her* fortune already."

"The only thing I'm counting on is myself, Rake Cordigan. That's all I've ever had to depend on. I got here and I'm going to stay here and you can just go to the devil."

He moved to block her way out of the dining room as she stalked toward the door, her anger palpable and violent.

"*I* got you here, and don't you forget it."

"I would have done it myself if you hadn't interfered."

"You'd be *dead* if I hadn't interfered."

"I'd be *happier*," she jeered.

"Happier dead, or happier if I hadn't interfered, Angelene?"

Dear Lord, she hated the way he said her name. The edge had gone out of his voice and he drew out each syllable lovingly, mockingly. And she hated the question too. If she said one word to him, she would be admitting something, and she didn't want to acknowledge anything about her weeks on the mountain with him.

"Or happier if I hadn't found you out altogether, *sister*, and you could have left the mountain as untouched as the nature around you?"

"I don't know what you're talking about," she said haughtily, trying to brush past him, and knowing, perhaps, he would never let her get away with a statement like that.

She sounded perfect, and she knew it and he appreciated it. She had slipped into the skin of a wealthy young woman with ease.

Maybe the ribbons constricted her breathing, or her brain, or something, he thought, grasping her arm and pulling her back to face his volatile anger.

"You know too well what I'm talking about, Angelene. Your problem really is that I remember your nakedness and I remember your kisses and the carnal caress of your hands on *my* body, and you just don't know whether it will be our little secret or whether everyone else will know too—eventually."

She wrenched her arm away. "Don't be ridiculous, Rake. I never did those things."

"I remember very clearly every last thing you did, Angelene, and so do you."

She felt her face wash with a fine burning heat. Oh yes, she remembered, and it seemed to her it was another lifetime ago, and it had just happened yesterday. She couldn't fix the reality of it in the context of where she was at this moment. The only thing tangible was Rake Cordigan and his animal power and those cool gray eyes that did not miss a thing—that held onto old memories with the tenacity of an enemy who refused to forget.

"We'll strike a bargain," she said resolutely.

"You have nothing to bargain with, Angelene."

"I can refuse to hold up my end of the story that you are my brother."

"But you're the one who lied in the first place," he pointed out, amused. "I think the old lady would toss you out on your ear first, Angelene, if you started rewriting your tale at this late date."

"I'll undermine you somehow, Rake, I swear I will."

"You don't have to do that. All you have to do is kiss me."

"I've done that already," she protested. Look where it got her: weak-kneed and at his mercy, and who needed that when she was trying to deny he had any effect on her whatsoever. "And besides, this is too public: what if that old dragon, Borden, happened down the steps? I think you must be crazy."

"How strange; I think you must be. A kiss, Angelene, to seal the bargain—behind the door if you like, if you're so scared—and I'll lower the light, and no one will ever know but you and me."

"I won't do it."

"As you wish, *sister*."

Oh God, there was that impassive face again. He truly was a man who could only be pushed so far, and she knew, she really knew that tight within him was a savage waiting to be let out. She felt it in that moment, the dangerous edge that both scared and exhilarated her.

"Fine," she said succinctly, ever willing to play with fire. "Wait."

"Yes?"

"Maybe."

"Angelene . . ."

She bit her lip. If it really came down to the truth, she wanted to kiss him. There was something about the situation, about walking that line, pursuing the past and daring the discovery.

"Turn down the light," she whispered.

He leaned over the table and reached for the chandelier which pulled down on a chain for just this very purpose. In a moment, the flames were but little tongues licking at the wicks in the lamp, and he turned to her, his eyes ablaze with the light of the fire.

He looked so strong and fine standing there in the middle of the room, shadowed by the dimmed light, the very shade of the dreams and substance of her memories: the two so very easily merged in the glow of the lowered light, and when he came toward her, as she gently closed the thick molded double doors to the dining room, she was ready to receive him, her body braced for the contact

269

against the thick heavy doors behind her.

The feel of him was thick and heavy against her body, his mouth hard, wet, possessive, perfect. She came to him willingly, seeking him, claiming him, reveling in the heat of his delving, demanding kiss.

Her body streamed with the memories of wanting him, and how she had teased him, taunted him and capitulated to his virile manhood.

She could feel it, hidden, mysterious, lusty, compressed against the crush of layers between them: the petticoats, the steels, the corsets, every impediment a civilized society could invent, when she could remember the pure opulent pleasure of being able to reach for him to touch him whenever, however she wanted.

She groaned, moving restively against the memory; this was not what she had intended, she hadn't meant to raise the spectre of her wanton response to him in a primitive place where no future existed.

She pushed away from him violently. "Enough."

"Never enough," he growled, reaching for her again.

She evaded his searching mouth, and braced her arms against his chest. "Rake . . ."

"I hear your fear, Angelene," he said, abruptly releasing her. "I hear your choices. And so I make mine."

"I made my choices a long time ago," she said, "and nothing is going to change them now." She dared him, by her very words, to say that he could change them, and that he would change them.

But all he said was, "As you wish, Angelene," in that mask-voice that she hated almost as much as the steely one, and it made her wish that not at all.

"It is exactly what I desire," she goaded him, turning and flinging open the door, and flouncing out into the hallway between the parlor and dining room.

Stubborn Angel Eyes, he thought, ignoring the aching in his loins and in his soul. "It is my pleasure to give you precisely what you wish," he said, following her out and into the hallway. "And now, *sister*, I will very properly escort you to your room in the way of a *brother* so you may rest secure in your choices."

The problem was, she decided later as she tossed and turned and could not sleep, that Josie was so far away she hardly represented a threat anymore. But Rake was too near, and her memories were too fine, too close, too compelling.

Her body was too treacherous.

Luxury was too seductive.

Her bed was soft with feather ticking and lustrous cotton sheets and coverlets. Underfoot, the thick carpet felt like a cloud, and across the room, the embers of the fire glowed rosily against the brass firescreen. Her nightgown, the one of cambric with the deep lace collar and cuffs, felt like silk against her skin. The sense of warmth and well-being that permeated the room had as much to do with her grandmother's unequivocal welcome of her as the unaccustomed abundance with which she was surrounded.

And Rake's presence?

She could do nothing about that—now. She had made her bed—and she was resting with her choices.

She was restless with them, shifting from one side to the other the whole night, fraught with the arousal of that one brief kiss, and determined to clamp down on every unseemly memory that threatened her sense of peace and homecoming.

In the morning, she arose early, long before Mary would appear, having slept for an hour or perhaps two, and she paced the floor, and she looked out the window at the gray dawn and let herself be amused by the amount of traffic that was abroad on the side street overlooked by her window.

It was a strange city, a restless city, full of movement and volatility, traps for the innocent, a wonderland for the deserving.

She could hardly remember the desperation of the day before. She could hardly account for how quickly everything had happened, from her moment of decision to board the train to her waking up this morning in her new life of splendor.

What had it been? Just a week, perhaps several days more. She had gone from bathing from a bowl of water in an attic to the opulence of an indoor tub, a maid and a feather bed, and a grandmother who wanted to indulge her every whim.

Or maybe her grandmother's own.

She couldn't let Rake spoil it for her.

She had to be extra careful not to do anything to botch it up for herself.

That resolution lasted exactly ten minutes, till the time she decided to try to draw her own bath because she couldn't think of anything else to do so early in the morning.

He had been there long before she ever thought of bathing, and he had obviously just stepped out of the tub, because he had wrapped the towel loosely around his hips and was just wiping himself down with another one when she pushed open the door.

"Good morning, Sister of Angels," he said calmly, his cool gray gaze raking over her body in the transparently thin nightgown, her pale face, and her edgy hand which kept pushing back the golden fall of her touseled hair.

"I didn't know you were here," she said—lamely, she thought.

"You knew," he said confidently, and she wasn't sure there wasn't some connection between them that had pulled her right to the door at the very moment he was most vulnerable and desirable to her.

But that was not to be considered: she had made her wishes clear.

So why did his brisk rubbing of the towel against his bare bronzed chest arouse something unnameable within her? She stood rooted to that square of tiled floor right inside the door, unable to move in or out.

He knew it; her indecision was as clear as glass to him, and something that did not fool him one bit. All her protestations came down to one thing: she had not moved away from the door and she had made no commitment to go and no decision to stay.

He tossed the one towel onto a chair, and stood looking knowingly at her, his hands placed firmly on his hips.

Her bolting blue gaze fixed firmly there too. There was no helping it. Her unexpected presence affected him visibly and insistently. The heat and the sultry dampness of the room enclosed them, pulled everything tightly around them thick and close.

She had only one overriding sensation: she wanted the mystery of him enveloped within the whole of her. It would always be like this, she would want him this way always, untamed and edged with that contained fury that could erupt at any moment.

It permeated the room, along with a tempering patience that she had never before recognized in him. He was the hunter, stalking the object of infinite desire. He couldn't hide it from her, he could only lure her with the ineffable mystery of it.

She wanted so desperately to reach out and touch him with the freedom of the wanton who had caressed him with such abandon on the mountain. She felt her whole body swell with the very thought of it, and the thought was like a caress, hot and silky against her skin, stroking her into a frenzy of memory and imagination.

Her heated breasts pushed tremulously at the thin material of her gown, aching for a lover's touch.

"I want—" she started, her voice quivering.

He helped her. "I know. Come take me, Angelene."

Her breath caught in her throat. Even after last night—it would ever be the dance between them, that she would deny her desire and never ever be able to hide it from him.

She walked slowly forward. "*Why*, Rake?"

"This is the way of it," he said calmly, and his words melted over her very core, and his perfect acceptance of

273

that statement aroused her desire for him still more.

She needed to touch him, to rip away the one hindrance to her overwhelming desire, and she needed to hold the mystery of him in her hands and to explore the jutting essence of him, to learn thoroughly the whole of his shape, his form, and never to know it in the aftermath and to need it still more.

How much more—how she had missed touching him like this; *this* was not to be denied. This touched the utmost femininity in her, as if there were an unseen link between them. She felt it deeply as she took him into her hands and began to stroke his towering manhood.

This was the way of it.

He kissed her deeply as she caressed him, he thrust himself into her hands, into her mouth, into her soul. He crushed her close to him and he sought the feminine curves of her body in a way he had not done before, wanting her, the essence of her, the thing she sought so avidly in him.

He pushed at the nightgown, he pulled at it, he buried himself in it, nudging urgently between her legs, and finally he managed to remove it, sliding it downward and letting it fall into a pool of virginal white at her feet.

Her perfect taut tipped breasts demanded his kisses, and he had not done this before either; he had not savored the lust in a woman's breasts, and she sagged against him as he sucked on her thrusting nipples and sent a flood of molten pleasure streaming through her body.

He sat her on the chair, the commodious chair where he had tossed the towel, and she picked it up and wrapped it around her shoulders so she could inhale the scent of him as he began a languorous exploration of her body with his mouth and tongue.

This was wholly new—the hot moist trails of excitement flicking all over her body, from the pebble hard tips of her breasts down to her stomach, her thighs, her legs, her feet, he tasted every golden inch of her and she reclined like a queen, giving him everything he wanted, her fingers digging into the towel and holding it tightly against her face.

And then his hungry mouth replaced the towel, avidly demanding her kisses, biting her lips, licking them, seeking her tongue, possessing her with a repressed violence that was nearly matched by her own.

He tilted her body forward and he slipped down onto his knees in front of her, a supplicant to his queen. Immediately, she wrapped her legs around his hips and pressed him toward her urgently.

"I need you now," he muttered hoarsely, and she whispered, "Take me now," and waited for that first shimmering contact of his lusty sex with her moist enveloping femininity.

It was the same as before, incandescent with feeling, as he plunged himself deeply within her and heard her low throaty moan of pleasure. She hugged him close, her legs entwined around him, and she felt him intensely, so thick and hard, so completely and indisputably there. She had held this living heat in her hands as tightly and lovingly as she held him deep within her body, and she didn't know which she loved better. She only knew she wanted his carnal possession of her.

He felt the shift in her, the break and the point at which he knew she wanted the possession, the movement, the pleasure.

He began with a long, slow, driving motion of his body so that she could feel him in all his potent power.

She pressed him closer, deeper, tighter, as if she couldn't bear to let him take her to the culmination, as if she wanted his possession of her to become an endless link between them.

Then the pure passion between them erupted; his body began a furious thrusting, driving movement, a frenzy of volcanic desire surging against her, with her, into her.

Her body went wild, bucking against him, shimmying and writhing in opposition to his movement to find the moment, the center, the crest of the building, mounting feelings; she was in the white-hot glare of it, begging for it, demanding it, exploding with it in a smoldering torrent of silver that glissaded over her straining body in one long streaming gush.

And then it was him, all of him, stretching against her, driving into her relentlessly, twisting, thrusting, rushing to that one last final lunge and his long convulsive culmination.

He held her tightly in the aftermath, with no words. Did they need words with so much else between them? Words were futile in any event; she always denied them, and he didn't need that, not after perfection.

She spent the rest of the early morning hours coiled in her bed alone, thinking of this unspeakable union between them. Then she slept until Mary woke her to take her bath.

"This," her grandmother said by way of curt introduction, "is Miss Crosby, who is to instruct you on the finer points of etiquette. Miss Crosby, may I present my grandson and granddaughter, Mr. Richard—" and she dared him to naysay her, "and Miss Angelene . . . Bellancourt."

They both stopped short in shock. "Grandmother," Angelene said warningly.

"Yes, my dear?" her Grandmother asked. "Surely you remember we discussed this."

"But we didn't discuss *that*," Angelene said pointedly.

"Well, there's no sense in discussing it *now*," her Grandmother said, glossing neatly over the name change as if Angelene's surname had never existed. "In any event, Miss Crosby is an expert in etiquette and fine manners and she will be coming here for the remainder of the week to make sure you are thoroughly grounded in the accepted mode. I'll leave you now. Miss Crosby."

Angelene watched her grandmother trip out of the parlor with mixed emotions, and then she turned to Miss Crosby, who seemed harmless enough.

She was tiny, with flawless skin and wren-brown hair,

but nonetheless she carried an air of authority that was almost daunting.

"Let's begin," Miss Crosby said, forestalling any comment Angelene might have made. "We'll start with Mr. Bellancourt."

"And what can we need to do for Mr. Bellancourt?" Angelene demanded belligerently.

Miss Crosby looked up at her. "Mrs. Bellancourt informs me that you have both arrived from—somewhere west,"—she made it sound so distasteful—"where manners are not in common usage and you need some . . . reeducating, shall we say? Mr. Bellancourt looks mannered enough to me, but perhaps he isn't sure, for example, when a gentleman bows and when he raises his hat. Or how to introduce persons to one another, or whether to introduce the youngest first or the eldest. And perhaps by the same token, the rules of introduction—out west—may differ from the way things are done in polite society. Perhaps you might dance at a party with someone you don't know, Miss Bellancourt, or perhaps you might shake hands with someone when you ought just to bow. These are things that are of prime importance to know.

"So—shall we begin?"

After an hour, it seemed as if they would never end, and Angelene's head was stuffed with useless information on the protocol of dealing with friends and family. The youngest was always presented to the eldest; friends shook hands, but young women should always bow to an unmarried man. She must always have an introduction before dancing with a stranger. She must have cards made up, and in fact, must be introduced by a mutual acquaintance via a card if *she* happened to be the stranger in town.

The wonder of it was that Rake was required to have cards too, cards to be left at the home of women whose acquaintances he wished to make, cards to send ahead and to leave behind on every conceivable occasion and for any situation, and specified hours during which to make these calls and connections. During these times, he was required to keep possession of his hat, as she was allowed to keep on her gloves, and they could not stay for longer than twenty minutes during the day and longer at night.

Protocol at night was less formal but the leaving and responding to cards was not. There was an etiquette for every situation, from the new neighbor in town, to visitors of friends and how to receive them, to the precise time in which to return a call from someone unknown to you.

Then of course, there was the discourse on proper conversation, which excluded everything from boasting to gossip, and required keeping one's temper at all times, and never talking about work, medicine, domestic concerns, fomenting arguments—and that was only in private.

There were a dozen rules and more for behavior in public, at the library, when travelling, in church, and even at home.

That was the first hour.

Afterwards, Mr. Darlington came, and he and Mrs. Bellancourt drew Angelene and Rake directly into the small parlor with the bay window where the table was set with four chairs and laid over with a white linen cloth and several decks of cards.

"Grandmother . . . !"

"Not now, dear. We have no time to lose. We have to start teaching you the finer points of several games of cards. Vernon has agreed to be our fourth, isn't it delightful? How did you find Miss Crosby?"

"She knows our name is Bellancourt," Angelene said dangerously. "Why is that, Grandmother?"

"Well—it sounded *nicer* than Scates. I sincerely believe that name grates on the ear, and you know society people like grand-sounding names. Now look," she scurried into one of the chairs, "we'll just go through the rules quickly before the dancing master comes for your first lesson—"

278

"Amelia, slow down," Mr. Darlington said, and to Angelene and Rake, "Sit down, children."

Angelene looked at Rake. His face wore that mask expression again, and by his silence and his acquiescence, he was the most polite person at the table.

Angelene sat down unhappily, and her disconsolate movement drew his eyes right to her. "I can see you are enjoying this enormously, *sister*," he said, a horrible touch of irony in his tone. He knew exactly what she enjoyed and it had nothing to do with manners or names or any of the trappings she so ardently desired.

But she had dealt the cards by coming here, and now she was faced with Mr. Darlington's eager little hands shuffling one deck, and her grandmother's avid voice explaining the rules of whist, euchre and bezique. She was hopelessly lost after the first hand and the explanation involving partners and leading and trumps and tricks and things she had never heard of before in her life.

Her grandmother looked at her speculatively, as if she were hoping desperately her granddaughter was not deficient somehow, and then she shrugged. "Well, after all, it's your first exposure to these things, I can't expect you'll comprehend them instantly," but Angelene saw immediately that she expected exactly that.

"Josephine loved to play whist," her Grandmother said, her voice tinged with nostalgia. "I know you'll learn it in reasonably good time because Richard has already caught onto the how of it."

"Oh, R—Rake was in the habit of playing cards in his youth," Angelene said spontaneously, and bit her lip. She didn't have to account for it, and he probably had, but that wasn't for her to say. It was his story now and he said nothing, as was his way, and she drowned in her own inventiveness and wished they had never come downstairs that morning.

Somehow the magic dissipated in the vastness of the high-ceilinged rooms. Even the intimacy of the card table was intimidating, and her grandmother no less so.

"Well, let's try it again," the old lady said brightly,

dealing the cards.

Angelene suffered. She hated the cards, and couldn't keep one rule straight in her head, and she wasn't sure if it was because of her morning of delights, or because her grandmother had tossed away her name the way she would throw away a tub full of water.

"No more cards," Rake said, when it became obvious that Mrs. Bellancourt and Mr. Darlington were entrenched for the afternoon at the card table.

"No dancing," Angelene protested, "not today. It's too much."

"Don't be silly, Angelene—just an hour, that's all. The waltz. You must learn to do the waltz, and who better to partner you than Richard. It's perfect. M. Ronet will arrive within the hour, and then we can have lunch."

M. Ronet was short, slender, pale, with a bushy mustache and a gentle manner.

"The correct position now," he directed in his thick Gallic accent after demonstrating exactly how Rake was to hold Angelene, and *he* had never felt so unmanly in his entire life as he did standing there, an arm's length away from her, his right hand awkwardly touching her waist, his left clutching her right hand.

"And so—" M. Ronet demonstrated. "Left foot behind—one, right foot now, *two*, right foot, three, right foot, four—Mr. Bellancourt, *what* are you doing?"

"They are hopeless," he reported later to Mrs. Bellancourt, and she sighed. "Did I say three months, Vernon? Perhaps we should not travel at all until next year."

"You didn't expect us to be *so* uncivilized that we had never played a game of cards—"

"Except I have," Rake put in maliciously.

"—or had gone out on a dance floor before, Grandmother, isn't that it?" Angelene demanded when M. Ronet had finally withdrawn for the day.

"I suppose so," her Grandmother conceded woefully. "I just took it for granted that Josephine must have—"

"Josephine didn't," Angelene snapped. "She just didn't. I wished she had, but she *didn't*."

280

Her Grandmother heard the overriding anger in her voice. "Oh please, Angelene, don't—don't be cross with me. I truly only want the best for you. There's plenty of time. I know it will all make sense to you once you become accustomed to it."

And it was true: within a week, she was faring better at the cards, although they had assayed no other games but whist, and she had some of the finer points of visiting etiquette firmly in her head at Miss Crosby's insistence, because that probably would be her first bridge to cross. She and Rake looked like a pair of rag dolls bumping around the dance floor, to M. Ronet's discouraged dismay.

"They must learn to dance," Mrs. Bellancourt decreed. "*That* is what I'm paying you for."

"Madame," he bowed himself out, his determination renewed. And every afternoon: "One, two, three, four; one, two, three, four . . . Mr. Bellancourt, *what* are you doing?"

It had been a week and there wasn't a moment of time when her grandmother did not have control over what they were doing. The smoldering memory of that past morning lay like a starry cloud stretched out between them. One, two, three, four; one, two, three, four.

"This is impossible," Rake said disgustedly. "A man's body just can't move this way . . ."

No, it could only move *one* way . . .

Every morning in that ensuing week, they were expected to join Angelene's grandmother for the obligatory carriage ride in the park, a ritual devoted to seeing and being seen.

"I do want my friends to comment on the fact that I am abroad again, and to wonder who these two handsome children are. Trust me, my dears, the cards will start to arrive."

Oh, the cards, the omnipresent, symbolic cards . . .

And they stopped every day to view the lawn tennis, which was a daily ongoing event in the park.

"How do they hit those balls?" Angelene murmured,

hardly able to envision herself holding a racket and swatting at anything, let alone something as *bouncy* as a ball.

"My dear, you will learn, of course. It's necessary."

Too much was necessary. The riding stables were located in the park as well. "But," her Grandmother said, "I'll assume Richard does ride, so we'll have to make arrangements for Angelene only. Do you ride, Richard?"

Rake's expression went stony. "No, he does not, but Rake does."

One, two, three, four.

"Music," her Grandmother pronounced one morning. "You said? You play a little?"

"Very little," Angelene confessed.

"No matter. There is no more charming sight than a young lady's graceful hands moving over the keys of a piano. Love songs only, of course, and you have only to learn a couple of them by rote. There must be a music teacher somewhere . . . a note to Mr. Darlington—"

Mr. Darlington was an unending fund of sources for every singular activity that her grandmother considered would be of social benefit to Angelene.

"I think she lays awake nights thinking of some new event of 'inestimable value'," Angelene said at breakfast one morning.

"I find nothing of value in tracking around a wooden floor in time to some music," Rake said dampingly.

"But my dear Richard," Mrs. Bellancourt said, coming into the room, "every young man from good family is prepared to take a lady onto the dance floor."

"I am *not* a young man from a good family," Rake contradicted darkly. "You cannot take a man in a cow suit and make him into a young man from a good family, ma'am. Although you could just let him be what he is."

"Don't be silly, Richard. You will be meeting the finest families in England. Of course you have to be a young man from a good family. There is no other way."

So now, every afternoon around tea-time, Mr. Darlington joined them for a round of whist, and slowly but surely, he introduced euchre, bezique, cassino, poker—just for the fun of it, but Angelene was not to tell her grandmother who did not have the patience to sit through an hour of play with two rank amateurs. Anyway, poker was more fun.

They travelled out in the morning, Angelene each day wearing some new confection of a dress, and Rake stiffly uncomfortable in either of his two alternating suits and scratchy cotton shirts.

Her grandmother pointed out the sights around the city, things about which they were supposed to be knowledgeable, everything from the best place to shop for ready-made clothes (McCreery's, of course) to the fashionable homes of the most wealthy, her neighbors, on Fifth Avenue: the Haight house, the Stewart residence, the Grinnell mansion which had been transformed into the ultra-fashionable Delmonico's Restaurant; they toured everywhere from the ongoing construction of the new elevated train at Columbus Avenue to its famous snaking s-shaped curve down near Coenties Slip. They drove on Broadway and down to Union Square; they looked at the new telephone building, and the grandiose hotels, the Metropolitan Concert Hall, the Pierpont Morgan House, the Studio Building—the first of its kind, housing for artists, and, said Mrs. Bellancourt, "a complete waste of money." They visited a multitude of churches: St. Patrick's Cathedral, the Church of the Transfiguration, St. Bartholomew's, and Trinity. They toured past the Stock Exchange, and marveled at the massive building that housed the Post Office, and flew past the Society Library and the Astor Library and the New York Historical Society and the Museum of Natural History, and they took refreshments at a place nearby known as the Dairy.

They saw all this and more over the course of the succeeding days, and the sheer magnitude of both the city and its cultural and public spaces left them awestruck.

Angelene glowed at the excitement of it; Rake glowered. "This is not a way for *civilized* people to live," he said pointedly, but it didn't matter: it was the way for Angelene to live at this moment and her *brother* gave serious thought to returning to his burned-out mountain top in Kentucky.

He did not know how he could take another moment of instruction from the precious M. Ronet or the monumental rectitude of Angelene's grandmother, who seemingly had gone mad with power with two untutored human beings at her disposal.

She couldn't bear to see anyone sit still, even for a moment. She ran them through the hours, day and night, until Angelene and he were exhausted and could do little else but collapse in bed. He felt Angelene moving further and further away from him, and he felt himself fast reverting to the things that he knew, the things with which he was in harmony, and discarding the trappings with which Amelia Bellancourt and Angelene sought to entangle him.

When he came downstairs to breakfast one morning in his *cow suit*, he thought Angelene's grandmother might faint.

"I'm sure I told you I never wanted to see you in that—that—"

"*Cow suit*, ma'am," he supplied.

"—again, Richard."

"Rake, ma'am, and I'm sure I'm getting pretty fed up with those starched collars and tight-fitting tailor-suits. I'll just have my coffee, ma'am, and then I'll be going."

"*Outside?*" Mrs. Bellancourt asked faintly.

"Yes, ma'am."

"Someone will *see* you."

"But they won't know me, ma'am. You can be sure of that."

"Out of *my* house," Mrs. Bellancourt said, her voice registering stronger as she pushed to get back in control.

He reached for his coffee cup, not daring to look at Angelene, but he was fully aware of her, all pink and blonde, band-box beautiful, her blue gaze holding him terribly accountable for upsetting her grandmother so.

"No one will see, ma'am. You told me yourself, no one is in town in August: they'll all go to Saratoga or Newport—at least," he added maliciously, "everyone who *counts.*"

"Well, he learned *something,*" Angelene's grandmother said waspishly as they heard the front door close.

"He'll be back," Angelene said, but she wasn't sure she felt as confident of that as she sounded. She felt bereft: he could be going around the block, or heading straight up to that monstrous building with the railroad lines, and she would never know which, not until later, and she didn't know how she was going to concentrate on *anything* today.

But there was still the indefatigable Miss Crosby and her endless rules to deal with this morning, a brief little learn by rote piano lesson. Instruction was now added in the various sports in which a lady was able to participate: she was now to conquer lawn tennis, croquet, archery, and to know the rudiments of bowls, golf, and cricket for "conversational purposes." She didn't need Rake's presence to proceed with that.

M. Ronet was cancelled for the day, and Mr. Darlington patiently went through the rules of the card games with her again, and so by dinner time, she was ready to take a nap, and missed Rake sorely.

How could he sit still while her overbearing grandmother tried to turn him into an effete young man of "good family"?

He would always be what he was and not what she wanted him to be. It made Angelene wonder whether her fairy wand of money could really change her as well.

But then, change wasn't the point. What she was learning were the things she needed to know to attract a man of substance. Another couple of lessons, a few outings among her Grandmother's few friends who did stay in town, and she would be ready, surely she would be ready.

*   *   *

He came back very late that night, and a disapproving Borden admitted him to the house.

"May I draw your bath, sir?" the butler asked disdainfully. Rake headed for the connecting hallway to the guest wing.

"No, you may draw yourself away," Rake said as unkindly as he could, not even bothering to hide his dislike.

He took the winding staircase two steps at a time, and let himself into his room.

He was not happy to be returning to this house; he could have continued wandering on, he could have taken a year and eventually come back to the place where he started.

But without Angelene. Always without Angelene.

He pulled off his shirt and tossed it onto the bed. *Cow suit*—no one had looked at him twice as he wandered the city until he finally came to the park of the parks, the place of the lawn tennis and trees and ostentatious carriages parading through the natural vistas corrupted by *civilization*.

He did not belong here either, and he was positive there was not one place in the whole of *civilization* where he would fit in.

And if that were true, it didn't matter what happened in this house: he would never fit here either, but he would be tolerated for Angelene's sake, perhaps even for Josie's sake because he was supposed to be one of her first-born twin sons.

But never for himself. He had no self here—or rather he was becoming aware of a self he never knew existed, the one who was attracted not so much by all this wealth and luxury as by the comfort that wealth could command.

He understood the lure of the things that surrounded him: the warmth of the fire, a pitcher of hot water to bathe his body, the softness of a bed or a carpeted floor, the surety of having these things on the following day.

The certainty of having Angelene.

He couldn't face another minute without seeing her, and he was thankful for the isolation of guest wing as he made his way across the landing to her door.

He knocked once, twice, three times before he shoved in the door and entered an empty room.

Every trace of her presence was gone. There was not a dress in the armoire, a brush on the nightstand, a nightgown laid across the bed, or a towel on the washstand.

She had been whisked away as completely as if she had never occupied the room. And so quickly. He wondered why so quickly, in the space of the day that he had chosen to roam.

He went downstairs slowly, not loath to confront Borden in spite of their mutual antipathy, and as usual, the butler was about, and appeared instantly the moment he sensed Rake's presence.

"Miss Angelene," Rake said.

"Miss Angelene has been removed to the family bedroom wing," Borden said haughtily, his eyes purposefully avoiding looking at Rake's bare chest.

"Thank you, Borden." He knew exactly what had happened: the old lady had offered Angelene Josie's old room and Angelene had had no choice but to accept.

He started to move toward the main staircase, and then he felt Borden's eyes behind him, watching him, daring him to mount the steps to the family bedroom floor, the outsider who was not yet considered family.

He pivoted suddenly, abruptly, quick as a panther, deadly as a snake if he had had a weapon in his hand, and he caught the butler in the act of spying on *him*.

A man did not play with his prey in the elegant confines of a mansion on Fifth Avenue. He waited until the thing he stalked realized its danger and scuttled away.

And slowly, painstakingly, he climbed the inner stairs to the bedroom floor to find Angelene.

She was feeling abandoned and trapped, and she was pragmatic enough to know that she had created the situations that precipitated the feelings.

Josie's room wasn't exactly a shrine, but she was sure her Grandmother had changed nothing about it since Josie ran off. It was the room of a spoiled young woman, frilled, puffed and bowed to the extreme.

She liked the guest room better, and more than that she liked being across the hall from Rake's solid presence. Now there was nothing, not even the assurance that Rake would ever return.

She had to grapple with what might happen if he never came back. And she didn't know why the thought of it annoyed her when it was exactly what she had wanted. Now she could continue her social lessons, her grandmother would take her to England, she would wear beautiful clothes and visit famous places and meet elegant people, and sooner or later she would be introduced to a man whom she could love. The end of the story was a glorious wedding, a fairy tale ending, with Josie locked out beyond the gates.

That was exactly what she desired: her evil witch of a mother destroyed by the man whom she would ultimately wed.

Well fine, but none of that had happened yet. The best she could enumerate was a wardrobe full of luscious dresses, and a passing comprehension of how to waltz, play cards, mangle two popular sentimental songs on her grandmother's grand piano, and a hazy understanding of the elaborate rules of etiquette that governed her Grandmother's society.

Not an enormous amount of accomplishment in the space of three or four weeks. She wondered if the fault lay within her, if she could even be educated in the most minimal arts needed to catch a husband.

Her grandmother had been extremely patient, and Mr. Darlington both accommodating and humorous, but warning her that there was a great deal left yet for her to learn.

She wondered why she had thought it would be as easy as coming to her grandmother's, asking to be taken in and then thinking her grandmother would just introduce her to the cream of her wealthy friends, among whom she had been sure there would have been *one* eligible, powerful man.

Even dreams had a price, and she wondered just when she would be asked to pay.

She didn't like Josie's room at all, and she wondered why her Grandmother had insisted she occupy it when she had protested she was perfectly comfortable in the guest room.

"But you are family now," her Grandmother had said, "and I want you close to me."

Angelene didn't know how much closer she could get—and she had been faintly alarmed by the sight of the connecting door between her room and her Grandmother's room right next door. She was almost afraid to make a sound lest she wake her Grandmother.

It was easier just to lay in bed and think her restive thoughts then to raise the gaslight and try to sit and read one of the ever-present magazines with which all the bedrooms seemed to be supplied.

She missed the privacy of the guest wing.

She missed Rake.

Damn him.

She should have known she couldn't demand that he stuff himself into the lifestyle that she so ardently yearned for. Still, his effort had been impressive, and even her grandmother had admitted that he *looked* the part.

She wondered if it were enough to look the part.

She fell asleep, dreaming of a life-size rag doll moving among the elite of society, dressed in one of the expensive creations that hung in her closet, propelled by a long wand held in the hand of her properly approving Grandmother.

She felt the mattress depress as the doll was set down in bed by the Grandmother after she had removed the beautiful gown and dressed it in a lacy muslin nightgown.

She heard her name—Grandmother approved . . .

Her name more urgently now, and someone's gentle hand shaking her, and she woke in terror as a hand clamped over her mouth.

"Angelene!"

Rake's urgent voice in her ear calmed her.

"You're back," she whispered as she pulled his hand from her mouth. "How did you get up here?"

"How do you think?" he asked lightly, his voice barely above a breath in her ear.

"You *crawled*," she hissed.

"Just to show you, Sister of Angels, that a man can exist successfully in many worlds—and still remain himself."

His tone, even hardly above a whisper, was chastising, a Greek chorus in her ear. "But I will not give your grandmother cause to question you. I will play the thing through," he added softly, and she went limp with the release of all her fear.

It broke right back again. Like a huge pounding wave as she heard her grandmother's voice through the connecting door.

"Angelene? *Angelene?* Is something wrong? Did I hear voices?"

"Oh lord, Rake—"

"Shhh . . ."

She felt him slip away from her, his enfolding warmth gone, a comforter pulled away from her abruptly, completely.

The door opened, and her grandmother stood in the threshold, a candle in hand held high over her head. "What's the matter, Angelene?"

She clenched her fists to calm her shaking body. The flickering candlelight lit up the room and outlined ghostly shadows in the corners. And *where* was Rake? If her Grandmother saw him here, now . . .

She eased herself into a sitting position, and pulled the cover up to her breast. "I'm fine, Grandmother. You need not have troubled to get out of bed."

"I thought I heard a noise."

"I'm sure you were wrong."

"Borden tells me Richard has come back."

She didn't miss a thing, her canny old grandmother. She couldn't show one whiff of emotion at that news. "I told you," she said finally.

"I will defer to your superior knowledge of his character," her grandmother said tartly, "but he can never take himself off like that again. It is very important that he present a united front with you. He is most attractive—except for that skin—and you are beautiful, and if you both heed my wishes, your social success will be assured."

"Perhaps," Angelene ventured, "*he* never wished for social success."

"Nonsense. How could anyone come out from the wilderness into the comfort and refinement of my home and not wish to emulate it? Look at you, my dear. You have yearned for it for years, and you have become an apt pupil, even though I have a feeling that all those social graces will be superseded by the sheer fact of your beauty. Sometimes that is enough. But that is another lesson for another day. Go back to sleep, my dear. I'm sorry I disturbed you."

The candle receded, the door closed softly, and beyond it, Angelene heard the faint rustlings that indicated her Grandmother had gone back to bed.

And she waited . . . and she waited, and then finally, painstakingly, she climbed down from the bed to look for Rake.

She hated the dark, she hated this room that she hardly knew, and above all, she hated the fact that her Grandmother slept with an eagle ear right next door.

She got down on her knees, to grope around the bed, and she almost fainted when his hand shot out from under the dust ruffle to grasp her arm.

He pulled at her urgently, and she couldn't protest; she shimmied her way under the bed to join him.

It was a close, tight fit. The mattress itself was perhaps

291

two and a half feet from the floor, and it was surrounded by the enshrouding drape of the white eyelet ruffle, and underlaid by a section of thick oriental carpeting.

It was a world apart from the elegance and civility of the bedroom. It was a primitive little cave, a fitting secret shelter for the most elemental of men.

He pulled her tightly, compellingly, wrapping his arms around her so that she was pressed uncompromisingly against the whole length of his body, his mouth settling on hers so that every inch of him was in urgent erotic contact with her.

Her whole body stiffened and stretched luxuriously as she aligned herself against him, and she opened her mouth eagerly to take his kiss.

His hands began to move, skimming downward to feel the curve of her body beneath the thin nightgown, and then downward still, to gather the skirt and pull it up so that his questing fingers could stroke the silky skin beneath.

Her arms twined around his neck, and she surrendered to the opulent feel of his hands exploring her, cupping her buttocks, pulling her closer to him, stroking her there in a different and arousing way, lifting her leg to drape it over his hip so that he could slide tighter and tighter against her sensual heat.

She shuddered with excitement as his hands possessed her now, seeking her from behind, from below, demanding her nakedness, coaxing her, pleasuring her as he found the haven of her velvet fold.

And his kisses, his hot wet alluring kisses claimed her, enthralled her, demanded everything from her, everything she was greedy to give him.

And they lay like this, in a hot tight connective union, savoring each other, feeling each other, no words between them—only his hands, his avid tongue, his thick hard surging manhood jutting out from his groin pressing so tightly against hers.

She loved feeling him there, powerfully contained against her, knowing that in one potent thrust he could possess her, and that she wanted him to, and she wanted him exactly as it was now, possible, exciting, intensely erotic, all sense and feel and knowledge of what was to come.

And it would come; there was so much time in a cave, even one of their own devising. There was time for him to play with her, to linger over his minute exploration of whatever part of her intrigued him, time to thoroughly examine, caress, kiss her pebble hard nipples, to suck and pull at the pure feminine mystery of them and to revel in her fierce primitive response to the tug of his greedy lips.

The hand exploring her back and buttocks clutched her more tightly against him, and she groaned deep in her throat, a long voluptuous sigh of pure pleasure from deep in the center of her being.

She arched herself against him luxuriously, loving the hard pull of his mouth on her nipples, and her body squirmed in an erotic mating dance to the lush sucking motion of his lips, and the hand that caressed her buttocks followed the movement of her as she enticed him to finally possess her.

Her own hands reached for him then, frantically pulling and unstringing the ties at the front of his deer-skin pants, until the throbbing length of him was within her grasp.

He drew in a harsh sibilant breath as her hands surrounded him. He would never get over the greedy way her hands always took him—both together, one above, one below, fully and eagerly possessing his length, wanting it with such a hunger to feel him and know him, and almost, it seemed, to never let him go.

He moved reluctantly to her mouth, claiming it again, urging on her shaking excitement of having the freedom to play with him yet again, crushing her against him almost violently as he felt the first vestiges of his own surrender.

It was too soon, or maybe it wasn't. He had waited too long to possess her again. His body constricted with the pulsating effort of restraining himself, and he whispered, he *had* to whisper, "Now, Angelene."

And she lifted her leg, bracing her foot against his lean hip, and she guided him softly, smoothly, deliciously home.

And they lay that way, connected now, wound around in each other's arms, legs, mouth to mouth, in a ravishing union of pure oneness.

"Now, Angelene," he sighed against her mouth when the perfection of possession turned to erotic urgency that could not be denied.

"Take me," she whispered, filling his mouth and his desire with her words, and she gave him her mouth, and she shifted her body, and deep in their man-made cave, in the sultry hot dark of the night, seductively invited him to drive his desire home.

He had never had her like this before. Everything became touch—wet, hot, urgent, at one, together, separate, distinctive; her body writhed with a new taut perception of him taking her, the length of him driving tightly and deeply into her, her body feeling every long hard inch of him in a totally new way.

They lay side to side, her leg propped against his lunging hips, and she was totally open to him, open to everything, to his hands, his thrusting force, to his mouth so hard and unquenchable on her own.

It was his hands; they reached, they stroked, they probed, they clutched her wriggling, gyrating body to center her, to feel her, to capture the movement of her sex somehow, and the thought of it excited her all over again.

His strong pumping body could not get enough of her. He felt a primitive savage need to have her always a part of him, claimed by him in a way so that no other man would ever want her.

And he knew, on this night of his capitulation to her desire and her dream, that he might never have her again.

It was all he could do to keep the howl of rage he felt in his gut from breaking into the air. He pushed it with every last ounce of strength into his torrid possession of

294

her, taking her, feeling her, wanting her with a shocking passion that he could only reveal in his potent conquest of her.

And she reveled in it, and the lush mystery of her body's response to the one pure male part of him that she could claim so completely and inexorably.

He became a part of her and she of him, and she knew this was the most inexplicable mystery of all. The wonder of it crowned her passion, and his tumultuous thrusts echoed resonantly in her and the rippling sensations began to build.

She loved this part, where everything was connected to and for the purpose of exacting those crystalline feelings of sensual release. She centered herself around them, girding herself as his powerfull thrusts guided her irrevocably toward the one pure moment of incandescent surrender.

She held onto him tightly, she wound herself around him, she urged him to take her, to give to her, to claim her, and in the last thick voluptuous moment before the peak, she even thought she loved him.

And then he twisted himself into her in one deep jolting clamorous thrust, and he pushed her over the peak into a fathomless paroxysm of culmination that wracked her body in a storm of churning sensation.

She couldn't stop; he silenced her moans by pinching her nose and still her body shimmered with eddying erotic emotion that just would not stop.

She clung to him, she pulled him closer and closer as if she could tuck the whole of him away deep within her femininity to know he would always be there. She sought his mouth, she devoured his kisses, she never wanted to let him go.

And he held her, as if he could keep her always, and slowly he eased himself into the unrelenting drive toward his own release of passion.

Ever so slowly at first, aware of the tight rippling feeling within her that was echoed in himself, aware that she was spent, but that she wanted the last wringing sense of his pleasure to be part of her own, he gave himself up to the primitive possession of her body, wholly and fully, with all his soul.

And then it was quiet, wet, thick with the scent of sex and repletion, edged with the danger of sounds that could have been heard, and the creeping menace of dawn and a household staff that knew nothing of the privacy of a man and a woman.

He held her, and she melted against him, reluctant to let him go.

"I *must* go," he breathed against her ear, and she agreed, and she hated feeling him slide away from her, and out from under the bed like a sinuous cat, silent, sure, keenly aware of every lurking danger . . .

She peeked out from under the dust ruffle, and he was nowhere to be seen, and she marveled at the quickness of him and the silence, as she slowly crawled out from under the bed and tried not to make a sound.

Her nightgown was up around her neck, and she felt a stinging feeling on her right thigh where she had lain naked against the nubby wool of the carpet.

Carefully, she slipped the nightgown down over her shoulders and inserted her arms into the sleeves. She could feel it was a wrinkled mess, and she knew she had to get into the bed before anyone saw her.

She got to her knees and crept onto the mattress, wincing as the springs underneath creaked slightly as her weight depressed it, and she eased herself onto her stomach, and reached backward to pull up the cover.

A minute later, the door burst open from the hallway, and a cheery voice said, "It's Mary, miss, with your breakfast. It's six o'clock, miss, and Madame asked for us to get an early start—so I'll just draw your bath, and you can choose a dress, and then we'll be ready in no time . . . Miss?"

Chapter 16

"I'm glad you came to your senses," Mrs. Bellancourt said testily the next morning when Rake put in his first appearance late at breakfast. "And I must say that suit becomes you."

"Thank you, ma'am. But I must warn you that I'm here only for Angelene's sake. Isn't that so, Sister of Angels?"

She lifted her golden head to meet his cool gray gaze. Oh, he was playing the thing to the hilt this morning: the emotion of the night before in him had been neatly set aside, while she could not forget a moment of it.

"What a charming endearment," her grandmother said. "Come, sit down. There is much to discuss."

Too much—and all of it entailed a new program of activities to be added to the ones that Angelene was slowly mastering. The next was riding. "Very important, my dear. Those English adore their horses, and love the hunt, so you must at least be able to keep up with them. I will assume that Richard is capable of doing that."

"Rake will be very happy to demonstrate," he said equably, determined that the old lady was not going to get the best of the name war.

"No thank you, Richard. You probably ride wearing those nasty cow leggings that all those western people seem to sport. I would really prefer you to go with Angelene and to make sure everything is as it should be."

"My pleasure, ma'am," he said. "Just how should it

297

be, to meet with your satisfaction?"

"Well, Angelene should have the services of a competent instructor; she is to ride sidesaddle in the accustomed way, and she should have at least a half-hour's instruction before she attempts to even mount."

"I see," Rake said, keeping his eyes firmly away from Angelene, who was squirming with annoyance with the way her Grandmother was treating her—as if she weren't perfectly capable to seeing to the very things she had outlined to Rake.

"Now, Angelene, you must change. I believe the riding suit came with your clothes, and then Borden will bring the carriage around and the driver will take you to the park."

Angelene stamped upstairs to change from her light-weight morning gown of patterned batiste, her ears straining to catch any piece of the conversation between her grandmother and Rake.

Maybe it was just silence. Maybe they were both so strong-willed, they could never have a conversation without clashing.

Maybe, in spite of last night, Rake hated her for forcing him into this position, and maybe it was solely his skewed sense of honor that was keeping him here now.

She couldn't believe that; she couldn't forget the previous night, and she had the strong feeling that neither could he, that maybe something had changed between them because of it.

Nevertheless, she was still determined to pursue her course, and if it meant hoisting herself onto some restive pony and prancing down a sylvan track, she would do it. She still had nothing to lose, and everything to gain—except that sometimes, she still had the eerie feeling that her grandmother was spending her money on the long-gone Josephine, and not *her*.

But she could still be seduced by the midnight blue riding dress that fit like a dream, with its tight bodice and eye-catching discs of buttons marching firmly down the front; these sleeves were close-fitting with no shoulder puffs, and the skirt was long and voluminous and without the ubiquitous steels to give her the freedom of movement to sit the horse. With it, she wore matching leather gloves and a delicious menswear-inspired top hat which Mary secured tightly on her wound and bound blonde hair.

She knew the result was stunning; the color of her eyes intensified against the deep blue of the costume, and her skin seemed almost translucent, her neck long and swan-like with the heft of her hair bound into a topknot and tucked under the saucy hat.

Even her Grandmother's eyes lit up as she marched grandly down the stairs, her riding crop tucked under her arm, and her boots making an authoritative statement as she walked across the parquet floor.

She couldn't look at Rake, but she had the skimming impression that he had changed too into something more informal and more apt for a casual morning.

Her grandmother had overlooked nothing. Everything was ready upon their arrival, and Rake had only to stand aside and let the supercillious instructor take over. He amused himself by going through the stable and examining the horseflesh available there, and finally, longingly, choosing one for himself to ride and boldly telling the stable master to put the change on Mrs. Bellancourt's bill.

After that, while Angelene struggled with the intricacies of maintaining her balance and her pride on the odious sidesaddle of conformity, he was able to take a long, revivifying ride into the forest of the park, veering away, despite the cautions, from the main track, and exploring all over its vast public environs.

He looked like a majestic centaur, appearing magically on the rim of a hill or galloping with abandon across the greensward of the sheepmeadow pasture.

He felt, when he finally reined in and returned to the riding track, as if he had reclaimed some little piece of himself from his past.

Angelene, however, could claim nothing; she hated

the side saddle and was still wrestling with it when he returned to the stable. "I hate this thing!" she stormed at him. "Why should I have to hook my leg over instead of just straddling the thing?" she demanded belligerently. "Who would know anyway?"

"But then you wouldn't be sitting to the side, ma'am, and that is most indelicate," her instructor, one Mr. MacNeill, said chidingly.

"This is impossible," Angelene said fretfully. "Why can't a woman ride like you do, Rake? That makes much more sense to me."

"Nothing concerning what women can do makes sense to me," Rake said, consolingly. "I think it's time to give up this lesson for today."

"But the hour isn't over," MacNeill protested, "and she hasn't taken the horse a foot from where we started."

Rake tactfully dismounted and handed his own horse over to a hovering stable boy. "Come, Angelene, it's not so difficult."

"You don't *know*," she said grittily. "I have to bend my leg and hook it into this thing, and it's the most uncomfortable position I've ever been in."

"Oh, surely not," Rake contradicted. "I can think of a couple of others, can't you, Sister of Angels? What couldn't an angel do, if she tried, Angelene?"

"I'm no angel, and *you* well know," she retorted.

"No, but you were the one who arranged this fantasy, Angelene, and now you must keep on with it. Just do it," he said, meeting her eyes meaningfully, "and remember I am watching, and I am aware of the stretch and the strain of your body, and nothing can be hidden from me."

Her face washed over with a faint tinge of color. He remembered, oh yes, he remembered, he just kept it close to his heart until he knew she needed to hear it. She squared her shoulders as he moved away from her, twisted her body and wound her leg around the saddle post and inserted it in the stirrup in proper form.

"That's the way, Miss," MacNeill said encouragingly. "Now the horse has stood patiently still for you, so you

x

300

must command him, just as I showed you. Just tell him what you want him to do, Miss."

She sent a lancing sensual look toward Rake from under the tilted brim of her hat, and then gently and calmly and firmly, she nudged her mount forward, in command and in control.

The ride exhilarated her, and she understood the necessity of learning the skill and all the possibilities that could open to her—among them, riding freely with Rake, alone and through the park.

This twenty or so minutes of privacy they shared in the carriage travelling to and from the park was not nearly enough, not after last night.

Yet he was the calm one, and she was ablaze with the memory and triumph. "I want everything, Rake. Why can't I have everything?"

"You can't. It isn't the way of things, and every decision has its consequences, and with every action, there is a price to be paid."

"I'd pay any price gladly if only you would kiss me," she whispered, reaching across the space between their seats to touch him.

"The choices are not pretty, Angelene: a moneyed and perhaps tilted husband or poverty and life on a mountain. You negated it once before, how can you be sure it is what you would choose now?"

"But I'm not choosing that," she said poutingly, "I'm choosing *you*."

"*That* is me, Angelene, in spite of appearances and in spite the circumstances. So, you will go through with your original plan because you will never get more than than that from me."

She recoiled as if he had slapped her. His words were not kind, and *they* negated the choice she had made the night before. She didn't know if she could forgive him for this self-righteous male rejection: it hurt, and it bothered her that in spite of her feelings and what she had brought him to, she might only be the equivalent of his "town woman" after all.

Of course, she had introduced him to the possibilities beyond the mountain. A man like this, one who had run from his past, and expended his rage to escape his future, knew nothing of this kind of life, whereas she at least had been immersed in the fairy-tale telling of it by Josie, whose potent renunciation of it had only fueled her own desire to have it.

She wondered if he even knew *what* England was, or whether he had ever seen an ocean, and even though she had not, she felt as if she had had worlds more experience than he just through Josie's resentful eyes.

And so those were the choices: returning to everything she had known, or going forward to conquer a new and exciting world. She could see there really was no choice. She could never go back, nor relinquish what she had been given.

The thing that had to be let go was *him*, and well he knew it. Maybe he had made it easy for her, she didn't know, but she was certain he would never amass any kind of money or own a stately home or a feather bed, or want any of the amenities that she had grown so used to in such a short time.

It was that simple. He had chosen his world ages before she had ever appeared in his life, and she had only just chosen hers.

They went to the theater, they went to the opera, they attended a crowded, fashionably catered party thrown by one of Mrs. Bellancourt's acquaintances in a large mansion rented just for the purpose.

"It is the new way of entertaining, and very exclusive," Mrs. Bellancourt told them. "My dear friend Helena and her husband merely tell the maitre-d' exactly what they wish in the way of food, decorations and service, and everything is provided. All they must do is arrive a half hour before, ascertain that everything is as they wish, and receive the guests when they start arriving. You can only imagine the convenience of this. The fact that it doesn't turn one's own home topsy-turvy makes it a very advantageous way to entertain a large group rather than squeezing them all into your parlor. There will be scads of people here tonight, my dears, and dancing and food and good conversation, and I promise you, it will be very hard to make a *faux pas* if you just follow all that you have been instructed."

Angelene shifted edgily in her seat as the carriage rolled up a long circular driveway fronting a large square house and long columns supporting its circular front porch.

"Here we are," her grandmother said. "If you are in doubt as to a course of action, come find me. Otherwise, you need only to be your own beautiful self, and everyone will find you very pleasing indeed."

She turned to Rake. "Have you any questions, Richard?"

"No ma'am."

"And you will try to be a little more forthcoming and a little less adamant, won't you? To please me?"

"Yes ma'am," he said obediently, but it would be for Angelene, all of it, and he had no illusions about that. This was her first test, and he meant to give her every help he could. He would forget the ache in his loins and the heartache in his soul.

Their carriage jolted to a stop directly beside the curving white marble steps that mirrored the shape of the porch overhang.

The footman climbed down and opened the door, and handed Mrs. Bellancourt out first, and then Angelene, who was wrapped in a luscious blue satin cape lined with cream silk, and then finally Rake, who was dressed in a severe black cutaway that emphasized his height and his coloring.

Angelene's heart sank. He was absolutely devastating in formal dress, and his air of aloofness was tantalizing rather than off-putting.

She wondered how many dozens of women would descend on him before he had entered the ballroom.

Mrs. Bellancourt led them grandly up the stairs and into the reception foyer, where a black-garbed maid took their wraps and a very tight-faced butler took their cards.

It was another dozen steps to the landing above the reception room, and here the butler stopped and called out to announce them, his voice booming sonorously over the noise of the crowd.

"Mrs. Horace Bellancourt. Miss Angelene Bellancourt, Mr. Richard Bellancourt."

Several people looked up, and one or two women detached themselves from little knots of conversation and came forward toward them as the butler motioned them to step down into the crowd.

"Amelia," one woman exclaimed, her hands outstretched and reaching for the old lady before she could move into the room. "I'm so glad you are out and about again."

"My dear Helena, permit me—my dear granddaughter, Angelene. And her brother, Richard. Isn't it wonderful? It's like having my very own daughter restored to me again."

"Come tell me about it. Children—" She made a discreet motion over her shoulder, and in a moment, she was joined by a graying well-set man with kind brown eyes who looked reasonably uncomfortable in his stiff collar and formal suit. "My husband, Oscar. Please, my dear, these are Amelia's dear grandchildren, Angelene and Richard. Do introduce them around, Oscar, and make sure they meet the most eligible interesting young people."

Immediately, the unprepossessing Oscar drew them into the swirl of conversation, and an hour later, Angelene learned the truth of things in her Grandmother's world: she had only to dress elegantly in a bosom-revealing hydrangea blue silk gown, toss her meticulously arranged golded head, smile mysteriously every

304

time she was asked a question, and she never needed to utter one word in conversation.

The other young women, some of them plain-faced, some of them intensely beautiful and even more daringly dressed than she, exhibited only a passing interest in the newcomer. Their eyes were fixed solely on the young men, and on one in particular, who towered darkly above the rest, and wore a forbidding expression on his almost pagan features.

She watched as everyone flocked to him, and begged a promenade around the floor with the romantic looking Mr. Bellancourt, of whom no one had ever heard. Immediately it was whispered about that there was some tragic story in his past that his grandmother had kept secret from everyone, and so instantly his companion of the moment, male or female, began asking searching questions, all of which left him at a loss because he did not know exactly what Mrs. Bellancourt had told anyone.

He was almost tempted to play with them, but these were innocent, perhaps not so guileless children, and he found that the best course, especially if he wished to keep his eye on Angelene, was to remain removed and quiet and let them all speculate on his colorful past.

Meanwhile Angelene was waltzed from one group of enthusiastic young men to another, in the company of one and another young woman, whoever was interested in someone in a group at a given moment, and she found herself dizzy with trying to keep straight all the names and compliments, and the heady sensation of being admired and desired by the kind of men she had always dreamed about.

They were young, maybe they were even slightly foolish—at least their social chatter was—but she found that refreshing after all these weeks of heavy-handed lessons in behavior and not a single example as to how to achieve it.

But now, she found it was easy. These men liked to do the talking, and they vied with themselves as to who could invent the most outrageous compliment, and barring that, the one that the beauty of the moment would even believe.

Their conversation was light and elegant and amusing, everything she had thought it would be, and the whole army of them were, if not all of them handsome, extremely pleasant looking and thoughtfully and gracefully turned out to seem as attractive as possible.

The stunning fact she realized was this: they were all looking for equally eligible young women in the same way she sought that powerful and eligible man. Not one of them passed muster as a candidate, and she could not define why.

At midnight, Mr. Randolph Trimble escorted her to dinner, chiding her ever so gently for being so shy, and telling her over and above that, how much he liked it.

Down the second of two long tables set up in a small ballroom, Rake, with his ever-observant cool gray gaze, watched intently to see exactly how he was to seat his lady, and then proceeded to hand Miss Antoinette Madrid properly and elegantly into her chair.

"The Madrids are paper," Mr. Trimble told her when she asked who was that lady with her *brother*. "Not the same as the market, or real estate, but by God, the country consumes a wealth of it every day."

"It sounds like a very wise thing to be invested in," Angelene ventured. "I mean, when you think of everything besides newspapers and writing paper . . ." her voice trailed off, but Mr. Trimble seemed much struck by her observation.

"You're right of course, Miss Bellancourt. I was thinking particularly of industry, and here you've gone and pointed out all the other facets. There's no end to the amount of paper products that are used daily: magazines, books, business forms, cards, paper boxes. Well, they own scads of land up north and they farm trees and cut them down and process them, and I think you're right— it is a very wise thing to be invested in. Now . . ." he paused and she breathed a sigh of relief that she had come

306

through that unscathed. Imagine telling someone like Randolph Trimble about wise investments. On the other hand, she hadn't particularly liked his snide tone when he had said, the Madrids are *paper*, as if the family and it both were disposable.

". . . Miss Bellancourt, take a look at this menu. Most delightful. Oscar and Helena do the most fabulous parties, don't you think? Oh, no—of course you don't. This is your first. Well, let me be your guide . . ."

Across the room and over the space of the two long tables, Miss Antoinette Madrid was saying much the same thing to Rake, who was becoming testy with the strain of remaining polite.

"Oh, the man with Miss Bellancourt—that's Randolph Trimble, you know—motors and machinery," she said, "all perfectly vile stuff. Not like being in the market or paper, of course, but there's a fabulous amount of money in the family. The father's a genius inventor, the boy's a gadabout and gossip. But look here, Mr. Bellancourt—Oscar and Helena always provide a menu, nothing stingy about their parties, which I expect you'll find out if you are to be in town much longer. You have only to choose what you wish. The waiter will come around in a moment or two."

It was exhausting, working at light conversation, keeping yourself cloaked in mystery, and otherwise trying to enjoy yourself while you wondered what your grandmother was thinking and what that clinging Antoinette Madrid was saying to Rake. Angelene felt quite intense about it, and she swore she wouldn't beg out of anything with a headache. She didn't have time to get a headache.

"I beg your pardon, Mr. Trimble?"

"I said, we had heard your father passed away many years ago and that your mother was a successful entrepreneur out west."

"Oh yes." *What was an entrepreneur?* And *successful?* If Grandmother only knew! "That's right." Now what did she say?

But then, he was intent on pursuing his own train of

307

thought. "Ranching, I understand."

"Yes," she grasped onto that gratefully. "Yes, she ran a ranch," which was just a little *tiny* misstatement.

"Cattle and all that."

"Yes, there are cattle on ranches," she agreed, a definite statement of fact, that, and not in the least to be linked with her mother the *entrepreneur*.

"Good money in cattle," Trimble went on.

"So I'm told," she said noncommittally.

"So you came east," he prompted her.

"Well, yes. Mother had sent me away to school—"

"A toast to your finishing school, Miss Bellancourt. A quite remarkable job."

"—and—and it was decided on my return that . . . it was time for me to come to my Grandmother's. Quite a lackluster story, I'm afraid, Mr. Trimble. Nothing romantic there."

"But you lived on a *ranch*—what was it like?"

"About what you'd imagine," she answered, spearing for any reasonable answer that would deflect his questions.

"A lot of horses and fresh air and that kind of thing."

"About that."

"Riding every day . . . ?"

"Well, no. I didn't ride everyday," and then, at his look of horror, she amended it to, "I didn't herd cows or anything like that. There's much to do on a ranch, Mr. Trimble. It doesn't run itself."

"Oh. Well. I thought there were cowpeople on a ranch who manage things just like servants."

"Cowhands, Mr. Trimble, and they manage the cows as their name suggests, while the family manages the ranch."

"Oh. Well, Miss Bellancourt, here is our waiter. Have you decided what to order?"

She had decided nothing except that she had to escape from the pointed interrogation by Mr. Trimble. She had told him too much already, and she could imagine him taking her down in front of his friends: can you imagine?

308

Lived on a ranch, never rode much, and dirtied her hands *managing* things. Of such small blunders was a social season ruined.

She buried her head in the menu, and she wondered despairingly how Rake was *managing* with the formidable and talkative Antoinette Madrid.

He didn't look any happier than she, but the one who looked most pleased was her grandmother, a perpendicular table away with her host and hostess, beaming across the finely groomed heads of the guests at her accepted protegés.

"That Madrid is a veritable tigress," Rake growled, settling back into the carriage for the short ride home. "She could eat a man alive."

"Well, that Randolph Trimble is a mountain cat, sleek and ready to pounce on you," Angelene said disgustedly. "I hardly knew what to say to him. And Grandmother—you with your tall story of my mother and her successful western enterprise."

"It's called saving face, my dear. We don't want *my* friends to know exactly what my *daughter* turned out to be when they can see with their own eyes how successful a granddaughter I have. And grandson, of course," she added belatedly. "If only Richard weren't so—ornery about the whole thing. I could almost believe that what Angelene said was true, Richard—that you'd rather go back to that western hovel that your mother ensconced herself in than stay here and enjoy all that this life has to offer."

"Angelene has it wrong, ma'am. I wouldn't rather go back to the—*hovel*, and I'm most interested in seeing everything this new life has to offer."

"Well! You see, Angelene. Well fine. I just hope you didn't give it away about your mother."

"I said yes to everything and offered no details, ma'am. I trust that is the correct procedure."

"You are a very smart young man," the old lady said

approvingly. "I knew there was some of the Bellancourt in you two. There's an example of discretion that cannot be taught. I am very pleased, Richard. Now, tell me how the dancing went; I was much too busy catching up on things with Helena and Flora Beauvisage."

"How can one describe *how* the dancing went?" Angelene wondered. "You just get up on the floor and hope you don't step on somebody's foot or fall on your face since you still can't get the hang of doing the waltz. I suppose it went all right. I didn't seem to do anything disastrous."

Except accept a partner to whom she had not been introduced, against all of Miss Crosby's strictures. But she had been so tired by that time, she truly could not remember whether she had ever met the gentleman or not, and he was so good-natured about her little gaffes in doing the steps that it didn't seem to matter.

"And you, Richard?"

"I chose not to go out on the dance floor," Rake said tightly, "in spite of Miss Madrid's penchant for issuing challenges and dares, and I can attest to the fact that Angelene did you credit."

"And did you enjoy this first party of the season, my dears?"

Angelene did not answer, her mind being occupied with the part about Miss Madrid's challenges and dares, and Rake, with his innate Bellancourt-like discretion, responded for her, "It was everything *we* could have wished for and more, ma'am," and only Angelene caught the tone of irony, the caustic *we*, the very proper phrasing of his gratitude and the pure venom underneath.

The cards poured in, and here at last they saw the end result of the meticulous instruction on the ways of the wealthy by the painstaking Miss Crosby.

Angelene was able to sort and discard, and send her own card back to several of the people she had met, and was rather astonished at the ease with which she accomplished this.

"Well, there is something to this card business. If you don't reply, then the sender knows, and tactfully, that you wish no further intercourse with him. And if you do, he only need come calling, nothing more, and everything is arranged, just like a dance—a step forward here, a backward step there, and nobody charges ahead unless they are learning to do that abominable polka."

The dance lessons were pushed to primacy: it was imperative that Rake be able to handle himself on the dance floor, and while he was having some success with the waltz, finally, he adamantly refused to hop around like a crazed medicine man attempting to do the polka. The line dances made more sense to him, and he patiently learned the intricacies of the quadrille, the Virginia reel and the lancers.

Above that, he began to learn the rules of sport from Mr. Darlington so that he would be well-versed in conversation with his peers. Mr. Darlington took him to all manner of games, from the lingering last games of baseball, to the elite country clubs where golf was the enduring pastime. He learned to throw bowls and the rudiments of cricket, and what the man even meant when he talked about shinny or athletics, which included everything from bicycling to ten pins to boating to quoits and a half dozen other energetic activities that were common pastimes among his set. He tried them all, and with some great success because of his natural athleticism and the pinpoint training of his childhood among his mother's people.

All of that combined to give him an edge in play, and the rules were easily learned, he found. The play was exhilarating and perhaps the one thing of all the nonsense that he didn't just tolerate.

He had an aptitude for anything physical, and he grew from being a novice in Mr. Darlington's company to an athlete of some stature among Mr. Darlington's friends. He became particularly fond of any kind of ball playing, including tennis and baseball, but more than that, he discovered he had a natural bent for playing polo.

He understood why that was: he was on horseback and he was in fierce competition with a set of other men, and it engendered still another memory of childhood; when his volatile combativeness was the only thing that made him stand out among his equals.

He had found the thing that would set him apart again. He was reckless on the field and cautious too. He had an instinct, and a real stalking patience, and he never lost his temper.

Mr. Darlington admired him greatly for his prowess on the playing field, and for his kind hand with the horses.

"A regular find, my dear Amelia. You never would have guessed from talking to him, or watching him clunk around the room with poor Angelene. The man is a real comer, amateur though he is. He just *knows* how to move and where to go. That is not a talent that can be taught."

Mrs. Bellancourt beamed with pride. "Horace was exactly like that," she said with satisfaction. "Richard must take after him."

Things were going swimmingly, and she hadn't enjoyed herself so much in years. It had taken her sweet beautiful granddaughter and her courageous stand against her mother to bring her grandmother back to life.

She would have paid any price for that and never gotten all this overweening joy too.

She began to make the final plans for their trip to England.

Chapter 17

Rake had found an outlet for his reckless desire for Angelene, but she had found nothing but a round of parties and visits and calls, and shopping, and all kinds of things that properly occupied unmarried girls of her station. She had found too the pitfalls that came with being both beautiful and the new unknown in town, and she had discovered that the girls of her set were not particularly friendly and were all in furious competition with each other.

They weren't above maligning each other or gossiping about each other, or pretending to be best friends in one moment and a spitting enemy the next.

She also did not have the cunning to ferret out secrets in the way of Miss Antoinette Madrid or Miss Charlotte Combes, both of whom were excellent friends or bitter enemies on any given day, and seemed to be the most adept at destroying a reputation or elevating it to the status of holiness.

They all paid their willing respects to the god of the card bearing Angelene's name because they all hoped they would just happen to run into the devastatingly mysterious Richard Bellancourt.

The fact he was now actively engaged in making the rounds of the clubs and participating in the sporting life of that set only made him that much more attractive to them.

"Well, Angelene, you must make sure that he is home some afternoon to help you entertain us," Miss Madrid said one day when she was well and truly disgusted because the object of her growing affection was nowhere around—again. "You know I feel like *I* was his first friend. After all, your grandmother did you a disservice hiding you away all those weeks until Oscar and Helen's party. Just think how much sooner we all could have had the pleasure of your company."

"And learned all about your fascinating mother," Miss Coombes put in. "And all those thick beefy cattle."

Angelene had never imagined that she would come to a point where she wouldn't want to share an afternoon with her newfound friends, but when they had at her like that, she wasn't sure who was whose friend at all.

"Must I continually see these same girls?" she asked her grandmother. "And those men—they are just fascinated by my mother and her *ranch*. You should have heard Charlotte Coombes the other day about the *cattle*. You would have thought she was talking about vermin."

"That's just how they talk," her grandmother said comfortably. "It hasn't changed at all since my time. Everyone's out to snare the most attractive and eligible man and they just don't care how they go about it, even if it means belittling someone else. It's part of the game, Angelene, my dear, and I think you should grow a thicker skin and learn to retaliate."

The thing was, she had been holding herself back from reprisal in kind, but it struck her that perhaps Miss Madrid and her ilk would have a lot more respect for her tart tongue than they had for her manners.

So why had Grandmother spent all that time and money on Miss Crosby? She could have handled Miss Madrid without all that copious instruction on the finer points *polite* reciprocation.

No holds barred with the pampered wealthy daughters of her grandmother's set: none of them could be offended and neither, now, could she. She was ready for Miss Madrid's next attack.

It came during an approved and properly chaperoned visit to the Museum where she and her group took in an exhibition of ancient bones which, in and of themselves, held no fascination whatsoever to any of them except for several of the men, Mr. Trimble included.

"Why, it's just like the pictures we've seen of bleached bones of *cattle* along those overlanding trails," Miss Madrid said ingenuously. "I don't see the difference."

"Indeed," Angelene said sweetly, "it's so nice to know that bones remain when paper is just ground to dust."

Miss Madrid looked up at her, startled.

"And they describe them, Miss Madrid, as *paper*-white bones. Imagine the merging of the two in all aspects. The paper wraps the meat that comes from those thick beefy cattle, but the paper is discarded and meat becomes a part of the body, giving energy and life. The body burns off the energy, Miss Madrid; the paper only burns. It is nice to think that the bones remain, isn't it?"

"Touché, Miss Bellancourt," Miss Madrid murmured. "I had no idea what a worthy adversary you could be."

"And I had every idea of how worthy an opponent you could be," Angelene said. "I think we may call this a draw, Miss Madrid, and become friends."

"Undoubtedly friends," Miss Madrid agreed, offering Angelene a tepid handshake. And mortal enemies, she added to herself. No one got the best of Antoinette Madrid; her father had taught her well. Blonde beauties never wore well, in any case, and her own blazing brunette volatility flamed brighter against the rasp of Angelene's new feistiness.

She had to tread carefully here, she thought, as the crowd of friends exited the Museum. Richard Bellancourt was still high on her list of most desirable catches, no matter what his mother had done somewhere out west where nobody cared. And she thought it fairly obvious that Angelene was the one preventing her from seeing him, that Angelene gave him the clue as to when her set would be visiting the house, and she vowed to become nicer to Angelene just to see what lay beneath, and to see

315

if the sister were the key to unlocking the mystery of the brother.

It was now deep into October, when the leaves turned and the air grew colder and the aspect of the city grew starker with the coming of autumn. It was the time of year Angelene did not like at all because it had meant, in the past, the advent of all the misery work she hated—the socks, the sewing, the making of feather ticks, the cooking to store up the pickle vegetables for the winter.

It wasn't that she expected to be handed a list of chores here, but she surely didn't expect the social scene to escalate into a frenzy of intimate engagements for cards or tea, or evening amusements involving someone's latest operatic treasure or author extraordinaire.

What she really hated was that Rake was nowhere to be seen. It was as if he had discovered another life, and he meant to live it to the reckless dregs, pulled along by the buoyant energy of Mr. Darlington, the perennial guest.

They really occupied two different spheres; she was being prepared to make a good marriage, and he was grooming himself to take his place among men. The difference between them were now sharply delineated: she was still the innocent young girl, and he was a grown and self-directed *man*.

But she wanted him no less; she just didn't know how to go skulking up to his room to ease her distress.

Maybe he didn't want to any more. Maybe he had found other willing women somewhere in town.

Maybe she had best not even give shape to the thought. She should be looking ahead, to England, to the next party, to the obvious attentions of Mr. Trimble.

But Mr. Trimble seemed like a mere boy in his effusive courting of her. It struck her that she probably had a great deal more knowledge about *things* than any other young woman of his acquaintance, and she wondered how she might ever explain *that*, when he consistently complimented her innocent eyes and the purity of her youthful womanhood.

She had gone two steps further than that, and she knew that she must disillusion Mr. Trimble very soon, but not sooner than it took to see the black angry mask settle over Rake's face when he happened upon them one afternoon, huddled together in the small parlor, where Mr. Trimble was singing his praises of her virginal beauty.

Yes, he was in a rage—he didn't like the thought of the Trimble touching her at all, and he hated the complicated quadrille that a man had to dance in order to pursue the woman of his choice.

It was an abomination that Angelene had turned him into her brother. He could do no more than act affronted at Mr. Trimble's forwardness, and get rid of him with as much Bellancourt-like tact as possible.

It pleased Angelene no end to see him all blown apart by Mr. Trimble's obvious sincerity.

"But of course, you are after a titled nobleman, Sister of Angels. Otherwise, why would you have agreed to this whole charade?"

"I had wanted a wealthy man, if you remember," Angelene pointed out silkily. "But none of these babies are *men*."

She could almost see the steam pouring out of his ears at the thought of the advantages a *man* might have over those immature puppies. She had backed them both into a corner so that there could be no resolution short of them both leaving Mrs. Bellancourt's home forever.

He knew she would never do that. Not with him.

"No, I expect all that fog in England makes a man out of a boy," he said nastily. "And perhaps a woman out of a pettish child."

"You don't have to be stinky about it. You can still leave."

"And waste this precious education in social skills? Do you know, I could have avoided the whole lot if I had just told them how much I know about horseflesh. Hell and damn, Angelene, this is *not* going to work, and you are

317

going to be deadly sorry you started it."

"Maybe I'm sorry about a lot of things," she said, attacking with the only weapon she had at hand.

"Maybe you're not the only one," he lashed back, and then he pivoted sharply as he heard a step behind him.

Borden stood in the threshold of the small parlor. "Miss Madrid is calling, Miss," he said, extending the salver with her card placed on it.

Angelene arose and came to take the card, which had scrawled on it, "I'm downstairs. Don't send me away."

"But now I'm upstairs," Miss Madrid's voice said over her comprehension of the note, "and it would be horrendously impolite to send me away, Angelene, so why don't you just order up some tea—Borden, if you please—and we'll ask your scowling brother to join us? Now what could be nicer—or cozier?"

There were more theater parties, card parties, dances, theatricals, masked balls, tableaux to be performed for charity all at the behest of Miss Madrid, where all the girls dressed in costume and recreated panels of historical scenes, for which they charged admission and then donated the proceeds to charity. They went ice skating and for long carriage rides as October drew to a close and Thanksgiving seemed to come impossibly near; they were leaving the week of Thanksgiving for London, and suddenly the house was aflurry with the chore of packing and making sure that every last dress was fresh and clean, and augmenting the abundance with still more.

Miss Madrid pursued Rake with the tenacity of a hunting dog, and he supposed if she had been beautiful, he might have been flattered. As it was, he didn't know quite what to do with her or about her, and so he wound up as her escort any number of times when he just could not politely say no again.

"Miss Madrid would be a likely match for Richard," Mrs. Bellancourt said complacently to Mr. Darlington at dinner one night.

"Rake would tramp her down in a week," Angelene said viciously. "She doesn't know anything about him, and he is too polite now to show his real feelings about her."

"Well, I hope not," her grandmother said. "The Madrids are going to join us in London."

Angelene felt like spitting. Try as she might, she had not been able to warm up to Antoinette Madrid. They were like two wary cats circling each other, and one had to strike soon or be left defenseless. Angelene was scared to death that she would be the wounded one.

"Well, as I said, he has become very polite, Grandmother," she said lamely. "I doubt if he would ever offer for her. Besides, there is our background, which would not bear scrutiny by someone as thorough and protective as Miss Madrid's father."

"Yes, that certainly could be a problem for Richard. However, it won't be for you, my dear, and I suppose that is our main focus. I'm so proud of you, you know. Three months ago you knew nothing about comporting yourself in a social setting and now there is nothing to be ashamed of, Angelene. Nothing at all."

And wasn't it true? She was a long way from the desperate hoyden who had tracked her way in disguise across two states running toward the very life she now embraced. And Rake had been a complication, nothing more, and she had allowed herself to feel too much for him, and to push what he was firmly into the background where she didn't have to think about it.

But now it was urgent that she think about it, imperative that she remember that there was only one thing he could offer her and that was not enough upon which to build a life with him.

It was as simple as that; she never wanted the kind of life in which her mother wished to imprison her and there was still only one way to escape that—and she meant to do it and damn the consequences.

She had learned all of her lessons well. She danced like a dream, played cards as if she had been gaming all her

319

life; she could now ride passably well, although she still hated the dreaded sidesaddle, and she knew to the finest degree the etiquette of her social set. She knew how to dress and enhance herself, how to converse about little nothings, how to deflect too probing questions and too ardent hands. She could return a tennis serve, and handle a bowling ball, whack a croquet mallet, and stay on her feet on a pair of ice skates. She could even balance on a bicycle, and Mr. Trimble had had the pleassure of teaching her that. She could play ten or eleven set pieces on the piano with gusto and confidence, and she had learned to enjoy various games of sport for which gentlemen seemed to have unwarranted enthusiasm.

She had learned to pour a pretty pot of tea and to preside over a lavish high tea which invariably was replete with a selection of meat, fowl, fish and ham as well as delectable cakes of every kind, muffins, toast, tea cakes and the like, and fruits in season and jugs of clotted cream served along with tea and coffee and good conversation; and she had learned to direct the elegant little tea, which was really a refreshment to be served when she and Mrs. Bellancourt indicated by card that they were "at home" and wished to receive company, and she knew the finite difference between this and a breakfast visit, as well as what distinguished a party from a ball. All of it was gradated to a fine point over cards and returned visits and it all seemed second nature to her now.

Her grandmother decided to throw an evening party to celebrate their upcoming trip to England.

"But *I* shall do it right, of course. We will open the ballroom here on the third floor, and we won't be catering anything either. Mr. Darlington shall take care of providing the libations, and you, my dear Angelene, shall think of how we can decorate, and we shall provide ourselves with a lovely party as a send-off before we leave town."

The list of invitees was extensive. Everyone was on it, and it required a personal visit from either Angelene or her Grandmother, or both, or leaving their cards to express their intent.

The very first week of November her grandmother sent out the invitations and set the date for just before Thanksgiving when everyone would still be in town.

The planning that went into this lavish event became something on the order of a military proceeding, with each general having command of his or her fort. No one dared let Mrs. Bellancourt down.

Of course the sheer size of the ballroom was daunting. It occupied the entire third floor of the house, front to back, side to side, and it was festooned with elaborate gilded molding over the walls and ceiling, and cherubs holding swags of plaster flowers at every corner. The parquet floor looked like a sheet of glossy ice with the sun pouring through the window, and all along the walls of the room were spindle-legged chairs, neatly upholstered in a very deep pink.

Beyond an archway, toward the front of the house, there was a dais for the orchestra, and to the rear, through two panels of discreet curtains was a supper room, large enough to accommodate a hundred people at a time.

"Well, it's a little dusty. It's been closed since Mr. Bellancourt died, you know," her grandmother said a little defensively. "Horace always liked a good party, didn't he, Vernon?"

Mr. Darlington nodded reassuringly. "Then we must provide him with one," he said, patting her arm lightly.

And how the invitation acceptances poured in. It didn't take but a week, and it was barely two weeks by then to the event, and Angelene had come up with no ideas about decorating the ballroom.

"Maybe simplicity is the best thing of all," she suggested to her grandmother.

"No, you must decide on something, Angelene, and

321

meantime, we will procure a new dress for the party."

Another new dress, another new shoe, all at the discretion of a seemingly bottomless income that could provide for any need, want or whim.

"Flowers," Angelene said, "*summer* flowers: we'll create the atmosphere of summer, grandmother, and make everyone forget that snow is on the way."

Her grandmother nodded approvingly. "And now you must find out how to provide them, my dear, and don't count the cost."

It was then she understood that this had been a test of sorts, that her grandmother had wanted to see if she were capable of assuming command, of taking control, of providing her guests with fantasy as well as comfort, as any good hostess should.

The flowers were imported from hothouses that specialized in such things, and she got together a willing crew of her eligible young men, captained by Mr. Trimble, to drape them, hang them, arrange them and otherwise create a summer bower for the delectation of her guests.

Her grandmother dictated the menu, and the tables were set for intimate conversation. Mr. Darlington engaged the orchestra and laid in the drinks and a tub of ice was put to cool outside the kitchen.

Her dress arrived in all its fairy-blue splendor and she couldn't wait for the night to arrive so that she could wear it.

"And of course, Richard will be your escort for the evening," her grandmother directed. "It wouldn't do to give Miss Madrid or Mr. Trimble *too* much hope."

"I thank you for that, ma'am," Rake said with irony. "It is purely impossible to get away from that woman in any other event."

"We will keep you very busy," the old lady assured him, "because you are to be my host as well, and I know I will require you by my side for a great deal of the evening."

"As you wish, ma'am," he said, but this time there was a faintly appreciative note in his voice instead of the usual tenseness.

Her grandmother had provided dance cards as well, and these had been hand-painted to match the decoration in the ballroom, to be given to every lady who came to the party as souvenirs.

The guests were to enter the house from the front, their coats and wraps were to be taken, and then they were to be whisked up to the third floor by an elevator in the hallways which had been installed just for that purpose when the house had been built.

The guests would be let out into a long narrow vestibule just outside the supper room, and guided by the maid into the dressing-rooms beside the elevator to freshen up, or directly into the ballroom.

It was most impressive. The first thing that struck the guest as he entered was the vastness of the room, which was overlaid by the scent of the perfume of the flowers. Beyond that, a window wall sent one hundred twinkling lights upward from an overview of the lower city. And beside him, his hostess, her grandson and granddaughter awaited his greeting, and there was something a little intimidating about the diminutive grande dame and her two intensely attractive grandchildren.

It was almost unseemly that one woman should have spawned such an extraordinary-looking second generation of family.

The old lady greeted everyone, friend and foe, and welcomed each individually into her home, and then presented Angelene and Rake before nodding him into the ballroom where her dear friend Helena took over the chore of making sure that guest was properly introduced, or found someone congenial with whom to converse until all the guests arrived.

Her grandmother had invited at least a hundred people that Angelene was aware of, but as the guests continued to arrive, she wondered if a hundred more invitations had not been issued.

Her grandmother knew each guest by name, and looked pointedly at Angelene as each introduction was made.

One of the very latest arrivals was the family of Antoinette Madrid.

"My dear Richard," she cooed, resplendent in dark green velvet and bold gold jewelry. "Surely Mrs. Bellancourt will release you from your receiving line duties *now.*" And she cast a meaningful look at her father who was staring at Rake, an odd, edgy expression on his face.

"I couldn't possibly, dear Antoinette. Richard must stay with me for a while longer yet," the old lady said with great satisfaction. "Angelene will take you inside. My dear—?"

"So good of you," Antoinette muttered, her envious eyes devouring Angelene's silk brocade dress of an eye-enhancing blue. She hated the way it fit her body, and it was almost indecent the way the apron tied across the front and draped down the back to a long train and ended in the front in two deep flounces. The girl had no taste at all, she thought wrathfully, and she had the nerve to wear such a deeply revealing bosom as well.

Helena met them and relieved Angelene of her burden. On the dais, under the arch, the musicians began a light unobtrusive waltz to underlay the conversation. The guests had already formed themselves into little knots of acquaintances, shifting like a quadrille in an intricate dance of acceptance as a newcomer came into each midst.

Angelene skirted the room, making sure that everyone had someone to talk to, ascertaining that no one wanted for anything, checking that champagne would be circulated among the guests by a waiter in the ensuing fifteen minutes, and then returned to her grandmother who was greeting the last of the guests.

Rake watched all of this busy activity with a skeptical eye. Angel Eyes had learned her lessons well. Grandmother had much to be proud of in the solicitous way

Angelene took care of her guests, and in her innate, natural beauty.

No one else could have worn that dress but Angelene, and no one else would have dared to wear her spun gold hair exactly the same way, parted and knotted in an upsweep, with one thick fall of hair resting lightly against her collarbone.

He knew men might die just to touch the soft skin where that sweet little end curl had lain. He might die too, but then he was becoming too accustomed to the excesses and he was starting to feel too comfortable among this crowd. All it took was a superior knowledge of horseflesh, just as he had told Angelene, and a man gained entree anywhere he wished.

"And here is the Richard Bellancourt about whom we've heard so much. Antoinette has told me all about you, son. Horsebreeding in Kentucky, eh? The bluegrass branch of the Bellancourts. Mighty impressive, son, with your mother in cattle and your sister breaking every man's heart right here in New York. Do you race? Where do you keep your stable, son? Need a place in New York?"

God, the scion of the Madrids was even more possessive than the daughter, and the story of his origins was getting more intricate by the moment. But why not? Who was to know, after all?

Angelene? Who had her own secrets to keep? Wasn't he proving to her the very thing he had promised, that he was to enter her world and negotiate it successfully? No one knew he had not been born in a mansion house in Louisville, and no one ever would.

What had that gotten him except a taste for comfort?

A man who was conceived in fury and born between two worlds did not deserve comfort. Comfort would smother his awareness of who he was and where he came from.

He couldn't let himself forget. He could not give it up for Angelene, and he had all the ready answers for

Antoinette Madrid's father and he hated himself for playing that man's game.

But he had not been dealt the cards; he could only work with what he had, and what he had been handed from the purposeful trip of a woman's lie.

"I'm so glad you're partnering me for dinner," Angelene said, choosing her words carefully because there was a look in Rake's eye that warned her not to be flippant or show any sign of contentment.

"I'm sure you are," he said harshly. "It's probably the first time in weeks you can actually be yourself. How refreshing that would be."

"Now, Rake—"

"I'm damned tired, Angelene. I've learned some hard lessons too. I've learned to smile at people I despise, and clamp down on telling people to leave me alone. I've stood by while people have outlined my whole social history to me, and lied when they asked for the details, and I swear I don't know what more I can do for you now."

"You can take me to supper," she said stonily, "and you can stop spoiling this evening for me, do you hear?"

"Mr. Madrid asked for the name of the family farm in Louisville where I raise thoroughbreds," he said, extending his arm so she could lay her hand on it. "Thought he might get in touch after I get home from England with Grandmother."

"What did you tell him?"

"Why, we call it Bellancourt, of course," he said caustically. "And everyone knows who we are. I told him, Sister of Angels, exactly what he expected to hear."

"And you're so good with the horses, I hear," she murmured. "That does seem to carry a lot of weight with these people."

"The lies are going to trip us up sooner or later," he warned.

"It doesn't matter," she said fiercely, "I'm still Amelia

326

Bellancourt's granddaughter, no matter what happens."

"And I," he said ominously, "I will be the outcast, Angelene, just like I always was."

Now he had scared her. The thing was rolling too fast, gathering mass like a snowball, almost out of control. A horse breeder in Louisville, with her mother running a ranch in Missouri—and her grandmother would approve of the whole thing.

There was something wrong with it, and she couldn't quite define what it was except that they needed to somehow pigeonhole Rake who neither looked, spoke, or acted as they. They needed to make him one of their own, and the fact that he knew so much about horseflesh was not coincidental to their placing him in Louisville. It was necessary.

And it was spoiling her evening.

Rake was absolutely uncommunicative during dinner, and after, when the music began again, this time for dancing, she forced him out onto the floor with her and made him dance the first waltz.

He had become passably good at doing that. But more, it was a chance to put his arms around Angelene in public, to be close to her in a way not possible under her grandmother's close scrutiny.

And her grandmother sat on the sidelines with her chums and said happily, "Don't they dance well together? I never could conceive of a brother and sister closer than they are. It's truly extraordinary."

"How lucky you are they came to you," her friend Helena murmured.

And in the corner by one of the windows, Antoinette Madrid cupped her hand over her dance card and scribbled Richard Bellancourt's name on every line.

The music swung from waltz to reel, stopping only long enough for the conductor to announce the choice of dance.

On the sidelines, Mr. Darlington daringly asked Mrs.

Bellancourt if he might have the next waltz. She protested she hardly remembered how to do it, but thought she might like to try.

In the center of the dancing throng, Rake held onto Angelene as if he would never let her go until Mr. Trimble forced him to relinquish her hand.

Out of the shadows, Antoinette Madrid glided onto the floor. "My dance is next, Richard," she said sweetly, holding up her card, catching him neatly in a crowd where he could not deny her without embarrassing her, which a discreet man would never do.

He took her into his arms reluctantly and slowly waltzed her around the floor, his eyes ever searching for Angelene, his attention totally focused away from Antoinette Madrid.

She rapped his arm, and his cool gray gaze skewed downward.

"But I'm *here*, Richard, and I don't know what you're doing looking at other girls."

"Perhaps I'm looking at the view, Miss Madrid."

"It is sensational. I envy you, having a room like this in your *house*."

"My grandmother's house," he corrected, almost stumbling over the word *grandmother*.

"Of course. You dance very well, Richard."

"Thank you, Miss Madrid." *Where was Angelene?*

"Of course you know you are pencilled in for all my dances."

He clamped down on his first impulse to just walk away from her. A discreet man would never do such a thing, and he tried to think of a Bellancourt-like solution to refusing her any attention at all for the rest of the evening. "I'm flattered, Miss Madrid, really I am, but I believe my grandmother indicated that she expects me to help with her hosting chores, so I'm sure you'll excuse me."

"No, I won't," she said tightly. "That's a lot of balderdash, Richard Bellancourt. Mr. Darlington is right by her side as you can plainly see, and she needs no help from you."

"I wonder that you presume to surmise my grand-mother's needs at all, Miss Madrid. Permit me to return you to your father."

And he abandoned her in the middle of the dance without a qualm at her father's side.

But where was Angelene?

Angelene was skittering around the edge of the crowd of guests, making sure that everyone's dance card was filled, everyone had a partner or someone with whom to converse, redirecting the waiters to serve more cham-pagne, and keeping well out of Mr. Trimble's way too.

"Slow down, Sister of Angels, you need a respite."

She bit her lip. "No, I don't know what I need. I don't want to dance, except with you, and I don't want to talk to that officious Mr. Trimble again this evening either."

"Then you're in luck," Rake said. "I'm being pursued by the rapacious Miss Madrid who had the audacity to fill her dance card with my name, and so the only thing either of us can do is get out of here before anyone sees us."

They ducked out through the supper room to the ele-vator. It was still early enough so that no one was yet thinking of departing, and no one was about except the maid who was in charge of directing the guests.

It was easy to elude her and slip down the steps to the bedroom floor and into Angelene's bedroom and lock the door.

"I feel guilty already," Angelene murmured, moving to the mirror over her bureau to make sure her hair was still in place.

"No, you don't, Angelene. You feel relieved, the same as I. We don't want all that above us. *We* want the reality of what is here in this room."

"No—"

"Don't deny it, Angelene. You would not have come down here otherwise."

"It was Mr. Trimble," she said faintly.

"And Miss Madrid, I know. How convenient for both of us that we are being intentionally stalked by the predators of the parvenus, my dear *sister*, because they thnk we're newer rich than they."

"We're newer, in any event, and we have no pretensions," she shot back.

"Except that *I* am the imposter."

"How nice that you have a conscience."

"With a past, Angel Eyes, which can easily be rooted out the same as yours."

"We have been here four months now and there's never been a question of—" she began heatedly.

"And there's never been a man ready to ask for your hand before this, nor a woman as determined as Antoinette Madrid. Your grandmother may have timed this trip to England exactly right, Angelene. We're getting out of the line of fire and into the den of lions."

"I don't care."

"Of course you don't. In England you will find the perfect man of power, the one who has enough money and the manhood to deal with you. And I don't envy him either, Angelene. But he'll be getting exactly what he deserves—a pretty little toy."

She wheeled on him then, her hand reaching for something to throw at him, at his arrogance, at his damnable masculinity that had spoiled her for anyone else . . . and then she slowly put her hand down. The choices had been made between them, and there was no bucking them now. They were set in stone and forever to be lived with and no words would change them—or heat or desire.

His frustration with her burned as hot as coals, waiting to burst into flame. He just couldn't make her *see*.

But she saw too well. Everything was before her eyes to see, just as he had said.

"I hear voices," she said suddenly, "I'd better go. I'll leave through grandmother's room, and get a handkerchief or something so I'll have an excuse for having come downstairs."

"You do that," he said, wishing she would just listen to herself making excuses for doing the things she wanted to do in the name of providing an explanation to people she didn't care about for things that were none of their business to begin with.

Well, he had learned, and he could see the larger picture and understand at least what it was within himself he was compromising.

At that, it was easier not to know.

He heard Angelene exit her grandmother's room and the fluty voice of Miss Madrid accosting her. "Why, Miss Bellancourt, so surprised to see you here."

"I came to fetch a handkerchief for Grandmother."

"Oh, how sweet. And have you by any chance seen Mr. Bellancourt?"

"I'm sorry to say I haven't," Angelene said sweetly. "I would surely like to have the last dance of the evening with him."

"Little witch," Miss Madrid muttered as Angelene disappeared from sight. "I wonder where he's hiding, Charlotte. I just know he walked out of that ballroom with Angelene."

And he ducked, coattails and all, under the bed the moment before the door opened to Angelene's room and Miss Madrid entered, relentlessly stalking her quarry.

Angelene did not dance the last waltz with Rake. *He* was nowhere to be found as the party wound down and the guests began to leave to the lilting strains of the last of the twenty dance numbers that the orchestra performed that night.

Ten days later, on November 30th, amidst a flurry of last-minute packing, recruiting an army of cabs and setting forth with a retinue of servants, friends and family, Mrs. Amelia Bellancourt set sail on the steamship liner *Brittalia*, bound for England and scheduled to arrive in London ten days thereafter.

Two days later, Borden answered the imperious knock-

331

ing at the door of the Bellancourt mansion to find a disheveled-looking middle-aged woman with gray-blonde hair and malicious blue eyes standing there, accompanied by a younger man who was obviously her son.

But the irony was, the woman demanded to see Mrs. Bellancourt in much the same arrogant tone as had Miss Angelene that night some four months before—and in exactly the same way, except that *she* was Miss Josephine Scates, and she was Mrs. Bellancourt's daughter, and she had come home today.

Chapter 18

He had never seen an ocean, and he had never seen a ship as massive and vast as this one, and he thought it was a credit to how much he had learned that he did not blink an eye when the cabs finally drew up to the dock and Mrs. Bellancourt pointed it out to him as the vessel on which they would be sailing.

Now that they were aboard and out to sea, and reunited with the Madrids and several other families from home, it seemed like the most natural thing in the world to be living on board a ship as if you were living at home.

The trick was to avoid Antoinette Madrid, and to make sure Mrs. Bellancourt was comfortable, and that Angelene did not succumb to the first wealthy bachelor she met.

Everyone was going to England that winter, but only Mrs. Bellancourt had the coveted invitation from Constanza Morales. And Constanza was already busy arranging the appropriate entertainments for the daughter of a wealthy American widow. Mrs. Bellancourt had only to present her beautiful, gorgeously attired granddaughter at Constanza's country estate outside London, and she would do the rest.

The idea was to storm the bastion of London society during the "little season" when society went abroad while the men stayed home and worked. Parliament was in session and so there was still a good deal of entertainment to be had, and more than that, accommodations, ranging from (for a rental fee) the most elegant town-homes in Mayfair or Berkeley Square (always making sure that there was a central staircase for making impressive entrances) to a suite of rooms at Claridge's or Brown's Hotel, also with the requisite grand entrance foyer, and preferably a duplex suite if possible, again for that sweeping staircase.

In any event, Mrs. Bellancourt had arranged to rent the Morales' massive town home, Oxendene House, as their base in London from which they would both entertain and travel, with Paris being the first item of business once they were settled in.

Of course, that was after settling in to the luxury of a ten day cruise to get there.

It was extravagance even beyond that to which Angelene had grown accustomed in her three months with her grandmother in New York.

For the first, the ocean was an awesome thing, and she had the horrible sense of having been spun away from everything she had ever known into a vortex of formlessness: she did not understand how the water supported the vast weight of the ship, and for the first two days, she was sure it was going to sink and she was going to die.

Nevertheless, she contrived to keep herself busy so she wouldn't think of the possibility of impending disaster, and indeed there were plenty of diversions, from a never ending buffet of food, to cards, dancing, billiards, bowling, quoits, entertainment by a professional musician in the lounge, a reading lounge with an unbelievable array of books, periodicals, and magazines. There were tables for letter writing on ship's stationery, and rows of deep leather chairs beside a viewing window that overlooked the lower decks of the ship and the limitless horizon beyond.

It was more than a little daunting: their days were filled with a little of this and a lot of that, depending upon

334

whom Mrs. Bellancourt wished to see or whom she wished to avoid.

Cards were not *de rigeur* on the voyage, and so it was not a matter of choosing not to respond to one. Rather, the lines were drawn along the choice of whose companionship would be the most advantageous, with the Madrid family straddling the line, solely because Mrs. Bellancourt wished to discourage Antoinette's unseemly pursuit of her grandson.

At the end of ten days, Angelene felt as if she had gone through a diminutive social season, complete with all the entertainments and maneuvers.

Rake felt like an accessory dangling from the arm of an increasingly selfish and avaricious Angelene in her unheeding fall from grace.

London was better. In London at least there was room to move, to pace, to explode. London was wet, foggy and cold, but it had a certain vibrancy about it after ten stultifying days in the enforced company of people who all had the same thing on their minds: storming the ranks of English society.

Mrs. Bellancourt was excessively pleased that she was already one step further along in this regard because of her astute move in enlisting the good offices of the American-born Constanza Morales, Duchess of Glanville.

"Of course, the Duchess is no fool either," Mrs. Bellancourt said the night of their arrival as they settled down in an informal supper around the parlor fireplace in a house so vast that no one had yet found his way around with ease. Nor had the covers been removed or the furniture dusted anywhere, and so the only viable thing to do was improvise. "*She* of course has removed to her country house and is charging me a most exorbitant rate to lease the house and provide the proper introductions. But, children, here is a case of a wise investment which will launch your social careers in England. So—"

Dinner was laid out then, soup, cold meats, plain steamed vegetables—Mrs. Bellancourt had had the forethought to bring her cook, and so was assured of everything being prepared exactly as she wished.

In addition to a phalanx of servants, Mary, her own personal maid and Angelene's, had come and was upstairs dusting the furniture and laying out clothes, while Mr. Darlington's man, Parkins, had been brought solely to attend to him and Rake.

The first order of business was to put the house to rights, a chore which Mrs. Bellancourt cheerfully handed over to her granddaughter with the advice, "It's all a matter of making a list and delegating the chores, my dear, and very useful knowledge to acquire, by the way, for any future event."

Angelene, dressed practically in a housedress made of brown homespun laid over with a big yellow and white striped apron, didn't miss the coy note in her grandmother's voice, and she supposed that any practice obtained in this circus-like atmosphere would be of some benefit, especially since her grandmother had had the forethought to bring her own servants. She could not see the servants of the lofty Duchess of Glanville taking orders from a commoner who barely knew what she was about.

In the end, it didn't prove that difficult a chore; it was a matter of organization. The bedrooms here, the public rooms there. Remove the covers, change the sheets, dust down every bit of furniture, clean the windows, mop the floors. Oh, she knew all about the mundane household tasks. The trick was to get the servants to willingly take on the additional work and not resent it.

Of course her grandmother would have said that they had had a very nice respite over the sea voyage where the majority of them had had very little to do, so that it was almost like a luxurious paid vacation for them.

But Angelene, who had mixed the grits and made the beds in a rustic road ranch not that many months before, remembered, and she never wanted to go back to doing that ever again. She infinitely preferred giving the orders, and felt a provoking distaste for the way Mr. Darlington and Rake left everything up to her and her grandmother, save stocking the liquor cabinet.

The next day, Mrs. Bellancourt was ready to sail forth and conquer the city. This meant appropriating a carriage, a driver, a map (through Parkins' offices), a reasonably dry cold and sunny day, and no little enthusiasm on Mrs. Bellancourt's part.

"We will know the city like natives by the time we are through," she prophesied, but all they knew at the end of several long hours of driving around in circles was that they had passed twice over the hugely crowded London Bridge, and that the city seemed to have a disproportionate number of parks, and the Houses of Parliament overwhelmed the landscape altogether.

In any event, they were close by Hyde Park and St. James Park, and not far from Piccadilly Circus, and most importantly, within walking distance of Green Park and Buckingham Palace.

Perhaps it was only a matter of securing the right location, and afterward planning a campaign.

The first step of this was to prepare for a side-trip of about a week to Paris. This required more trunks, more packing, travel reservations and a hotel accommodations arranged by telegraph.

Then they were off again, with Mr. Darlington and Rake staying behind, assuring the ladies that everything would be exactly as they wished upon their return.

"Thank heaven we wrote ahead," Mrs. Bellancourt said—and often afterwards—when they were ushered into the hushed recesses of the dress salon at the House of Worth. It was enough to make a person cranky to see how many mothers and daughters awaited the attention of this most sought-after designer whose dressmaking establishment was housed in a five-story building on the Rue de la Paix with a plain sign over the entrance that merely stated his name.

"Everyone who is not travelling in the little season is here, and I count no less than eight mothers and daughters waiting in that anteroom, and I don't know if any of them have appointments as we do. The only saving grace is that his designs are exclusive and will never be duplicated from one client to the next."

When he joined them, wearing his signature beret and artist's smock, he began by making it perfectly clear that he was not appreciative of receiving measurements and instructions at all. "I never create a gown for someone I have never seen," he told them concisely and not a little arrogantly as he paced around Angelene and looked her over quite thoroughly. "That is not why a woman comes to me to be dressed. I must see the woman, the posture, the coloring, the shape of her body, Madame Bellancourt, all of which cannot be conveyed by a set of figures and a description of her coloration. What words could communicate the blue of Mademoiselle's eyes or the gold of her hair? We will measure now," he added, snapping his fingers crisply to an assistant waiting nearby.

"It is only fortunate that you wrote far enough in advance," he added, as the assistant disappeared for a moment and came back bearing an armful of material and a measuring tape. "So."

When one had money, Angelene thought, as she allowed herself to be twisted this way and that and wound up, down and around in the ubiquitous length of measuring tape, one could command the world, and wait seven days for the high priest of fashion to finish it. Her grandmother was handing her the world in the form of five gowns of unparallelled fit and finish, in colors appropriate to her skin and hair, in a drape and design that proclaimed to the world that she had been dressed by Worth.

She was to wear green with a cream lining for that evening at the theater. And there was a watercolor of blues, greens, creams, yellows, pinks, handpainted on a drift of chiffon for afternoon tea, as well as embroidered virginal white for both tea and tennis. There was a party

338

dress of a striking bronze color, assymetrical, and draped two different ways across her bosom and on the over-skirt.

Finally, there was the ball gown, a most outrageous confection with a long train lined in an unexpected fuschia color, which she would drape over her arm while dancing, and chiffon puffed sleeves, see-through and illusory, that were perfectly matched to the royal blue color of the body of the gown which was of a thick silk brocade shot through with silver threads. When she walked, light glimmered over every inch of her body.

There were accessories too, everything from shoes to underwear of the finest, most delicately embroidered linen, to the proper stockings and matching shoes.

There were fittings, three of them, before everything was perfected enough for the master to agree that the final finish could begin.

Finally, there were four lovely days and nights at the Hotel Cambon, once again in the most discreet luxury, and there was the obligatory sightseeing tour, which ranged over every mile of the city, because "a worldly woman will have explored the best and the worst of wher-ever she travels," her grandmother said. "You must be prepared to talk about everything from can-can to the Sunday crush on the Boulevard as if you have known and done it your entire life, and you must wear your lovely dresses as if they were the only clothing you had ever known. You will present yourself like the princess you are."

Last but not least came the trunks, the packing of which her grandmother left in the hands of the experi-enced helpers at the Rue de la Paix. These were expressed over to the Hotel on the last day of their stay, and added to the wagon-full of trunks and suitcases with which they had come.

Another two days' travel returned them to London just days before the onset of the Christmas season.

And finally, to crown this triumphant, but brief, visit abroad, awaiting Mrs. Bellancourt when they returned was the much desired invitation, as promised by the Duchess of Glanville, to a "little tea," during which they might become acquainted with several gentlemen and ladies of her acquaintance with whom they would have much in common.

The date was set for the week before Christmas, just before everyone adjourned to their country estates to celebrate the holiday.

The timing was perfection. It meant the possibility of invitations over the New Year, and Mrs. Bellancourt just knew that both Angelene and Richard would take these stuffy country-house aristocrats by storm.

The tea dress was taken out to hang and to be pressed, and to be admired. Mrs. Bellancourt then began to plan everyone's attire down to the last detail. If anything were missing, she promptly dispatched Parkins to find it or buy it. If anyone protested, she rolled over their objections like a breaking wave that swept everything in its path onto the rocky shore.

She would have it her way and no other, and Mr. Darlington and Rake must take the utmost care with their appearances. Not a hair could be out of place.

They were going to tea at the Trowbridge's, whose town house was located not far from theirs on Curzon Street. They would take the carriage in spite of the short distance, and they would be sure to be just on time so as to make the best possible presentation.

Again, the timing was most favorable. The combination of Angelene's blue-eyed blonde beauty in contrast to the height and brownness and starkness of Richard's looks made them instantly recognizable and objects of great curiosity when they entered the Trowbridge townhouse.

Here was a five-story red brick building that occupied the whole corner of Curzon Street where it intersected with and turned into the private enclave of Chesterfield Gardens.

It was a most elite address, and Mrs. Bellancourt was justly proud that her children looked very much a part of the social strata they were about to breech.

It really was merely a matter of whom the Duchess had arranged to be present who was of any note. All it would take was one socially well-placed gentleman who might take a liking to either Angelene or Richard and issue the invitation that might place them within the company of the Prince of Wales, and that gentleman's roving eye could not help but notice Angelene.

It became obvious, as Lady Trowbridge introduced them around, that Constanza, Duchess Glanville, had done a little preliminary sowing of seeds. Already they all knew that Angelene was an American heiress who had lived on a cattle ranch, and Rake owned stables in two states and bred thoroughbreds under a very well known name, having done so, it was said, to prove to the family that his talent with horseflesh was something to be both respected and prized as another adjunct to the family fortune.

Everyone was humming with curiosity about the striking man with the forbidding expression and the sun-dark skin, and positively agog at Angelene in her water-color silk tea dress, instantly aware it had been designed by Worth.

But the ranch life fascinated them more, and the conversation was lively and easy. If Angelene had any compunction about restructuring the truth of the matter, she only showed it by her refusal to look Rake directly in the eye.

Their reticence on those matters, particularly Rake's, was viewed very favorably by a somewhat hardened cadre of social trend-setters who had met all manner of American women over the previous two or three years. They really were rather taken with these two, not only because of their striking good looks, but because they were not as brash and bold as some of the newcomers, and yet they had an easy manner that did not back down from the probing personal question and gave back the same with graceful good humor.

Mrs. Bellancourt sat back in silence and enjoyed the

spectacle of the reluctant Richard, all trotted up in his tightly fitting suit and Angelene, drifting like something ethereal among the other guests, taking this little corner of London by storm.

"Dear Richard, you should have no qualms at all about telling people what they want to hear," Mrs. Bellancourt said complacently the next morning as they reviewed the previous afternoon's triumph over chocolate, pastries, cold meats and fruit.

"It seems to be a predominant theme among those with whom we are involved with socially," Rake said without rancor. He had about given up on trying to reshape the morality of the thing. There was no morality, no balance, and he had been forced to deal with the substance of that observation every moment he had been in Mr. Darlington's company. A man's worth was judged solely by what he said he did and not by who he was, and therefore the more a man could elevate himself in the estimation of others, the more acceptable he became.

It held true for every area of a gentleman's life. Whatever he said was the norm and the underside of that was never to be brought out into the light of day.

"We're going to the club," became a euphemism understood by a brotherhood of men who sought to protect the women in their lives from their baser natures.

Mr. Darlington was particularly adept at evading specifics when it came to details of where he and his protegé had spent any given evening. There was always an invitation from someone, an old friend, a letter of introduction, a colleague—Mr. Darlington seemed to have a legion of friends and friends of friends who could run interference to deflect a question about where he had been all night.

And the club, above all, was a privileged sanctum which existed, Rake sometimes thought, solely in the minds and hearts of the men who ostensibly belonged to it.

A man could be a breeder of horses or a member of a club and the words simultaneously cloaked the lie and the profanity. A man in this extravagant society hid behind words and the certainty that no one would ask an indelicate question.

Indeed, Mrs. Bellancourt never pursued that line of thought at all. It was as if men had a subordinate life that was not subject to any framework whatsoever, and they could go about their business—whatever it might be—with impunity and the sure knowledge that no explanations would be required of them.

"Well, it's the wenches, you see," Mr. Darlington did say by way of trying to initiate Rake into the intricacies of the amusements for men of greater than usual appetites. "That little Mary now, doesn't she get your heart just ticking away?"

"She's fair enough, I suppose."

"Didn't she ever offer to give you a good steamy rubbing down when you were taking a bath?"

Rake shrugged. "Not yet."

"Well, you see, she wants you to ask. A girl like that can't come forward. You have to make it known that it would be something you would really appreciate, if you understand me."

"I understand you now," Rake said, the mask coming down over his face and shuttering his eyes.

"Any of the girls. A little money. A stranger on the street—you can always tell the working girls, and they're always glad of a couple of extra pounds. A friend of mine makes a damned career out of seducing innocents he accosts on the streets. There's something very appealing about that—you can take any amount of pleasure with no complications. A man can't ask for more than that."

Sister of Innocents . . .

"Of course, if the street doesn't tempt you, we can always make the rounds of the clubs. The houses that cater to every taste. I found a few connections after we arrived, glad to say, and I can recommend several good places to go."

"I'd rather have a drink," Rake said, and Darlington laughed. "It isn't like Paris, Bellancourt. They don't dance up a storm in these places and then offer to go home with you."

"What do they offer?"

"A little toss and turn in the back room, my friend, and I wouldn't doubt someone's watching behind the wall. But if that's your taste . . ."

Rake hid his disgust. "I think your taste is that little girl across the way, waiting for a bus. I think you and your friend make a great sport of competing with each other as to who can take the most virgins in a night, don't you, Darlington?"

"I confess to a preference," Darlington said with no hesitation about admitting it. But these things were understood among gentlemen, and there were any number of well-dressed men prowling the streets of London at night seeking voluptuous delights. "Let me show you so you will know how it is done."

And that first time, he went across the street and said a few words to the girl. They disappeared and they came back again within fifteen minutes, and no one would have known any assignation had taken place at all.

Except that Mr. Darlington was flushed with success. "Oh, she was cheap, Bellancourt, and damned fresh. A worthy conquest that whets my appetite for more. Come join me."

This was how his nights had been spent with Mr. Darlington, among the fresh and fair, the jaded and the jezebels and somehow he had made it through the maze without ever having to prove his manhood on the fields of profligacy.

But Mr. Darlington wouldn't take no for an answer long. "What's wrong with you, boy? There's a tasty morsel every which way you look. Just put out your hand and pluck it off the vine. Or maybe you don't care for the fair sex?"

"Which fair sex is that?"

"Now look, Bellancourt, a man can be restrained, but

344

you're a positive monk. There isn't anyone who doesn't run amuck when they come here. I've heard of places in town that do things that would curl your toes, man. Things I want to try in this one life, boy. And I'll tell you what else heats up my vitals, Bellancourt—that sister of yours."

"Isn't that interesting," Rake murmured, keeping his tone neutral.

"She's something. I tell you, I go to a house now, I'm always looking for a blonde little hussy just like her."

"That's good, because if you touch her, I'll kill you," Rake said, and his voice was so even and so low and so steely, that Darlington almost did not catch the threat in his words until it was too late. But even he recognized the tone of a man who cannot be pushed *that* far, although he thought privately that Richard Bellancourt ought to be first on line to sample that sweet virgin, and relationships be damned. Any woman who looked like that was game for any man, and he was almost willing to put himself on the line to try.

But that stony hard look of Bellancourt's stopped him. There was something primitive there, something that could give pain with no mitigating pleasure.

"I never said anything," he said good naturedly. "The desire will never get past the thought, I promise you, Bellancourt."

"And the thought had better not get past your lips again either, Darlington."

"My word," Darlington swore, but after all, what could one expect when you took a savage and put him into decent clothes and introduced him to the gratifying pursuits of normal men?

He almost didn't want to give up. In fact, Bellancourt was a damned challenge, and besides, a man of morality belonged in a monastery, pure and simple.

It was just a matter of finding out what was Bellancourt's weakness, the thing that would make those stony gray eyes come to life and blaze with lust.

"An altogether successful debut for you too," Mrs. Bellancourt concluded, as they rose from the breakfast table that morning after the tea. "I can't wait to see who will send cards. Tomorrow, my dears, we will make our thank-you calls, and on this occasion we may walk—at least *to* Curzon Street, and then we'll have the carriage pick us up."

She was so satisfied with her plans, and how perfectly everything had worked out at the tea. Even the Duchess Glanville could have no complaint, and she wondered how much of the success of the afternoon would get back to her.

"It is only a matter of a week or two. Christmas is difficult; one always wants to be with family and not so much with strangers. I'm counting on the New Year weekend to set us up exactly where we want to be, and meanwhile, we will celebrate ourselves right here in our cozy little house."

Well, she was prone to exaggeration, Angelene thought. There was nothing cozy at all about the Glanville House. It was a cavern, vast and dark and full of ancient furniture of the fashion of another age, and hung with portraits of disapproving relatives all up and down the stairs, and indifferent landscapes in cracked gilt frames in the bedrooms.

It was cold and drafty too, and the furnace took incessant stoking to spew up even a little heat until Parkins finally got it going, and then the expense of keeping it filled with coal and swept became another story.

But all of that her Grandmother cheerfully dismissed with a wave of her hand and an infusion of a few shillings here, a pound there. Anything unpleasant could be washed away in a sea of money.

Mrs. Madrid came to call from the family's elegant suite at the Claridge Hotel.

"Do you really think *renting* a house was preferable to staying at the hotel?" Mrs. Madrid wondered aloud with rare bad taste. But of course, she had to make it look as if they had made the superior choice because Amelia Bellancourt had gotten neatly ahead of her by tricking that pallid Angelene out in clothes by Worth and getting that invitation to the Trowbridge's.

The best they had been able to do was to contact Eliza Ottridge who, while she had connections, couldn't arrange anything in the way of introductions so close to Christmas, and made promises of securing them a New Year's weekend somewhere wonderful, for which they would never have to apologize.

"Well, we're just *surrounded* by Glanville history," Mrs. Bellancourt said contentedly. "I don't find that a *disadvantage*."

"But all that extra work when the hotel could be doing it all for you."

"But think of all the people who will know about the Bellancourts. You know—the wealthy American family that is staying at the Glanville's in Mayfair. I don't think you could pay any amount of money for that kind of conversation, dear Flora."

Mrs. Madrid gave up. Mrs. Bellancourt had always been very knowledgeable and a step ahead of everyone in their crowd before she went into complete mourning after Horace died.

But she hadn't missed a step and had eased her way back into things as though her way had been greased with butter.

Besides, Mrs. Madrid's main intent had not been to come and belittle Mrs. Bellancourt, at least not initially, even though she was stewing over the inroads Mrs. Bellancourt had already made.

She was really scouting out the whereabouts of Richard Bellancourt and perhaps a little more of his background, since Antoinette seemed so head over heels about trying to captivate him.

"Antoinette is so enjoying the city. I trust the same is true of your grandchildren, Amelia?"

"I can speak for all of us," Mrs. Bellancourt said,

motioning for Mary to serve the tea. "We're enjoying it enormously. And Mayfair is the perfect location. So close to everything, including the Royals. I'm very pleased. Tea, Flora?"

Flora took tea and lot more of this genteel abuse before she gave up and made her farewells.

"There wasn't a thing that old witch would tell me about her grandson, Antoinette, and I do wish you would get him out of your mind as an eligible. I couldn't bear to be around that Amelia Bellancourt more than the half hour I put in with her today. Do you hear me? Do you?"

"No, Mother, I won't listen to you at all. I want Richard Bellancourt, and I swear I will have him."

"There must be some damned thing that makes you stand at attention, Bellancourt," Mr. Darlington said despairingly on yet another night when they were going to the club. Mr. Darlington meant to sample some fine young ladies at a place where not one of them was rumored to be over sixteen. "Something young? Something lush, Bellancourt? You know, with a little flesh to her? Something a little out of the ordinary? Perhaps you have a taste for a little violence with your main meal, eh?"

"I haven't yet seen the thing that appeals to me," Rake said calmly—again, not stating the out and out lie, but skirting painfully close to the truth while he was caught in the bind of not being able to refuse Mr. Darlington's twice-weekly forays into the belly of the city and not having any good reason to stay at home.

Of course Darlington had introduced him to more savory fare: several afternoons sitting in at Parliament, and tour of the galleries at the Hall of Justice. He knew the best and cheapest vintners in town, and the location of every beer hall in the city.

He was a man with a secret life in much the same way as the city, and he prettied it up with cordiality and availability, and an overlay of the appearance of a bottomless pocket. He wound up with the reputation as the guest everyone wanted, and he had parlayed that into a trip to London where he could indulge his excesses and Mrs. Bellancourt didn't have an inkling of what was going on.

"I'm enjoying this riddle, Bellancourt; I don't believe I've had so much fun in years. You haven't seen the thing that appeals to you! That's wonderful. Not a woman in the whole of the kingdom? How about the Queen, my friend?"

He knew them all—dark, exotic, young, old, bosomy, plain fat, slender, boyish, girlish, experienced, virginal. "You don't have any taste, Bellancourt. What was wrong with little Fanny over there? Come on, man, I want to see you take a ride."

"I ride enough in my life," Rake retorted. "Leave it, Darlington. There's nothing worthwhile here for me."

It made Mr. Darlington wonder what this remote and reserved man considered worthwhile. He was aching to find out, and it was almost as good as an unexpected opportunity in the excitement it engendered.

He spent a lot of time thinking about Bellancourt and his "taste," and everything he had shown him, and some of the more exotic things he had not. There was room there yet: every man had an appetite of some sort. He made a bet with himself: he would discover it before the end of the "little season", and long before they ever had to return home.

Chapter 19

The invitation came from the Duchess Glanville herself for the Bellancourt household to join her and a gathering of friends, at her country estate in Sussex, just outside of Colchester.

It was a preening moment of triumph for Mrs. Bellancourt. "There it is, could anything be better? Angelene— *a gathering of friends*—surely some of the people we met at the Trowbridge's, including *them*, of course. They must have reported most favorably about our visit, and it is all a credit to you and Richard. You two are the ones who made the excellent impression. And now, and now— there's no telling how far you will go. I am *overwhelmed.*"

She never noticed that everyone else remained decisively silent.

"We'll take everything with us, all the servants, our clothes—we'll make a grand entrance—you'll need some new suits, Richard; tweeds in the country, especially in the winter. I'm sure there will be excellent shooting, riding, wonderful company. I am head over heels over this invitation, children. Now let me think . . ."

Mr. Darlington eased out of the room, annoyed that Amelia was going to lift him out of his sensual playground for the space of a whole week.

Rake paced around Mrs. Bellancourt like a caged lion, wondering how he could get away from the encroaching old woman, and Angelene realized that this moment was the beginning of everything, and not the headlong flight that had put her at her grandmother's mercy.

This was the moment she had so ardently wished for, and now it had arrived in the form of a creamy sheet of thick stationery. She was not prepared for it or what it would mean for her. Everything else, as even her grandmother knew, had only been preparation for this moment when she and her family would be invited to mix with nobility.

Anything could happen from here on in; this was the end of her long road of choices, and it was the place where she should reach out with both hands and take whatever was offered.

Then she lookd at Rake, tall and forbidding and horribly remote, and she didn't know that any choice was the right one at all.

She had spent hours with him, treating him like the best of all brothers during the voyage over, and he had spent hours with her and her grandmother, never uttering one word that could be misconstrued or acting anything more than grateful for all her grandmother had done for them.

At any time, he could have walked away. More than that, he could have revealed her little deceit. But he had made choices too, just as he had said, and now that she was on the brink of the most important choice of all, she didn't find much happiness in it, or in anything for that matter, since they had departed New York.

Rake was as distant as if he were across an ocean and she wondered for the first time if that had been deliberate on his part. *She* hadn't even noticed.

She saw it now, and that it had been coupled with the faint hope that Mrs. Bellancourt could not make any inroads into the tight English aristocracy, and that eventually they would all go home.

He had been willing to be patient, to see her through the end of it, so that the choice would then come around again and she would have a second chance, another opportunity.

351

But the circumstances would still be the same: he would always be Rake Cordigan, the man of the mountain, isolated in silence, a man of his past; she would always be on the run from Josie, and a prisoner of her secret. The plain fact was, she needed security and safety more than she needed him.

He saw the decision touch her face briefly, his beautiful, treacherous Angel Eyes, and he knew that he would make one more sojourn with her and her grandmother and that the end of his pain was finally in sight.

Grassmere, the Glanville country house in Sussex, was not the typical half-timbered sprawling Tudor edifice that Mrs. Bellancourt was familiar with. It was rather more classical, constructed of brick, with three thick chimneys rising symmetrically from its roof and long windows on all sides of the reception floor, and delightful gabled bedroom windows above. It rose from a full basement that housed the kitchens, laundry, pantries and cold storage rooms, and its grounds were terraced upward from a long winding road that led to a circular drive and a basement entranceway for luggage and a stone staircase to welcome the guests.

It was an extremely manageable house with a long parlor to the left of the entrance hall, off of which there was a more intimate drawing room, a library and a billiard room. Its dining room was laid out adjacent to the kitchen stairwell, the business office and a little sitting room on the other side of the house. Upstairs there were ten bedrooms, six of them aligned on the side of the house above the parlor, the others laid out over the dining room wing, and one small bedroom over the drawing room ell.

It was a most elegantly laid out house, and it was one which made its guests feel comfortable because there was nothing overdone about it.

Mrs. Bellancourt and Angelene were escorted to their separate rooms, Angelene's being the small bedroom over the ell, and her grandmother situated in the larger corner room overlooking the rear garden.

At first she took offense at where she had been put, until she reflected that more guests were expected, and probably of noble rank too.

Rake and Darlington were together in the dining room wing, and the Trowbridges across the hall in the large front bedroom. Opposite them were the Hallandales, who had already arrived but had not been introduced. Constanza, Duchess Glanville, indicated there were several more guests expected.

"This is my protegé," she said, extending her hand to Angelene.

"And this is *Mr.* Bellancourt," she added, as Rake exploded into the room and stopped abruptly as he caught sight of the assembled company. "Mr. Bellancourt."

"Ma'am?" He came forward and took her other hand at her imperious command. She was an imperious sort of woman, tall and large-boned, impeccably dressed, with a long narrow face and deep dark eyes.

"You do live up to advance expectations," she murmured. "I'm so pleased to have you both here. Permit me now, my husband, Henry, Duke of Glanville. Lord and Lady Hallendale, Mrs. Bellancourt, welcome, and Mr. Darlington, I'm so pleased to see you. You all know Lord and Lady Trowbridge. Our other guests will be arriving imminently. Please make yourselves at home."

But the Duke immediately drew him aside and before he knew it, he was engaged in still another discourse on horsebreeding and thus proving his worth to both his hosts and the assembled guests.

By the time they retired to dress for dinner, the remainder of the company had arrived. They included the Earl of Rottingham, George Endicott and his wife, Beatrice; Lord Edward and Lady Alice Walbridge; Mr. and Mrs. Victor Madrid and their daughter, Antoinette.

"I don't believe this," Mrs. Bellancourt fumed. "How in the world did she *ever* inveigle an invitation *here?*"

To make things worse, they were quartered in the two bedrooms side by side that of Mrs. Bellancourt, and the only gratification she got from any of it was that the remainder of the peers occupied the bedrooms across the hall. Even so, that meant Flora Madrid had equal access to them as well.

However, she determined not to let that disappointment dim her pleasure in coming. Antoinette Madrid could never outshine her Angelene, nor would she ever get one foot near Richard if she, Amelia, could possibly prevent it. All it really meant was that it was going to be a very interesting weekend.

It was the perfect time of year to fill the house with guests: desolate outside, cold and inhospitable, and warm, comforting, cozy and congenial inside, with the scent of Christmas still in the air, and the crackle of logs on the fire underscoring the lively conversation.

They spent the first day in perfect leisure, eating, talking, touring the stables, taking walks around the property, in the billiard room, in the library, in the drawing room, doing nothing but staring into space.

The servants tended to everything. There was food laid out in the dining room at every hour of the day and access to a generous wine cellar.

There would be cards that night as well, and entertainment by the Countess of Rottingham who was a notable pianist.

It was a chance to relax in an atmosphere of conviviality, but Angelene found herself totally on edge, and not totally because of the august company either, she thought. She tried to analyze her disquieting feeling, although it was enough to make one quake to be among earls and dukes of the realm and still have no idea how she had gotten among them with such ease, no one discovering she wasn't quite what she seemed.

On the contrary: the story of her mother the cattle baronness was making impressive rounds among the guests concurrent with their fascination with Rake and his thoroughbreds.

The Duke in fact was quite anxious to show off his horses and the good shooting to be had in the vicinity, and a party was scheduled to take advantage of that early in the morning. The women could elect to ride or spend the morning at leisure. In the afternoon, they would partake of a lavish lunch and either nap or settle in for cards or billiards, and then change for dinner.

After dinner, more of the same, with perhaps lighter entertainment provided by the guests along with a detailed recapitulation of the day's events.

"That Bellancourt chap, he really knows his stuff about horses," the Duke was heard to say admiringly.

"*And* can handle a gun," Lord Hallandale put in. "There really must be something to this American west business. Those two children have led a life right from the pages of a novel."

"So we are a unit," Angelene said to Rake as they sat before the fire and sipped some claret. "We are a pair, the Bellancourt siblings, and you, my dear Rake, are the star."

"That wasn't exactly what I had pictured," Rake said bitterly. "It must be equally exhilarating to be admired for your beauty as much as I am for my skill. I would never have thought that the abilities that are so natural to me by virtue of the training and the games of my youth would be so coveted by people like these. They are trained for nothing but occupying their leisure days, and they find people like us to fill the void, because they don't know how to fill it themselves. I am not happy being an appendage to a woman who is not my grandmother, nor the brother of an angel. This will be the place, Angelene, where the next decision is made, and I promise you I will stand by this one, and it will be the one made for my peace of mind and not yours."

She reached out to touch him, all white and golden— and tainted with the desire to persevere, and her fingers settled lightly on his arm that was clothed in the very finest of tailored fabric, and Antoinette's light voice said behind them, "Ah, Richard, I wondered where you had got to. I have extraordinary news to tell—the Prince will be dining at Grassmere tonight, isn't it incredible? He sent word to the Duchess not an hour ago and will be arriving shortly before five. This could be the night our reputations are made!"

From Grassmere and the approbation of the Prince who, always in search of something new and novel, took immediately to the breeder and the daughter of a *cattle* baroness (which he found quite amusing) who was the most beautiful woman he had seen in years—and dressed by Worth too—from this small seed grew a positive plethora of invitations to evenings of dining, dancing, more country house carnage, a mountain of cards from everyone who was in town, and a resulting need for even more dresses, more gowns, and perhaps a long-unrequited weekend of doing just plain nothing.

It was enervating, having the Prince's approval, and Rake found to his dismay that he was going nowhere fast and Antoinette Madrid was following him right on his coattails.

They met at the opera, at Covent Garden, a theatrical, a ball. She was there when he went riding in Hyde Park in the mornings, or toured the National Gallery with Angelene just for want of something to do.

He couldn't leave town: everyone knew who he was and everyone wanted him and Angelene and there was no getting away from it, because the *London Tatler* chronicled every last thing they did.

Rake was almost sure he knew who was dispensing the information: the inexhaustible Mr. Darlington, who had found Grassmere greatly distasteful and limited, and had nonetheless tried to foist one of the maids off on Rake, only to have him refuse. His abstinence made Mr. Darlington look all the more vulgar, a sensation to which he took great exception.

Darlington was determined to get him one way or the other, and the *Tatler* had all the up-to-the-minute gossip, including the searching question of why this eligible American hadn't yet formed an attachment. Darlington was still trying to lure him out at night once they returned to London, and pretending he knew nothing about the scurrilous stories in print.

And Angelene had finally met the man of her dreams.

He was Charles Endicott, Rottingham's son, who had appeared one evening unexpectedly at a musicale which, in the normal course of events, bored him silly.

But this particular evening, Miss Angelene Bellancourt was to be among the guests, and his curiosity had been well and truly piqued about her after his parents' return from Grassmere.

He was tall and slender and finely made, and he moved with an economy of motion that was one of the first things one noticed about him. More than that, he was handsome and strong in a gentle kind of way—there was no edge of danger about this man. There was rather a quiet competence and the surety that came from having possessed great wealth all his life. He knew that every door was open to him and he had no arrogance about his position in life; he was polite, mannered, appreciative, selective, and in many ways, bored.

He had met many American girls over the years as they began to take regular trips to England, but he had never met anyone quite as beautiful or intriguing as Angelene.

The first thing he saw that night at the musicale was her glorious hair which was piled carelessly into a topknot but for that one fall draped enticingly over her shoulder.

And then the shoulder, swathed in silk brocade and velvet in a bronze color that made that fall of hair look like silk.

And then her skin, ivory against the dark color, and those eyes, so deep a blue he thought he could drown in

357

them, set in the perfect oval of her face.

She had been raised on a ranch somewhere in the Wild West one was always reading about, and she still looked and acted like a perfect lady. She had so entertained the Prince of Wales that everyone wanted her on their guest list.

What could be better?

The forbidding-looking gentleman with the stony gray eyes would have to go, of course, but that would be easy. The music would be over soon (none too soon, he thought), and everyone would rise and mingle, and finally, he would have his chance.

"What is love after all," Angelene wondered, shaking out the newest issue of the *Tatler*, only to find her name gracing the front page for a change.

"It is definitely a useless emotion when one is in pursuit of a peer," Rake said dourly as he entered the parlor. "And Mr. Endicott, I might add, is less than useless."

"I really think it is time you returned to your racehorses, *Richard*. This London air seems to be fogging your brain. Charles is perfection, I promise you, and rather a nice change from the volatile personalities around here."

"But have you checked the list of invitations pouring in, Sister of Angels? Surely there are twenty-five you would like to accept, always assuming Charles will deign to put in an appearance."

"You make it sound as if I'm expending a gross amount of time and energy on being entertained."

"Yes, I think that's exactly what I'm implying, Angelene. You've gone overboard, to say the least, especially when you tried to coax your grandmother to stay until spring so you could go down to Cowes for the sailing just because the Prince was going to be there. There is a limit, although I don't think your grandmother knows what it is, and you, in your wild success, haven't fathomed it."

"But you of course hold the key to everything in your hand."

"I hold nothing in my hand, Angelene, least of all you, and if you think I have forgotten or that you have buried all that is between us, I will tell you now that it can never be erased."

"Nonsense—look—it's gone!" she said lightly, clapping her hands.

"Do you really want to test that, Angelene?" he asked dangerously, and she backed down instantly, which gave him some satisfaction.

"No, I don't," she said bravely. "I just think the best thing for you to do would be to go back to America."

"But I too have all manner of engagements to attend to," he said officiously. "All the riding I could possibly want, endless mornings of shootings anywhere within a fifty mile range of London. I'm wanted for polo when the weather heats up, dinner with the Madrids, who just never give up; I believe Lady Sanborne has invited me to the opera; there's an upcoming session of Parliament which Lucretia Lady Dornborough wishes to attend . . . I believe my calendar is as full as yours, Angelene."

"And you find no satisfaction in it whatsoever."

"I find no satisfaction in watching you flounder around here. There's no threat to you any more, Angelene, and even if there were, there are ways of outwitting Josie."

"That's not the point," she said heatedly.

"Tell me the point; after five months, I tend to forget the point."

"The point is I never want to go back to that again."

"And *that* is . . . ?"

"The lack of amenities, the poverty, the memory. I'll stay here forever, Rake, even if I never find a husband, rather than return back home and go right back to where I started from."

"It seems to me you started this sojourn from the wealthiest part of New York with a thousand dollars worth of dresses by your side."

"*You* don't understand."

"I reckon I don't, Angelene. Or maybe you *won't*. But that's been the problem all along, hasn't it? You didn't expect to want me the way you did, and I never expected to be sitting across a room in the heart of London arguing with you about what is right before your eyes."

"Charles never says such things to me."

"And Charles never will, Angelene. But Charles will never ache for you, nor will you ever beg for him, and that is the difference between what you have and what you really want."

"Well, then—go home."

"There is no home," he said stiffly, or maybe it was that he just didn't know where to find a home without her.

"What *is* there, then?"

"There is life, Angelene—the life we have made between you and me."

And then, at the end of January, they were off as part of an exclusive party to Shillingford, the country seat of the Rottinghams in Kent.

This was a seat of grand proportions with halls and walls every which way a guest turned, a pillared entrance hall with a wide sweeping staircase surrounded by statuary, and Axminster carpets covering the floors in great sweeps of faded splendor.

The main body of the hall was shaped in an ell with the utility room all at the foot, and the main living room all off a long hallway to the backstairs and the butler's pantry.

On the second floor there were ten bedrooms surrounding an open ceiling that looked down like a gallery on the entrance hall, and above, there were still ten more, plus accommodations for children, bachelors, maids and attendants, servants of guests, and the household help.

There was no intimacy here, only the sense of entering a house steeped in history that looked more like a church than a home.

Nonetheless, once a guest understood that all of the rooms in the central section of the house fed off of the squared corridors, it became easy to navigate his way back to the public rooms.

This time, in addition to those with whom they were already acquainted, the Bellancourt family met the Duke and Duchess of Buckton, assorted Lords, Ladies and Honorables, the Lady Moren Craig who was down with her parents from Lincolnshire, and two other American families—the Madrids and the Coombes' who had just arrived in London, just in advance of the next wave of American emigrants who were coming in time for the long season.

"Of course the quality of person arriving now leaves much to be desired," Charlotte Coombes said loftily to Charles Endicott. "You would not believe some of the people who travelled over with us. There was one particularly vile woman . . ."

At which juncture, Charles excused himself as he caught sight of Angelene wafting down the stairs in one of her tea dresses and looking impossibly fragile.

"Has anyone ever called you an angel?" he demanded possessively, grasping her hands and looking up into her cool blue eyes.

"Now and again," she smiled, "but never as charmingly as you."

"Well then, you can be my guardian angel," he said, handing her down the last two steps, "and help save me from these predatory young ladies who only care about titles and not about the man."

"I care about the man," she said instantly, and he patted her hand and tucked it into his arm.

"Well, in that case, you deserve the royal tour of Shillingford, my guardian angel, and you'll never be able to hide from me again."

"No, it will be that much easier to find you," she said teasingly.

"I should never want to lose you," he said fervently.

"So here we go. Notice the billiard room and the fact the table is almost as big as the room itself, so there is no room at all to play the game. Next, across the hall we have the dining room of the army: a hundred thousand men and more can fit into this room at one go—no? It is rather vast, isn't it? It certainly sits fifty, in a pinch. And look—see that cunningly fitted out wall over there—come behind and see: it's called a servery and it is where all the dishes are stacked just before serving. It's also the place, sweet Angelene, where I mean to give your first kiss—"

And he bent toward her and his lips touched hers just a little bit experimentally, and she reared back just a little bit, and he immediately released her.

"It's too soon, isn't it?" he whispered, trying to be kind and respect the delicacy of her feelings.

"Oh no . . ." Oh yes. Oh no. She didn't know what to think, except that she had wanted his kiss up until the very moment he tried to claim it.

And yet, what pretensions had she, after all she had been through with Rake Cordigan. She knew what she was about, she could have kissed him, at least.

She couldn't—not yet.

But if she did—if she could bring herself to—it would be the first step down the long dark corridor of winning him for herself. It was necessary, vital that she command his interest.

But still—she didn't know whether he expected this of her, the sheltered grandchild of a wealthy widow, or whether her willingness would be taken as an invitation for him to pursue.

She decided quickly that reticence was best: a man could always be charmed by what he could not have. More than that, he could never hold it over a woman, all that nonsense about aching and begging. Charles was not a man she could ever see herself importuning, and she liked the thought of that.

He could plead with *her*.

And he did.

"Then let me have my kiss, sweet Angelene. Don't

362

deny me now, when it's all I've thought about for days."

She forced herself to hold rigidly still as his lips just gently pressed against hers and sought no more contact than that.

Was she disappointed? Did she care what his kisses were like? She could live with tepid kisses, if only he would decide that she was the one he wanted.

She did have the edge: she was American, and blonde and beautiful and well-to-do, and she had some exotica in her background. She could compete with any of the young women strutting down the hallway at that very moment, and in more ways than they would ever know.

"That was lovely, Charles," she whispered, reaching up and touching his lips.

He kissed her fingers.

"It's only the beginning, sweet Angelene, the enhancement to all of our coming pleasures."

One pleasure she was not looking forward to was Rake's disparaging remarks, but surprisingly, this time, he seemed not to be disposed to make them.

He and Darlington, along with several other of Charles' friends were quartered in the bachelors' rooms down the long hall of the ell toward the front of the house on the second floor.

Angelene, Mrs. Bellancourt and the other single ladies were given bedrooms just off the square corridor with the open ceiling to the entrance hall, and the married couples occupied the bedrooms surrounding the corridor itself.

It was a very nice arrangement, with at least two private stairwells at the disposal of anyone who wanted to make an assignation and who, if he had been clever enough to explore, would have found any number of private rooms on the third floor.

Dinner was the next event after arrival, and when the guests came down from changing, they were directed into the dining room which had been rearranged and now contained four large tables instead of one long one. Each of these tables was elegantly set with linen and silver and place cards to insure the proper mix of guests and to make sure old friends didn't just sit and talk to old friends.

Angelene had been placed directly beside Charles, a definite mark of preference at a table that also included two peers of the realm, the hot-eyed Moren Craig, Charlotte Coombes and Flora and Vincent Madrid.

Rake drew the table with the Coombes', the Endicotts, Antoinette Madrid, the Craigs, and her grandmother.

For her, the others didn't matter. Except for Moren Craig whose eyes strayed very definitely across to where Rake sat, and Charlotte who couldn't seem to get along without Antoinette by her side. Charles was uncommonly charming, but she could feel his reluctance to have any kind of intercourse with Charlotte, because she was a little gauche and terribly naive.

"Well, isn't this lovely," Flora Madrid kept saying, as she tucked her napkin nervously away between each course. "This is lovely, Charles."

They wound their way through all manner of meat, fish, game, vegetables, breads, soup, desserts in a selection large enough to offer in a restaurant, and they finished off with coffee. The gentlemen retired for brandy in the library, with the ladies joining them afterward in the drawing room for a musicale.

There was nothing spontaneous about this outing in the country. Every moment was planned by the extremely consciencious Countess, who, for this evening, imported an orchestra and invited her guests to dance.

She hated country weekends where guests were left to their own devices; invariably they got bored and then passed the word around that the Endicotts, or whomever their hosts happened to be, could not get up enough to interest even a weekend guest.

To that end, there was to be a hunt in the morning, or riding, a shoot in the afternoon, cards early evening, a musicale after dinner.

She had no expectations of any Princes dropping by with an hour's notice, nor did she expect her guests to amuse themselves, although they could choose to do so. She only expected that everyone would dress for dinner and that no one would bow out of cards or whatever games she had planned for the succeeding evening.

And after the orchestra had played a selection of musical numbers, the Countess announced the dance, and in the informal environs of the country house, there was no need for formal introductions. Everyone knew *who* everyone else was; a dance gave them an opportunity to get to know them a little better.

Only Charles commandeered Angelene for the first dance and then would not let her go.

"Were we in London, dear Charles, the censure I would receive would be almost unbearable."

"But we are here, sweet Angelene, and only my mother is the arbiter of propriety, and I promise you, she is stricter than any patroness you ever heard of."

They danced again, and then he took on Charlotte Coombes while Angelene pried Rake away from Antoinette Madrid.

"You are inordinately silent, Rake Cordigan," she whispered fiercely under the cover of the music.

"Perhaps I'm beginning to see the worth of all of this," he said easily. "I'm told Lady Moren Craig is an avid horsewoman, and I mean to ask her to accompany me tomorrow."

"How nice," she murmured. "I'm so glad you have found someone who can be useful to you."

"Yes, we did talk about use in connection with Charles, didn't we? Well, Lady Moren is a woman of experience and I'm looking forward to getting to know her."

"I'll wager you are," she said sweetly, "but you're not going to bamboozle me, Rake."

"Nor you me," he said in kind. "We know each other so well, Angelene. Neither of us can outwit the other. Excuse me now, will you?" And he left her there, as the music died away, and immediately solicited the attention of Moren Craig.

She felt a pang at that, she didn't deny it, but she couldn't possibly demand that he refrain from finding happiness when she was on the brink of it.

Charles rejoined her as the orchestra began to play a pretty waltz. He swept her into his arms and around the floor, and in that moment, she thought she could want nothing more.

She rode in the morning with Charles, she took breakfast with him and other early risers later, after an exhilarating gallop across the rolling fields of Shillingford, neck in neck in competition with the excellent seat of Moren Craig.

But she was confident now, in no small part due to her grandmother's insistence on lessons; and it helped immeasurably that Charles was perfectly attentive to *her* and ignored the flagrant allure of the fickle Moren.

She wanted *every* man, Angelene thought, and she would take whichever man succumbed to her enticements. She had a front row view of Rake being taken into the deep well of those smoldering eyes which all the while were assessing exactly how interested Charles Endicott was in the pallid little American.

Charles had gotten awfully interested. He escorted her to her room to change for lunch; he stole a kiss and playfully tried to enter her room. He whispered suggestive little nothings through the keyhole.

He took Rake shooting in the afternoon and came back in awe of Rake's ability with a shotgun. "Why, the man can hit anything on the ground or in the air at two hundred feet. Amazing."

"What about with an arrow?" the Honorable Joseph Linbaugh, one of Charles's sporting cronies, asked. "As long as we're at it, old chap, why don't we test the fellow's mettle. Make you a wager on it. Any takers?"

Immediately he was surrounded by the crowd of

eligibles who had been listening idly to this conversation.

"They're betting on Rake—my *brother?*" Angelene asked in disbelief.

"Why not?" Charles shrugged. "They're bored silly and you two *are* the novelty of the moment. It's that western thing: they think everyone is either a cowboy or an Indian, and you have to admit, Richard knows his horses and guns."

"He does at that," Angelene said, her eye fixed on Moren Craig who had inched her way into the center of the crowd and declared loudly, "One hundred pounds *for.*"

She bowed to a scattering of applause at her audacity.

"Of course, we need a crack archer to go up against him," Charles said, trying to bring some order to the thing.

"Well, then—that's you, old man," Linbaugh said. "You can't get bloody better than firsts at Oxford."

"You can damned well not bruit it about, Linbaugh. That's a part of my past I keep undercover. Nor have I ever told about the one time you shot me out of the box, old son—so it looks like you get to try the champion."

"A hundred pounds on Joseph," Moren declared, "and rescind the bet on the stranger. I'll bet on an Englishman any time."

"Done," Charles said, and proceeded to take the bets in an orderly fashion, in spite of the growing excitement over the idea of a match between Bellancourt and Linbaugh. "Your fellow peers have great faith in you, Joseph," he said after the wagering was done. "It's up to you now, for Queen and country. Only two bets on the American—"

"Three," Angelene said suddenly.

"Three? Well now, ladies and gentlemen, here's a wager that changes the face of things—Mr. Bellancourt's sister, full of faith and confidence. All takers? No? You all know Joseph and nobody knows the dark horse—so to speak. Very well then. The bids are up and I'm locking them in the safe and they can never be touched again until the match is over."

They followed him then to the library to what his family called the "public safe", the one that could be opened with impunity for just such foolishness without giving away the family secrets.

He popped in the paper and swung the door shut with a flourish.

"And now my dears, let us go and challenge the formidable Mr. Bellancourt and see what kind of sporting man he is."

It really was like being charged by the enemy, Rake thought as Charles presented the proposition in such a way that he couldn't possibly back out. He didn't want to back out. These damned jaded aristocrats thought they were going to get some entertainment for their money.

"Your challenge is taken," he said politely.

"Well done, Bellancourt! We'll set up in the courtyard and have the gamekeeper arrange a selection of gloves, an arm brace and a quiver of arrows. You'll choose your own bow of course, and we shoot by standard scoring, the highest total out of twenty shots, with the best score being one hundred and eighty."

"I'm agreeable to that," Rake said.

"Then we'll change and reconvene in twenty minutes in the stable courtyard. Come, Angelene—" and he grasped her arm and pulled her away when she would have gone to speak with Rake. "Now tell me true, sweet Angelene—does he have the faintest chance of oversetting Joseph in this contest?"

"I don't know; how good a shot is Joseph?"

"He's the best."

"Then—" she hesitated a fraction of a second, "they are probably evenly matched, Charles, and while I have faith in my brother, it is not for me to call the winner." And look at her, playing it safe and sane among the weary nobility who really only wanted to make sport of Rake and his differences.

368

She recognized that finally, and the fact that there were only so many occasions when they would be the novelties of the evening or weekend. They had now had their shot, and she had within her grasp the attention of Charles Endicott, and it was up to her to see that he remained interested and if it meant reducing Rake's prowess—in all things—to that of a schoolboy flexing his muscles, well then, that was what she had to do, even while her loyal bet won her points for family fidelity.

Twenty minutes later, in the courtyard of the stable, a dozen young men and women reconverged to find that Rake was already there, trying the gloves and testing the bows.

Charles had arrived early as well, and was pacing off the distance between the targets and back to the shooting range.

The guests ringed themselves in a circle behind the two players, each of whom now had chosen his glove, his bow and his draw of arrows.

Charles had aligned two targets ten feet apart, and had designated himself the scorekeeper. "The guest will have the opening shot," he decreed, and Rake lifted his exellent bow which was made of Italian yew and had a sweet elasticity, and which he had already fitted with his first arrow. He lifted it almost carelessly, focused his eye, corrected his angle and let the first arrow fly.

Thunk! A quivering hit, right on the edge of the gold for the first high point.

"Nine for Mr. Bellancourt," Charles called out sonorously. "Mr. Linbaugh."

"A lucky hit," Mr. Linbaugh said in a stage whisper, and loudly to Rake, "Good shot, Mr. Bellancourt."

"Make yours count," Rake advised him lightly, and everyone laughed.

Mr. Linbaugh lifted his bow easily, fitted his arrow, took careful aim at his target, readjusted his alignment and let go the arrow.

"Nine points Mr. Linbaugh, first round tied," Charles called, as they drew the next flight.

And so it went: "Nine points, Mr. Bellancourt." "Nine points, Mr. Linbaugh," until they were tied at the end of ten rounds and neither had made a mistake.

"Perhaps we should increase the distance to create an additional impediment," Charles suggested, bored by the monotony of a neck and neck race. He wanted Joseph to win and he saw nothing wrong with increasing the odds.

"By all means," Rake said. "How many feet? Ten, twenty? A hundred, Mr. Endicott?"

"Do I hear an objection?" Charles asked cagily, because he knew he heard something in Bellancourt's voice, he just didn't know what it was.

"No objection at all. I am yours to command, Mr. Endicott. Whatever will make the challenge more interesting for *you*."

Charles missed the irony as he counted off twenty additional feet behind the shooting line. "Joseph?"

"Not a problem, Charles."

"Mr. Bellancourt?"

"Agreeable to me," Rake said tersely, his eye following and judging the line of the arrow's course from this distance.

"Your round, Mr. Bellancourt."

They all watched it, and they swore that he had barely looked at the target and no one had seen him even taking precise aim, and still the arrow landed squarely on the gold.

"Nine points," Charles said, his interest piqued now. "Joseph?"

Linbaugh took more time, fussed, aimed, realigned his arm, aimed again, recalculated for the extra footage and aimed again—and let it fly.

Thunk! "Nine points," Charles said, bored again. Linbaugh was as good as this American rustic any time. "Bellancourt?"

And so it went: "Nine points," "Nine points," down to the final three arrows, by which time Mr. Linbaugh seemed to be sweating and Rake's expression was positively cold-blooded.

He lifted again, with that same ease and seeming carelessness and took his twenty-seventh shot.

"Nine points."

Linbaugh followed, still fussing, still edgy, wondering how the damned American had the hang of it with such ease. He felt the pressure now—Queen and country: Charles wasn't far wrong.

Thunk!

Silence.

"Seven points," Charles said tersely, walking over to examine the point of the arrow, which was a shade over the line into the red circle. "Just. Mr. Bellancourt."

Rake moved in for the kill.

Thunk!

"Nine points."

Thunk!

"Nine points, Linbaugh."

Again—"Nine points."

And Linbaugh: "Nine points."

Linbaugh prayed as Rake lifted his bow for the last show.

Whang! The arrow split through a previous one in an emphatic testament to Rake's skill.

Damn him, Linbaugh thought, and raised his bow.

Thunk!

"Seven points," Charles called out. "Just." He walked forward to retrieve the arrows and hide his annoyance. The damned upstart, and all that money!

"And guess who takes the bank, Bellancourt?" he said pleasantly as they dismantled the targets and brought them back to the stable.

"You, if you had been smart."

"Well you see, I wasn't. No, it's a great big go for family pride, Bellancourt; sweet Angelene bet against the house, and she takes home the pot."

"Aren't you the faithful sister," Rake murmured, catching up with her as she walked back to the house on the fringes of the hugely disappointed knot of Charles's friends.

"Aren't you the epitome of the man of the West. Don't tell me—they taught you to shoot the bow and arrow the minute your mother brought you back to the camp of her people."

"Pretty much," he said complacently. "We were also taught to study the habits of the animals we stalked, and that everything was of significance and worth a second look. I scarcely see much difference between your Charles and a mountain lion playing with his prey. He just could not be aware that the supposedly lesser animal is endowed with means to survive as well, and in this case, he was well and truly outwitted. And you, dear sister, reap the reward."

She wasn't sure what the reward was, besides the bag full of money that Charles grudgingly handed over to her. *He* was sulky, and Rake now became the center of attention. Every woman was very eager to hear just how he had become such a master of the bow.

It was a *lot* of money she counted later that evening, when her grandmother had already gone downstairs to join the older guests for a pre-dinner game of cards. The profligate young lords and ladies had wagered close to a hundred pounds each—almost a thousand dollars in American money.

The etiquette of it bothered her. She almost thought she ought to give it all back. But they had been so serious, and she was certain that if Linbaugh had won, they would have happily taken her money and never thought twice about it. It was that kind of crowd.

She dressed for dinner that night in a gauzy white with blue velvet trim, and deep puffed sleeves that narrowed to an eye-catching point at her wrist. It was a pretty thing, with a rich white satin apron that draped over the lace-flounced underskirt and looped into a modified bustle in the back and tied with blue velvet ribbon.

She knotted matching ribbon around her neck and threaded it through her hair, worn as always in a loose knot to display the long line of her neck.

She carried her blue gloves in her hand, only drawing them on as she began to descend the stairs.

Charles awaited her anxiously, drawing her to him as she dismounted the bottom step, tucking her hand in his arm. "You're not angry with me, are you?"

"I should think not," she said, feeling much relieved that he was not angry altogether.

"It was a good match, and who was to know?" he said slightly, but she thought she detected something in the question that was censurious.

"And a man can rise to the occasion," she added. "It is an aspect of . . . my brother that I am not familiar with. You understand he has been away from the ranch for many years." She had no qualms at all about willfully embroidering the lie. She was only protecting Rake and her own greediness, because she wanted to keep the money.

"Well, that explains it then," Charles said, the expression in his eyes lightening. "And now to dinner, and then to play."

But still, she wondered about just how serious that little contest was. A great many flicking little taunts passed around the table, which was the grand dining table she had seen the night before which grandly seated every one of the guests, with room to spare.

A cadre of servants provided service, a stream of them coming from behind the service wall, one after another, offering, removing, pouring, passing and never listening to one word of the conversation which went on right below their ears.

"You look deliciously innocent," Charles murmured into Angelene's ear. "Are you?"

She caught her breath. "Are *you*, dear Charles?"

He clapped his hands lightly. "I do love that about you—you're so quick and quick-witted. I daresay someone like Hester Trowbridge over there would have

373

fainted dead away at the question. I do believe you have unplumbed depths, Miss Bellancourt. I hope I may be the one to discover them."

She wondered if she hoped that too, or whether she just coveted everything she saw around her, from the ancient tapestries covering the walls to the largesse that encompassed an unending number of servants to do every bidding and the leisure for her to do nothing at all.

A day or two more and she would know the truth of the matter, whether Charles was interested in her or not, and then she could make a decision. In the meantime, she could play words with him, there was no harm in that, and she could allow him to steal a kiss or two and whisper daring and suggestive things in her ear which titillated her not at all, but which certainly could not harm in having him believe she was not as innocent as she looked and perhaps more worldly than she seemed.

The key appeared to be to envelope herself in mystery, to intrigue a palate that already had a taste of more mundane treats and yearned for something infinitely more rare.

He would want variety and diversity. An innocent might fascinate him one minute and bore him the next. She wondered how many women she might have to become in order to win him.

The cost was escalating moment by moment as he moved back her chair so she could rise from the table.

"To cards now, sweet Angelene. We are paired with the mercurial Moren and the restive Richard, and perhaps I can recoup some of that money which he so handily deprived me of. I daresay I'm better at whist than he is, but only time will tell."

It was an interesting after-dinner quadrille. A distinct cadre of friends posted themselves in the gentlemen's room across from the library. Several couples followed *them* into the library proper, and good-naturedly argued partners. Other couples divided and re-paired with another partner and disappeared, presumably for billiards or conversation in the drawing room. Mr. Darlington wandered aimlessly from room to room, seeking diversion of a sort he could not define in polite company, while her grandmother held sway over one table of card players in the library where she had settled herself well before dinner.

"Ah, the redoubtable Mr. Bellancourt. Please be seated. And Moren, my dear, such a pleasure."

"An ongoing one," she murmured, seating herself opposite Angelene. "Shall we play? Charles?"

The game commenced, a play to the death type of game, with Angelene partnering Charles and trying to tone done his combative recklessness, and Rake looking over his cards with that same steely look with which he had approached the bow and arrow.

It did not bode well for Charles, and in the end, after an hour of hard driving play, Charles came away the loser again and he had a very hard time putting the best face on it.

"You'll have to console me," he told Angelene. "You'll have to do whatever I want in order to make things better. Two losses in one day is a bit much to bear."

And what was the right response to that rather sulky little speech? "I'm at your command," she said lightly, and he threw down the cards and reached for her hand. "Come."

Angelene threw a quick look at her grandmother who beamed her approval, and then at Rake, whose expression radiated pure animal danger.

No matter. She wanted Charles, she was sure of that, and she grasped his hand and allowed him to lead her from the library.

"Where are we going?"

"To find some privacy, sweet Angelene. I'm tired of that man staring at me like I'm some kind of lecher. I want you to myself now, and I hope you want me."

I do. I do. What do you mean by want?

"Angelene . . . ?"

"I'm here."

"Please be here," he murmured, turning her into the alcove that enclosed one of the several back staircases. "This is a stairway that leads to heaven, Angelene. Are you willing to come?"

She hesitated again, and he backed her up against the staircase wall.

"I'm willing," she whispered, sliding her hands up his chest and waiting to feel those thickening feelings that the thought of his kiss should arouse.

He moved closer to her. "There are more things between heaven and earth, sweet Angelene, and I can show them to you if only you'd let me."

"I'm here," she murmured, but only because she thought she ought to. She didn't know where the luxurious feelings were. She felt stone-cold with no excitement at the thought of him so close to kissing her.

"Let me taste heaven, Angelene—"

"And let *me* give you a taste of *hell*, Endicott," Rake said grimly from behind him, his large hand clamping down hard on his shoulder.

"Oh, bother it, Bellancourt, you're a damned nuisance," Charles grumbled, shaking Rake's hand away. "Make this man understand, sweet Angelene, that you have some free will in the matter of what you do, and perhaps he won't trouble us again. *I* will wait for you in the drawing room."

He stalked off and Angelene felt of a mix of emotions that crossed from gratitude into dismay.

"I am going to lose him," she said angrily, moving to go after him.

"My dear Angelene, you have never had him."

"I'm playing with the possibility I could have."

"Don't be naive. You know exactly what he wants."

"Indeed I do, Rake. He wants someone fresh and new and interesting to whom he can offer to share his life."

"You are going to find that the novelty of your being someone foreign and faintly exotic will pall very fast in this set, Angelene. The thing Charles is looking for is boatloads of money and a vast tolerance for his nonsense

376

and his transgressions, and he'll take those two attributes in any woman he can find and he'll marry her like a shot. You can offer him neither."

"I can give him—"

"But you can't, Angelene, and you should be damned grateful to me that I didn't let him force the issue."

"But I can," she said loftily. "What could be so difficult about giving myself to the man I want, freely and without reservations? A man finds it easy to do, Rake. Don't you find that's so? A new woman, an uninhibited word here, a touch there, a man succumbs so easily and he never is so selective as a woman."

"You're the only one who has succumbed to anything, Sister of Angels, and it hasn't taken but a fast prodding by money and consequence to send you reeling into some man's arms. I don't call that selective, I call that downright avaricious. But you've made it plain from the start that was your intent, and you have played it through admirably, right down to betting with the nobility and pocketing a healthy handful of their pin money. You *are* amazing, Angelene. You have achieved everything you set out to do."

"So have you, Rake Cordigan. Don't you haul me down for giving you the chance to move in a world you never could have entered under ordinary circumstances. You can walk with anyone now and you can bury your past as deep as it will go and find your father and do all the things that were impossible in your youth. Why castigate me for that?"

"Because I'm *bored*, Sister of Angels, and I'm tired of being the newest toy for these people to play with and torment. And it is time to find my place and make my peace and find the thing that will bind the wounds once and forever. What I need, more than anything else in the world right now, is to kiss you, Angelene."

"*No!*"

"I hear your fear."

"This is too public, Rake. We cannot destroy the lie, we *can't*."

"Brother to sister," he goaded her.

"There is no such thing," she whispered.

"No, there is only the life between us, the one you seek to deny."

"There is only one life I seek to embrace with both hands," she contradicted angrily.

"As do I, Angelene," he said, slowly moving toward her.

She backed away, and bumped up against the wall again. "You can take anything—and anyone—you want, Rake," she whispered furiously. "I've seen them all looking at you."

"But is that what you really *want*, Sister of Angels?" he murmured, casually cornering her between his body and the first step down to heaven with Charles Endicott.

"I want Charles," she hissed.

"You want both, Angelene; you wish I were Charles and he were me and then you could kiss him with compunction and take everything he offered—"

"*No!*"

"—and not be afraid," he finished, slanting his head so that he could just breathe the words against her lips.

"I'm not afraid," she lashed out boldly.

"No, you are walking into his arms with your eyes wide open, Sister of Angels. You know what you see." His lips touched hers. "You know what you will give." He kissed her again. "You know what you will lose." And again, whispering those hateful words of unerring perception against the very mouth he coveted, knowing he would arouse her anger and her resolution.

"Yes, I know what I see," she said coldly, clamping down on the skittery little feelings those kisses aroused in her vitals. She couldn't give into that, nor his prescience, nor the rising heat of her desire which stoked up like a furnace whenever he was too near.

There was that between them, and she was very well aware of it, and that she had to keep her perspective: she couldn't give anything up to him, not now.

Not ever.

She pushed against him with the strength of her determination. "I see that I want to find Charles," she said, her voice firm with purpose.

He shrugged and moved aside with a mocking bow. "As you wish, Angelene," he said in the masked-up tone of voice she so despised. "But you and I know you're going to the devil."

Mr. Darlington was as happy as a fox in a henhouse. "Oh, those plump little maids, they know exactly what they're hired on for, Bellancourt. Those Endicotts train their staff well. Anything to please the guests. Anything. You really ought to try one."

"I see nothing to my taste," Rake said calmly, reiterating the phrase that absolutely stuck in Mr. Darlington's craw.

"You must have very bizarre tastes, Bellancourt—look at that saucy brunette who is wiggling her way across the room. Look at that bosom. It makes a man want to—"

"And how many have you?" Rake asked scornfully.

"Any one who would let me, Bellancourt, otherwise, what is the point?"

"You surely know what it is," Rake retorted.

"Well, let me introduce you to that sweet little girl over there, standing by Endicott. She looks like your type—fair, slender, anxious to please . . ."

"I beg your pardon, Darlington, I have no type. I have selectivity."

"I'm telling you, man, the Endicotts have provided and we have only to take. Didn't you watch them pairing off earlier? What do you think that was all about? There are major assignations occurring in this house even as we speak. Only everyone is too well bred to comment on it."

"As am I."

"What do you think these envoys of ennui *do* on these

country weekends, Bellancourt? It's just a damned excuse to play in the hay. Or hadn't you got your invitation?"

Rake froze. "I haven't checked my room since I came down to dinner," he said carefully.

"Maybe *they* are selective in whom they invite. Maybe the fact of whether you bed the acolytes of passion is a test as to whether you are issued an invitation or not. *I* imagine I was one of the first."

"You talk too much," Rake said dourly. Or maybe not enough.

"They really believe in the precept of *do what you will*. When they are in that kind of a mood, anything is possible, including nubile maids to tempt anyone's palate, even the most discriminating."

Rake felt an absolute chill course down his spine. Darlington was talking nonsense. There couldn't be a more conventional scene than the one before him in the drawing room, with couples or individuals promenading around the room, or sitting and talking or playing an idle hand of cards, and being served intermittently by those eager smiling maids who passed champagne and laughed at a passing jest and disappeared as smoothly and unobtrusively as they had come.

Charles held court in the center of the room, with his admiring train seated all around him, and Angelene right by his side.

"Champagne, sir?" It was the fair slender maid whom Darlington had pointed out to him.

"Thank you." He took a glass.

"Anything else, sir?" she asked archly, and he wasn't at all sure he misread her tone of voice.

"What else is there?" he asked cautiously.

"Oh, there's a menu of tidbits, cakes, tarts, nectar . . . sugarplums . . . would you care to see?"

"When I am ready," he said evasively.

"*When* you are ready, we can service you in the dining room, sir," she said pertly, and turned on her heel and left him.

"Tarts sound good to me," Mr. Darlington said, smacking his lips. "Or don't you believe me now, Bellancourt?"

"It's your overactive imagination, Darlington, coupled with your nasty nose for gossip."

"Oh? You figured that out, did you? Well, never mind. There's enough nastiness to fill a book here, and I'm going to get my share of it. Come along, Bellancourt. Let me make you into a true believer."

He balked, he really balked at that. Darlington's imagination was running rampant—or maybe his was, and probably because of that damned Endicott.

He wasn't going to give in and follow Darlington. He would just stay where he was and watch the stately pavanne of guests leaving the room and other guests taking their place, with Charles orchestrating the whole from the center of the room.

But now that he was looking, he began to see a pattern of arrivals and departures, and he marveled at the complete discretion of it, still and all while everybody knew.

The maids would enter the room bearing silver trays of not more than four stems of champagne, and it seemed after a while, they were not handing them out randomly, that they were choosing to whom they offered the drink and their seductive bill of fare.

Then when their trays were empty, they slipped from the room and a few minutes later, the first of their patrons got up and followed, and always in the order that they had been selected.

So everyone knew, and everyone was watching so that no one left out of his turn.

Or else he was just imagining it, and things had gotten so out of hand, he was ripe to believe anything that scurrilous Darlington chose to tell him.

Or maybe he should just see for himself.

He eased himself away from the threshold of the drawing room and made his way across the gallery to the kitchen hallway which, apart from the closed double doors giving onto the main stairwell corridor, was the only other way to enter the dining room.

He heard the voices long before he got to the service room door, the laughter, the soft squeals of accommodation, the rumble of a male voice making a suggestive play on the menu of the evening.

And Mr. Darlington's distinctive words: "I came for my tart, ladies. I am *ravenous* for a tart. Can anyone accommodate me?"

He felt a pair of long sinuous arms wind themselves around him, and he inhaled the thick seductive scent of Moren Craig, whose body pressed tightly against him, and whose voice came huskily out of the darkness to entice him. "You don't need to try the maids, Richard. You can have the priestess. You have only to say the word."

"I find nothing to my taste," he said prudently.

"Ah yes, word has circulated about your much vaunted selectivity. But I am the one who is supposed to make a man forget his vows and promises, Richard. I find you a most interesting challenge. I don't think there has ever been a man come to Shillingford who hasn't partaken of its pleasures. Endicott is known for it. The weekends here are coveted by lesser men than you."

"And yet here *I* am."

"Indeed, and a more tactful man would not have gone out of his way to displease his host so thoroughly this afternoon."

"Nor would a host have set his guest up to be attacked so thoroughly, if he were a tactful man. And so all the proof points to the fact that Mr. Endicott is not."

"And you are a man who wants taming, and by a woman who is more than your equal. I am the goddess of love, Richard, and even Charles Endicott obeys my command."

"And a mere mortal has no free will whatsoever?"

"Mere mortals are not given invitations to Shilling-

382

ford, Mr. Bellancourt, unless Charles is sure they will want to participate."

"And how sure was he of me?"

"He wasn't, dear Richard. But he was very sure of your sister. Sometimes accommodations must be made. But then, I have seen your potential, and I can't wait to test you out."

"You are so sure of yourself, Moren."

"Let me take you someplace delicious and erotic and I will show you what those poor fools can only dream."

She enfolded him like a great living butterfly, and she led him into the billiard room, and gently chased away the other occupants who looked at Rake with a combination of envy and distaste.

They all knew, he thought, and they did not question her command or her need for the room or her presence there. They knew exactly what would transpire in this room, and perhaps one or all of them had played out similar scenes with Moren and would be envisioning exactly what she would do.

They knew already that she would hoist herself up on the billiard table and lay herself down, propping her head on her arm. They knew she would smile alluringly and begin stroking her thigh with her free hand, lifting her dress inch by inch as she went along, exposing her delicate lacy underthings, made exquisitely revealing by a connoisseur's design. They knew her legs were bare and her garters were black and surrounded a lush thigh that was barely covered by a scrap of lace. They knew, too, that she would lift her leg seductively and invite him to envision further delights and that eventually, when she had played with his senses and his mind, she would command him huskily, "Come and take me." No man had ever refused.

Except that a caustic voice behind them at the door intruded a jangling note of reality to the scene. "If I were you," said the voice of Angelene, "I would take that two ball in the side pocket. It's a very *easy* play."

383

Chapter 20

"*You* have some nerve lecturing *me* about 'forcing the issue,' Rake Cordigan," Angelene spat furiously. "I could . . . I could—"

"So could I," Rake said, that steely note in his voice once again as he backed against the billiard room door and closed it emphatically. "But maybe you could just tell me why you even followed me in the first place."

"*I* was following *her*," Angelene said loftily. "And *you* were positively *tracking* her scent."

"In the custom of my people," he murmured, with just a touch of irony. "Or perhaps you were protecting what is yours, Sister of Angels. In the custom of *your* people."

"*You* are not *mine*," Angelene retorted sharply.

He folded his arms across his chest. "And you have no defense whatsoever for why you burst in here—where you were presumably not wanted."

Angelene sent him a long look that was purely feminine and downright perverse. "Oh, I think you *wanted* me."

"I've been telling you that, Angelene."

And so it backfired. She stamped her foot. "Don't tell me you didn't want to be rescued."

His cool gray eyes glinted. "Let's just say I wouldn't have minded drowning, Angelene."

"I feel like holding you under myself," she muttered, disliking the look in his eyes very much.

"I do believe we *under*stand each other, Angelene. Neither you nor I will relinquish what is ours."

She drew herself up exasperatedly. "Nor am *I* yours, Rake Cordigan."

"But you surrendered so long ago, Sister of Angels."

"*I* yielded when it was politic to do so," she said frigidly.

"You could not have put it better, Angelene. That was my very thinking not ten minutes ago."

"Men only think with what is between their legs," she shot back.

"And women with their heads and hands. We do go deep, Sister of Angels, each in our different ways. But the fact remains, you are here and Moren Craig is not."

"And which of us would you rather have?" she asked nastily, prickly with expectation.

"The one who goes after what she wants, Sister of Angels."

"And which of us does that?" she demanded in irritation, put off by his glib answers.

"The one who surrenders to life, Angelene. But I won't beg *you* to lay on the billiard table with me."

"But why not? It's all of a piece."

"But you would give me no peace. And this place is not nearly as private as Moren seemed to think."

"*I can't bear this.*"

"Nor can I," Rake said tightly. "You trade substance for shadow and you may yet take Moren's place on this table."

"Nonsense, Charles is a gentleman. Moren Craig is a tart, and you—you are a savage still."

"And rutting in satin and breeches instead of leather and breechclout," Rake said, the hard stone-face mask slipping down over his features. "I am what I always was, Angelene. You are what you have become. But the life between us remains and nothing you can do will crush it away."

"Nor you," she said stonily.

"No," he said, his patience beginning to wear thin.

"You need no help on that score, Angelene, and the only thing I will offer you now is to escort you back to the library."

"I'll stay here thank you."

"Perhaps that *is* best," he agreed gravely. "You will have time to arrange yourself on the billiard table until Charles comes looking for you. I believe you had a good look at Moren when you came in?"

She felt like smacking him then. "I believe you did too," she said snidely, and gathered all her courage to march past him and out the door. Charles would never, and Moren would, and she didn't know which dismayed her most.

But none of that showed on her face as she made her way to the library, aware that Rake followed but a few steps behind. She had forgotten her grandmother was planted like a fixture in the corner of the room, inviting all comers to join her at cards. When she caught sight of Angelene, she jumped up and darted over to her.

"Oh, wonderful, you're both together. I must tell you, I don't know when I've enjoyed myself more. In fact, even Mr. Darlington says the hospitality here is unsurpassed. He is absolutely charmed by the willingness of the servants to do anything to please. You have only to ask, he says, and the thing is as good as done."

"Well yes, Grandmother, they seem to be very obliging. Now tell me, have you seen Mr. Endicott anywhere about?" she asked, slanting a goading glance at Rake, just daring him to interfere.

"I believe he is still in the drawing room," Mr. Darlington said, sidling up to them. "And undoubtedly watching for you, Angelene, and wondering just when you will return."

"Well of course he is," she agreed, and smiled tightly at Rake. "I will relieve his vigil as of now. Goodnight, Grandmother, I don't know if I will see you again before you retire. Ra—Richard, Mr. Darlington . . ."

They watched her graceful white-gowned figure exit the room, and Mr. Darlington shook his head. "She is so beautiful," he began, and immediately clamped down on the next thought at Rake's steely look.

"Well, Vernon, are *you* ready to retire?"

"Oh no, Amelia. I have a long gratifying evening planned with several of the guests. You just go on ahead and be comfortable this evening, if you are tired of cards. I know the servants will do everything to attend to our needs."

She bid them all goodnight then and Darlington turned to Rake and said jovially, "She is such a naive woman, Amelia. It would never occur to her that respectable and wealthy widows and certain other families have been invited as well to be smokescreens for the *real* entertainment of the weekend. And they'll do everything to be sure her stay is everything she could want it to be. They specialize in that, you know—fulfilling fantasies. It doesn't matter whether it's the desire of a randy young bachelor or the golden dream of a capricious American. That's part of the fun, planning it down to the last detail, including everything extraneous."

He shook his head again and clucked at Rake. "You shouldn't look so disapproving, my boy. This weekend is like a big plate of luscious ripe fruit—you just bite into whatever tempts you."

"While underneath, the fruit is rotten," Rake said.

"But you don't get that part until you've had your fill of the rest."

The man was a pig, wallowing in mud, and he didn't give a damn where he rutted—the streets of London or the elegant salons of Shillingford, it was all the same to him.

"And then you choke on it," Rake finished inflexibly.

"Oh man, bend a little. Think about how tart and fresh and sweet it can be—you roll it around in your mouth, you taste it, you suck the nectar from it . . ."

"You are just full of allusions this evening, Darlington. You reek of juices, and I have a feeling this is only the beginning."

"Join me and find out," Darlington said coyly. "Anything is fair game tonight, Bellancourt. Just remember I warned you."

"I know what is *not* possible," Rake said grimly.

And Darlington slapped him on the shoulder with all the comeraderie in the world and put the finish on it by saying, "But Endicott wouldn't have it any other way."

Ominous. The whole thing was ominous and all he could do was stand by and wait. And fend off Miss Antoinette Madrid, who had seemed almost cowed for the past two days, and had not seemed to be able to fit in with the able set of peers with whom she had aspired to consort. She was a fish out of water, floundering around to get a fix on some direction which would make her more acceptable. She hadn't yet found it, and she was a little in awe of the fact that both Angelene and Richard Bellancourt had.

But in the two days she had spent at Shillingford, she had not seen one woman evince any interest in the enigmatic Mr. Bellancourt, except that street woman, that Lady Craig. And what was she but some experienced jade who had had her pick of noblemen and probably discarded them all.

Anyway, Richard didn't seem in the least bit interested, and it raised her spirits immeasurably to think that he could be proof against such an experienced seductress.

He was waiting for her.

Well, maybe not *waiting*; he didn't know he was *waiting*—but she did, and she wondered how to approach him, forbidding as he looked, in the comfortable and crowded confines of the library.

Surely a brief conversation couldn't hurt—

"Good evening, Miss Madrid," he barked at her.

"I—" she faltered and then went on, "Are you enjoying your stay?"

"I will enjoy my leave-taking," he retorted. "What about *you*, Miss Madrid? Is Shillingford everything you had hoped for?"

388

"It's breathtaking."

"There certainly are things about it that do take your breath away," he agreed trenchantly. "I'm happy you're enjoying yourself."

She hated him just then because he was looking through her and not *at* her. "You are rude, Mr. Bellancourt. I recollect you don't remember that I was your very first acquaintance and you've done nothing more since we've met than cut me every time you see me. You would be kinder to say you don't want my company and we would leave it at that."

He looked at her then and he thought about all the useless social posturings he had been forced to bear, and it suddenly seemed like the thing had come full circle, with this very arrogant, very spoiled and naive young woman who had had the misfortune to be attracted to him.

He didn't know how to be kind, but he knew how to be gentle. "I don't want your company in the sense that you mean, Miss Madrid. I'm always pleased to have you as a friend."

She recoiled as if he had slapped her, and her chin went up and her mouth thinned to a grim line. "I will never take up any more of your time, Mr. Bellancourt. I appreciate your candor."

It was a brave speech for her and it had badly cost her her pride; the first thing she thought to do was run upstairs into the sanctuary of her father's arms and cry "Father, father, that Mr. Bellancourt was horribly rude to me downstairs, he's horrible, horrible. And in front of everybody too. I'm going to get back at him, Father, I swear I will, but you have to help me. You have to find out the one thing about Richard Bellancourt that will hurt him the most. Will you do that, Father? I want to hurt him as badly as he has hurt me. I can't bear it, I *can't!*"

And when her tears were spent and her father had agreed to do just that little thing, she put herself to rights and let herself out of her parents' suite and found herself confronted by the Honorable Joseph Linbaugh, who just happened to be passing by; she recognized him from the afternoon debacle, and she was curious that he showed no effect for having lost his host and guests a fair amount of money.

"You're Antoinette Madrid," he said suddenly, wheeling back toward her.

"Yes, I am," she said haughtily, remembering of course that one didn't talk to strange men unless someone had introduced them.

"I'm Joseph Linbaugh, but I expect you know that," he said cagily. "I saw you in the crowd this afternoon. You're a beautiful girl."

"Thank you," she said, preening just a little. An Honorable . . . a *something*, not like that gutter piece, Richard Bellancourt.

"Everybody must tell you how beautiful you are," Linbaugh said, reaching out just to touch her thick dark hair. He would wager it was long and lustrous and probably it reached right down to her feet. "That's why you get everything you want: everybody pets you and just loves to be around your beauty. Men probably fall all over you, and you stand here so patiently and listen to my poor effort."

"Oh no, you're quite charming, Mr. Linbaugh."

"And beautiful girls are always kind," he said mournfully, offering her his arm. "You will take pity and let me escort you downstairs? Oh, good. And perhaps you would like to get together with some of my friends, men who admire beautiful women tremendously and would do anything for them if only they would deign to be kind? Could you be kind, Miss Madrid to some poor fellows who would love to adore you for all the beauty you possess?"

"I might," she said coyly, just as he was sure she would. He recognized all the signs, the wild wet hungry eyes, the bruised begging mouth, the stiffened backbone and the trampled pride.

"Wouldn't you love to just mete out your favors to men who would crawl at your feet to beg for them, Miss

Madrid? You could be as bad as you wanted to be, but they would have to plead for the merest kiss, beg for every caress, and you could accept or reject at your whim. That is the power of beautiful women, Miss Madrid; wouldn't you love to take your place among them?"

"I might," she said slyly.

"All men want a beautiful woman," he went on, "and all men love to try to kiss and fondle her, and a beautiful woman adores having as many men as possible make love to her. She will seek them out, and then she will make them beg and she will always choose to reveal herself to many and never exclusively to one. But you know all this, Miss Madrid. A beautiful woman is always surrounded by men and she is never alone, especially when she is giving and kind. So I return to my original question—can you be kind, my beautiful Miss Madrid?"

"Tell me how I can be kind," she whispered, her head full of visions of all these lovely men, all wanting her.

"Let me kiss you now, Miss Madrid."

"Right now, right here?"

"Right here," he said, turning her on the stair and pressing her tightly against the wall. "Don't deny me, Miss Madrid."

She savored the words of the first man to beg her, and she opened her mouth to his hot, devouring kiss.

Sometimes Charles thought the waiting was the best, that the anticipation was almost climactic and the rest just petered out into sameness and nothingness.

Or was he getting even more jaded as the years went on? He had beside him the epitome of everything he had ever dreamed of in a woman, a cool blonde virginal beauty with an angelic name but with fire in her eyes, and a bit of snap in her tone of voice. She had money from the healthy backing of her grandmother, but more than that, *she* wanted a life in England, away and apart from everything she had ever known.

She was perfect, and he didn't want to despoil her, not ever; he wanted nothing to touch her that wasn't good and clean and as beautiful as she. She would grace the house, provide him with sons, and eventually when that mundanity dulled into pure boredom, he would begin all over again—secretly. He could do it, he had years of experience planning these revelries, and he did them discreetly and he had made them into something desirable to be part of. That was the sticking point: why she wouldn't want to be part of them.

She sat beside him, so animated, so beautiful. The life in her eyes came from some other place deep within her, a place perhaps to which he would never go, and she had such a refreshing femininity about her; nothing about her body shamed her, she used it shamelessly, her hands and her devastating smile, even the daring décolletage of her dress as she leaned forward to make a point, and touched and pressed and all but drove a man out of his mind with wanting her.

And he watched the servants, the girls who willingly entertained the guests in the manner he approved, and as each selected guest left the drawing room, his imagination ran riot with erotic pictures of what was happening behind the service buffet. There was nothing like those creative sensual images to stimulate a man and keep him excited all night long. Especially when he knew what he had to look forward to.

And then there was the ingenious punishment he had devised for Linbaugh, to recruit that prissy American Madrid to be one of his girls. He got a fantastic erection just thinking of all the ways Linny could have accomplished that impossible task. He couldn't wait to see.

And to add the final filip, there was that randy Mr. Darlington run amok among the servants and the hired girls, and hardly knowing which way to stick it when every wench was available to see. The man was a treat, with a sexual purity and directness that was very refreshing. He was a man who deserved to be rewarded for such racking energy.

So now, he only had to wait. Everything was in place, all his guests had partaken of the luscious dessert tray and had nibbled away on some tasty morsel, and now they all awaited the main course.

He himself wanted to just lick and suck away at the delicate shell of Angelene's ear, but just the thought of doing it was almost enough for him, and of course, out of respect for his elders, he always waited until the other members of the party had gone to bed. This too took time and whetted the appetite still further.

To prolong things still further, he would be the last to arrive, so that his mental imagery was in full swing even before he descended to the gates of heaven. The difference this time was he would have his queen on his arm.

She sensed something in the air, a thick atmosphere of portent that she couldn't quite understand when everyone seemed so relaxed and even soporific.

She felt happy as she looked up at Charles and took his hand in a gesture of affection. She could foresee a future filled with evenings like this, weekends like this, a life like this.

She wondered if he had any feeling for her at all. She wondered if any were necessary if she fulfilled all his other requirements.

She wondered if she could forget Rake and that snaky Moren Craig. What if he were with her now, and there would be the culmination of the moment she so precipitously interrupted?

So what. It was Charles she wanted and Rake would become a fiction of her past, a story she might tell sometime to her children about how she had come to England and met their father. About lies, and choices, and decisions and determination.

A long story.

She noticed that some of the men were leaving, and she relished the thought of the moment when the drawing room would be empty and she would have Charles all to herself.

She looked up at him again and felt full of pride for his aristocratic manner and his gentility—and for the obvious protuberance between his legs that told her that he was as anxious as she.

Yes, she wanted him to kiss her now, and she wanted that evidence of his passion for her. She wanted to be alone with him so she could convince him she could love him.

Could she? . . .

She *would*.

The last guest departed and the sense of excitement in the air escalated.

"Charles," she whispered, and he pulled her to her feet.

"Sweet Angelene," he murmured, sliding his arms around her waist and pulling her tightly against his lower torso so she could feel the jut and thickness of what he offered her. He kissed her cheeks and brow and finally the shell-like curve of her ear, and her reaction was everything he could have wished, a squirming, writhing attempt to escape from the heated wet exploration of his tongue that excited him all over again. "Do you know I was dying to do that to you all night, my darling?"

His words thrilled her, if his actions did not. He had been watching her, wanting her, and she understood the power of the dream.

"Come with me now, Angelene."

"Where are we going?"

"To heaven, my darling, if you'll only let me show you the way."

He took her hand and he led her through the empty hallways to the rear staircase which was dark and enveloping, and he backed her against the wall and began kissing her all over her face, imprisoning her with the sheer force of his bulging lower torso.

"Where is heaven?" she panted, wanting to push away his kisses and still wanting to welcome them so that he would want her.

"Heaven is what I create down in my *voudrais*. Do you know *voudrais*? It means 'what you will', and it is the place where I give my friends license to do anything they want, *anything*. Do you understand?"

"I don't know, what do you mean by anything?"

"I mean, I mean sweet Angelene, we all have unquenchable appetites that we have to suppress for the greater good. But mine is never satisfied, nor my guests, and we do everything to gratify every lust in the *voudrais*, and no one is exempt and no one ever has to pay any price but silence."

"I don't understand."

"Then you shall see, sweet Angelene, and then you shall join us because your passions are inflamed already with the greed of desire. Come with me, Angelene . . ."

She licked her lips. She didn't know what he meant, she didn't know that she wasn't just a little afraid of what he meant, and she allowed him to pull her down the steps, down and down again a winding staircase until the very bottom where a flickering candle in a sconce lighted up a heavy wooden door.

"Behind this door is heaven, my darling. Open your mind and your heart to everything you see, Angelene, and you can enter heaven too."

And he drew out a key and inserted it in the lock, turned it once, depressed the catch and threw open the door.

She drew in her breath sharply at the scene before her. Heaven—or hell?

In the steamy darkness that was lit only by guttering candles, she saw a cavernous room filled with people— people she recognized, the men she had shared the dinner table with in free naked sport with any available woman who allowed them to pull her down; the women, partially naked, sashaying around the room, playing with the men who importuned them, or sitting right down in their laps

395

in rank invitation; in the distance, lushly upholstered sofas, occupied by couples caressing and kissing each other in pairs and in combinations of threes and fours; on a dais on the other side of the room, a woman with long lustrous hair, partially clothed, reclining on a platform, her breasts bared, listened to the petitions of men who urgently desired to make love to her.

In the center of all the erotic frenzy was Moren Craig beneath the hard pumping body of a man Angelene could not see in the throes of an ecstasy that was the property of all who cared to observe.

Beyond this room there were other voices, other moans, a cornucopia of delights to be had for the price of naming the name and removing one's clothes.

Charles had taken off his jacket and shirt, as he watched her, and he began to unfasten his pants when he spoke. "Let me undress you, Angelene, and we'll explore the freedom of the senses together, you and I."

She couldn't keep her eyes away from Moren Craig and the perfection of her body and her sleek response to her lover. "I can't."

"Don't do this, Angelene. I want to share this with you."

"You mean you want to share me with everyone else."

"I want to share your nakedness," he agreed, his voice hard with displeasure. "Look at your friend Miss Madrid. Look at how she revels in the way those men want her body. They'll do anything to kiss her and caress her. Look at how she consents to let this lover suckle her sweet little breasts. She has no qualms or fears, Angelene. She has the surety of a beautiful woman who knows she is desired."

"I don't need that kind of surety," Angelene said, her eyes fixed in fascinated horror on Antoinette Madrid and her arching body that met the wet fervent kiss of the man whose mouth surrounded her breast.

"Don't spoil this for me," he warned, and she turned away in disgust. He grabbed for her, and pulled at her dress, and the delicate chiffon and satin ripped in his hand.

He should have thought of that sooner, he thought, just tearing away all of his blonde beauty's virginal inhibitions. That was what they all wanted anyway, to be taken until they could allow themselves to select.

"That's better, sweet Angelene," he said, holding up the remnants of her beautiful dress in his hand. "Much better." He slipped the length of gauze and satin around his neck so he could inhale the scent of her while he completed the task of removing his clothes, and held her thin underwear tightly in his other hand so that if she so much as moved, he would strip off her clothes and she would have nowhere to hide.

Her body heaved with fear, or maybe not fear—anger, violation, rage, all manner of things she could not understand, in the service of an orgiastic lecher who could not tell when enough was enough or where to draw the line to contain his base nature.

And above all, she felt stupid and used and clear in her mind that fixing Charles's interest in her was no fair exchange for having to endure *this*.

"Just let me go, Charles. I can't do this."

"But you've done it, my beautiful Angelene—and there is nothing more enticing than firm young flesh in beautifully made underclothing. See how your breasts are quivering? Perhaps they would like some attention."

"Don't touch me."

"Angelene, you are making me very angry and as a consequence I am losing my desire to sample all the delights available tonight. You don't know how long I have planned this night, and how I prolonged the moment before we would come down here. I thought for sure you were a woman of the world and understood these things, but I see you aren't. You are provincial and narrow-minded and you don't deserve to be rewarded for your prudishness.

"Just sit there, my dear, because I am going to take my

turn." He motioned to one of the men, who abandoned the eager kisses of the woman with whom he was dallying, and came up to the bench where Angelene had been pushed and took his place beside her almost like a guard.

Angelene watched in horrified fascination as Charles waded into the squirming mass of bodies, stopping to thrust himself at any pair of hands that reached for him, and finally falling into the hands of one bold woman who offered her charms, with barely any idea who had just entered the *voudrais*.

He wasn't done after her. The thought of Angelene watching urged him on, and he took kisses and caresses, and he made quick explosive love to every willing woman until he had made his way across the room to Miss Madrid, who was being avidly kissed by a lover who grasped her hair and demanded her kisses. He was supplanted by Charles who demanded her body and she was so warm with wanting, she gave in to him with no protest whatsoever.

He hoped that stupid hopeless American bitch was watching and learning just how an accommodating woman got what she wanted from a man of strong appetites.

Maybe the Madrid was what he was looking for, with her pliant little body, and her rich father and arrogant little ways. Maybe she could tame him with her delicious little breasts and her odd idea that he must beg for her favors. Linny had somehow brought her to that point. It was masterful, it was climactic.

He left her to her next lover and went on to Moren Craig. He loved the sleek uninhibited Moren who could never be gratified and loved to wring a man out trying.

It was a while before he could finally look around to make sure Miss Priss Bitch was watching.

But she wasn't there, and the man he had assigned to guard her was writhing in pain on the floor.

The worst thing was Mr. Darlington. The moment she

saw him in the midst of the fray she decided to run; she didn't even think, she just unleashed a sharp jab of her elbow right into the most vulnerable point of her guard's anatomy, and jumped the moment he fell, howling in pain.

She didn't stop, not for a second: she raced up those stone steps in her stockinged feet, slipping and sliding, sure that he was behind her and if he ever caught her, he would kill her.

Up the steps and up: she didn't recognize anything in the dim light, and she was blinded by her fear. One hallway looked like another, and there wasn't a soul about.

She climbed until she could not go any further and she ran back down again; she had to get to the bedroom floor, to the safety of her room—she had to find Rake.

Oh God, Rake—and what had *he* been trying to tell her? And what she could tell him about Moren.

Everything had to be complicated. She wanted to grab her clothes and run out into the night, away from Shillingford and England and everything it had represented. How would she explain that to her grandmother? How could she explain it to herself?

She had done nothing wrong except failing to recognize his salaciousness. But there were no guidelines for that either. What a mockery the *voudrais* made of the mystery between a man and a woman.

What a mockery she had made of herself.

She was on the second floor now, the bedroom floor to which they were all assigned. Somewhere to her left was her bedroom, and the other way, down another long corridor, was Rake's room.

Slowly, she eased herself away from the landing and tiptoed down the hallway. Useless precaution. They were all down in the *voudrais* and she was the only one who was not.

Where was Rake when she needed him?

Oh, he was off somewhere laughing his fool head off, loving the fact that he had been right about Charles and she had been wrong.

She heard footsteps, and she flattened herself against the wall—another piece of rank foolishness to think she could become as inconspicuous as an insect on the wall when she was creeping down a hallway dressed in torn white underclothing.

But still . . .

She held her breath, waiting, the images of the *voudrais* flooding her mind, pumping her heartbeat as she thought of the possibilities that those footsteps brought closer. If it were Charles . . . if he were coming after her to silence her—

She slid down the wall, and crouched low on the floor. Maybe she could trip him up if she came at him unexpectedly. Maybe she could injure him permanently so he could never again succeed in seducing another naive woman into his shocking practices.

It was a moment of pure terror as she waited, hunched over like a trapped animal in the dimly lit hallway.

And then—

"Angelene?"

"Rake!" She got up slowly and walked toward him uncertainly.

"*Angelene—*"

She ran the few feet of distance between them into his arms. "I want to get out here, I want to go back home. Please take me, please . . ."

He gathered her tightly against him, his rage spuming into life against the tearful shuddering of her body. "Hell—" he muttered, half-lifting her, half-supporting her as he got her to her room. "Hold on, Angelene—here, lay down. I'm going to cover you. Damn it, where's the damn light?"

He bundled her into her bed, raised the gaslight and sat down on the edge of the bed.

She raised herself into a sitting position immediately. "We have to get out of here. I don't know if he followed me, but I never want to see that debaucher again. Rake—"

400

"Tell me," he commanded, grasping her hands, containing his fury.

His tone of voice alerted her. "You know something," she said accusingly. "You let me go off with that man, that satyr, and you never said a word . . . ?"

"*Tell me.*"

But his thunderous expression gratified her enough. Whatever he knew, he could not have known the whole. "Down the back stairs, all the way down the stairs in the basement, there is a place—he calls it the *voudrais*—a room where you enter and do whatever you want. He presides—and Lady Craig, and he grants his followers every license, any sensual gratification they desire—and they all conspire to keep the secret because they all want to keep doing it . . . it's horrible . . . he takes anyone, everyone who is willing—they're all willing, they all want, they invite—they deliberately entice him, and all the men to take any liberty. To take them, one after the other, endlessly, as if it had no meaning, no other purpose other than the moment of seduction. He wanted to initiate *me*—"

"Pack your bags," he interrupted, his voice threaded with steel. "We'll leave tonight, you and I, if not your grandmother. I will come for you within the half hour."

She didn't like the expression on his face; it was more than just that forbidding mask she so despised: it was the face of a man in the grips of a primitive emotion. "What are you going to do?" she demanded as he knelt by the fireplace, scooped up a handful of ashes and began to smear them on his face.

"I'm doing nothing more than protecting what is mine," he said grimly. "I'm going on a revenge raid."

It had welled up from deep inside him, that elemental powerful desire to take vengeance, from a time he had been used to sitting in a corner of the lodge and watching his uncle in those long ago days when morality was

401

simple: when someone struck against you, you struck back.

He felt it now, plain, searing, primitive.

He eased himself out into the hallway and over toward the back stairwell, and then down the flat steps, silent as a cat, listening, always listening. As he came closer and closer to the basement door, the thing that struck him was the silence. But a lecher who had planned his version of heaven had to be careful: he had to be sure that it was exclusive, and that the wounds of revelry could never be heard by his respectable parents or the friends that had been invited as a smokescreen for the orgy.

The door was thick, several massive pieces of wood tied together with hard iron hinges. He could just hear a trace of the noise from beyond, and he tried the door, certain it would be locked, impenetrable.

But it wasn't, it swung open easily, almost as if Endicott hadn't bothered to lock it after Angelene's defection. Almost as if he wanted someone to happen down to the *voudrais* and find his heaven.

Rake flattened himself against the door, and inched his way over the threshold. The scene was a libertine's dream, with the one shocking element the complete corruption of the arrogant and relentless Miss Madrid, who was laying naked now on her sofa, accepting the attentions of a half dozen adoring men. In the center of the room, on a raised dais, Moren Craig reclined on a bed of thick pillows, idly reaching for the nakedness of whichever passing man interested her. In corners and on the floor, couples copulated with abandon and reached eagerly for other partners as soon as the thing was done. On another plump couch in a corner, the randy Mr. Darlington lay naked with a crowd of nubile young servants massaging his body and offering him tempting sweetmeats.

The mind could hardly grasp the whole. There was still more: there were things not seen or presented in public that still could be heard and appreciated in other rooms beyond the *voudrais*. And the man who had created this

402

lewd revelry was now ensconced on a pillowed throne and attended by eager voluptuaries who begged for his attention.

How did a man exact revenge against such a licentious abyss? He knew—he consigned the whole thing to hell.

To be done subtly, so that nobody perished, but so that the thing was destroyed once and perhaps forever.

He edged back outside the door, and reached for the innocuous, sputtering stump of a candle.

A hunter always learned how to outwit his prey before committing himself to the hunt. He had been taught that as a child, and he felt the primitive seduction of the old ways as he set the candle firmly against the wooden plank door that separated the back rooms of the *voudrais* from the kitchen cellar behind, which he had found scouting through the service ell, the part of the house directly over the *voudrais*. He didn't know if that discovery were luck or skill: he had tried every door, thumped every wall to find an entrance other than the one down the rear staircase, because he wanted them to escape, naked and ashamed, and he wanted them to watch their decadent hell crumple to ashes.

Still, it took several long breathtaking moments until the flickering little flame licked its way into the wood of the door; heartstopping moments, because he didn't have the time to rummage through the kitchen to look for matches or another candle. He didn't have time for anything but to set things in motion and escape as fast as he could with Angelene.

He felt a bloodcurdling yell welling up inside him, the age-old signal of a revenge completed and a warrior's return, and he clamped down on it ruthlessly, and watched the little fire flame into life suddenly, and race up the wooden hinges and doorframe, and seek the air of the room beyond.

He ran then, up into the kitchen, and through the labyrinth of hallways that led finally to the front door,

403

and he pushed open the door and ran for the stables.

It was so late, so dark, with only moonlight to show him the way. It was fitting for the new-born warrior to rely on the moon, it was the way of the old ones and the things he had forgotten in the seduction of the new.

He aroused the stableboys without a feeling of pity. "Get me a driver and a carriage, boy. I need to return to London tonight."

"'Oo says?" one of the boys demanded arrogantly.

"The wealthy American lady, the one with all the money who will make it worth your while. *Get going!* If you're not at the door in five minutes, I'll come back and take a whip to you."

They scurried, and he ran back to the hell-hole, back to the house. Everything had to mesh perfectly. He dashed up the stairs to Angelene's room to find her waiting, dressed in her riding habit with a small bag by her side.

"Grandmother can take the rest," she said succinctly. "I want to leave *now.*"

He grabbed the bag, took her hand and they ran once more down the staircase to the main hall and out the front door.

"I need some of that money you won from Endicott; I had to bribe the stable boys—here they come now."

The carriage jounced to a halt beside them and the driver jumped down. "I want me money now, lady. I ain't goin' to London without I 'ave some pay off."

Angelene reached into her bag just as they heard the faint sound of a scream. "Here—" she thrust a handful of silver at him. "Get us away from here *now.*"

The driver mounted his perch without another word. "You ready, lady?" he shouted down, and then without waiting for her answer, he snapped his whip and set the horses running, and the carriage lurched away from the manor house and the horrified screams of the patrons of the *voudrais.*

Chapter 21

None of the guests of Shillingford were astonished by the speed with which they were asked to leave after the fire. The halls were filled with smoke, the basement and the underfloors of the kitchen ell were damaged and dangerous, and there was no help for it whatsoever.

"It was rude of you to leave," Mrs. Bellancourt scolded Angelene as she stepped down from her carriage and sailed angrily into the house. "I can't think of a single reason for a person to skulk away before daylight without properly thanking her hosts, and especially the man who has been so particular in his attentions to you."

"Nevertheless . . ." Angelene said, loath to supply even one detail.

"And that messy, smoky fire—so distressing after such a lovely weekend. In any event, I am not proud of your behavior, Angelene, nor yours, Richard, in abetting her in this way."

"Sometimes a gentleman has no choice, ma'am."

"And what does that mean, young man?"

"Sometimes a gentleman can't tell."

"You both are talking in riddles. This has positively ruined everything. Mr. Endicott is not one to forget an incivility like this," she warned.

"I wouldn't think so," Angelene said defiantly.

"This could be the end of our social career in London."

"Then we'll just go home."

"That wasn't my intent, Angelene. I wanted you both to experience the full range of opportunity in London, especially when the season is in full swing in April."

"That may still be possible."

"Perhaps—but only if you apologize to Mr. Endicott and hope that he forgives you and even deigns to call upon you again."

"I won't apologize, Grandmother."

"I don't understand. We are talking about the Rottinghams."

"How aptly they are named," Rake murmured from across the room.

"You are talking in riddles, Richard. I wish someone would explain what is going on."

Still, the solecism did not diminish the number of invitations they received, nor the habitual influx of visitors in the first week they came home.

The first to attend the Bellancourts at home were the Madrids, *and* Charles Endicott dancing attendance on Antoinette, hanging on her every word, and just daring Angelene to open her mouth and say anything relevant to the weekend.

"So sorry things came to such an abrupt end," he murmured suggestively, "but we've all come up to town and we're going to do our country weekends here. Can't have too much of a good thing, can we, Angelene?"

She shuddered.

"And of course you'll all be invited," he said sweepingly. "And now, I've promised to take dear Miss Madrid on a special little tour of the city. I hope to see you all soon," he added, bowing out and leaving Flora Madrid in perfect raptures over the Bellancourt tea table.

"Can you imagine? He's so taken with Antoinette he insisted on coming up to town as soon as he could just to be with her."

"Taken with Antoinette?" Mrs. Bellancourt said faintly, her eyes slanting accusingly at Angelene.

"Oh yes, it happened on the weekend. It was almost as

if he had just *discovered* her out of the blue. He hasn't let her out of his sight for a moment. I am in transports. The Rottinghams and *my* little girl. It's everything a mother could dream of."

"Or grandmother," Mrs. Bellancourt put in dryly, but later she vented her distress in no uncertain terms.

"I don't know what happened between you and Mr. Endicott that allowed that little snit to step in and steal him from you, but I will tell you, you will never get him back."

"I don't want him back. I want to go home."

"Well, we can't do that; we cannot let this become a setback, Angelene. We have to sail forward as if Mr. Endicott's defection meant nothing to us, and we'll just try to fix someone else's interest as soon as possible. Things are really fine: Mr. Endicott may be misguided but he isn't angry. All isn't lost, Angelene, take heart. The season has barely begun."

Of course, he could have seen to it that they were ostracized socially, and grandmother was radiant with relief that he had not. But everywhere they went, and wherever they encountered *him*, his malicious dark eyes challenged them, and his whispered conversations were the stuff to make any aspiring newcomer shiver.

But now Antoinette Madrid was the recipient of his confidences and the snide little sidelong glances she habitually sent their way when they met in company made Mrs. Bellancourt, at any rate, decidedly uncomfortable.

Antoinette had not forgotten her vow to make Richard Bellancourt pay for the way he had treated her. She went at her father constantly about it.

"But what's the point, my dear? Here you have Endicott practically grovelling at your feet; why waste your time on Bellancourt?"

"I want to. I want to know." And in fact, so did Charles when she confided that her father was going to track down Richard Bellancourt's particulars to see if he found anything untoward in his background. "Charles is curious too. I mean, they just came out of nowhere, Angelene and Richard. What if we found out they were fakes? What if they've taken in the old lady so thoroughly she has made over all her money to them? And what if she dies suddenly, then what? And all because you wouldn't do this one little favor for me, father. You could be doing Mrs. Bellancourt a bigger one."

But Victor heard almost none of that. His attention was caught by the idea that Endicott was interested too, and that was reason enough for him to comply.

"I'll do it, my dear, but I'm sure you are chasing rainbows."

"Thank you, Father. I'm sure *none* of us will be sorry."

But she meant to make Angelene Bellancourt sorry. She meant to make her pay for making Charles so unhappy until Charles had found *her*. And she meant to pull the rug right out from under Richard Bellancourt, to make him so unacceptable that he would never be received anywhere in the world ever again.

Mrs. Bellancourt coerced them out driving, and accepted invitations to tea, and took them to the terrace at Parliament so they could be seen, and so Angelene would not appear to be languishing over the defection of Mr. Endicott.

"I hardly consider Mr. Endicott's attentions to Miss Madrid a defection," Angelene said stiffly over tea in the open air in the shadow of the Parliament buildings.

"But things have slowed down so. There is still that little ongoing interest because of the Prince but we just can't count on that carrying us through the rest of the season."

Angelene was barely listening; she had the odd sensation that someone's eyes were on them and she twisted around in her chair, but the terrace was so crowded, she thought she must have been imagining it.

But the feeling persisted as they emerged from the terrace and she only wanted to go home to shake off the feeling of dread.

She was sure it was Charles. He had just the kind of malicious streak, if his visit with the Madrids was anything to judge by.

But what did he mean to do, scare her? Make her regret she had rebuffed him? Flaunt Miss Madrid in front of her whenever possible and dare her to tell all that she knew?

Her sense of malaise continued when they arrived back at the Glanville house.

"I have had enough of this season," she said testily, and her Grandmother's mouth tensed up into a prim shape of disapproval.

"I have not spent all this time and money on you to have you back out now," she said tersely. "We have a number of invitations, which I have accepted, and the ball at the Windmere's, where I was looking forward to having you wear that wonderful dress. You just can't change your mind about things now."

"After the Windmere ball—" Angelene began.

"After the Windmere ball things may have changed so substantially that you will wish we had never had this conversation."

But the atmosphere did not lighten.

"This house is too gloomy," her Grandmother complained one day. "I wonder if we shouldn't remove to a hotel."

"I would prefer it," Angelene agreed—because even Rake was restive, and she had the feeling he had had quite enough of being dangled in front of society as the loving brother of the American novelty.

Everything had gone so very wrong; all of her plans had exploded in her face. She felt fragmented and without substance, a figment of her Grandmother's imagination—and maybe her own.

She had nothing to run to, nowhere else to go.

Choices. She had made them and they had almost brought her down low.

Mr. Darlington had defected, now that he had been taken up the Endicott's set, and he set up living quarters at Brown's, and made himself available to Charles as the extra guest, the compatriot in the quest of the streets. There was no doubt about it, he had found a kindred soul, and because of it, Angelene wondered if it were he whom she felt watching them on behalf of Charles, just as he had spied on them for the *Tatler* beforehand.

It would make so much sense if it were Darlington. It meant she could relax a little, not necessarily let up her guard, but at least she could understand who and how and why and it would be less *threatening*.

But her sense of unease did not abate.

They went to a musicale at the Trowbridge's (who knew nothing of her flight from Shillingford, assuming she had only left early and so were still on friendly terms); a dinner at the Claxton's, another Trowbridge connection, an evening of theater by themselves, all of it to sludge through January to the bright light of the upcoming ball at the Windmere's where everything might be made right again.

She was not liking the life of a lady of leisure. There were too many inconsequentials, most of which were embodied in the ritual of the daily call. She saw too that her grandmother relished them and returned every last one with a vengeance and would not let her bow out of her social duty.

But Rake was another matter.

"What *is* he doing these days?" she demanded one morning as she sorted through still another stack of endless cards, resisting the temptation put all of them into the non-acceptance pile.

"Why, he's out buying horseflesh, my dear, didn't you know?"

"I beg your pardon? *Horses?*"

410

"Good bloodstock he says, and of course we have to keep up the story of the thoroughbred farm. So . . . horses."

But what was she but good bloodstock, she thought, being paraded around as blatantly as any horse. At least the horse got to do a job. She didn't know exactly what she was supposed to do, and sometimes the inactivity drove her to distraction. She envied the fact that Rake could go out of the gloomy mansion and *do* something, and he didn't have to sit and wait for *invitations.*

"Well, there is always a let-down at this time of the year," her grandmother assured her, "even in New York. And you've done so much better than I ever dreamed of. It's like having a daughter all over again who understands the rules."

Oh, but don't be too sure of that, Grandmother, she wanted to say. She hadn't played by any rules since the moment she had decided she was going to come to New York, and she was chafing under the restrictions even now. A feeling of dread followed her around like a little cloud.

It had to burst—and soon, and maybe when it did, she would find another choice.

It happened two weeks before the Windmere ball.

Mrs. Madrid was the bearer of the happy news—for her at least.

"But Amelia—you're not listening to me. Mr. Madrid was most appalled that he had recommended Richard's farm to a friend for boarding, and when his friend tried to send his stock there to be trained and boarded, he couldn't find the Bellancourt stable anywhere in the state."

"I'm sorry to hear that," Mrs. Bellancourt said complacently. "Maybe he had the name wrong? Or the town?"

"You never did say what town, Amelia."

"What town *is* it, Angelene?"

411

Angelene bit her lip. This was Charles's instigation, she just knew it, and she hoped to the gods that Mrs. Madrid's friend had never heard of the place where Rake had lived on the mountain.

"Crossville Junction, Grandmother."

"That's right. It's not up near Louisville, as I understand it, is that right, Angelene?"

"No, it's closer toward the Missouri border."

"Exactly, and that is why your friend couldn't find it; he was looking in the wrong end of the state. So all your excitement was for nothing, Flora. Mr. Madrid just got the facts wrong."

Mrs. Madrid didn't think so at all, but she was livid that Amelia had taken the wind right out of her sails. "Well, we shall see, Amelia. But I still think there is something to this. I always thought Richard wasn't one of us."

This was getting worse and worse—*not one of them!* Mrs. Madrid was seeing tiaras and coronets in her dreams, Angelene thought, just because the Endicotts had approved of Antoinette. If only she knew what Antoinette was up to, and how Charles Endicott was counting on no one ever telling.

Her tension escalated as she recounted Mrs. Madrid's visit to Rake. "Endicott is after your hide," she warned him.

"Fine, and I'll hang the bastard by his. I'm not afraid of him, Angelene. Are you?"

Choices. She waited for the axe to fall as the days to the ball wound down to just a few.

Someone was watching them, and now she wasn't so sure it was Charles or even someone hired to look into Rake's affairs. Maybe it was Mr. Madrid. Maybe it was her imagination.

Not even the beautiful blue ball gown with the fuschia silk-lined train could buoy her spirits the night of the ball, as Mary helped her to dress.

The doorbell rang, ominous and intrusive.

"Oh, it's Mr. Darlington come to call, miss. He's visiting with Mrs. Bellancourt now. So hold still, we're almost done."

Darlington. Who wanted to see him? He represented a threat now, a link with an enemy that was not to be trusted.

"But my dear, you looked stunning," he murmured, as she tripped carefully down the stairs and met him and her grandmother in the parlor. "Just stunning. Endicott is a blind man. If he ever saw you as you are now, he would give up every vice and lay his soul at your feet."

"And I would step on it," Angelene said nastily. "Where is Richard?"

"He'll join us in a moment, my dear. I just cannot get over the cut of that dress. Come into the light and let me really look at you."

The doorbell rang shrilly again.

"Now, I *know* we're not expecting anyone else," Mrs. Bellancourt said, motioning to the butler to indicate they were not at home.

A fury burst into the room. "Not at home? Not at home? Isn't that like you, Mama. You haven't changed a bit. Won't even give a greeting to your own daughter, and I went to the trouble to track you down all the way over here, even after all these years."

"Josephine," Mrs. Bellancourt said faintly, and then she crumpled to the floor right where she stood.

"Well, aren't you something, Angel Face. Your gramma got you all trussed up and tricked out. I would hardly know you were my daughter."

"And no one would know you're Grandmother's daughter with that hard-hearted indifference. I hate you."

"Oh, we know that already, daughter. We didn't expect anything from you after you disappeared."

"I know what you expected," Angelene said tartly. "I'm glad I outwitted you. What do you want here? And

413

what do you think you can expect with Grandmother laid up in bed in shock?"

"I came to visit my mother, Angelene, just like a good dutiful daughter. Which is more than I can say for you."

Angelene ignored her, her eyes anxiously on the door, waiting for the moment, Mr. Darlington would return with a doctor. Rake was upstairs with her grandmother, having lifted her frail body as easily as he would have lifted a child's, and carried her to her bedroom.

She felt uneasy being alone with Josie. She felt the same amorphous threat emanating from Josie that had disquieted her for the last several weeks. She wondered about the fact Josie was alone, and that she was well-dressed and well-groomed in a way she had never seen her before in her whole life.

Josie had spent money on herself; she was wearing a travelling suit of a dark charcoal gray cashmere which had a velvet collar and cuffs and a matching belt. Her hair had been trimmed and tucked up fashionably under a coordinating velvet hat that perched tipsily on top of her head, and looked about to topple off.

She looked the same and different, and her fashionable clothes made her look younger, if not less bulky. But her face was still hard and determined, and she had come for something and eventually her grandmother was going to find out exactly what.

Mr. Darlington scurried into the hallway, followed by a stately man with gray hair and a very businesslike manner.

"She's upstairs," Angelene directed them, and Mr. Darlington motioned the doctor to the stairway.

A minute or two later, Rake came racing down the stairs.

And that was the redoubtable Josie, so tall like Angelene, so like Angelene, only older and thicker and radiating a malevolence that she could not disguise with beautiful clothes and a semblance of manners.

And he had left Angelene alone with her—

"Who are you?" she demanded when he reached the bottom step.

"Why, I'm your loving oldest son Richard, ma'am," he drawled as he came into the room.

"I'd love to have a son like you," she said with just a hint of suggestive flirtatiousness. "You're fine. I just know you know what you know, son. Such good looking children."

"Grandmother thought so," Rake said blandly.

"Yes, I hear she had a high old time spending *my* money on Angel Face here and some tall western stranger, making a grand show all over London. Seemed to me I had to move to protect my interests."

Angelene felt a cold chill. "Where's Bobby?"

"I left him at Gramma's house in New York to enjoy a healthy dose of fine living, just like you've been doing."

"Then you came here to scare Grandmother out of her wits."

"Or maybe I came to keep you from going to that fancy party you was heading to, girl. That dress could keep me in style at home for ten years. So I just upped and decided you shouldn't be getting everything I was entitled to, daughter, and here I am."

Her words had a menacing undertone, her sentences slightly incoherent as if she were boiling inside and spewing out whatever came to mind.

She was ragingly jealous of Angelene, Rake thought. She always had been, and a woman in a rage was dangerous, explosive, uncontrollable. She might attack Angelene; he might have to subdue her.

There was something in the air and he couldn't define it. The woman had to be watched; Angelene had been right to escape her.

The doctor brought them down the news that Mrs. Bellancourt was resting comfortably, and aware that it truly was her daughter Josephine who had arrived this evening. She could eat if she wanted, he would prefer broth, tea, and a good night's rest with no excitement.

Angelene snapped her fingers and the maid appeared, scurrying to comply with her request to put the kettle to the boil and make sure a broth would be available should her grandmother wish to have some.

"Ain't you the lady of the house," Josie said snidely. "You got to defer to your elders, girl. That makes me the boss now."

"I was so hoping you would return to wherever you have been staying and come back in the morning when Grandmother is feeling better," Angelene said.

"No, I was planning to stay with you and Mother. Do you have any problem with that?"

"I can't begin to tell you all my problems with that. You cannot stay here."

Josie shrugged and turned to Rake. "She always was a rebellious one."

"Josephine!"

Her grandmother stood, wavering at the top of the steps.

"Grandmother—"

"Perfect," Josie muttered and reached for her purse.

Rake saw her; her hand delved, her arm lifted, she removed a gun, she raised her arm, she aimed it—he jumped just as she squeezed the trigger, he fell on her heavily and the shot went—he couldn't tell where the shot went—screams, Angelene pounding up the stairs to her grandmother; Josie, like a wildcat beneath him, screaming imprecations in his ear—his hands clawing the gun from hers. A voice from close behind them:

"*Angelene!*"

He heard the voice, he pulled the gun from Josie's hands by sheer desperation; he rolled on his back in a split second decision aimed at the figure in the shadow of the doorway and he fired just as the killer aimed his shot.

He dropped, Josie screamed: "*Bobby!*" and crawled over to his body where it lay.

Rake got up slowly, the gun still smoking in his hand. "The doctor, the doctor . . . Darlington, get that

416

damned doctor back here. *Rake!*" Angelene's voice, frantic, in control.

"You little bitch!" Josie screamed, looking up at her. "Taking everything away from me you weren't meant to have. Taking away my mother, leaving me with nothing—*nothing! I'll kill you*—" she shrieked, reaching for Bobby's gun—"*I'll kill you,*" she screamed, getting to her feet as Angelene disappeared from the edge of the landing. "You're dead, girl," she shouted and raced for the stairs.

The gun went off wildly, and Josie reeled crazily up the steps after her daughter.

Rake took aim again, calmly and coolly, and fired one shot that stopped her dead in her tracks.

The scandal was the talk of the town for weeks, and it was Darlington who betrayed them again, Darlington who ran for the doctor past the inert bodies of Josie and her son, Darlington who returned with Endicott in tow.

The thing was delicious, and Endicott saw it as his last final act of revenge against the woman who had spurned him and the man who had defended her honor.

The *Tatler* had the story before the night was over: on the evening of the most talked about social event of the season, the murders of Josephine Bellancourt Scates and her son Bobby became the most talked about event of the season. And the scene, as the reporter saw it in copious detail, was scandalous and suggestive: Mrs. Bellancourt lying in a pool of her own blood; her grandson, dead, on the reception room floor; her daughter Josephine slumped on the stairs. Her granddaughter Angelene directing the doctor and the police with great calm and self-possession. The gun on the floor beside Richard Bellancourt. The grandmother near death in the hospital. A fortune in inheritance in the offing. The possibility that Richard Bellancourt was not what he seemed.

But there was only one story that Angelene would

417

allow to be told. "Josie shot at Grandmother, Bobby shot her and Richard shot him to prevent him from coming after me. Is that clear? Does everybody have that clear?"

The *Tatler* didn't believe it, and the society doyennes who had welcomed the fascinating Americans into their homes spent many hours denying it, and gossipping about it while Angelene stayed closeted with her grandmother in the hospital and Rake fended off reporters.

"When grandmother recovers, the stories will be laid to rest," Angelene said stoutly. She was sure of it.

The Glanvilles asked them to foreshorten their lease and leave. Claridge's wouldn't take them. Brown's might, but perhaps they wanted to try the Mayfair.

They moved, servants and all, to the smaller and less exclusive hotel. Grandmother's money could not buy everything.

The police investigation went on exhaustively.

The *Tatler* detailed the story exhaustively. They had it on authority that Richard Bellancourt was not in fact Mrs. Bellancourt's grandson. He was not a top-rate breeder of horses in Kentucky. He was not anything connected with the Bellancourts at all and the speculation arose, fueled by the gossip, that he was Angelene's lover and her accomplice in the murder of her mother and the attempted murder of her grandmother in order to claim her fortune.

The public believed it, the ostracism was complete. Everyone had always known there was something not quite right about the Americans. It was just that the Prince had taken her up and who dared to question his judgment.

The lies piled upon the lies. Bobby, in death, had become Rake's brother, Josie his mother. There were questions that were unanswerable except with more lies: why had Josie come. Had they expected her? Why would she want to attack her mother, why would the boy shoot her, why would Rake take aim at his brother?

Still, it was a more reasonable story than the truth: that Josie had been stalking them and had meant to kill both her mother and Angelene for the sake of the money after she got tired of waiting. But how did one explain the lifetime corruption of a soul that could never be satisfied.

The resolution was not much more satisfactory: Richard Bellancourt had discharged the gun in defense of his family, and the verdict was abetted by the testimony of Amelia Bellancourt from her hospital bed.

Society snickered; the *Tatler* had told them the real story—the man was her lover and the old lady still wasn't safe.

They never got another invitation anywhere ever again, but her grandmother never knew it while she lay recovering in her hospital bed.

The worst blow was yet to come.

"I'm going home," Rake said one morning as he read yet another scurrilous story in the *Daily Times*, excerpted from a "confidential source", and he hardened his heart against the expression on her face. "It is the only thing I can do, Angelene. The longer I stay, the worse it affects you. I am the murderer. I killed your family and I can barely come to terms with that."

"You and Grandmother have become my family," she protested. She hadn't cried since she had arranged to have Josie's and Bobby's bodies sent home to Missouri.

She didn't have much to cry about, she thought. She had had a run at the life she had dreamed of, and she had even attained a little success. Now, she felt like a cypher, blurred, in limbo, not sure of what to do next. The tears for Josie refused to come. She cried a little for poor misguided Bobby and thought she would never understand why he wanted to kill her.

She sat by her grandmother's side and made plans to go home and never told her about the invitations that didn't come.

She said yes, she understood why it was time for Rake to go home.

*　　*　　*

419

He left the clothes, all but one suit, and he took the horses, and he kissed the tenacious old lady goodbye.

He held Angelene until his soul cried for mercy. "Goodbye, angel of my heart," he whispered into her lustrous hair. *Remember me always, sweet angel eyes.*

He sailed on the steamer *Queen of the Sea*, a less luxurious liner which catered to the pragmatic needs of the business traveller with more cargo space and smaller staterooms.

That suited him fine. He was a man who had to make peace with who he had been and what he had become—and how he had reverted back to being a killer at the drop of a gun.

He had defended Angelene and destroyed her family, and he had made himself into a man who had forgotten his past. In the space of six months, he had lost his soul and now he needed to find where he belonged.

Rake's absence did not make anything easier. She became Love's Lady Lost in the *Tatler*, and they always pictured her dressed in mourning.

Her Grandmother lingered on, losing strength every day, asking after Richard when she finally understood he would never come around again.

"He's gone home, Grandmother, to tend to his farm," Angelene told her gently. "He had taken too much time away from business and he had to go home."

"And he took Josephine and Bobby with him to bury them on the farm?" her Grandmother asked, and Angelene said, "Yes."

There was just no sense telling the truth about anything any more, but she dearly wanted to tell her Grandmother the truth about Rake, but after a while, that didn't matter either.

"I loved our time together in England, Josephine," her Grandmother said one day. "So handsome a pair, you and Richard, it was just the way I dreamed it—you and a handsome young man."

It was too late after that. Her grandmother's memories drowned in a mist of love for Josephine who had turned into perfection, the very daughter she had always wanted, and so "everything I have will be yours, dear daughter. I arranged everything before we came, a gift to you because you gave me this gift of yourself."

Two weeks later her grandmother died, holding her hands, and Angelene finally cried. It came from a well deep down inside her of nameless emotions she had shoved away and buried tightly. It came up in a flood, a primitive scream, and it felt like she would never stop. She felt like she was cut loose from everything and there was nothing to which she could anchor.

She knew what it meant to be alone.

And then she knew what it meant to be rich. The bank in England extended her a letter of credit; her grandmother's lawyer cabled that she was the beneficiary of the will. She had not meant Josephine, or maybe she had just gotten the two of them intertwined and interconnected. Maybe as she approached death, the disparity didn't matter anymore. Whether they were one and the same, or two different people, they were equal to her in her fierce love for them, and in the end, Angelene had become Angelene, even if she had been called Josephine in the doorway of death.

The money eased nothing, none of the pain, none of the snubs. The news of the inheritance became the next ten days' wonder in the press, which culminated with the speculation as to what might have happened in the hospital to speed things along.

Mr. Darlington attempted to pay a condolence call. She heard his words, she saw only his betrayals, and she finally refused to listen to anything he had to say.

The family Madrid, flushed with social success, risked censure to pay their respects, and tactfully left their daughter home.

Even the Duchess of Glanville, taking pity, paid a discreet call. She said how sorry she was and she hoped that Angelene would consider returning to America, and how happy she was that Angelene had been the beneficiary of her grandmother's estate. In between the lines she said: *how nice now that you're rich; you won't have to ask me for help.*

Angelene made arrangements to sail in early March. She would leave just as the little season was ending and society was gearing up for the influx of families from overseas to begin the social swirl.

She would leave as the horses were being primed for the first spring races at Ascot. She would leave without ever having been presented to the Queen.

But she would leave her Grandmother safely at rest, in the city where she would have enjoyed all those things.

Chapter 22

The road ranch was deserted.

Angelene picked her way through the overgrown track that led to the house, and pushed her way inside the dank musty interior.

No one had lived in that house for months, and the scent of blood and disuse hung over the place like a pall. Rats had invaded the place, holing up in the kitchen until all the food had been devoured and then moving into the bedrooms or wherever vermin could be found to feed on.

She had the eerie sense someone was watching her.

Folly to have come here alone, or to even think that a little ceremony to celebrate the life of her mother would be appropriate in the place where she had finally found some . . . some what? Some unsuspecting prey.

There was blood all over the place, from the nameless bodies buried in and around the house to the streaks that had trailed down to the floor and gotten scuffed in the grain of the wood.

A memorial would be a travesty: there had been no celebration of life here.

Nevertheless, she made the attempt. She took the shovel which she had brought with her, and she scratched a pit underneath a tree which was a fair piece from the house and marked it with a plain wooden cross

423

she had bought in the town where she had rented the wagon.

The deed was done. Perhaps Josie was content now, and Raso and Tice would come back and find her.

She scratched Josie's name on the cross with a stone, and Bobby's beneath it.

For the evil at heart, there was no resting in peace.

In the end, he had had no choice at all about where he wanted to go. The mountain drew him as if it claimed his soul.

When he arrived in Crossville Junction, it was the dead of winter, and there wasn't a soul in sight.

He took the horses and he went to Carter, whose front door was closed against the cold and whose stove radiated welcome heat into the night.

"Man, I never thought I'd see you again," Carter said. "Sit down, sit down."

"Never thought I'd be back," Rake said, rubbing his hands over the stove. "I need a place for my stock and somewhere to stay until I get my sights on what's going on up the mountain."

"I could tell you, man, there's nothing up on the mountain. The whole top of it burned down, and burned out at the stream where there was a natural fire break. Lucky. Otherwise it could have blazed through the town. Don't tell me you're thinking of going back up there—"

"Maybe, maybe not. I'd appreciate some coffee, Carter. It's been a long damned trip."

In the morning, Carter accompanied him up the mountain, and his first overriding thought was it wasn't as bad as he thought.

It was barren, it was bruised, it was naked, but here and there little signs of new life sprouted—a burgeoning branch, a tuft of grass, the seed of a leaf.

The sky was closer now, unbroken by the silhouette of

leaves and canopy of green. He could reach up and touch it, he could warm himself in the sun.

The hardest thing was the cabin, which was just a desolate ruin over which twining fingers of ivy had crept from the path down near the barn.

But the cookstove still stood, a charred iron mass, and the stone fireplace, and crackled broken dishes, and the battered coffeepot.

He turned away from the desecration and went to search for the bones of the dog.

And he found them, exactly what he expected to see.

"We will bury the dog," he said, but he couldn't bear to inter him under the ground. He rigged a little hammock and he wrapped the dog around, and he suspended the burial place between the trees in the time-honored way of his youth, and he released the dog to heaven, and his grief to the sky.

He rebuilt the cabin when the ground thawed, and when the weather warmed, toward the end of March, he brought the horses to his place.

His place, the place of sorrow and the place of redemption. The work had done him good, the sorrow had eased, and once again he felt the lifting of the burdens of his past.

The man who had killed did not want to die.

He felt the mountain come to life all around him as nature eased into Spring. He felt his blood quicken in the warming of the sun. He felt the hope of renewal and his heart began to sing.

He made his obeisance to the sun and his peace with the moon. His memory of his time away from the mountain receded like the tide. The song in his heart chanted, *Angelene*.

A man could not make a life on a foundation of lies.

The truth of the matter was he would never know whom the lie had touched; he would never know if things would have been different.

He thought of the old lady often and he wondered if she had survived. But he never said the word out loud: *Angelene.*

Carter told him the killers had ravaged the mountain after the fire had burned down, and then they had come into the town and wrought destruction there. They had sworn they would return and they had, like circuit preachers, once a month, looking for the girl and the man who had stolen her away.

"The girl is gone," he said, and he thought he really meant it, and that it was meant to be.

"They'll be back anyway," Carter told him, "but they didn't come last month, too cold most likely, but I don't like the idea of you're being up alone against them."

Rake smiled grimly. "Neither do I. You don't think I'm planning to stick my damnfool neck out for that, do you?"

"You went to town for the girl, Cordigan."

"Town? Hell, I went to England, man. Remind me some day to tell you. I wager those two won't come back again, Carter. They couldn't be that stupid as to spend five months over the same hunting ground and come up empty and keep on coming anyway."

"Who knows what a killer will do?" Carter shrugged, and Rake reflected he had gotten that right. A killer could do anything, even swear his life to peace and then kill again.

The months on the mountain had made it better, but the pain of it still hadn't washed away. Nor was his guilt mitigated because of the circumstances and who his victims were.

They were Angelene's family, and no matter what they were, that could never be erased.

But he tried. He worked hard on the mountain bringing it back to the lush life he remembered, but he worked at it now with a different heart. This time, a man worked who had come around in a circle and ticked off stations through which he had successfully passed. And this time, he was travelling slowly, and savoring every miracle, including the one called Angelene.

No one had seen Tice or Raso for months, and no one knew where they had gotten to, and Angelene felt a little frisson of foreboding. For all she knew, they both could be dead.

She travelled up to Cairo to visit with Mother Margaret and Sister Philomena at the convent school and left them with a contribution to the church on the heels of the news of her good fortune and the revelation that Mother Margaret had approved the Sister's helping her escape Josie all those many months ago.

So—everything had come in a circle, and if fate were kind, somewhere just over the Kentucky border, a man would rescue her with a reluctant lifeline.

But now of course she travelled by coach and in the company of other travellers, and she had no destination at all. . . . Or maybe she had. Maybe she had swung around to Cairo just to follow her course of nearly a year ago.

Maybe she knew exactly where she wanted to go because she felt a certainty that that was the only place he could be, even though, all these months, he had known where to find her. Even though, with the passage of time, England had become a dream and her wealth a reality, and it seemed as if she had always had it, and she had never had her mother.

She would *not* give in and go to Crossville Junction.

He could have come for her any time in these past several months.

But he mightn't have known she was back.

He could have *tried* to find out.

Angel of his heart . . .

Hadn't she folded that endearment to her heart all these months, and taken it out in the bleakest of times, the blackest of moments? Or had that too been a dream,

427

the words, the love, the *life* between them . . . ?

How could she know if he wouldn't tell her?

She left the stage in Madison and took the train for Lexington, to the place where she would be within a day's travel to Crossville Junction.

April had come and with it blue skies, soft spring rain, a sense of renewal and a calm resigned peace.

The curious thing he found as he labored up on the mountain was that now he did not deliberately seek to isolate himself from companionship, and he was making regular and periodic trips to town. He was feeling a sense of community.

He was not a man to accept that lightly; he could feel himself leaning into a friendship, warming to a kindness, and ceasing to search for the condemnation behind the curiosity.

He was the man who was reclaiming the mountain, the breeder of horses, the man who had returned.

They knew him by name. He was starting to know them. They thought he was congenial and mannerly, and very different from how they remembered him. He thought of the fearsomely proper Miss Crosby and was amused by the idea that her injunctions were as correct here as they had been in any drawing room in London.

He was starting to understand, just a little, that a man was the sum and substance of all his parts, all his past, all he had learned, all he desired. He wasn't one thing or another: he wasn't a halfbreed or an alienated son of his mother's tribe—he was both and neither. He was the thing he had made of himself, and the restitution he had made beyond that.

He was both a primitive man, who needed none of the embellishments of civilization, and he was a creature who liked the comfort and sustenance it could offer, and he could always choose.

Choices.

He had made them. He had relinquished Angelene

428

deliberately and decisively so that she should not continue to bear the pain of his instinctive brutality.

Choices. He had sworn it would never happen, but he had killed again.

Choices. He had unleashed the malevolent force of a nobleman's vindictiveness by his unquenchable thirst for revenge.

Choices. He had come to the mountain as a symbol of repentance, as he had chosen never to try to see her again.

And so why did he think he was seeing her, one bright late Spring afternoon as he emerged from Carter's store.

But no—it was a woman, richly dressed in blue, trimmed with fur and sun-gold hair blowing in lustrous wisps about her face in the wind of the mountain. How could it be Angelene?

In his youth, when the urgency was upon him and his peers, and the elders were guiding them into the rites of manhood, they had isolated him in the woods, in the forests, on mountains, in the sweat lodges to insure he had every possible chance to experience a vision.

The practical part of him, his father's part he often thought, had never understood the necessity of it, the complexity of it, or the importance of it, and he had never reached that exalted state when men achieved visions and portents of the future.

He only saw the things around him, the concrete and the immediate, and he saw the derision of his companions, the hopelessness in his uncle's eyes, and spinning decision of the elders to label him a contrary. He fought the identity and the symbolic branding of him for all time. He fought harder than any one of his rivals, counted more coup, led more raids, forged a more reckless and death-defying trail through the ranks of the tribe to prove that even without the visions, he was as much the man as any of his equals. And he proved their point.

But here was a vision, clearer and more dimensional than anything he had dreamed in the two months since he had last seen her, a woman so complete that she even moved like Angelene and smiled like Angelene.

But she was not dressed like Angelene. This woman wore an aura of wealth, and she was so beautiful that it was suspect what she was doing in a small town like Crossville Junction at the outset of spring.

She was the vision that he had always sought and never attained, the one he could never allow himself to reach for because the differences had always been too great.

He turned on his heel and he walked away from it.

"Good morning, Mr. Carter," a feminine voice said briskly, and Mr. Carter looked up from counting his inventory into the flashing blue eyes of a very exasperated and beautiful woman.

"Ma'am?"

"You don't remember me,"she said.

"Well—" Well, he didn't, or rather, she seemed familiar but she was much too richly dressed to be a farm lady from anywhere nearby.

"I was with Mr. Cordigan the day the mountain burned," she amplified, and his eyes lit up speculatively.

"Well now, I do remember, ma'am, but I have to wonder what you're doing back in Crossville Junction."

"I'm looking for a man to train a string of horses that I own, sir. I don't suppose you can tell me why he turned away the moment he saw me."

"Do you reckon he thought a fancy lady like you couldn't be looking particularly for him?"

"I don't reckon; I want to *know*," she said, smacking her purse on his counter in frustration.

"No one knows the workings of a man's mind, ma'am. He's been different since he come back, and he's worked up the mountain the last few months and he's brought it back, just a little, and he's building the barn in preparation to mating them two fancy horses he returned with. He settled his accounts with me, and so I don't ask too many questions. But he's been different, ma'am, that's the one thing that I can tell you."

She was different too, she reflected. She was now a woman of means, instead of a woman scheming to attain them. She had gotten what she wanted, and she had lost a lot along the way.

And he thought he was the murderous one.

She had killed the life between them.

And then she planned to walk back into his life to flaunt that success to a degree. It was not the way to do things with a man like Rake Cordigan. He had seen her elegant dress and he had turned his back, certain the line between them could never be crossed—after he had proven that he above anyone could successfully do it.

"I need some clothes," she said suddenly, decisively. "You know, plain clothes—calico, cotton—a sun bonnet—Mr. Carter, I am not sunstruck. I am going to give Mr. Cordigan exactly what he wants."

He wanted Angelene. The unexpected sight of her haunted him. His unbendable code of ethics would not let him give into it.

When he saw the wagon emerge from the far end of the pasture as he was chopping wood in the course of completing the framework for the barn, he was sure it was Carter because no one else knew the way of coming up the mountain, and no one else had come.

But it was the vision of his wildest, most improbable dreams, a woman of simplicity with long streaming golden hair, racing to come to him—and almost there.

She jerked the horses to a halt a foot in front of where he braced his body on the teetering edge of a black-bladed axe, and he squinted up at her.

"Angelene." His deep voice was so noncommittal, except for that faint thread of longing edging his husky tone.

He looked fine, unscathed. His body was browner and leaner than she remembered, his bared upper torso flexing with an impatience to continue—or an impatience about something else, she couldn't quite tell.

431

"Shall I just turn around and leave?" she asked tartly, flicking the reins lightly on the backs of the horses who stamped restively against the wagon.

"I probably should tell you to," he said at length, his steely eyes just feasting on her in her thin cotton dress that looked like it was a size too small for her. Everything about her was emphasized, from the crush of her breasts against the button-front bosom to the pattern of blue flowers that deepened the color of her eyes. Angel eyes.

"But you won't," she said decisively, dropping the reins and sliding across the seat. "I'm coming down, Rake Cordigan, and don't you dare stop me."

She swung her legs over the side of the wagon, and her dress hiked up over her long bare legs as she jumped down beside him.

"You have nothing on under that dress," Rake observed calmly, tossing the axe to one side. "That was a pretty daring thing to do, Angelene."

"Or desperate," she muttered, turning her burning gaze away from him.

"Sister of Angels is always rash and reckless," he said, his voice expressionless. "I will show you what I've done."

He took her arm and walked with her and soon she could see the cabin, its hand-hewn logs still naked with the marks of the axe. This time, he had built the cabin with only one floor and two rooms, one for his bed, one for his kitchen, and he had built the whole up and around the erstwhile blackened and charred iron stove which he had lovingly scraped and cleaned.

It was small, the cabin, smaller than the previous one, and it looked almost forlorn among the blackened stumps of the surrounding trees.

"It is sad up here," she said at length as they walked around to the back of the house and the framework of the barn he was constructing. Inside, within newly built stalls which were not secured from the elements, his beautiful sleek horses stamped and munched away on grasses and oats.

"Wanton destruction is sad," he agreed. "And rebuilding is hopeful."

"And why you returned," she said.

"I may say the same for you."

He was so perceptive to understand that, she thought, as they went back to the front of the cabin. She couldn't bear to look around at the waste and to think of all the years it would require to bring the mountain to the place where it had been when she first saw it. Did a man have that much patience?

Did she?

"My grandmother died," she said after a while.

"I knew it," he said. "I saw it in your face and the clothes you chose to wear. There really is nothing more to be said, Angelene. Your life is now set and there are no more limits to anything you want to do."

"But there are," she said in frustration, "and you have set them. I am the one who made the choice this time—and *you* chose to turn away."

"I haven't turned away now," he pointed out.

"One can turn one's mind as well as one's body," she said disgustedly, "and don't pretend you don't know that."

"I know too much, Sister of Angels, and only heaven knows whether I ever sleep. Tell me of your last days in London and the death of your grandmother."

"Your leaving made it worse. Grandmother passed away, thinking you had returned to your horses, and she thought me to be my mother until the last. I buried her there, and I kissed her for you. The tabloid dubbed me 'Love's Lady Lost,' and they as good as accused us of murdering her. Everyone was glad to see me go, and I was glad to leave. I understand Endicott will be marrying the Madrid this same time next year."

"And the whole now belongs to you," he said, a statement of fact that seemed to put a whole chasm between them.

"*Everything*," she said boldly, and dared him to walk away from her. She walked away from him instead, and

433

then turned back. "I went back to the ranch and put up a marker for Josie and Bobby."

"Good." And she had done it alone. He felt the first stirring of compunction: she should not have done that alone. She should have come to him. He should have gone to her sooner.

"There was no one at the ranch. I don't know where my brothers are."

"They stayed around here, by all accounts, but they haven't been seen for months now. They are men who are destined to die, Angelene."

"I know," she said unhappily. "And so was my mother and so was Bobby."

She understood that much at least, and a little of his pain eased away, fanned by a little flicker of life.

"Let me take you back to the wagon," he said, and her little resolution of hope slowly died away.

As they entered the pasture, she closed her mind to the barrenness of the place, and the fruitlessness of her quest. He would never yield, not when there was steel in his voice and ice in his heart. He had not forgiven her choices or the necessity for his own.

He was denying life and choosing repentence: the mountain was the monastery for his gesture of renunciation.

He had become the untouchable and she was now the greedy.

Her fingers dug into the hard bronzed muscles of his arms as he lifted her to the wagon with the same urgency she had gouged him during the height of their lovemaking; he had never forgotten.

He stopped in mid-motion and shifted her body toward him, aligning it against his and letting it slip sensually down the length of his until she was pressed tightly against him and wrapped in his arms.

She was so perfect against him, her beautiful eyes begging him, her mouth so conveniently there.

He wanted her. Every fiber of his body reacted to her seductive heat, to the squirming little movements of her body in reaction to the hard jutting thrust of his. He wanted her.

She had told him without words that she was willing that he take her. Her body, under the flimsy cotton dress, was naked and enticing, inviting him to imagine the way they used to be. The entwining closeness stoked the feverish heat of his memories. His tentative searching kiss exploded into dominating possession.

The moment he enslaved her mouth, she owned his soul. The kiss went on and on and on, hot, greedy, merciless in its voracious need.

His hands ripped away the obstruction of the dress and bared her beautiful body to his hot hard need. He cupped her buttocks and lifted her to press her harder and tighter against the forceful thrust of his manhood, and she wrapped her legs tightly around him to demand still more.

He carried her in this position to the rear of the wagon and he set her down on the lid of its bed, never breaking the kiss, to strip himself so he could take her. Her hands flexed in their excitement against the hard bronzed wall of his chest.

In a blazing moment, she felt him lift her again, and felt the probing tip of him against the welcoming fold of her desire.

She felt the push, she felt his hands guiding her downward to his perfect possession of her quivering need.

He held her to him, supporting her solely with his large hands cupping her buttocks and the tight fulfilling hardness of his manhood.

She surrounded him, perfect in her acceptance of him, loving the feel of him and the immutable connection to him, the pagan and primitive possession of him in her nakedness.

But the desire for completion pumped through his veins. He loved not moving and being at one with her and he wanted to plunge into her deeply and drive her to her culmination.

He lowered her to the wagon again to give him

435

purchase to move, and she braced herself to receive the surging pumping thrust of him. She wanted him now, she wanted his love. She arched herself to him in mute invitation, she opened herself to him and demanded his full driving possession of her.

He felt the radiance of his unspoken love for her devour his senses. He leaned over her and possessed her kiss once again, and he surged into her deeply, powerfully, over and over, primitive and virile, consumed with the hunger of taking her, owning her, surrendering to her.

He gave everything to her that hot racking spring afternoon, and when he felt her body twinge, and he felt her surrender, he drove into her in a white-hot fury of tumultuous possession.

She took it, and she wanted it, and she never wanted another man in her life to love her because she could never want anyone else but him.

Her body told him what she could not. In his last driving thrust, he caught her and the galvanic feeling in her center burst into a shattering shower of heat that convulsed her body in a sizzling succession of spasms, all molten and golden, streaming through her body, once, twice, three times, a fourth—and he surged into a volcanic climax simultaneously with her completion.

And she stayed. She had only the one dress, torn in the violence of his need for her, and she wore it proudly as a badge of his need for her.

It aroused him to see her in it, and she loved to watch that light of wanting deepen in his eyes. She loved to lay beside him and handle him, the mystery of him still a pure and primitive wonder to her. He loved to feel her hands stroking him into a granite hard arousal so that then he could come to her.

Time stood still again. There was no yesterday, no tomorrow. There was only the moment, and their luxurious mutual ongoing arousal of each other, and the

436

luscious fulfillment of desire, each at the free command of the other.

She loved his kisses. He adored her breasts. She loved to watch him walk around without his clothes. He loved to tear hers off of her so that there were just strips of her dress left by the end of the week.

She loved to lay with him in long lingering deep kisses, whispering and confiding all the different things that were so desirable in him. He loved the deep hard kisses of pure male possession that told her he had branded her as his own.

He wanted her endlessly. She couldn't get enough of him.

They rediscovered all the ways they had had of loving each other and they invented new ways.

He took her in the wagon again, this time with his eyes fixed on the sensual provocation of her face. They lay in the woods and in the water, on the path and in the hay.

He took her under the sky and under the moon and he could never fathom the sheer flagrant femininity of her, and he swore to give his life over trying.

And after two weeks, it was coming to a point where they both needed to make a committment in words and look toward a future.

He didn't know what to offer her, except himself. And she had too much. His problem was he couldn't see a way around that.

His life was in Crossville Junction, and the problem with loving someone was that other things came in to complicate it.

"Angel of angels," he murmured to her sleeping form as he caressed her spun gold hair. "Angel eyes."

Angel of my heart . . .

She heard the endearments and she tucked them deep in her heart. She felt his desire, all molten and alive, and she felt her own rise to meet it.

In the heat of the night, with no decisions made, she

turned to him, and she offered him her soul.

He took it and possessed it.

And he withheld his own.

In the dim light of dawn, he heard it in his dreams, that shrieking whooping animal howl that drove away his dreams.

His mind and body bolted awake—he wasn't dreaming and the sound echoed all around him, and he knew they had returned.

"Angelene—" he shook her hard, relentlessly, rousing her from her wildest dream of passion. "*Listen*—"

There was an eerie silence.

"Get dressed," he whispered, reaching for his pants and tossing her a shirt. "Hurry."

The silence was deafening, every insect sound magnified by the sheer torture of waiting.

He took down his rifle, crawling across to the other side of the room to get it, and crawling back again to the front door.

Angelene crouched beside him. "What is it?" she whispered tremulously.

"Intruders," he said tersely, not wanting to elaborate because he couldn't be sure—but he *was* sure: her brothers, scavenging on the mountain because they had heard he was back.

Nothing mattered now but his vow of revenge as he braced himself against the coming dawn.

The day radiated into light slowly, the matte gray gradually turning into light bright blue on the horizon as the sun slowly rose.

The stillness deepened into something ominous, a battle of wills, stretching the limits of concentration and patience.

But he knew they had no patience. They had a keen animal cunning, and a monster's sense of when to strike.

Nothing moved, except Rake's bronzed body across the pasture floor.

He heard something, he braced the rifle, he raised himself to his feet and gave a bloodcurdling yell.

438

It echoed off the stumps of trees, bounced into the hollows and resonated down the mountain.

And somewhere, in the distance, an animal howl answered it in kind. From the edge of the pasture at the far end away from the cabin, Angelene heard a dull thumping thud of horse hooves.

Rake stood watching it, his rifle set and aimed—there two of them, racing like mountain lions across the pasture toward him . . .

. . . Dear Lord—Raso and Tice!—

Rake's rifle exploded and one of them fell . . . the other came at him as he reloaded his gun.

. . . her brother—

She raised her rifle and aimed it somewhere in the distance—her heart pounded wildly, *Rake, Rake* as the rider bore down on him to get the closest possible range—

Rake!

She thought she shouted his name as the rifle went off—he fell—she heard another report . . . hers?

"Rake!" she screamed as the rider kept coming and coming . . . he was riding for the cabin—he was coming for her—!

She dropped the rifle and ran for the little rear kitchen door—she heard a blast of a shot behind her, and the scream of the horse as he rammed through the cabin door.

She wheeled around in terror to see the horse picking itself up in a daze, and behind its bulk, she could just see the boot-clad foot of a prone body. Rake was behind it, the smoking rifle still in his hand.

Chapter 23

He took her back to town the same day, and made arrangements for the sheriff to remove the bodies.

He didn't ever think he would go back up on the mountain again, but he didn't know where he would go instead.

He could not now go with Angelene.

He could not escape from the boy who had been a killer or the man who had destroyed the family of the woman he loved.

He wondered if there were some kind of impulse within him that could never be suppressed, a monster riding in the dungeon of his soul.

He had never healed. He had never changed, and the overlay of civilization had only been a veneer that had cracked under the first little pressure.

"We'll go to the hotel," he said in his mask-voice, and Angelene knew he had gone far away from her. "I'll get you a room, we'll see about burying your brothers."

"All right," she said evenly. "That's what we'll do."

But she didn't want to give them a decent burial. She wanted them to lay where they had fallen, to return them to the earth that they had soaked so thoroughly with other men's blood.

She was glad he had killed them; they couldn't have lived, misfits that they were, without Josie's firm hand behind them, and if she had lived, they would have only continued on their killing spree.

"I meant to get them," Rake said suddenly. "They killed the dog."

She hadn't forgotten, and maybe that was the most important thing, that their violence extended to a helpless animal—any helpless animal.

They were buried in a plot in the far corner of the cemetery the following day. Angelene requested no homilies, no service.

"Those who liveth by the sword shall dieth by the sword," the minister intoned, and that was their epitaph.

Maybe hers too, Angelene thought.

When she got back, Rake was gone.

So he had told her and he had left her, because there could be no life when he had taken that of her family.

There could be no life when a man tried to sever his own roots. She wondered how far he would run away.

"He'll be back," Carter said comfortingly, but his assurances pulled no weight. Rake was a man undergoing the torture of change. Because of England, he could no longer claim to be a savage, and because he had blood on his hands, he could not claim to be civilized.

Where did a man go who was caught in the middle?

He went in search of his past, she thought, the thing that had made him the way he was; he looked for answers now, and no longer in the arms of a woman. He had willingly given her up to go on his quest.

"Where are the horses?" she asked Carter.

"He took the stallion, he left the mare."

She closed her eyes, her heart resigned to his symbolic abandonment, and the wellspring of pain.

No, *never*—

Her eyes flashed open as she resisted the temptation to just let him go.

Never, because of the life between them and the life they might have created—

Never, because he knew what rejection meant—

He had never accepted it either.

Never, damn it—*never!*

She swallowed painfully. "I will need your assistance."

Carter said, "He rode away like the wind."

"Who can catch the wind?" she asked. "All you can do is stand in its path, and let it possess you." *And let it blow itself out so it would come back to you.*

"Tell me what I can do for you," Carter said.

But at that moment, she didn't even know what to do for herself.

It came to her on the train, as the marvel of modern travel pulled her away from the primitive little western town. It was a strange, disconnected thought: *he would not seek his mother's people.*

He would go to the place where he had become a man.

The man who was born in the child.

But the father had made the man—by his treatment of the child. The father, the governor, who couldn't soil himself with the likes of the child.

And his anger had spilled over two continents and touched the life and the family of the woman he loved.

She was the spawn of a murderer; they were as well-matched as any two people could be. She would just go to Illinois and hope to find him, and then she would just have to make him see.

She loved being rich. A woman with money could command any whim, even that of stopping the train and getting off long before it was due to arrive in Lexington and then hiring a carriage to take her where she wanted to go.

Money bought anything, and it was a cushion of protection against any obstacle she might encounter on her eccentric quest.

For one moment, she thought she was crazy, running off to someplace she had never been to find a man she did not know.

442

But still, there could be no harm in that. The worst he could do was send her away. And the best that could happen was that Rake would be there.

Still, it was a long trip from mid-state, and her reservations grew that she was taking this one large step from such a nebulous clue.

But at that, the die was cast. The more she thought about it on her long journey north, the more sense it seemed to make to her.

It was the only place to which he could have possibly run.

Springfield had been a city that was exploding in growth that time ten years before. He remembered it as being crowded, unfathomable, but less chaotic perhaps than the scene that confronted him now as he pursued his way down one and another of the broad avenues of the business section.

It was built up even more now, lined side to side with brick and brownstone buildings compressed around large squares with shops and services of every conceivable description lining the interspersing side streets.

He remembered riding down a similar street all those years ago in agony and pain, but he couldn't remember where he had come from or how he could get there again.

He had only the same resource at his command as he had had before: the power of a politely asked question.

It was simple, actually, as it had been before. The repository of a city's history was in its daily newspaper, and it was a stranger who courteously suggested this to him. From there, it was easy enough to find the six-story brick building on one of the squares, and to breech its formidable front door to enter its main office.

Everyone looked up as he entered, a tall, impeccably dressed stranger who commanded attention immediately.

"I'm looking for Governor Cordigan, gentlemen. Can you give me his direction?"

"You mean ex-Governor, son. His term was out two

years ago, so it's been a damn long time since you've come by," said a man who was taking notices at the front desk.

"I reckon it has," Rake admitted. "Any reason for me not to know?"

"Not in the least son," the man at the front desk said easily. "Let me draw you a map to show you the way."

His father now lived far out of town in an elegant mansion situated in a grove of trees. It was a stately house, a forbidding house, the kind of place where a man didn't just walk up and knock on the door.

Rake dismounted, tied his horse, and walked up to the door.

Ten years before, he had walked up to a different house with a different door. He had been a different man. He had been a child, a boy-man without visions unwilling to suffer the vicissitudes of his mother's people's beliefs. He had been a boy without identity then, with no one to make him amulets, or to enlist for him the power of the turtle; there was no one to give him a name, and no one to pierce his ears as was the custom of his mother's people, and the ears that bore no earrings identified him forever as the outside of the tribe.

Ten years before, on the day he had walked up to another house and another door, he had been a boy playing man's games, and he, as the outsider, had played the hardest of all, had run the fastest, had developed into the best rider, learned the ways of the plains, captured the most animal fare.

But there was no one to give him his ceremonial clothing, no warrior society that would take him in.

He had been the man-boy who walked alone, and so, when it came time to put his commitment to the severest test, he ran away to his father—and the man who had answered the door had denied him.

He didn't know, as he walked up the path to the stone steps of the porch, exactly what he would say this time to the man who answered the door.

In his mind, the man would look exactly the same, with that haughty, inturning look that he himself knew so well.

His father would reach out his hand and greet him.

He pressed the bell before he could think of the consequences.

The man who answered the door was not his father. "May I help you, sir?"

"I'm looking for Brandon Cordigan," he said carefully—and then he saw him, striding across the entrance foyer, a man who could have been him but for the gray-black hair and the absence of a mustache.

"Who is it?" Brandon Cordigan demanded.

And he knew the voice.

"A stranger, sir," his father's majordomo said.

"What do you want?" Brandon Cordigan asked, coming to stand in the doorway, and looking as if he were about to bar the way to some vagrant. "Who are you?"

His voice was rough, impatient, intemperate.

"My name is Rake Cordigan," Rake said, not one shade of emotion coloring his voice, and the man he called father looked at him, hard, and motioned him into the house.

"Now, who are you?" he demanded. "Who sent you?"

There was a mirror in the hallway, a long gilded pier mirror above a matching console table, and Rake walked over to it and stared at his father from within the reflection.

And it seemed to him that he was of the same age and had the same look of the man who had turned him away so many years before.

"My name is Rake Cordigan, sir."

His father moved up closer so that now their faces were almost aligned in the mirror, and even though they were not standing side by side, the resemblance was remarkable.

He *was* the man who had rejected him ten years before.

And he was himself. He felt the connection deeply, irrevocably. He was the son and the father both, and he always had been.

The man beside him saw it, felt it. "There was a boy once . . ." he said, his voice shaking a little. "I sent him away. I was sure he had died."

"He did," Rake said, turning to face his father. "And now he is reborn."

Her feeling of urgency was compelling, and she had travelled long and hard to make up for the fact he had had a day's advance on her. And she still didn't know if she would find him.

The whole thing was made worse by the fact she was confronted by a city the size and expanse of which seemed so similar to New York, that she almost turned around and returned to Kentucky.

Her knees were shaking as she debarked at the train depot in Springfield, and her fear escalated into a living palpable thing.

She was that close now—and that far.

He could be gone already. Or he might never have come.

Ask questions. She remembered. A woman with money and enough gumption could command anything, including the right of her future.

She found a carriage and asked the cab man to drive her around the main part of the city for a while, and then finally she got up the nerve to pose the hypothetical question: if the driver were a stranger in the city, where would he go for information?

Simple as that. "The newspaper's the place, ma'am. They can tell you anything you want to know about the city."

He drove her there, and she went in to inquire, and her heart pounded wildly, erratically, bolstered by the fact the counterman had said, "Well, you're the second one today."

The cabman knew exactly where to go, and she directed him to park right in front of the door.

She was the first sight Rake saw when he finally emerged from the house.

He was a man who had now walked successfully in two worlds. He had confronted his father and confronted his fears, and he had travelled a very long road to come right back to where he started from.

He was a man who had walked with impunity in his father's house and now he knew from where he came.

He had walked into his future with his woman on his arm.

It didn't matter what had been said in that house that afternoon; it only mattered that he was there and his father had known him. And it didn't matter that he would never see that man again; the knowledge was there and his father now owned it.

Now he wanted to complete the chain—to be father to the man and conceive the boy.

One more time they went back up on the mountain to bury the wounds, and lay the dead to rest.

"This time you must tell me how to love you," Rake said, "so that I never hurt you again. This time, Angelene, I will never let you go."

"You must take everything I offer you," Angelene said instantly, "and never say no to anything I ask of you."

"What do you offer me, Angelene?" he asked warily.

Her beautiful eyes glinted with mischief. "I offer you the money with which to buy a ranch, a place where you will raise those thoroughbreds we created for you in England—*yes* . . . you can't deny me. I want us back in England next year, Rake, with a reputation for horse-flesh that precedes us, and I want that Endicott and all his friends grovelling to buy your racers."

"Yes, angel of my heart, and what else?" He took her arm to guide her back to the wagon, amused and amazed by her ferocity and her ambition.

"I offer you my heart," she whispered, "if you promise to treat it gently."

"I love you," he said, turning her so that she was backed up against the side of the wagon.

"Then I offer you my kiss," she sighed, lifting her mouth to take his ardent kiss. And the beginning was here, in the surrender in his kiss, and the way that he held her, and the need in his eyes that warmed when he looked at her.

"And I offer you my body," she whispered, reaching for him, and he did not need another invitation.

"I offer you mine," he answered softly, and he lifted her gently and carried her to the back of the wagon. There was a throw there, and he spread it out for them, and he lay her down on it and climbed into her arms.

They lay there, entwined in the warmth of the sun, kissing, touching, murmuring, arousing each other gently, slowly, luxuriously.

The beginning, the surrender—ignited with a rush as her hand began a slow course down his belly to the root of his manhood.

He adored it when she loved him there and when she reached for the mystery that complemented her own.

She was ready for him quickly, lifting her dress, exposing her eagerness, and when he lifted himself over her, and poised himself to possess her, she arched herself upward to meet his first thrust.

He eased himself into her and her body drifted downward, taking him with her as deeply as a sigh.

And he lay there quiescent with her, connected, bonded, filling her, loving her, drowning in the mystery of her seductive angel eyes.